Praise for the novels of

'Read on, adventure fans.'
NEW YORK TIMES

'A rich, compelling look back in time [to]
when history and myth intermingled.'
SAN FRANCISCO CHRONICLE

'Only a handful of 20th century writers tantalize
our senses as well as Smith. A rare author who
wields a razor-sharp sword of craftsmanship.'
TULSA WORLD

'He paces his tale as swiftly as he can with
swordplay aplenty and killing strokes that come
like lightning out of a sunny blue sky.'
KIRKUS REVIEWS

'Best Historical Novelist – I say Wilbur Smith, with his
swashbuckling novels of Africa. The bodices rip and the
blood flows. You can get lost in Wilbur Smith and
misplace all of August.'
STEPHEN KING

'Action is the name of Wilbur Smith's game
and he is the master.'
WASHINGTON POST

'Smith manages to serve up adventure, history and melodrama in one thrilling package that will be eagerly devoured by series fans.'
PUBLISHERS WEEKLY

'This well-crafted novel is full of adventure, tension, and intrigue.'
LIBRARY JOURNAL

'Life-threatening dangers loom around every turn, leaving the reader breathless . . . An incredibly exciting and satisfying read.'
CHATTANOOGA FREE PRESS

'When it comes to writing the adventure novel, Wilbur Smith is the master; a 21st century H. Rider Haggard.'
VANITY FAIR

Wilbur Smith was born in Central Africa in 1933. He became a full-time writer in 1964 following the success of *When the Lion Feeds*, and has since published over fifty global bestsellers, including the Courtney Series, the Ballantyne Series, the Egyptian Series, the Hector Cross Series and many successful standalone novels, all meticulously researched on his numerous expeditions worldwide. An international phenomenon, his readership built up over fifty-five years of writing, establishing him as one of the most successful and impressive brand authors in the world.

The establishment of the Wilbur & Niso Smith Foundation in 2015 cemented Wilbur's passion for empowering writers, promoting literacy and advancing adventure writing as a genre. The foundation's flagship program is the Wilbur Smith Adventure Writing Prize.

Wilbur Smith died peacefully at home in 2021 with his wife, Niso, by his side, leaving behind him a rich treasure-trove of novels and stories that will delight readers for years to come. For all the latest information on Wilbur Smith's writing visit www.wilbursmith-books.com or facebook.com/WilburSmith

WILBUR SMITH

NEMESIS

WITH TOM HARPER

ZAFFRE

Copyright © Orion Mintaka (UK) Ltd. 2023
Author photo © Hendre Louw

Typeset by IDSUK (Data Connection) Ltd
Printed in the USA

10 9 8 7 6 5 4 3 2 1

Hardcover ISBN: 978–1–8387–7955–9
Canadian paperback ISBN: 978–1–8387–7954–2
Digital ISBN: 978–1–8387–7956–6

For information, contact
251 Park Avenue South, Floor 12, New York, New York 10010
www.bonnierbooks.co.uk

SUSTAINABLE FORESTRY INITIATIVE
Certified Sourcing
www.sfiprogram.org
SFI-01681

Logo will apply to text stock only

This book is for my wife
MOKHINISO
I gambled on love and it paid off handsomely
Thank you for being the best bet I've ever made

THE
COURTNEY
FAMILY
IN
NEMESIS

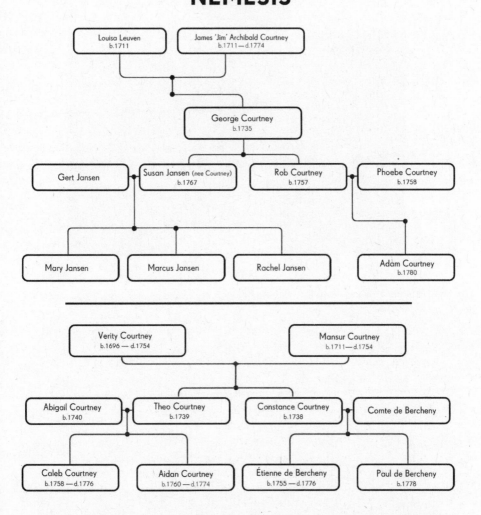

Find out more about the Courtneys and see the Courtney family tree in full at www.wilbursmithbooks.com/courtney-family-tree

PARIS, 1794

A white dove flew from a rooftop above the former Place Louis XV and landed on a tall wooden structure in the middle of the square. It was something like a tree, though unlike a tree, it had hard right angles and unnaturally smooth trunks. It had grown all in one night and been fully formed by morning, as if it had suddenly erupted from the stone cobbles. Straight and rigid, it stood as if guarding one place from another. It smelled of blood.

The dove had no interest in the violent conflicts of men. She settled on the crosspiece that joined the two uprights and preened her soft feathers busily.

Below, sparks flew as the executioner rasped his steel against the whetstone. The guillotine blade, blunted with use, was being honed to a fine edge. Death should be quick and painless; this is how Joseph-Ignace Guillotin wanted it to be. Aristocrat or commoner, their fate would be equal – cold steel was indifferent to class. The blade would be busy today.

The executioner oiled the blade's edges to aid its downwards velocity, then wiped the surface clean. He fitted it into its housing and screwed it tight. He ran his hands over the cord, checking for weaknesses and snags. He hoisted the blade into position, high above the square like a battle standard. The housing clattered against the crosspiece. The dove, momentarily startled, took to the air quickly, as if gravity held no burden.

The executioner considered his task. The world had been turned upside down. Terror was the rule, killing was routine and nobody was safe. Blood sacrifices had to be made on the altar of the revolution. So many were condemned to death, the guillotine was the most efficient means of execution, designed to dispatch swiftly, not to torture – unlike the breaking wheel of old, which crushed bones and lacerated flesh. And yet the executioner had witnessed many times the eyes and lips of his decapitated victims moving as if pleading for clemency, the pupils of agonised eyes focusing on him. He shuddered at the reception he would receive at the gates of Hell.

Today a restless energy gripped the crowd. The taverns surrounding the square had emptied and people jostled for the best viewing position. Children crawled through the legs of grown-ups, laughing and racing one another to reach the front, right under the imposing contraption that was the guillotine on its high platform. Their mothers pushed after them, they, too, not holding back, not wanting to miss any detail of the spectacle.

Wooden wheels rattled on the cobblestones. The crowd's raucousness descended to a murmur, necks craned to catch sight of the tumbrel rolling down Rue Saint-Honoré. The cart was packed with all manner of nobility and low-born, clothes torn, heads hanging, but among the bedraggled victims one shone out like the sun between clouds. Tall and slim, dressed in a clean white gown, she stood upright and swayed easily with the motion of the cart. She was more than fifty years old, but even after weeks in prison she could be reckoned to be twenty years younger. Her pale skin was as smooth as marble; her golden hair had lost none of its lustre. The guards had cropped it short, so that it would not cover her neck and impede the blade, but the bobbed style only made her look more beautiful. She raised her head to the sky as if searching for an indefinable meaning, exposing her throat, which was supple and pink and beginning to flush with emotion.

Today was the execution of the Comtesse Constance de Bercheny.

Before the revolution, she had been the most notorious woman in Paris. Her name was synonymous with glamour and scandal. She had slept with King Louis, people said – and, it was rumoured, with Queen Marie Antoinette. She had murdered two husbands and cuckolded a third so many times he had died of shame. She had seduced most of the courtiers at Versailles, and blackmailed the rest with an intimate knowledge of their innermost secrets. It was whispered she was as powerful as the king; others said more so. In the web of sex, influence and intrigue that had been the *Ancien Régime*, she was the deadly spider at its dark heart.

Now the revolution had caught her.

The cart came to a halt. A soldier took her arm roughly and tried to lift her down, but she shook him off with a toss of her head and scrambled to the ground unaided. Barefoot, she stepped through the mud and detritus smeared over the cobbles and mounted the scaffold. The stairs were steep and crusted with blood, but she glided up them as if ascending the grand stairs of a palace.

Boos and jeers rose around the square as she reached the top of the platform. Envy and hatred lubricated their voices. A woman in the crowd started shouting '*Putain! Putain!*' – whore. Others took up the cry. Eggs were thrown. Constance turned and her ice-blue eyes flashed, and instantly the crowd fell silent. It was as if her beauty had robbed them of their contempt.

She unwrapped her shawl, baring her shoulders to the top of her breasts. Her skin was as white as her dress, virgin-pure in the cold, cleansing air; her slim figure showed no sign of the five children she'd borne. More than one man in the crowd felt a heaviness in his heart at the waste it would be to remove that beautiful head from such a flawless body.

Constance de Bercheny could feel the iron glare of those lustful gazes. It did not intimidate her. She knew what men were capable of, and how much power she wielded over them. For one last time, she let herself savour the majesty of her femininity, and how feeble she made them look.

She was not afraid of dying. She had seen men die, had let men die, and – when necessary – had resorted to murder herself. She had faced death many times and survived through cunning, resourcefulness and force of will. Even in the stinking hole of the Conciergerie prison, where the condemned awaited the guillotine, she had refused to accept defeat. She would seduce one of the guards or persuade an admirer to smuggle her out. But most of her admirers were dead, and the chief jailer was not a chivalrous man. He had put himself in her mouth and forced her to pleasure him, then called her a whore when she appealed to his kindness. Out of malice, he had manacled her with the heaviest set of chains. If a prisoner escaped, it would be the jailer's head on the guillotine.

Constance wouldn't give in. Even on the scaffold, a part of her refused to surrender. She scanned the crowd for a familiar face, a spark of hope. But there was no one. She would not give her captors the victory of seeing her doubt herself.

She touched the wooden neck brace of the guillotine, rubbed smooth by the bodies and fluids of the men and women who had lain there before her. The oblique-edged blade hung above like a gash in the sky, glinting in the light. She was glad to see it had recently been sharpened.

The other women in the prison had talked about this moment many times. Their minds were fevered with anticipation.

'I've heard that your whole life plays out before your eyes as the blade falls,' one had said – a girl of seventeen who played endlessly with her rosary. Constance had laughed.

'I've lived too many lives for that,' she'd said. 'So many I barely remember.'

But in her heightened state, memories came to her like fireflies in the dark. From the height of the scaffold, the crowd below seemed to dissolve. They weren't the Paris mob, but dark-skinned Indians in turbans and cloth armour; and the clouds above were not the powder-puffs of a French spring, but the heavy thunder-heads of the oncoming Bengal monsoon, so dense you could feel them press on your shoulders. A different continent, another life-time: a young woman called Constance Courtney, a merchant's daughter, far from innocent but still a blushing rosebud compared to the woman she had become.

She would confront death, laugh in its face. If she entered an afterlife, she would charm the angels to let her into Heaven despite everything she'd done.

Constance lay on the guillotine's hard bed. The executioners tightened the leather straps across her chest, her belly and her thighs. The two upright posts towered above her like a doorway waiting for her to step through.

'I am going to meet my children.'

She said it quietly, as if to herself, but loud enough so it would be heard. She knew people would repeat her last words, and because they were sentimental fools, they would believe them. Perhaps they would say that beneath her scandalous reputation, she had been a good mother. They would recall that of her five children, two had been killed in the wars with England, one was taken by disease, and one executed in the revolution. Her legend would grow. She would be immortalised on canvas by great painters. In time, she might become a martyr.

The executioner placed his hand on the lever. The black-clad judge began reading the final sentence. The crowd surged forward, urged by the scent of blood, by the sight of beauty, privilege and excess brought to its knees.

One man hung back. A youth, wearing long trousers and a short carmagnole jacket which sagged on one side from the weight of an implement hidden in the lining. His head was bowed; he was concentrating on the charcoal sketch he was composing of the scene. He had been in his place since early morning, and the drawing was nearly complete.

Everyone who saw his work agreed that the young artist had an exceptional talent. The picture before him was uncannily realistic: the marquise, in particular. The artist had captured every curve of her grace, her fierce beauty and her defiance. In delicate charcoal strokes, she almost came alive on the page.

'I will give you ten sous for the picture,' the man beside him offered.

He wore a red cap, and a butcher's apron smeared with animal blood. He knew he could sell it to the handbill printers for at least triple the price, such was the interest in Constance de Bercheny.

The boy shook his head and remained silent. He didn't trust himself to speak. He barely looked up, except to glance at the scene through the long fringe that hung over his eyes. He was sixteen years old, though he seemed younger: buttery smooth skin, clear blue eyes, and feathery flicks of dark hair sticking out above his ears. There was a musty scent about him from the stable-yard he had been sleeping in. He had been on the run for four months, stealing to eat and snatching shelter where he could. There were so many other dispossessed homeless on the streets that he melded with the crowds. The authorities couldn't round them all up. If they had caught him, they would certainly have sent him to the scaffold.

His name was Paul de Bercheny. The woman strapped to the guillotine was his mother.

The last time he had seen her was a year ago. By then, the vast château where he had grown up had long been abandoned to the mob. Paul and Constance had taken a cottage in the country near Rouen, far from their former lives. Inconspicuous, but not invisible. A peasant dress and a shawl could hardly hide Constance's famous beauty.

They thought they were safe. The revolution was faltering: half the provinces were in revolt, foreign armies were camped on French soil, and Toulon had fallen to the British.

'We will wait them out,' Constance declared. 'The revolution will pass like a storm on a summer's day.'

Paul, comforted, had believed her.

Then one day an old servant, a woman whose loyalty to her former mistress had not been dulled by the revolution, had come hurrying across the fields.

'They are coming, madame. The Watch Committee.'

Constance had not so much as flinched.

'You must say "Citizen" now,' she reminded the woman gently. '"Madame" or "Monsieur" will get you killed.'

'But the Committee . . .'

'I will be ready for them,' Constance promised. 'Do not fear on my account. But go. If they find you here, they will kill you.'

The old woman had kissed her hand, trembling with emotion.

'You were a better woman than all of them put together,' she declared.

As soon as she had gone, Constance pulled out a small valise from a cupboard by the fireplace and thrust it into Paul's arms.

'Here is everything you need.'

Paul had opened the valise, and felt a sickening creep of dread as he saw the blued metal of a pistol barrel gleaming up at him. He snatched it up and brandished it wildly. Through the open door, he could see dust rising from the freshly harvested fields as a crowd approached.

'I will defend you,'

'*No.*' Constance's voice was as hard as a slap in the face. She tore the gun from his hand, almost breaking the finger that had curled through the trigger guard. 'Use it to survive.'

Paul's face flushed. Tears threatened. 'But, *Maman* . . .'

'You must run.'

They could hear shouts now coming across the field. She gripped his face, fixing him with those impenetrable blue eyes.

'You were my last, my best hope,' she whispered. 'For your brothers I wanted glory, power, but you were always my baby. My own. One good thing, for all my sins.'

He did not understand, but her words stung his pride. Growing up the youngest, his brothers had been almost mythical creatures: stiff and remote, always in a hurry, talking of tactics and battles and important people Paul felt he should have heard of. He remembered how stiff their shirts had been, and how their spurs struck sparks when they crossed the stable yard flagstones. Paul had always thought that one day he would be as grand and confident as they were.

'I am as good as any of my brothers.'

'Yes. And where are they now?' She held his face so tight his cheeks hurt. 'Keep yourself alive. Will you do this for me?'

Paul nodded. Not enough to convince her. She gripped him tighter still, as if she could impress her will directly into his brain.

'Do whatever you must, endure anything, say anything, become anything. But promise you will survive.'

Specks of dust and chaff drifted through the open door, caught in a shaft of sunlight. A fly crawled over the crumbs of the bread they had had for lunch. He noticed the tiny beads of sweat glistening on his mother's cheeks, a red spot on the bodice of her dress where she had spilled a drop of wine. The smell of her perfume, sweet like ripe lilies, wafted off her warm skin and enveloped him.

'I promise,' he whispered.

She released him. Blood flooded his skull; he felt dizzy.

'Now go.'

'But what about you?'

She shook her head. 'It is too late.'

'But—'

Her eyes flashed with fury. 'They know who I am. They will not stop until they find me. But I can delay them long enough to save you.'

He hugged her, burying his face in her chest, and would still have been there when the revolutionaries arrived if she had not prised him off her.

'Go. And *stay alive.*'

He picked up the valise and ran out of the back door. Over the garden wall, across the fields and into the copse: his mother's perfume still caught in his hair and her final words ringing in his ears.

Stay alive.

In the Place de la Révolution, the man in the butcher's apron was straining to get a better view.

'For Marie Antoinette I was in the front row,' he said. 'This far away.' He held up his finger and thumb, an inch apart. 'She was a sight to behold. Makes me hot just to think about how her headless body spasmed and kicked, you know what I mean, lad?'

Paul gripped his pencil so hard it snapped. Charcoal flakes fluttered over his picture, smudging the lines. He wanted to gouge the man's eyes out with the splintered end.

His hand went to the bulge in his jacket, feeling the weight of the loaded pistol in the lining. He imagined blowing the butcher's brains out. He forced himself to resist. He only had one bullet.

The time was now. The judge had finished reading the sentence. He nodded to the executioner. Paul gripped the pistol, unfamiliar with its shape and complex mechanism.

What am I going to do?

The night before, when he had hatched his plan, he had plotted it so clearly. He would leap onto the scaffold, brandishing the pistol. The crowd would back away. He would cut his mother free, commandeer a horse, and ride all the way to the border to escape.

But now he was here, the reality was all wrong. The crowd was too thick. Not wanting to draw attention to himself, Paul had hung back: he was too far away. The ring of soldiers around the scaffold did not look as if they would be intimidated by one man with a pistol. They had seen so much killing, their attitude was as hard and sharp as the bayonets that gleamed on the ends of their muskets.

His heart beating frantically, and close to panic, Paul pulled the pistol out of his coat. No one noticed. All eyes were directed at the scaffold.

He cocked the gun. Even that seemed to take all his strength. The pistol was heavy; he held it with both hands. The crowd was tight around him. He hesitated.

Stay alive. The words were so vivid in his head, he thought his mother must have spoken them from the scaffold. *Do whatever you must, endure anything . . .*

Time froze. He felt his soul tearing in two inside him. Obey his mother, or save her? The shame he had carried ever since that day at the cottage swelled through him. His brothers would have known what to do. His finger tightened around the trigger, but it seemed to have rusted solid.

He was still trying to decide when he heard the rattle and rumble of a falling blade, followed by an abrupt thud, terrible and complete.

A sigh rose from the crowd as if a chasm had opened up in the earth. Constance's head tumbled into the basket at the foot of the guillotine. Blood cascaded in gouts, splashing the faces of the nearby crowd. A few wisps of golden hair fluttered down like straw and settled in the lake of flowing blood. Soon they were soaked crimson red.

The crowd moaned. Some ardent patriots raised *huzzahs*, but the cheers died as quickly as the prone figure, which jerked once or twice like a final insolent valedictory. No one relished the death of such a beautiful woman.

Paul dropped the pistol and staggered back, as if an invisible cord that tethered him to the world had been cut and left him unmoored. His own mother, murdered, and he had stood fifty yards away and witnessed it all.

A scream rose inside him. Paul felt it as a physical presence, a weight like a vast snake coiled in his chest. He tried to choke it back. If it emerged, he would draw attention to himself. People would wonder why he was mourning so passionately the death of an enemy of the people. They would find out who he was. If he was lucky, they would drag him to the Conciergerie to await trial. If not, the mob would tear him apart where he stood.

Endure anything.

The man in the butcher's apron turned and stared at him.

'Citizen?' he said. 'What the devil is wrong with you?'

The scream rose through Paul's lungs. He felt it pressing against his ribs.

His legs buckled. Paul fell to his knees, bending double over the dirty cobbles. His mouth dropped open, and the scream was rushing up through his throat like a rat along a sewer. He gagged.

No sound came out – only a flood of bile that spattered over the square and soaked his shirt front.

Blood swam in front of his eyes. The butcher was upon him. A meaty hand took his elbow and hauled him to his feet. Another hand proffered him a dirty handkerchief. Paul wiped his lips and spat.

'Your first time? I was the same. You will soon learn to enjoy the entertainment,' said the butcher in a tone between glee and envy.

Paul pulled away and scrabbled on the ground for his belongings. He found his sketch, but where was the pistol? He would place it in his mouth and blow his brains out.

It had disappeared. But then he saw a small girl, her hair in pigtails and her smock stained with dirt, had picked it up. It was almost as big as she was. She held the barrel with both hands as she peered into it.

'Give it to me,' Paul croaked.

He reached out. The girl regarded him with solemn eyes. Without a word, she turned on her bare feet and scurried away through the legs of the crowd, dragging the pistol behind her. You lived by your wits in Paris: the gun meant she would eat that night.

Paul gazed at his drawing, his last image of his mother, and let out a cry. The picture was covered in his vomit, the paper soaked through. The image of Constance was a smudge of charcoal and blurred lines.

The butcher looked over his shoulder.

'She is ruined. A shame.' He shrugged. 'But with your talent, you can always make another.'

The guards were already shoving the next victim up the steps of the guillotine. Constance's death had unsettled the crowd: they needed another execution to calm them, to restore a sense of order.

Paul held his hand over his mouth. He had nothing to say; he had survived. But the scream remained trapped inside him, echoing around his soul forever.

CAPE OF GOOD HOPE, 1806.
TWELVE YEARS LATER . . .

Admiral Sir Robert Courtney stood on the deck of his flagship, the *Nestor*, and felt the huge Cape rollers surge under the hull, the turbulence of cold Atlantic water meeting the heat of Africa. His body moved easily with the motion. He had been at sea since he was seventeen years old, starting as a common forecastle hand. Now he was a vice admiral of the Red, a knight of the realm, darling of the British press, and curse of any French captain unlucky enough to cross his path. He had accomplished a lot in the last thirty years.

'It seems like yesterday when we started out together,' said the man beside him, reading Rob's thoughts as true as a compass. Angus MacNeil was a barrel-chested Scotsman who had sailed with Rob on his first voyage in the navy, and somehow contrived to follow him aboard every vessel he'd served on since. They had saved each other's lives more times than either man could remember.

Rob leaned on the rail, half listening as he stared out at the great flat-topped bulk of Table Mountain looming above the bay. He could almost smell its scent, though with the stiff onshore breeze he knew he must be imagining it. Africa was where he had been born, where he had lived all his youth until dreams of big ships and the promise of adventure lured him away. Now, nearly fifty, he felt a powerful urge to return, as if the dust of the continent had lodged in his bones and was at last beginning to stir. He had lobbied the Admiralty for this command for months. Now he was almost home.

But the Lords of the Admiralty had not sent him halfway across the world for shore leave. He had work to do. He put the telescope to his one good eye and swept it over the bay with a practised motion until he found the fort. Its white walls sparkled in the sunlight, its five corners thrust outward like spear points.

'My great-great-grandfather helped build those walls,' said Rob. He searched out the open parade ground on the shore below the castle walls. 'And *his* father was executed there by the Dutch.'

'Then you've a debt to pay,' said Angus. He swept his arm across the horizon, where the full line of Rob's fleet spread over nearly ten miles of ocean: four ships of the line, two frigates and a dozen transports, with several thousand Highland troops quartered aboard. 'And the men to give it back to Holland with interest.'

'It is not Holland any more. It is the Batavian Republic,' Rob reproved him.

The Batavian Republic had been formed after the downfall of the old Dutch Republic, when French revolutionary forces intervened in 1795.

Angus spat over the side. 'A turd by any other name. What's the matter about all this change?'

The world had been transformed out of all recognition since Rob first emerged from his isolated childhood in the African bush. He and Angus had cut their teeth fighting American revolutionaries, but that had been the prologue for the greater contest that had erupted ten years later, with the French revolution. First France had been sucked into the maelstrom, then Europe, and finally the world. For a time, it had looked as though France might drown in the bloodbath the revolution had unleashed. But as her cause looked lost, a charismatic soldier named Bonaparte had emerged from the chaos to redeem his country. In less than ten years, he had risen from cadet to general. In another five years, he was dictator. And five years after that, he had crowned himself emperor. Now, there was not a corner of the globe where France and Britain did not fight for mastery.

That was why Rob was here. Cape Town was the key to the East, to the new British empire rising in India. Holland held the Cape, but the country had been overthrown. The Batavian Republic was a vassal state of France, with a chokehold on Britain's most vital trade artery. And so the Cape had to be captured.

Rob felt a touch on his arm – lighter than the breeze that plucked at his sleeves, but he knew it at once with a joy that had not dimmed in all these years. His wife, Phoebe, had come up beside him. He slipped an arm around her waist and hugged her to him.

Many things had changed, but not his love for her, or her looks. Even when he met her, a teenage slave abused on an American plantation, she had had a calm self-possession beyond her years. Despite the terrible suffering endured at the hands of cruel slave masters all those years ago, age had made her more beautiful, a more perfect version of the young woman she had been. Her almond eyes were deep with love and wisdom; her soft face was kindness itself, while her golden-brown skin bore no trace of the storms she had weathered.

Since Rob married Phoebe, they had not spent a night apart. The Admiralty frowned on officers bringing their wives aboard ships; sailors swore it brought bad luck. None of it swayed Rob. The war had kept him at sea almost continuously. If he had left her behind, he would hardly have seen her for three months in ten years. Life ashore was hard enough for any sailor's wife; for Phoebe, living in a different country and with a different skin, it would have been intolerable.

Whatever people might think, Rob's extraordinary run of victories had quieted both punctilious admirals and superstitious sailors. He had become known as a lucky captain, and then a lucky admiral; his ships were never short of volunteers. And in the unique world of seamen, her race was irrelevant. Ships' crews were made up of men from every country that had a coast: Scots, Irish, Cornishmen, Africans, Indian lascars, Chinamen, and stout men with strange tattoos from the islands of the South Seas. Anywhere in the world that British ships called, men came aboard and entered the Royal Navy's bloodstream. Many men volunteered, eager for the pay, board and the chance to travel to exotic lands, but those who were press-ganged would arrive with nothing but the clothes they were wearing, and sporting a bruise or two. Rob knew how brutal the experience could be – he had been forced into service many moons ago, and understood the men's fears.

Now the crews loved Phoebe. She was their talisman, their Madonna and their mother. If Rob had tried to leave her ashore, they would have mutinied.

Phoebe shivered in his embrace. Cape Town was not a happy memory for her.

'The last time I was here, it was in the hold of a slave ship.'

'Now you are Lady Courtney. And soon, slave ships will be a thing of the past. The Saints are planning a new bill to abolish the trade, and they are confident that this year at last they have the votes to pass it.'

'The Saints' was the nickname for a group of Members of Parliament who had spent twenty years fighting against slavery. Many of them were Rob's friends, and he had been their enthusiastic champion. Of the considerable fortune in prize money he had amassed during his career, much of it had been dedicated to supporting their cause.

'Imagine if we could turn our guns on those slavers.'

'The French abolished slavery more than ten years ago,' said Phoebe.

'Until Bonaparte brought it back,' Rob reminded her. 'Which is why – among many other reasons – it will give me great pleasure to seize Cape Town from him.'

Phoebe studied the gleaming fort. 'It looks heavily fortified and strongly built.' Having been in so many battles, she had developed a captain's eye for tactics. 'Will you be able to manoeuvre the ship close enough to shore for it to be in range of your guns?'

Rob kissed her. 'Your assessment is astute. We cannot assault the castle directly. Fortunately, I have a plan.'

He sought out his flag lieutenant, a terrier-like Welshman named Jones.

'My compliments to the captain. Ask him to prepare my launch.'

Jones saluted. Phoebe arched her eyebrows.

'I hope you are not planning anything rash?'

'As you rightly observed, I cannot get close enough to the shore in the flagship. I am transferring my flag aboard the *Valiant*.'

'You are an admiral,' Phoebe said, a note of concern in her voice. 'Your job is to let younger men fight the battles, and win the glory.'

Rob smiled. 'I need to be present to tell them how much better I would have done it at their age. Besides, you know what the *Valiant*'s captain is like. Impetuous, headstrong and insubordinate. Who knows what he would do without a firm hand on his shoulder?'

'He takes after his father,' said Phoebe.

'I think that is his mother's side.'
She let go of her hold on him.
'If I told you to be careful, would it make any difference?'
'If I said I will, would you believe me?'

Rob surveyed the landscape through a telescope as he sat with
Angus in the rear of the launch approaching the sloop *Valiant*.
Phoebe had been right: a direct assault on the castle would have
been an invitation to disaster. They needed to find a different landing place. For a week, Rob's ships had been making feints close to
shore, testing the defences and leaving the Dutch guessing where
the final assault would come. He knew from his intelligence that
the Dutch had over three hundred guns mounted on shore batteries along the coast. He needed to land almost ten thousand men,
and he would not send them ashore to be slaughtered.

Rob had decided on landing on a site at Losperd's Bay, some
sixteen miles east of Cape Town. It was far enough from the castle
that the Dutch could not reinforce the area quickly, and unpro-
tected by any permanent batteries. The drawbacks were the strong
current that swept the beach, and the high sand dunes screening
the interior. If the Dutch brought up troops, the dunes would
provide a natural defensive rampart. But as best Rob could tell,
the place was deserted.

He felt the familiar heat rising in his veins at the prospect of
action. He knew it was unbecoming for an admiral. Phoebe was
right about that, too. He should stay back, directing the fleet from
a safe distance. But some impulse forced him onwards, his rational,
strategic judgement giving way to the promise of the thrills he
used to experience in his youth: the camaraderie, the shared purpose, the knife-edge between life and death. For a long time he
had been missing the visceral excitement of battle, and he knew he
had to answer its siren call. And he could never ask his men to face
danger that he would not.

The boat came alongside the sloop. For another admiral, a different captain might have rigged a boatswain's chair to hoist the
flag officer aboard safely. But Rob would rather fall in the sea
and drown than be lugged aboard like livestock, and the *Valiant*'s
captain knew that better than anyone.

The red vice admiral's pennant broke out from the masthead as Rob came on deck. The captain saluted crisply. Then, forgetting decorum, he stepped forward and embraced Rob warmly.

'Father.'

'It is good to see you, Adam.'

Rob gripped his son's shoulders and looked into his eyes – the same green eyes that had flickered open in Rob's arms as he held a newborn baby on a stormy sea in the Bay of Biscay. He had grown into a fine young man, Rob thought. He was a true mix of his parents, with his mother's irrepressibly curly hair, his father's ready grin, and a light-brown complexion halfway between the two.

Though their ships had been separated by only a few miles of ocean, they had barely seen each other on the voyage out. Before that, years would pass between their reunions. From the moment Adam took his warrant as midshipman, Rob had insisted he serve under other captains.

'My son must earn his own place in the world, as I did,' he had told Phoebe.

He had known the charge of nepotism would hang over Adam's career, however it progressed. He did not want to add any substance to it.

But Rob had read avidly every letter from Adam. He had scoured the *Naval Gazette* for reports of his son, delighting in news of his exploits. He had watched with pride as Adam grew from a callow midshipman to a dashing lieutenant, and now a commander with his first ship. Only now had Rob used his rank to bring Adam into his squadron.

It was the right time. Adam had African blood in him on both sides, but had not set foot on the continent in nearly twenty years. He should return to his ancestral home, to see his grandfather, his aunt and uncles and cousins.

But first they had a battle to win.

'Is everything prepared?' Rob asked.

Adam frowned. 'General Beresford was unable to land his troops today because of the gale. He decided to move north with the bulk of his forces and land at Saldanha Bay.'

'But that is a hundred miles away,' Rob protested. 'A hundred miles they will have to march back, across a waterless desert.'

'He did not consider he could make a safe landing here.'

As if to underscore Adam's words, a wave slapped against the side of the ship, throwing a spume of spray over both men. At the east end of the bay, Rob could see the sea foaming around the rocks of the razor-sharp reef that protruded from the beach.

'Our men would be dashed to pieces in this,' Rob conceded.

'Scipio promises me that tomorrow the wind will change.' Adam said it lightly, but there was a gleam of intent in his eye.

Scipio was another man Rob had helped free from slavery on the same plantation as Phoebe. With Angus and Phoebe, Scipio had stayed with Rob throughout his career, until Adam moved to his first ship. Then Scipio had joined Adam, and served wherever he was posted ever since.

'If Scipio says the weather will change, then it assuredly will.'

Scipio had grown up on the great river deltas of West Africa. Later, he had served as a boatman in the mazy coastal swamps of South Carolina. He could sniff out wind and weather three days away.

'Will you bring the army back?'

Rob shook his head. 'General Beresford is in command of the army. I have to defer to him.'

'Now you sound like a desk-bound admiral,' Adam chided him. 'Waging war with protocol and pieces of paper.'

'I *am* an admiral,' said Rob, a touch of petulance in his voice. In truth, he was as eager as Adam for a quick, decisive strike. 'It is a great deal more complicated being an admiral than a sloop captain, haring over the horizon and engaging every ship you see.'

'Then I hope I never get promoted.'

Rob was about to give a sharp retort. Then he remembered himself and smiled.

'I believe I said the same when I was your age. But ... circumstances change.' He sighed. 'Everything catches up with us in the end.'

'Then let us drink to good times and good friends, and pray I never get old like you.'

'An excellent idea.'

Adam led Rob aft towards his cabin.

'You remember that French schooner I captured off Marseilles? Her captain was fond of claret. He kept a hold full of the finest Margaux wine. I managed to save a few bottles.'

'I will gladly swap them for a bottle of the fine cognac I took from Admiral Gaspard when I accepted his surrender.'

Deep in conversation, father and son headed below. Two men watched them with deep affection. One was Angus, who had come aboard with Rob. The other, a strongly built African with ritual scars on his face and his hair tightly cropped, was Scipio.

'It is good to be back together,' said Scipio.

'It is that,' answered Angus.

The two men were firm friends, united by their love for the sea, and for the Courtneys.

Scipio nodded towards the shore. Shadows were lengthening over the dunes, hiding whatever might lurk in their hollows.

'It will be hot work tomorrow.'

'If the weather changes.'

'It will change. And he will attack.'

'A rare day, seeing the admiral and his bairn in the same fight.'

It was another – unspoken – reason why Rob and Adam did not sail aboard the same ship. Phoebe had never said a word of complaint, but Rob knew she fretted long sleepless nights about her menfolk, and the dangerous profession they had chosen. He had not dared risk both Courtneys' lives in the same battle. Until now.

'Let us hope they do not regret it.' Scipio sounded troubled.

Angus laughed – too loudly. Deep down, he felt the same misgivings as his friend.

'It's yon Dutchmen we should be worried for,' he said stoutly. 'With one Courtney coming at 'em, they wouldn'ae stand a chance. With two of 'em . . .'

He clapped Scipio on the shoulder and led him forward.

'We should celebrate. Claret and brandy may be fine for the likes of Admiral Rob and Captain Adam, and grog's all right for them, but I need a good dram of whisky.'

The wind dropped that night, as Scipio had predicted. Next morning, it blew stiff and steady, licking the waves with crisp white foam. At first light, Rob sent a boat ashore to reconnoitre the beach. The men returned and pronounced it clear of defences.

'How is the sea?' Adam demanded.

'A fair swell,' said the coxswain. 'Nowt we can't handle.'

'What about it, then?' Adam asked Rob. 'Sir,' he added hastily, remembering there were others present. 'We have seven thousand men in the transports. If we put them ashore now, we could cut off Cape Town from the rear. The garrison would have to come out and give us open battle, away from the castle.'

Rob studied the shore through his one good eye. If the wind turned, or rose again, the boats would be trapped in a nexus of currents, waves and rocks, with no escape. The high dunes behind the beach offered cover for marksmen or artillery if the Dutch managed to bring them up.

'What do you say, Scipio? Will the weather hold?'

Scipio nodded. 'For a few hours.'

Still Rob hesitated. 'I do not like the look of that reef. The current will draw the boats on to it.'

'We can run one of our sloops aground against it,' said Adam. 'The *Bluebell*'s hull is so rotten she would never survive the journey home in any event.'

'That is an excellent plan.' Rob swung around to his flag lieutenant. 'Mr Jones! Signal the fleet. We will commence landing forthwith. The troop ships will disembark their men, while the bigger ships lay down a bombardment.'

'There is no one ashore to hit,' objected Jones.

'Then let us keep it that way.'

The men jumped to their orders. A string of signal flags was hoisted to the masthead. Adam hung back.

'General Beresford will not be happy when he learns he has made a two-hundred mile round trip to assault a fort we have already taken.'

'That presumes we will have taken it.'

Rob checked the wind again.

Does it feel stronger already?

Seven thousand men's lives depended on the decision he had taken.

Adam grinned. 'With Lucky Courtney leading us, how can we fail?'

My luck will run out one day, Rob wanted to say.

Every time he heard his nickname, he felt a twinge of super-stition. His instincts, his courage, his seamanship and his judge-ment, he trusted absolutely. But luck, like fate, was a capricious goddess. It could turn at any moment.

He would show no self-doubt.

'Death to the French,' he said loudly.

'And confusion to our enemies,' chorused his officers.

The men on deck huzzahed and threw their hats in the air. A cannon's roar split the sky. The sixty-four gun *Diomede* had already begun the bombardment of the beach.

'You will not regret this,' Adam promised.

Boats were lowered, troops mustered and weapons checked. The deck was a frenzy of activity as the crew attended to their allotted tasks: to an outsider it would have looked like chaos, but in reality it was highly ordered and disciplined. Rob stood still on the quarterdeck, the eye of the storm, observing the commotion he had unleashed. Thousands of men were moving to a purpose – some maybe to their deaths – because he had given the word.

'Over there, sir.'

Jones, the flag lieutenant, saw them first. Riders, galloping over the crest of the dunes, reining in as they saw the flotilla making for the beach. Through a telescope, Rob could see they were not uniformed as regular soldiers, but civilians: sober-suited farmers. Each carried a long rifle holstered by his saddle.

'Not enough to make a fart's difference,' sniffed Angus.

As he said it, a cannonball from the frigate struck one of the riders square on. Rob saw his torso torn in two. The Dutchman's head and shoulders cartwheeled across the ground. The panicked horse galloped away across the beach, the rider's legs and waist still held in the saddle by the stirrups, fountaining blood.

'That'll learn 'em,' said Angus.

'They'll bring others.'

Three of the riders turned and spurred back towards Cape Town. The others dismounted. They tethered their horses out of sight, then took up position on the back of the dune ridge, where the bombardment could not reach them. Rob glimpsed the flash of a spyglass.

'More will be here soon.' The tension was building inside Rob. He hated being out of the action. Against his better judgement, he felt himself giving in to the red mist. 'I am going ashore to reconnoitre.'

'Sir?' said Adam in shock.

'I will not ask my men to face dangers while their admiral sits in comfort in his flagship.'

'But that is your job. What has got into you?'

Rob was silent. Maybe it was older age that was prompting him – goading him to emulate the fearlessness of his youth, to recover the spark of being truly alive.

'I will accompany you,' said Adam.

'No. I need you at your post commanding the ship. If the Dutch bring up troops, we will need to react quickly.'

There was a boat alongside, ready to ferry men ashore. Before Adam could argue further, Rob shinned down the ladder, as nimble as the topman he had once been. The men on the oars began to protest as he squeezed between them, then hurriedly knuckled their foreheads when they saw who it was. Broad grins broke out on their faces. They were going into battle with Lucky Courtney.

The landing was in full spate now as the ships disembarked their troops. The boats crowded the bay. The rowers had to feather their oars, trying to find pockets of water among the press to make progress. Steering was out of the question. They moved en masse, as the boats knocked and bumped one another forward.

Rob crouched and scanned the beach. There were rocks close to the surface that would capsize the overloaded boats in an instant if they struck. With no steerage way, there would be nothing the crew could do to avoid them. Worse still was the danger from the beach. If the Dutch brought up artillery, they could cut bloody swathes through the landing flotilla.

The beach was clear for the moment. But what lurked in the undulating dunes beyond?

Coenraad Voorhees cursed the British. Then, for good measure, he cursed the Dutch governor, General Janssens. It was hard to say whom he hated more: the British invading his homeland, or the government, who had summoned him from his farm on the Zuurveld frontier, on the colony's eastern border, to fight in the militia.

He had almost refused. He had a wife, eight children, a hundred head of cattle and eighteen Negro slaves on his farm. The Xhosa tribesmen on the other side of the Fish River were always looking for a chance to cross and steal his livestock, while the governor ordered the Boers to stay behind a line that some official in Amsterdam had drawn on a map. As if the blacks had any right to that land when it was so fertile and ripe for grazing. When the blacks got too uppity, Coenraad and his fellow farmers would form a *commando* and traverse the river. They would slaughter a few of the Xhosa menfolk, burn their villages, and give their women a lesson they would not soon forget.

That was what it meant to be a Boer. You defended yourself and your property, whatever the law demanded.

And that was why he had answered the governor's call now. Not out of loyalty to the government, but to defend his land. He scrambled up the back slope of the dune, holding his rifle clear of the ground to prevent sand from fouling it. It was a beautiful weapon, though immensely heavy: so long that you could rest its butt on the ground while sitting on horseback and reload without having to dismount. He had carved the stock himself from stinkwood, curving the butt like the thigh of a male baboon.

He had cast the bullets himself, too, tempering the lead with tin to make it hard enough to penetrate even the toughest animal hide. He was wasting them on men – human skin was a soft target – but he wanted to hurt these men. He wanted the bullets to smash their bones and organs and come out the other side to strike the man behind as well.

If you provoked the Boer, kicked sand in his eyes, he would put a knife in your guts.

He edged to the ridge of the dune. To his right, a crew of Malagasy slaves were manhandling a gun into the emplacement they had dug out of the sand. They made too much noise – if they had been his slaves, he would have given them a lash of his *sjambok* – but the crash of the surf hid the sound from the men who were staggering ashore on the beach. They were Scotsmen, kilts flapping in the breeze and bagpipes wailing. They looked like seasoned fighters,

but that didn't worry Coenraad. The joy of the hunt was pitting yourself against a worthy adversary. And if he missed the landing party, there were always the men in the boats behind, packed so tight it would be like shooting cattle in a *kraal*.

He laid out the cartridges and his powder horn on the sand, and sighted his rifle. He unwrapped the cloth from the lock. This was the moment he enjoyed most – the power of holding a man's life in your hand, the power of the hunter over his prey.

There.

An officer, with a weathered face and plenty of gold lace on his uniform jacket. He would be a fine kill for Coenraad's bag.

Coenraad closed one eye. He nestled the stock against his cheek, wrapped his finger around the trigger – then squeezed.

The gun spat flame, smoke and lead. His aim was true. The hardened ball hit the officer below the ribbons on his chest and flung him backwards into the water.

That was what happened when you fought the Boer, Coenraad thought. Try to take his property, his land, and he would take your life.

Even above the roar of the surf, Rob – out in the landing flotilla – heard the shot. His head snapped up, homing in on the source. He saw everything in an instant: a puff of white smoke from the sand dune, and, on the beach, a Highland colonel staggering back into the surf, clutching his chest. The gold braid on his uniform coat had made him an obvious target.

More shots cracked from the dunes. Reinforcements had arrived. There must be a whole company of Dutch sharpshooters entrenched at that spot. But what if they were only the vanguard?

A deep roar boomed behind Rob. The ships were returning fire, pounding the beach with the full weight of their broadsides. Cannonballs screamed overhead, throwing up high plumes of sand. The men in the boats crouched low, while the Highlanders who had already gained the beach flung themselves to the ground.

None of the men were novices. Almost all had been in battle before. But the soldiers were out of their element, trapped in bobbing boats on a tossing sea, caught between the cannons behind and the rifles on shore. Some started to panic. Boats rocked; the rowers missed their strokes, and as soon as they faltered the current took them. It swept them sideways, pushing them east along the beach towards the reef.

The sailors in Rob's boat saw the danger and tried to pull away, but there was a boat butted up hard against their windward side which gave their oars no room. Now the reef was so close they could almost touch it. The sailors tried to fend it off, but their oars might as well have been toothpicks. Some snapped; others were wrenched from the men's hands.

The boat shuddered as it struck. Men were trapped. As the oars wedged against the rock, they jammed, pinning the men to their benches. One almost caught Rob's knee, but he wrenched it away and managed to scrabble to his feet. Stepping over his own men, Rob lunged for the side of the vessel.

The boat had already started to tip. Frantic soldiers were trying to climb over the side, scrambling into the neighbouring vessels. But those were overloaded, too: any more men would capsize them. Chaos would spread from boat to boat; the flotilla would be lost. With their equipment weighing them down, even the soldiers who could swim would drown.

Rob unbuckled his sword belt, pulled off his uniform coat and leaped onto the rock. The surface was wet and worn smooth by the waves: he slid straight off it into the water. He clung on, seeking a foothold underwater. He found a crevice in the rock and wedged his foot in. If he misjudged his next actions, there would be no escape.

The boat drifted towards him. Low in the water, she looked as huge as a whale. A splintered oar floated on the surface nearby. Rob grabbed it. Propping it against the rock, he tried to fend off the oncoming longboat. He knew he could not stop it. Instead, he bashed at the hull, trying to turn the bow away from the rock.

The boat slid so close to his face he could taste the tar from the caulking on his lips. Men were leaning over the side, staring down at him and yelling. Water muffled his ears, so he could not hear. He held his breath. Another inch closer and the hull would grind him against the rock like a millstone.

Behind him, he heard the hull scrape against an outcropping and for a moment he thought his time was up. The stern of the boat was swinging round towards him, inch by inch. It grazed his

cheek, pushing his head back against the rock. He felt his skull begin to crack like a nut.

Suddenly the pressure eased. He could breathe again. He had managed to push the boat away; a small pocket of space opened out on the water. But another boat, caught by the current, was already bearing down on him.

'Grab hold of the painter!'

He had to shout to be heard. Salt water swept into his mouth and made him gag, but he spat it out and shouted again, waving frantically. He saw an oar sweeping low over the water towards him. He duck-dived a second before it would have stoved in his head.

Resurfacing, he saw a man in the bow of the second vessel take a rope and throw it to the boat ahead. The line was taken in and went taut.

Past the rock, free of the crowded flotilla, the lead boat was able to manoeuvre. Her crew worked the few oars that hadn't broken, pulling clear. They dragged the trailing boat away from danger. That allowed the second boat's crew to row, opening more space. The jammed flotilla began to drift apart.

As quick as a squall, the panic that had threatened to engulf the men subsided. Sailors dug in their oars and sent their vessels cruising forward. Highlanders found their balance. They kneeled on the thwarts and poured a brisk fire at the beach, while the ships behind pounded the dunes with their cannons.

In the confusion, Rob had been left on the rock. But he was a strong swimmer. He kicked his foot free and turned towards the beach.

There was a shadow in the water.

Shark, said a voice in his head – he had seen them often enough, growing up – but no sooner had he thought it than he realised he was wrong.

Sunlight glinted on brass buttons. It was a soldier. He must have fallen from a boat in the panic and was sinking fast. In a moment, he would be out of reach. Without hesitating, Rob dived down and wrapped his arms around the man's torso.

The body was limp; hair floated like weed. It was impossible to tell if he was alive or dead. Rob pushed hard, lifting him to the light. They broke the surface, and almost went under again as a wave smashed over them. The waterlogged soldier, with the full kit and sodden woollen jacket of a corporal, was nearly three hundred pounds of dead weight, but Rob did not let go. He raised his head above water again and thumped him hard on the back.

A shudder convulsed the man. He was alive. Rob paused for a moment, treading water and taking his bearings. He was two hundred yards off the beach, with an ominous line of white breakers to pass through. Up on the dunes, he saw the muzzle flashes of rifles firing at the landing force. He doubted the Dutch could see him. At that distance, low in the water, he would be lost in the waves.

He took a breath and struck out towards the beach. The sea was high, and a vice admiral of the Red does not go swimming very often, let alone carrying a half-dead corporal. But Rob had spent his childhood exploring the coves and inlets of Nativity Bay; his grandmother had joked he was half porpoise. The movements returned effortlessly. He powered through the water with strong, purposeful kicks, his arm under the soldier's shoulders.

The noise rose as they approached the boiling breakers. The corporal's weight tried to drag Rob down, but he tightened his grip and kicked harder, paddling as hard as he could with his one free arm. A wave was coming in. Rob let it lift him and the corporal, kicked towards its crest, then gave himself over to the merciless wave to carry them both forward on its surge.

The wave broke. Rob stopped trying to swim; instead, he wrapped himself around the soldier and held his breath as the surf tumbled them over and over in the maelstrom. For a moment, he felt weightless. Then his foot touched solid ground. He launched himself up; his head broke the water and he saw the beach only a few yards distant. Dragging the corporal by his shoulders, he staggered onto the beach.

He had returned to Africa.

A bullet hit the ground beside him. The marksmen in the dunes were still in full action, and the Highlanders forming up on the beach were too far away to provide cover. Rob had left his sword in the boat and lost his pistol in the water; the corporal had his ammunition pouch attached to his belt, but the powder was soaked. Rob scanned the open beach for a rock to hide behind, but there was nothing.

The corporal was coming to. Rob dragged him towards the shelter of the dunes – closer to danger, but at least they would not be out in the open. From the corner of his eye, Rob saw a silhouette rising, an impossibly long rifle levelling at him. Rob could make it to cover if he ran, but that would mean abandoning the corporal to certain death.

If he did nothing, they would both die.

The air hummed as a cannonball screamed overhead and slammed into the slope above. The marksman ducked away, as a column of sand exploded into the air and rained down around them.

Rob was convinced it was more than luck. Adam must have been watching from the quarterdeck. He would have seen Rob emerge from the sea, and assessed the danger from the riflemen in the dunes. Now any Dutchman who wanted to shoot Rob would have to expose himself to the full force of the ship's broadside.

Rob dragged the corporal over the stretch of beach and found a hollow at the foot of the dunes. The corporal rolled over and purged lungfuls of water.

'Christ, but that was a cunny hair from drowning.' The salt water had done nothing to douse the man's broad Scots accent – or the colour of his language. He was a small, terrier-like man, with a red moustache and a corporal's stripes on his shoulder. He stuck out a trembling hand. 'Frank Waite.'

Without his uniform coat, Rob had nothing to indicate his rank. He had lost his fine boots and stockings, and his tailored breeches had been torn ragged in the surf. The corporal had mistaken him for a common sailor.

Rob shook the proffered hand. 'Robert Courtney.'

Corporal Waite's firm grip went suddenly limp.

'*Admiral* Courtney? Vice Admiral Sir Robert bloody Courtney?'

'I will be when I get my fleet back. In the meantime, rank is no protection from a Dutch bullet. We are equals on this beach.'

'Aye,' said Waite doubtfully.

Rob's mouth was parched. 'Do you have anything to drink?'

The corporal unbuttoned his tunic and fetched out a small flask. Rob took a deep draught to wash the salt water from his mouth – and nearly choked as the raw taste of whisky burned his throat.

'I didn't think the Highlanders needed any extra courage,' he said.

'No more we do, sir,' said Waite. 'But fighting's a sore thirsty business.'

'That it is.'

Rob glanced up. At the foot of the steep dunes, with Adam's cannon covering them, they were safe from the sharpshooters above. It would be possible to wait out the rest of the battle, until the Highland regiment formed up and made their advance.

It was not in Rob's nature to lie low while his men were being shot at.

'I am going up there,' he told Waite.

The corporal looked unsurprised. 'I'll follow ye.'

'Maybe we will get you a sergeant's stripe before the day is out.'

Rob clambered up the slope. Sand ran into his shirt and his breeches. He paused at the top of the rise – then, in a sudden bound, sprang up and rolled over the top.

A cry of alarm told him he had been seen. Before he had stopped moving, he located the source of the sound. A burly man, with a sunburned face and the blue uniform coat of the Cape *Dragonder* militia, was loading a long rifle, ready to fire at Rob. He handled the rifle with ease; less so the militia jacket. The tight-fitting seams cramped his movements, giving Rob half a second more time. He hurled himself at the Dutchman.

The man pulled the trigger. Rob was so close that the discharge scorched his face: surely the man could not miss. But in his haste, the man had snatched it. He hadn't finished reloading. The ramrod flew an inch past Rob's shoulder and stuck quivering in the sand behind him.

Rob drove into the Dutchman and wrestled him to the ground. On the soft sand, neither of the men could keep their footing. They rolled to the bottom of the slope, locked in each other's grip.

Rob was first to his feet – but it was scant advantage. He was not a weak man, but in the last ten years he had spent more time wielding a pen than his fists. The Dutchman was a farmer who could carry a springbok across his shoulders. He pulled himself upright, spitting curses.

For the first time, Rob felt afraid. He squared up to his opponent, keeping his fists high. He tried a left feint, followed by a right jab, but the Dutchman dodged them easily. He answered with a straight hit to Rob's face, a punch like a kicking horse. Rob managed to block it. Too late, he realised that it had been a feint. The attack with real purpose was a fist to his belly that doubled him over. Before he could recover, the Dutchman brought up his knee, trying to smash Rob's nose. He caught Rob's chin instead, snapping his head back so hard it almost broke his neck. Rob flew back and landed on the sand.

The Dutchman pulled a blade from his belt. It was the hunting knife he used for flaying the carcasses of the game he shot, or sometimes the blacks who trespassed on his land. Rob lay helpless, dazed from the blow he had taken. The glimmering blade was a blur of white light. He tried to crawl away, but the Dutchman put a foot on his leg and pinned him fast.

The knife dropped. A heavy weight thumped into Rob, knocking the breath out of him. He tasted blood. But it was not the killing blow. The Dutchman had collapsed on top of him, bleeding where his scalp had been cracked open. Blinking, Rob saw Waite with the ramrod in his hands. It had broken in two with the force of the blow Waite had struck.

Before the Dutchman could recover, Waite picked up the fallen knife and stuck it through his ribs.

'You saved my life,' Rob gasped.

'That's why the Lord moved you to pull me out of the water,' said Waite.

He wiped the knife on the Dutchman's jacket, then expertly frisked the corpse. A few guilders disappeared into his ammunition pouch. He picked up the dead man's long rifle and reloaded it.

'What now, sir?'

Rob's head was clearing. He stood, scanning his surroundings for any new dangers.

A sharp crack sounded from the narrow valley that wound through the dunes. It was different from the report of a rifle – more like the snap of a whip. It was followed by a cry and a groan.

Rob and Waite exchanged glances. They crept through the spiky rhinoceros bush, over a saddle in the dunes to a valley leading down to the beach. It looked like a well-trodden path that stray livestock and antelope might take to the shore; now it was blocked. Timbers had been thrown across it, and the sand dug out to form a makeshift embrasure. Eight black slaves, naked to the waist, were serving a small eight-pound field gun under the direction of a white officer. They must have dragged the cannon all the way from Cape Town. Their hands bled, and their feet were shackled so they could not run away

The officer struck one of the slaves. The man tripped on his fetters and stumbled into the gun. The scalding hot barrel scorched his skin. He screamed and dropped the cannonball he was carrying. That earned him another sharp lash of the officer's *sjambok*, which left a bloody welt across his shoulders.

Rob felt his blood rise. Growing up on his family's homestead in Africa, it had never occurred to him to judge a person by the colour of his skin. The people of the local tribes had been friends and guests; their children had been his playmates. He had not forgotten the horror he had felt the first time he saw how British and American planters treated their slaves – the barbarism they meted out in pursuit of their profits. Twice in his early career, he had freed slaves from their owners, and both times it had nearly cost him his life. Since then, every slaver on the oceans feared crossing paths with a ship under Robert Courtney's command.

The sight of the slaves being forced to fight for the men who oppressed them made him boil with anger. He grabbed the rifle from Corporal Waite and stepped into the open. It was an age since he had fired a long arm, but it settled against his cheek easily. With a single fluid motion, he sighted and fired.

The hardened bullet hit the Dutch officer between the eyes, drilled through his brain and emerged from the back of his head. He stood for a moment, almost too surprised to die, then collapsed. The slaves, accustomed to violence, reacted faster. They threw themselves to the ground, burrowing into the sand.

'Go!' Rob shouted.

The Africans looked up, but did not move. They didn't speak English, and they would not trust the word of a white man.

'Go!' he said again, more urgently. He slipped effortlessly into the Qwabe language he had learned as a child with his playmates, the language he spoke sometimes with Phoebe. 'Go before the Dutch come back.'

The sight of a white man speaking like an African astonished them. One, bolder than the others, rose to his feet. He backed away, never taking his eyes off Rob. Rob smiled encouragement and waved him on.

Waite found a set of keys on the Dutch officer's belt and tossed them to the slaves. The leader unlocked his manacles, then freed the others. One by one, they climbed to their feet, rubbing their ankles and staring uncertainly at Rob.

Then they turned and ran into the dunes.

Rob knew it was only eight men – eight, against the tens of thousands who would be kidnapped and brutalised every year. But eight was better than none.

'There's more'n a few Scotsmen who'll be alive tonight because you took that gun out of service.' Waite was examining the cannon, wondering if it could be turned on the Dutch. 'You're not like any admiral I've ever seen before.'

But Rob didn't answer. Above the noise of battle, Waite had not heard a shot, let alone the wet plash of lead hitting flesh. Yet now Rob was lying on the ground, blood pumping from his chest.

Coenraad Voorhuis could not believe his luck. The Englishman had stepped out into the open, careless of his own safety. He had lost his coat, his hat, his sword – everything that marked him out as an officer. Yet Coenraad wasn't fooled. The eyepatch, the thick dark hair and the firm attitude of command gave the man away as surely as any gold lace or epaulettes.

The battle on the beach was over. He could see the militia sharpshooters streaming from the dunes towards Cape Town and the main army. They had known they could not stop the British landing – only extract a price for it. Perhaps if they could have brought their cannon to bear, they might have held out longer. But the British admiral had seen to that, with his daring strike.

Down on the beach, the British were forming up in lines and advancing. If Coenraad didn't retreat now, he would be captured.

He had time for one last shot. He had already notched up a colonel that morning; now he wanted an admiral in his game bag. The Englishman was out in the open, inspecting the captured cannon. Coenraad was convinced he was an admiral – a sixth sense told him so. Hidden by seagrass and a dip in the dunes, Coenraad was invisible. He wrapped one of his hardened balls in a leather patch, then rammed it down the barrel. He steadied his arm on the sand so there would be no tremor, no mistake.

The rifle kicked hard, but Coenraad's broad shoulders rolled easily with the recoil. The Englishman fell. Blood gushed from his chest as he lay beside the overseer he had shot. A small measure of revenge, an eye for an eye, thought Coenraad. It was the same sweet feeling he had when he brought down an old bull elephant.

That would teach them to take on the Boer, he thought.

As a commander, Adam Courtney was used to being in control of his ship, master of his own destiny. Now, all he could do was watch through his telescope, trying to stifle his unease for his father. He had seen Rob's boat drifting towards the rocks; held his breath while Rob guided the vessel to safety and emerged safely onto the beach. But then Rob had disappeared into the dunes, where the Dutch sharpshooters were entrenched. That was over half an hour ago.

'The admiral'll be fine,' said Angus's steady voice beside him. 'Most likely he's marched to Cape Town and taken the castle by now.'

Adam nodded, though his hand that gripped the rail was white at the knuckles. He lifted his telescope and scanned the beach impatiently.

'What is that?'

A party of Highlanders had emerged from the dunes with a stretcher, heading towards the boat. Adam could not see the man they carried – only a glimpse of a pair of bare feet, unmoving.

The Highlanders waded into the sea and lowered the stretcher into one of the troop boats. There seemed to be an air of deference and melancholy about the sailors on the oars; Adam imagined he could hear a groan rise as they saw the man in their midst.

He knew, immediately, who it had to be.

The boat came alongside. Adam looked down and saw his father's body lying stretched out over the benches, his skin white from loss of blood.

A black veil passed across Adam's eyes; he thought he might faint. Then Rob's hands twitched, and his one eye blinked. He was still alive.

They brought Rob aboard and carried him to Adam's cabin. They laid him on the chart table, so the surgeon could observe him by the light coming through the stern windows. The soldiers had staunched the bleeding of the wound with a balled-up shirt, but the blood had soaked through it and was oozing out. How much blood could a man lose?

The surgeon laid out his tools: a gleaming, sharp-toothed arsenal of knives and saws. He slit the front and sleeves of Rob's shirt, then pulled away the cloth from the wound.

Blood slopped out of the hole in his chest like wine from a bottle. Rob cried with pain, but Angus was at his side. He cradled Rob's head in his arms as he tipped brandy from a tumbler into his mouth.

The surgeon took up his scalpel and passed Angus a thick piece of leather.

'Put this between his teeth so he does not bite off his tongue. This will hurt.'

Adam was no coward. He had fought in scores of engagements with the same careless bravery he had learned from his father. But the sight of Rob, in agony and helpless as an infant, was unbearable.

'Tell me when it is done,' he said, and walked out from the cabin.

Phoebe Courtney stood on the rampart of the castle, fanning herself against the hot January sun. She gazed at the bay where the ships lay anchored, dominated by the great flat top of Table Mountain and the vast African sky above. On the slopes below, the town spread out in a wide arc: neat, white houses and the elegant buildings left by the Dutch East India Company who had first settled here.

The sight stirred strange emotions. This was her homeland, but not as she had known it. European architecture planted onto

African soil, a hybrid that was an awkward clash of cultures. Like her. A proud daughter of the Qwabe tribe, standing in a Dutch castle that flew a British flag, dressed in silks and muslins that had been the height of London fashion when they sailed. Her life had taken her to three continents. She had played on the banks of the Umgeni river, slaved on a South Carolina plantation, and been presented to the king at St James's Palace. Often, she thought she did not know what she was or where she belonged.

'I am Robert's wife,' she told herself.

That was the fundamental truth. He was the rock on which she had rebuilt her life, after the slavers had tried to destroy it. He was the reason she could walk down Pall Mall and not care about the curious looks she attracted. With Robert and their son Adam, her world was complete no matter where she went.

Now her world hung by a thread.

Bare feet slapped the stone behind her. She half turned, and saw Scipio coming up the steps. The scars on his face were creased with concern.

How is he? The look on her face asked the question without words.

'Asleep, still.'

He joined her at the parapet and stared out into the bay.

'Remember the Nile?' he said.

The Battle of the Nile was the worst battle she had ever experienced in all her years sailing with Rob. Napoleon's army had invaded Egypt, the first stage of a planned conquest that was meant to go all the way to India. But a British fleet under Admiral Nelson had found Napoleon's ships anchored off the Egyptian coast. With their flank protected by the shore, the French fleet should have been unassailable.

Rob had been a captain that day, leading Nelson's line. It was Rob who had read the pattern of the sea in the uncharted bay and realised that there must be a channel of deep water on the landward side of the French fleet, where they did not expect to be attacked. He had taken his ship across their bows, so the French were battered from both sides. The ensuing battle had destroyed the French ships, cutting off Napoleon's army and dooming his campaign almost before it started.

The victory had been terrible. The French flagship, the *Orient*, had caught fire. As well as a full magazine of gunpowder for a hundred-and-eighteen-gun ship, her hold had been loaded with munitions for an entire army. The explosion when the flames reached it had been heard as far away as Alexandria. In an instant, the ship and her thousand-man crew had been blasted into a million fragments.

One piece – a chunk of iron, no larger than a shilling – had struck Rob in the eye. Phoebe shuddered as she remembered standing beside Rob's sickbed in the bowels of the ship, a lamplit hell of blood and broken men. The surgeons had been operating so quickly that severed limbs spilled out of the buckets, and the blood flowed in waves across the deck. She had held Rob's hand as the surgeons extracted the missile from the eye socket, praying the eye was all he would lose.

'That was eight years ago,' she murmured.

The wound had been terrible, but clean. The red-hot metal had cauterised the flesh around the eye. Once the pain and the shock eased, Rob had recovered. A mercy.

This was different. Rob had been unconscious since the Highlanders brought him to Cape Town, three days ago. Even after the surgeon had done his work, Rob had been too weak to move. Phoebe had tended him night and day. This moment, taking the air up on the ramparts, was the first time she had left his side in seventy-two hours, and even that felt like a betrayal. She told herself she did not want him waking up without her there. The truth was, she was terrified he would die without her.

Angus's head appeared through an open window.

'He's awake.'

Everything confused Rob. The wide, unfamiliar bed he woke up in. The pain throbbing in his chest. The view he could see through the windows: Table Mountain, far nearer than it should be.

A moment later the door opened. Phoebe, Angus, Scipio and Adam rushed in. The relief on their faces told him more than any surgeon's report about what must have happened. Flashes of memory returned. Sand dunes and sea grass. A long-barrelled rifle. The taste of whisky in his mouth. Then – darkness.

The visitors clustered around his bed. But not too close. Rob noted they kept a wary distance, as if afraid of damaging him.

'Was it that bad?'

'The bullet missed your heart by this much.' Adam held up his finger and thumb an inch apart. 'But it shattered your collarbone. It will be a long time before you can use your arm again.'

If ever.

The alternative hung unspoken between them.

Rob levered himself onto his right elbow. The strain was immense; sweat ran down his face and a tear beaded in the corner of his eye, but he kept pushing until he was nearly upright. Everyone could see the amount of physical effort he put into it, but no one tried to stop him.

'Where are we?'

Sitting up, he could see he was in a handsome room, long and spacious. The four-poster bedstead was carved of stinkwood, while the yellow-wood floorboards were waxed to a lustre. The wide bay windows were set with stained glass like jewels. Through one window, he saw his fleet at anchor in the bay, while through the other a large Union Jack blew from a flagpole.

He struggled to take it in.

'A victory?'

'Aye,' said Angus.

'The battle was two days after the landing,' said Adam. 'General Janssens took up position on the ridge of a hill named Blaauwberg. The Highlanders charged it, and in a short time broke the Dutch lines decisively. They chased Janssens into the mountains, while the rest of our army marched into Cape Town. The garrison commander surrendered without firing a shot.'

Rob processed the news.

'And our losses?'

'Two hundred and twelve casualties.' Adam gave a tight smile. 'Two hundred and thirteen, including you.'

'I do not intend to be a casualty for long.' A hint of the old steel returned to Rob's voice.

'On the contrary, my husband,' said Phoebe, 'the surgeon insists you must rest at least two months. If the wound reopens, there is a danger of infection.'

She did not need to explain what that meant. All of them had seen men die of gangrene: the rot that devoured a man's flesh until it poisoned him. If it set in in an arm or a leg, the limb could be amputated to save the man. But with this wound, so close to Rob's heart, there would be no remedy.

'My men . . .'

'In a few weeks, the India convoy will be arriving under Admiral Bolt, and he will take command. Until then, your ships will sit at anchor in this safe harbour and refit after the voyage. They do not need you.'

Only Phoebe would have dared put it so baldly. Adam looked away, while Angus could not meet Rob's gaze.

Rob gestured to his surroundings. 'Where am I?'

'The castle.' Adam said. 'The governor's quarters.'

Rob felt the finest linen made of best Chinese silk, the goose-down pillows and the yielding mattress. Compared to the narrow cot and paper-thin mattress he was used to at sea, it was like a king's bed. But . . .

'I must return to my flagship.'

'Nonsense.' Phoebe pointed to the windows overlooking the bay. 'You can watch your fleet from here. They will not run away.'

'No,' said Rob.

'It will speed your recovery.'

'No,' Rob said again.

A note of impatience came into Phoebe's voice. Rob knew from long experience that it meant she would not be contradicted.

'You must.'

Rob tried to lift his arm to stop her, but the effort defeated him.

'Enough. I know you are right. I will stay ashore.'

Phoebe folded her arms.

'But not here.'

She didn't understand.

'Where, then?'

'Nativity Bay.' He saw the doubt in her eyes. 'If I must recuperate, where better than with my family, in the house where I was born?'

A distant look came into his eyes. Even the thought of home brought colour to his cheeks.

'But to get there—'

'It is a week's easy sail up the coast. I will detach a sloop – I am still admiral of this squadron, am I not? – and Adam can take us. He has not seen his cousins and his aunts in years.'

He knew his plan was fanciful, and not a little indulgent, but he had the authority to insist it would happen. He stretched out his arm to Phoebe and took her hand in his.

'It is your home, too.'

Phoebe did not let go of his hand.

'Robert Courtney,' she murmured, 'you never know when to give up.'

FRANCE, 1798. EIGHT YEARS EARLIER . . .

Paul had never seen the sea before. He had spent his childhood moving between the family's town house in Paris, and
their estates and châteaux in the country around Orléans.
Constance never took him to the coast. Once, in a dusty room
that had been left unlocked, in a house they rarely visited, he had
found a portrait of a young man in a navy captain's uniform, with
a warship in the background. The man's fair hair and fine features were so familiar, he thought he was looking at his mother –
but when he showed her the portrait, she had smacked him and
locked herself away in tears. Later that day, he watched a footman
burn the picture in the garden. When Paul asked who it was, the
footman told him that the man was Paul's own brother, Étienne, a
dashing sea captain who had been killed in battle with the British.

'Her favourite,' the footman whispered. 'Her greatest hope.
After he died, she never set foot in a boat again.'

Ever since, Paul had brooded about the brother he had never
known. Sometimes he thought he could feel his presence, like
a ghost at his side. He obsessed about it. And every time he did
something wrong, or disappointed his mother, he thought: *I am
not as good as he was.*

Now he was going to sea himself. He stood on the quay at
Toulon, formed up with his regiment, staring open-mouthed
at the bustle of the harbour. There were ships everywhere he
looked, a grand parade of nautical power, sails, pennants and flags
dancing in the wind like a magnificent carnival. Thousands of
men stood arrayed in confident ranks, exuding purpose and lethal
intent. And beyond the breakwater, the vast expanse of the open
sea, like a mouth waiting to swallow him.

He turned his gaze on the largest ship, the hundred-and-eighteen
gun flagship *Orient*, the pride of the French navy.

'Admiral Nelson will shit himself when he sees her,' the sergeant said.

His name was Bastiat, a squat man from the Dordogne, with a face like a monkey and a nose for human weakness like a pig sniffing out truffles. He had taken a dislike to Paul since his first day in the regiment: tripping him, cursing him, humiliating him, making him an example to the others of everything a soldier should not be. He had not let up since then, or missed any opportunity to bully him.

'What do you say, *Couillon*?'

Couillon was the nickname he had given Paul. It meant 'little balls'.

'*Vive la république*,' said Paul.

He hated the army. Hated the other soldiers. Hated fighting for the revolution that had murdered his mother. But in those desperate days after her execution, it was the only place he could go to find refuge. France had introduced conscription: any young man found wandering the roads would be accused of being a counter-revolutionary or a deserter. Either way, he would be shot. Paul had assumed a false name and a false past, and buried himself in the last place that anyone would think to look for the son of the late Comte de Bercheny.

He had fought in the Low Countries, then invaded Italy behind an unknown general named Napoleon Bonaparte. He had fought in thirteen battles, thirteen victories. Before each one, he had emptied his guts. Sergeant Bastiat called him a faggot and worse; the other soldiers spat at him and pissed on his blankets, so that he woke up damp and stinking of urine. But Paul had survived.

Now the sight of the *Orient* stirred something in him. Not pride, revolutionary fervour or martial desire. It was the beauty of it. He pulled his sketch pad and a pencil out of his haversack and began drawing. His arm moved easily, bringing the ship to life on the page with bold lines. Sketching let him forget the relentless misery of the army and set him free.

Drawing the ship demanded all his attention: the intricacies of her rigging and spars, the complex shadows that fell between the sails. He was transported. In the void between the eye and the hand, it was no longer Napoleon's flagship, but the ship in the portrait in the locked room; and the tiny figure on the quarter-deck was his brother. In his imagination . . .

A fist knocked the pencil from his hand. Bastiat snatched the paper away.

'Give me that,' said Paul in a low voice.

'Come on, little bitch,' said Bastiat. The other soldiers had gathered round, forming a tight circle. 'Take it from me.'

Bastiat showed him the paper – then, as Paul grabbed for it, he punched him hard in the gut. Paul doubled over, gasping for breath. Bastiat laughed and kicked his feet from under him, dumping him on his back on the quayside.

The other men guffawed. A few aimed kicks at Paul.

Lie still, Paul told himself. *Let them lose interest. If you fight, you will make it worse. Endure what you must to survive.*

But the picture was of his brother, and Bastiat was still holding it above his head. Paul leaped up and lunged for it again. The sergeant brought up his fist.

Paul moved faster than he expected. Before the punch was thrown, Paul was inside Bastiat's guard. Paul was scrawny; Bastiat was built like a brick wall. Paul's fists would bounce off his barrel chest without making a dent.

Paul kicked him between the legs with all the power he possessed.

The look of anguished surprise on Bastiat's face made everything worthwhile. Then the sergeant's fist hit Paul's face very hard, so that he felt his nose crack. He fell to the ground, blood streaming over his lips.

'I will kill you,' said Bastiat.

The other soldiers stepped away as Bastiat stood over Paul. He crumpled the drawing and tossed it aside. Paul saw the wind blow it across the quay towards the sea.

'I will break every bone in your body,' said Bastiat. 'When I have finished with you, you will not even be able to hold your cock.'

Paul had nothing to fight for. He curled himself into a ball and prayed for it to be brief.

The blow never came. Paul heard a sudden shuffle of feet and stamping of boots. Opening an eye, he saw the platoon standing to attention. Bastiat had stepped back into line. He snapped a salute.

A group of officers had appeared, men with fine leather boots and expensive swords. But that did not explain the look of awe and terror on Bastiat's face.

Then Paul saw the general, so short he was hidden in the throng of men, yet the moment you noticed him everyone around him appeared insignificant. You could describe his appearance – delicate features, a narrow bow mouth and tousled dark hair – but that barely captured his presence. He glowed with energy, like the haze around a candle flame. The hero of the revolution, the man who had saved France and conquered Italy: Napoleon Bonaparte.

He was holding a rumpled piece of paper. It was Paul's picture.

'Who drew this?'

Paul said nothing. Inwardly, he cursed his fate. He could have survived Bastiat's beating, but now he had come to the attention of Bonaparte himself, he was doomed. What if they thought he was an English spy, drawing the French forces? Or – worse – if they found out who he really was?

Bonaparte began to get agitated. He was not used to asking twice.

'Who drew it?'

Bastiat did not know why the general cared. But he knew that if he did not give Bonaparte what he demanded he would be cleaning latrines for the rest of his career. He pointed at Paul.

'Him.'

The general turned. Paul shrivelled under his gaze. Bonaparte's grey eyes were as hard as steel, eyes that seemed to take in the world and shrink it to nothing.

'You have rare talent, Private.'

Paul blushed and bowed his head. He hated compliments.

'What is your name?'

'Private Paul Courtenay, sir.'

Courtenay was the name he had assumed when he joined the army.

'You know where we are going?'

'No, sir.'

The army's destination was a closely guarded secret, though that did not stop rumours spreading. Some said Sicily, others Malta. Some of the wilder guesses said they were going to invade England itself.

The general gave a small smile. 'I am glad there are still some secrets in this army.' The aides around him laughed sycophantically. 'I can tell you, citizen, we are going where no Frenchman has ever been before.'

Paul understood he was not expected to ask where that might be.

'I am assembling a group of the most talented scientists, engineers and artists to accompany the expedition. They will document what we discover and bring our newly acquired knowledge back home to display to the world. They will demonstrate beyond doubt the glory of France.'

He leaned forward and addressed Paul. 'For a man of such humble origins to be elevated to the group, purely on account of his talent . . . you would be a living monument to the ideals of our revolution. Do you wish to join this group?'

Paul had little idea what the general was proposing, or what he would say if he found out Paul's origins were not humble at all. But it was obvious that Bonaparte was offering him the chance to escape, away from the front line – wherever they were going – and away from Bastiat. That was all Paul needed to know.

'It would be the greatest honour of my life to be part of the expedition,' he said.

'Lefebvre.' Bonaparte snapped his fingers. A tall man in a well-tailored grey coat stepped forward. His appearance was immaculate, except for the cuffs of his shirt, which were smeared with charcoal and spotted with paint. 'This private is assigned to your commission. Take him under your care and see he has all the equipment he requires for the task ahead.'

The commotion on the dock seemed to halt as Lefebvre's gaze fixed on Paul. He had eyes full of appetite that drank in the world; an artist's intensity that seemed to strip away Paul's clothes and see into the flesh beneath. Paul felt uneasy.

Lefebvre offered his hand. He had long, slim fingers that tickled Paul's wrist as they shook hands. A benevolent smile touched the corner of his lips.

'I look forward to working with you on our mutual mission.'

Bonaparte passed Paul's picture to an aide, who returned it to Paul. Paul saluted, sniffing back the blood that still trickled down his nose.

'*Vive la république!*'

Bonaparte saluted, then continued along the docks with his entourage. The moment they had passed, Bastiat gave Paul a murderous look. Paul ignored it. For the first time in nine years, since he had heard the church bells ringing in the revolution, he felt he had a purpose.

He glanced at Lefebvre.

'Where are we going?'

Lefebvre gave him another of his appraising stares. Paul blushed; he became keenly aware of his bloodied face, and the dockside muck that clung to his uniform after his fight with Bastiat. Lefebvre reached out and brushed a piece of straw from Paul's shoulder.

'The first thing we must do is get you bathed. We cannot have you making dirty pictures.'

The fleet sailed a week later. Paul had thought that sharing a tent with eight other men in the army had been cramped, but that was like the Palace of Versailles compared to life at sea. The flagship, the mighty *Orient*, was more crowded than a cattle market. Her regular crew of a thousand men had been joined by two thousand soldiers and another two hundred officers and other hangers-on. At mealtimes Paul and Lefebvre ate at a table set for two hundred and fifty men, so tight one could hardly lift food to one's mouth without clashing elbows.

It was still better than life in the army. As a new member of the Commission of the Sciences and Arts, Paul was no longer treated as a private: he was a gentleman. He had no chores, no duties and no discipline. He was free of Sergeant Bastiat, who had been assigned to one of the other transports.

He began to draw. He sketched the officers in their fine cocked hats and dashing uniforms. He drew the sailors, working the ship or off duty, smoking their pipes and dancing their jigs. He sold some of his pictures: a sou each for the sailors and a franc for the officers, because, after all, the revolution had not yet made men *completely* equal. He drew Bonaparte, standing on the poop deck staring at the horizon. He captioned it *L'homme du Destin* – the Man of Destiny. When Bonaparte saw it, he exclaimed with delight and put it on his cabin wall.

'But where are we going?'

It was the subject they always came back to, their endless specu-
lation unhindered by hard fact. This time, the question had come
from an engineer named Gaillard, sitting at supper one evening.

'You should know,' said a major of dragoons across the table.
'You're a *savant*.'

There was widespread laughter. The '*savants*' was the nickname the men of the Commission had been given: 'the experts'.

'Ask Lefebvre,' said Gaillard. Lefebvre was the head of the
Commission. 'He knows, but he won't tell.'

All eyes along the crowded table turned to Lefebvre. Paul, sitting next to him, shrank into the bench. His colleagues were emi-
nent men, erudite, quick-witted and impeccably mannered. Paul
felt lumpen in their company. He let them ignore him, for fear of
what they might say if they took notice of him.

Only Lefebvre paid him attention. For reasons Paul didn't
understand, he had adopted Paul as his protégé. He complimented his drawings, tousled his hair and always sat next to him
at meals.

Lefebvre looked around conspiratorially.

'Happily, the general has permitted me to reveal all. We are
bound . . .'

He let the silence deepen until every man was hanging on his
next word. Then he thrust his knife upwards, where the night sky
glimmered through the open grating.

'For the moon! Bonaparte means to conquer the stars themselves.'

His companions clapped and cheered. They raised their glasses
and drank toasts to the moon and the stars. Paul joined in, glowing with the good humour and camaraderie in the room. One of
the *savants*, an astronomer, stood up and began to sing a ribald
song about a peasant girl who took a walk under a full moon.

Paul felt a nudge at his elbow. Lefebvre was holding out his
fork with a morsel of beef on the end of it. He put it in Paul's
mouth to bite off.

'Thank you.'

Paul was squeezed so tightly he could barely lift his fork to feed
himself. Not that he cared. The food was weevil-infested biscuit,
rotten beef, and vegetables pickled in so much vinegar they made

him gag. After every meal, there was hardly space along the side of the ship for all the men emptying their stomachs.

Lefebvre wiped a spot of gravy from the corner of Paul's mouth.

'Come to my cabin after dinner.'

As head of the Commission, Lefebvre enjoyed the ultimate luxury: a cabin to himself. It was still no bigger than a hen coop. Lefebvre was sitting on the small bed when Paul arrived, with a sketch pad on his knee and a row of pencils lined up beside him.

He poured two glasses of brandy and gave one to Paul.

'I want to draw you.'

'Me?' Paul was flattered.

'As a life model.'

It took Paul a moment to understand what he meant.

'Undressed?'

Lefebvre nodded. Paul felt uncomfortable, but he supposed it was not an unusual request. Artists drew female nudes all the time, so why not men as well? He knew little of such things. The brandy had loosened his inhibitions.

He took off his clothes while Lefebvre readied his sketch pad and pencil. Lefebvre had trained as an architect, and it showed in his work. When he drew people, the images were brusque and functional, as though the people were blocks of stone. Paul found it slightly unsettling, though he would not presume to criticise his mentor.

Lefebvre walked around him. He adjusted the angle of Paul's head. He lifted Paul's hand and put it on his bare hip.

'Now move your right leg out – like so.'

He grabbed Paul's thigh and tugged it forward so firmly that Paul stumbled into him. For a moment the two men were locked in an awkward embrace. Lefebvre wrapped his hands around Paul's waist and clutched his buttocks. Paul smelled the brandy on his breath.

Paul pulled out of Lefebvre's grip and resumed his pose. Lefebvre sat on the bed and took up his pencil. He studied Paul for a long moment, then jumped up again.

Before Paul knew what was happening, he felt Lefebvre's hand slip around his member. Paul was so surprised he didn't know what to do. He froze. Lefebvre's slim fingers encircled the shaft, tugging back and forth. Paul felt himself harden. He was embarrassed – he wanted to resist – but his body responded automatically. In an instant, his penis was standing proud and hard as a pistol barrel.

Lefebvre drew back, admiring his handiwork.

'This is how I want to draw you. The potent French hero.'

Paul stood painfully still. The ship was alive with the sounds of men, ropes, spars and waves, but all he could hear was the scratch of the pencil. Lefebvre drew quickly, a flurry of sharp jabs and deft slashes, almost as if he were attacking the paper.

When he was finished, he patted the bed beside him.

'Sit here.'

Paul did as he was told. Lefebvre spread the paper across his knees. His hand rested in Paul's lap, trailing between his thighs.

'Do you like it?'

Paul could hardly concentrate with Lefebvre's hand touching him. But he did not like the picture. Lefebvre had drawn him with hard angles and sharp lines, geometric precision that some-how reduced him to an object. Lifelike, but without life.

Lefebvre's hand moved up Paul's thigh and closed around his manhood once again.

'Do you like it?'

Paul realised Lefebvre was no longer talking about the painting. A hundred thoughts confused his mind and left him tongue-tied.

Endure anything. Become anything.

'It is nice,' he stammered at last.

'Good,' said Lefebvre, smiling. 'Because there is something else I want to do with you.'

He unbuckled his breeches and reached for a jar of pork lard sitting on his sea chest.

Paul left the cabin reeling. His body ached from the things Lefebvre had done to him; his mind was in turmoil. He was not ignorant. After three years in the army, he was aware that men did these things together. When Bastiat taunted him as a faggot, he knew what it meant.

He had always thought such things were unspeakably wrong. Yet Lefebvre was his mentor, a man he trusted. He was good to him. How could he do anything bad to Paul?

Lefebvre was also Paul's superior. Bonaparte had organised the Commission along military lines and given every man a rank. Lefebvre was a general; Paul only a lieutenant. If Lefebvre took against Paul, he might demote him to a private and expel him from the Commission, send him back to his regiment. Whatever Lefebvre had done to Paul, it was still kinder than what Sergeant Bastiat would do.

Paul took his place in his hammock, stacked three deep with a man above and another below. The snores and belches and farts of three thousand men made sleep almost impossible. It was hard to nod off with a man's filthy body sagging six inches over your face.

He lay there, his soul aching, until daylight seeped through the gunports.

He told no one what had happened.

Every day the vast fleet of over a thousand ships sailed east, and still no one knew where they were going. Paul, raised on stories of the ancient myths, thought even the Greek fleet sailing to capture Troy could not have been more splendid. It was impossible to think that any force on Earth could challenge it.

Yet the crew were nervous. The captain posted double lookouts, and was often on deck with his telescope. Even Bonaparte seemed uneasy.

One afternoon, Paul eavesdropped on the conversation of two sailors he was sketching.

'The English cannot be far away,' said one.

'Let them come,' scoffed the other. 'Bonaparte will give them a taste of French iron. He is unbeatable.'

'On land, *bien sûr*. But at sea? The English admiral Nelson will have something to say about it.'

The second sailor pointed at one of the twenty-four-pound cannons lashed to the bulwark.

'This will take care of Nelson.'

'It is not only Nelson. His captains are as fierce as he. There is a rumour – I heard it from a brothel-keeper in Toulon before we sailed – that Captain Courtney is with Nelson's fleet.'

'*Putain*,' the second sailor swore. 'I fought Courtney off Guadeloupe. Our two-decker against his frigate. We shot his ship from under him, but he kept coming at us until he had battered us to the waterline. The sharks would have taken me, if Courtney had not lowered his boats to rescue us. That man does not know when he is beaten.'

Paul had stopped drawing. Spoken in French, the English name 'Courtney' and the French name 'Courtenay' did not sound similar. No one had noticed the resemblance between Paul's false surname and this notorious British sea captain's; if they had, they hadn't thought it worth any comment.

Paul had taken the name 'Courtenay' because he thought it had once been his mother's – though she had never told him that. In the library of the château, aged about ten, he had found an English book among all the dusty French tomes: *Moll Flanders* by Daniel Defoe. The cover had fallen open, and on the inside, in a neat school-girlish hand, he had read, 'This book is the property of Constance Courtney'.

When he asked his mother about it, she told him Constance Courtney had died many years earlier. He had not pressed her. He was intelligent enough to know that his mother had many secrets. But the name had stuck in his memory, a solitary clue to a past he could only guess at. When he took it for his own, he had francised it to 'Courtenay' so it would not stand out.

To hear the original spoken now, aboard ship, made him uneasy. He told himself it must be a common English name.

'Where does this Captain Courtney come from?' he asked the sailors.

They looked at him in surprise. They hadn't realised he was listening. Paul saw the first sailor readying a sarcastic response, before remembering that Paul ranked as an officer. He adapted his answer into something impeccably patriotic.

'He comes from the Devil's arse.'

And that was all Paul found out.

Bonaparte's famous luck held. Nelson did not find them, and nor did Robert Courtney. After three weeks, the fleet arrived in Malta, but only to reprovision. The Knights of Malta refused them access; Bonaparte responded with a furious twenty-four-hour assault that reduced the defenders to abject surrender. Another vestige of the old world swept away – another territory added to the might of

France. Bonaparte was unconquerable. The army was invincible. Bonaparte at last revealed that the fleet was bound for Egypt, but even then his men whispered that this was not the final destination. Once he had conquered the land of the pharaohs, he would march across the deserts of Persia and Arabia to India itself, like Alexander the Great. He would seize the jewel of the British Empire and cut off the riches that funded her mighty navy. And after that, who knew? The world was at Bonaparte's feet. In those heady days, who could doubt it?

Paul never forgot his first sight of Egypt. He stood at the rail, jostling with every man aboard, until the captain ordered his marines to push them back for fear the ship would capsize. Paul had his sketchbook ready to capture the moment. He had imagined a skyline like some ancient oriental cityscape, studded with pyramids and obelisks and colossal statues of pharaohs, fringed with palm trees and graced by flocks of exotic birds.

There was nothing to see. Just a shimmering ribbon on the horizon, as if someone had taken a paintbrush and drawn a white line where the blue sea met the blue sky.

Paul drew a pencil line across the centre of his page. He licked his finger and smudged it. The starkest image imaginable, like the beginnings of a picture he had quickly abandoned. Yet it unsettled him. The line throbbed on the page: a border, a divide. As if by crossing it, he would be doing something transformative and irrevocable.

Lefebvre squeezed beside him. He ran his hand down Paul's back to the base of his spine.

'You know what the Arabs do to the men they capture?'

Paul shook his head.

'A particular treatment for which the Orient is famed. But it is not so bad as men say.' Lefebvre gave him a wink and a slap on his buttock. 'I have heard some men even enjoy it.'

The fleet landed on the coast near Alexandria. The Mameluke cavalry charged them, but the brave desert warriors were no match for disciplined French troops. Another victory for the Republic. Alexandria fell, and Bonaparte took up residence in a house overlooking the ruined foundations of the great lighthouse, once one of the Seven Wonders of the World.

Two days later, the first battalions set out towards the Egyptian capital, Cairo. Bonaparte was impatient. The easiest route was to follow the Nile, where water was plentiful and boats could supply their advance. But the river meandered in disobliging loops that lengthened the route and offended Bonaparte's efficient mind. Instead, he drove his army in a straight line across the desert. Flies, thirst and Arab raiders tormented the men. They burned by day and froze at night.

Paul's only consolation was that Lefebvre left him alone. He was too busy worrying about food to think about satisfying his carnal appetites.

They were in the desert for almost three weeks. One night, they struck camp after midnight and marched across the moonlit sands, formed up for battle. As day dawned, they heard the cry of a muezzin's call to prayer wailing through the mist across the river. The call was taken up by another, then ten more, then a thousand others.

'Cairo.'

The word went up and down the line in excited whispers. The air glowed as the sun rose. The parting mist revealed a city: a shimmering fabric of domes, towers, battlements and spires, piled up and almost too fabulous to be real. Paul grabbed his portfolio and sketched it quickly, soft inky lines blending into one another like a dream.

Ahead, three peaks pricked the morning sky. They floated suspended above the desert haze, too high to be buildings. They had to be mountains, but when Paul drew them the lines were so undeviatingly straight they could not be natural.

The sun rose higher, revealing them more clearly. The pyramids. Then the sun touched the ground of the plain, and Paul forgot his wonder. Stretched between the river and the pyramids, spanning nearly ten miles, was the enemy army.

The battle lasted for only two hours and confirmed – yet again – Bonaparte's military genius. Paul spent the time cowering with the pack mules, trying to keep the animals from bolting. Afterwards, he sketched what he could remember.

He drew the Mameluke cavalry parading like glorious tropical birds in their bright silk robes and turbans. Some had decorated their helmets with egret feathers. The sun burnished their helmets and scimitars, the points of their lances and their mail armour, so that they looked like a line of fire sweeping across the desert. Their horses were the finest Paul had ever seen, their weapons flashing with the inlay of gold and precious stones, as if the Arabian Nights and the Romance of King Arthur had all melded into one.

He sketched them again an hour later, when their corpses lay heaped five or six deep. Dying horses thrashed their limbs, jerking the dead like puppets. Some of the Mamelukes were still on fire where spent musket wadding had set their fine silk robes alight.

The battle was a victory for brutal mathematics over chivalry. The French infantry formed squares, so that every horse was opposed by at least nine muskets, and no amount of courage or daring by the Mamelukes could beat those odds. The cavalry dashed themselves against the infantry squares like rabid dogs. When their morale broke, the French soldiers executed a perfect evolution from square to column, and drove the Mamelukes back across their lines and into the river. Many drowned, weighed down by their splendid armour. Paul drew the French soldiers who swam out to the bodies to loot them. They had to compete with the crocodiles, who swarmed off the banks to devour the living and the dead indiscriminately. Several of the looters lost hands, or worse. Paul titled the picture *Feeding Frenzy*.

The Mameluke commander, Murad Bey, escaped the battle and withdrew south, abandoning Cairo to her conquerors. Victorious soldiers rampaged through the city, stealing anything they could carry and debauching the women they found. Paul did not enjoy the victory. That night, Lefebvre found him. He stank of wine, and had a manic look in his eye.

'*Vive la république*,' he slurred. 'Did you think I had forgotten you, my pet? Now we have something to celebrate.'

Paul knew what was expected of him. Flushing with angry shame, he unbuckled his trousers and rolled onto his stomach, wondering if it would not have been better to be captured by the Bedouin after all.

INDIAN OCEAN, 1806

The *Valiant* beat up the African coast, keeping away from the rocky shoreline and the currents that swirled around them. Rob was out of bed, standing at the rail despite Phoebe's attempts to make him sit in the shade.

'This is our home,' Rob reminded her. 'The sight of it is better medicine than anything that old sawbones could give me.'

Phoebe squeezed his hand. Together, they stared at the wild land they had both grown up in.

'There,' said Rob.

To the north-west, a whale-backed hill rose above the coastline, its profile unmistakable. It was where his ancestors lay buried, back to his great-grandfather, Tom Courtney, who had first built the settlement at Nativity Bay.

'We'll never get the *Valiant* through there,' fretted the sailing master. 'That channel's not wide enough for a longboat.'

'I have seen a fully laden Indiaman thread that passage.' Rob's face was alight with energy, flushed with colour that had finally returned after his convalescence. 'I will guide you through it without scratching the paintwork.'

Balancing himself on his cane, he shuffled forward to the bow. The sight of home could cure the spirit, but Rob's flesh would take longer to heal. Angus and Scipio followed close behind, ready to catch Rob if he fell.

Rob braced himself on the stays and leaned forward, surveying the sea ahead. It was a treacherous coast, with steeply shelving beaches and rugged headlands that offered no protection from the high surf. From the ship's deck, it was impossible to see any way in.

'Wind's behind us,' muttered the sailing master, eyeing the foam that surged over the rocks.

'There'll be a devil of a job beating off this shore if the channel's not there.'

Rob lifted his right arm. The helmsman eased the wheel a point to larboard.

'My father knows these waters,' Adam reminded the sailing master. 'He grew up here.'

'Aye. But how long ago was that?'

Rob waved his arm again. The helmsman paid off a little further. The ship rounded the point, and suddenly there was a narrow opening between the hill and the mangrove forest that came to meet it.

The sailing master chewed a wad of tobacco and kept his mouth shut. The helmsman kept his eyes on Rob.

'Put a leadsman in the chains,' Adam ordered. 'Who knows how the channel may have silted up or changed its course since last time.'

The ship glided under the shadow of the promontory, so close that a topman on the yardarm could have touched the cliff. Adam scanned the landscape with mounting excitement. Memories of his last visit flooded back dimly, like dreams. Would he recognise his grandparents? He looked to the slopes above for a welcoming signal. Rob had told him that in the old days they often kept a lookout on that hill, when the world was full of enemies who might seek out the Courtneys.

Today there was no one. These must be more peaceful times.

Rob guided the *Valiant* round to starboard, following the ribbon of deep water that was the only safe channel. Past the mouth, the bay opened out into a broad lagoon. A small river fed into it, with mangrove swamps on one side and a golden beach on the other. A long whaleboat was drawn up on the sand, high above the tideline.

'Somebody must be at home,' said Adam hopefully.

They dropped anchor in the lagoon, the same place where so many years ago a ship called the *Dunstanburgh Castle* had arrived to take Rob away.

'And now I have returned,' he murmured to himself. 'I have travelled so far, and here I am where I started.'

It should have been a happy thought, but somehow it seemed too final, like the end of a journey. The wound in his chest throbbed, as if to remind him of his own mortality.

Phoebe read his thoughts. 'You are only forty-six,' she reminded him. 'You have many years to live.'

'It does not feel that way.'

'Do not let Adam hear that. He is worried enough for you already.'

Rob nodded, but the years he had been away weighed on him. What if something had happened to his father – or, worse, to his sister Susan and her children? It had been years since he had received a letter from them, although that was not uncommon. It needed a rare synchrony of shipping routes, weather patterns, naval operations and luck for a letter to travel from Nativity Bay to wherever in the world Rob might be.

The sun had slipped behind a cloud. The water, the sand and the mangroves had turned grey. Even the chattering of birds and monkeys from the trees sounded muted.

They lowered the jollyboat and rowed in. Rob kept waiting for someone to appear, either his family or one of the locals who lived in the neighbouring village. But no one came. When they splashed ashore, the only footprints on the beach belonged to animals who had come down to swim. The whaleboat Rob had seen from the ship turned out to be derelict, her timbers bleached and cracked by the sun. Beyond, the neat fields he had tended as a boy were wild and overgrown. No cattle grazed. Fort Auspice, the family home, was only half a mile from the beach, yet he could hardly see it through the tangle of thorn bushes and saplings that had sprung up.

Metal rasped on metal behind him. Scipio had drawn his cutlass. Angus did likewise. No one spoke: everyone felt the menace fouling the air.

'Did we land in the wrong bay?' Adam wondered.

'This is the only safe harbour for a hundred miles,' Rob answered.

Every inch of the landscape was familiar, and yet it felt terribly wrong.

The track to the house was hard to find. Scipio led the way, using the cutlass to hack away the branches and vines that choked it. Thorns tugged at Rob's sleeves. The sun stayed hidden, but its heat pulsed through the clouds. Rob's shirt clung to his body, drenched in sweat. His mouth craved water, but they did not carry any. He prayed there would be an innocent explanation, that Susan and her children would be waiting on the porch for him.

The swish of Scipio's cutlass was like a goad, driving him forward. Sweat ran into his eyes and blinded him, so he did not see where he was going. His toe stubbed a hard object in the ground; he tripped, and fell on his knees. He let out a curse as a stab of pain coursed through his wound.

Adam pulled him to his feet, looking concerned. Being pitied by his own son made Rob angry.

'It was a tree root,' he said.

'No,' said Scipio. He pointed to the ground where Rob's foot had scuffed away the topsoil. A golden object gleamed in the red earth.

Adam dropped to his knees, scrabbling until he had dug it out. It was a knife, beautifully wrought. Its golden hilt was set with pearls, and the pommel was in the form of a snarling tiger's head with two rubies for eyes. The curved blade had the dappled pattern of Damascus steel, engraved with exotic writing. Adam thumbed the edge and winced with surprise as it drew a bead of blood. Even after being buried in the ground, it had not lost its edge.

'Is it Arabian?' Adam guessed.

'There are no tigers in Arabia,' said Rob. 'And that script is not Arabic. It is from India. It must have belonged to some great rajah or prince.'

'Then how did it get here?'

'When I was young, East Indiamen often called on these shores,' said Rob. 'They could load up with the ivory my father sold them, off the books, and then trade it on their own account in Bombay or Calcutta. Perhaps this was a gift from one of those captains.'

'If it was a gift, why's it out of its sheath?' said Angus.

Adam tucked the knife in his belt. They carried on, silent except for the swish of Scipio's cutlass. They were in a kind of stupor, filled with unease they dared not voice. When the clash of metal on metal rang out, they started as if they'd heard a shot.

Scipio cursed. His cutlass had snapped off below the hilt.

'A rock?' said Adam.

Scipio shook his head. He pulled away a handful of the vines, revealing what was beneath. It was a smooth iron cylinder, tapering towards its base where it had been set upright in the soil. A black iron hinge pin had been welded on to its breech.

'That is a nine-pound cannon,' exclaimed Adam.

'It was the gatepost,' said Rob. His voice was choked with despair.

There was no sign of the gate now. Every scrap of wood had rotted or been eaten by insects.

They passed through the gateway. The vegetation thinned as they crossed the invisible threshold, leading into a clearing. It had once been grounds and gardens. Now it was a wilderness. And in its centre . . .

They stared in horror at the ruins of Fort Auspice. The windows had fallen in. The elegant verandas had collapsed. Trees thrust through the broken roof like giant hands tearing the building apart. Roots wormed through the walls and cracked them open. The whitewash that had sparkled with crushed shells was now black with soot where part of the building had been set on fire.

'What has happened here?' whispered Adam.

Rob let out a deep groan. Dropping his cane, he ran towards the building, trampling the weeds that sprouted in his grandmother's old flower beds, and in through the entrance. A termite mound was all that remained of the wooden doors that had graced the fort.

He paused on the threshold. He was no stranger to carnage: he had seen the decks of a man-of-war after battle more times than he could count. But nothing had prepared him for this. This had been his home.

He wandered through the rooms as if in a nightmare. His grandmother's harpsichord was smashed to pieces, the ivory keys scattered across the floor like a pile of bones. The books in his father's library had been pulled off their shelves. Dark marks stained the walls. Some looked like scorch marks; others like blood.

He entered his own old bedroom. The last time he visited, it had been given over to his niece Mary, his sister's eldest daughter. It had not been spared the violence; if anything, it had suffered worse. The mattress had been eviscerated with savage strokes. The nightstand lay in splinters, the porcelain basin smashed. A piece of embroidery showing a ship under sail had been torn off the wall and sliced apart, leaving severed threads hanging loose like entrails. A bed sheet lay balled in a corner, soaked with what could only be blood.

Rob's chest was in a vice. He stumbled outside and dropped to his knees, gasping for breath.

Adam found him there.

'Perhaps they left Nativity Bay,' he said, clinging to hope. 'Perhaps drought or famine drove them somewhere else. Then a gang of pirates, or a local tribe, found the empty house and vandalised it.'

Rob crawled to his feet and crossed to the back of the clearing. Adam followed, as did the others: Scipio, Angus and Phoebe.

The vegetation had grown more thinly here, as if something in the soil was toxic. Blood-red flowers blossomed from a vine that curled around its edge. At the back, six stone markers stood in a row, set upright in the earth. Each had a single letter carved into it: G; S; G; M; M; R.

Hope died that instant. The patch of ground was a mass grave.

'George, Susan, Gert, Mary, Marcus.' Each name was torn out of Rob's heart. His father. His sister and her husband. His niece and his nephew. 'I do not know who R could be. Perhaps Susan had another child since we last saw her.'

The thought that he might have had another niece or nephew – a child who had been born and lived and died, all without him even knowing – felt like the cruellest loss of all.

'Who buried them?' Adam wondered.

Who would wreak such terrible destruction on the house and then give the victims a proper funeral? They must have been thorough, burying the bodies deep and covering them with stones. The initials on the grave markers had been gouged deep, scratched into the stone by the point of a knife, gone over again and again. It must have taken an enormous effort.

Rob didn't answer. His face was wax-white, his expression fixed like a mask. A patch of blood was spreading across his shirt front.

'Your wound has opened!' cried Phoebe.

With a muffled cry, Rob fell from Adam's grasp and sprawled unconscious. Blood leached into the red earth that covered the graves.

CAIRO, 1798

Cairo was a madhouse. You could smell the insanity in the air, like Paris in the revolution, but a thousand times stronger. Even Bonaparte's genius could not tame it. He installed street lighting, cleared the rubbish, and in one night poisoned all the wild dogs whose barking kept him awake at night. It made no difference. Even with soldiers posted on every street corner, the city was gripped with a crazed atmosphere. Nothing was safe; everything was permitted. Generals were seen careering around the city on donkeys, dressed in exotic Arab robes. Egyptian women who had not shown their faces since they were twelve years old tore off their veils and walked about scandalously bareheaded. Some changed more than their clothes. They threw off their husbands and became the lovers and mistresses of the occupying French.

By night, the city became an open-air camp. There was nowhere to billet the army, so every courtyard and square was crammed with soldiers sleeping outdoors. Paul was not with them. Lefebvre used his rank to commandeer a mansion on the banks of the river that had belonged to a Mameluke noble. It was luxurious accommodation, elegantly decorated with beautiful tiles and silks. For Paul, it was a prison. Every night he went to bed clutching his blanket, waiting for the footfall that would announce Lefebvre had come for him.

Daytimes were his freedom. He roamed the city, sketching people and the markets, the mosques and the great gates. He painted in the bright colours of the women's robes and the play of light through the smoke that suffused the air from the dung fires. The bazaar was his favourite place to work. He could lose himself among the crowds, unnoticed and invisible, painting the vivid hues of the spice bowls like a garden of exotic flowers.

One day, he was sketching a monkey sitting on a pile of melons in the bazaar. Nobody seemed to mind it. It sat on the topmost fruit like an emperor on his throne, washing its face with its hands. Paul liked sketching animals – he felt less self-conscious than when he was drawing people.

He had started to lose himself in his work when a shrill scream sounded from an alley behind him. Paul jerked up from his picture. The monkey darted down and hid behind a barrow. No one else took any notice. There were a thousand people in the bazaar, jostling and haggling, all of them acting as if they had not heard the scream.

I should do the same. But the scream erupted again, terrified and helpless. It was the cry of someone who did not have a friend in the world.

I should not get involved. But – as if an invisible hand had taken hold of him – he found himself moving down the alley. The noise and colour of the market faded behind him. The crumbling walls closed in. Ahead, he saw three soldiers hurrying along, dragging a girl between them. She had stopped screaming, probably because one of the men was holding a bayonet at her throat.

Paul's insides clenched in sympathy. It was obvious what they meant to do. They would treat her as Lefebvre treated him.

You have survived it. She will, too, said a cold voice in the back of his mind.

I should turn back. There was nothing for him to do here. One more anonymous local woman, enduring the fate of conquered women everywhere. At best, getting involved would draw attention to himself. At worst, the soldiers might turn the bayonet on him.

Yet he did not move. He couldn't take his eyes off the girl. The soldiers spread-eagled her against the wall. Two men held her arms, while the third dropped his trousers and lifted her dress. Paul knew how she felt: intimately, agonisingly, helpless. Still he did not run away.

The man with the bayonet noticed Paul. He had a flat face with a straight nose, and a sergeant's stripe on the cuff of his coat. A look of brief panic crossed his face, quickly turning to indifference as he saw Paul's civilian clothes. He beckoned Paul in.

'You want to join us?'

There were lots of things Paul could have done next. The most sensible would have been to turn around and walk back to the market, pretend he had seen nothing. All his life he had shirked conflict. The shame and fear and guilt he had carried since the day his mother died had been hidden deep inside. But they had not gone away. In the dark cave of his soul, starved of light and air, they had nourished a shapeless monster.

He put his hand to his waist. French officers were not safe in Cairo: several had been murdered in broad daylight. Everyone, even Paul, carried a pistol.

The sergeant jerked his thumb.

'If you don't want to join in, piss off, eh?'

Paul pulled out the pistol and trained it on the three men. His hand trembled, but only a little. He was no longer the boy who had struggled to even lift the weapon at his mother's execution. After three years in Bonaparte's armies, it was second nature to him. The pistol was not a burden: it was power.

'Leave her,' he said. 'I order you.'

The sergeant stared at him. Disbelief turned to a smirk.

'Who are you to give me orders?'

'I am a lieutenant in the Commission of the Arts and Sciences.'

The soldiers holding the girl's arms looked uncertain; their grip slackened. The girl turned her head. She was young – barely eighteen, Paul thought. Her long dark hair fell over her face, but the eyes that peered from behind it were bright with almost painful hope.

'Sergeant,' said Paul, as slow as talking to a child. The gun in his hand calmed him. 'You are molesting the locals, in direct disobedience to General Bonaparte's orders. I order you to let her go.'

The three soldiers looked between them. Despite the gun, Paul felt a cold fear trickle down his spine and lodge somewhere in his loins. If they attacked, he would not be able to shoot all of them before they overpowered him.

The sergeant's muscles twitched with aggression, the bayonet alive in his hands. But the two soldiers seemed less sure, shrinking away under the sergeant's glare. Neither wanted to be hanged for assaulting an officer.

'No girl is worth dying for,' one of them said nervously.

The sergeant stared into Paul's eyes, maybe wondering if this dishevelled young man would really pull the trigger. Whatever he saw, it made him draw back. He lowered the bayonet.

He is afraid of me.

Paul realised it with a rush of elation. It was the first time in his life anyone had ever been afraid of him. Paul savoured the feeling, like strong sweet wine. It made him feel invincible.

Maybe the sergeant felt it, too. He turned away and spat at the girl. A glob of spittle landed on her hair and dribbled down onto her dress.

'*Putain*,' he swore.

Then, with a twitch of his head, he beckoned his comrades and stalked off down the alley.

The girl stayed where she was. She stared at Paul, wide-eyed, her whole body shivering despite the heat. She did not even move to pull down her dress, but left it bunched above her thighs where the sergeant had lifted it.

Horrified, Paul realised he was still holding the gun. She thought he was pointing it at her. He lowered it quickly, smiling like an idiot to show he meant no harm.

The girl stared at him a moment longer, unwilling to trust him. Paul took two steps back, arms out in innocence.

'You are safe now.'

The girl wriggled her body so that her dress fell back down to her feet. She picked up a scarf that the sergeant must have torn off, and tied it over her head, sweeping her hair back off her face. Paul caught his breath. She was beautiful, on the cusp of womanhood, with pouting lips and round cheeks and those wide, innocent eyes.

She saw Paul staring and lowered her gaze. Paul felt ashamed.

'I am Paul,' he said, pointing to himself. She didn't understand. 'Paul,' he repeated.

'Abasi,' she said, pointing to herself. And then, '*Shukraan*.'

Shukraan was one of the few Arabic words Paul had learned. It meant 'thank you'.

'You are welcome,' he said awkwardly. It sounded horribly trite, no recognition of the ordeal she had faced.

Silence hung between them. Abasi stared at Paul, as if she expected something, but even if he could have spoken her language, he was utterly tongue-tied.

You are safe, he wanted to say. *I will protect you.*

The memory of the way the sergeant had looked at him – the fear of his power – glowed warm inside him. He wanted more. But how to explain that to the girl?

She grabbed his hand. Her fingers were slim and soft. Before Paul could ask what she was doing, she pulled him down the alley and back out into the light and bustle of the bazaar. If anyone had ideas about what a Frenchman and a local girl might have been doing in a back alley, it did not distract them from their business.

Abasi led Paul out of the market, walking beside him and half a step ahead. As they carried on through Cairo's narrow streets, Paul saw the groups of soldiers on street corners turn to look at Abasi – even under a headscarf, her beauty was captivating – but when they saw Paul alongside her they turned away.

Again, Paul felt a glow of power. She was with him. She was protected.

Abasi led him to a crowded tenement near the al-Azhar mosque. A stout woman in a black dress ran out the moment they arrived, embracing Abasi to her bosom even as she chided her in a stream of scolding Arabic. From this, Paul gathered she was Abasi's mother. Half a dozen children of different ages leaned out of the doorway, watching the entertainment, while from inside came the smell of cooking.

Abasi's mother pulled back and fixed Paul with a suspicious look. Paul smiled and gave a little bow; again, he wished he knew what to say. But Abasi spoke urgently; there was no missing the passion in her voice. Her mother's gaze softened. She hugged Abasi again, kissing the top of her head, then ushered her inside the house. Just as Abasi crossed the threshold she glanced back, and the look on her face was something Paul had never seen before. More than gratitude: it was adoration.

Abasi's mother gave Paul another appraising look. She pressed a finger against the cheekbone below her right eye, then the left, and said something Paul did not understand.

'*Pardon?*' Paul spread his arms in the universal gesture of ignorance.

'You.'

She pointed at him, then at the sun, then made a circular motion with her hand. Lastly she pointed back to the house.

'You want me to come back tomorrow?'

How she knew if he had understood, Paul had no idea. Evidently she was satisfied – or perhaps she simply wouldn't waste any more time on the conversation. She shooed him away and went inside, leaving Paul with a confused grin on his face, and the memory of Abasi's final gaze making him long for tomorrow.

'Bonaparte will visit the pyramids tomorrow,' Lefebvre said that evening. 'The engineers intend to blow them open with gunpowder.'

He stroked Paul's face, and Paul forced himself not to recoil. He remembered the way it had felt aiming the pistol at the sergeant in the alley. The memory was so vivid it made him shiver.

Lefebvre misread the emotion. 'You like that, my pet? Then you can come with us. We will be the first men to see inside for four thousand years. Who knows what we might find?'

Paul fought back his hatred.

'Thank you,' he said humbly.

But the next morning he did not rise from his bed.

'I am sick,' he pleaded from under his sheets. 'My bowels were running like a tap all night.'

Lefebvre made a face. 'I warned you not to eat food from the market. A pity. You will miss the pyramids.'

'They've waited four thousand years. I am sure they can wait a little longer.' Paul groaned. 'You will have to make some good pictures for me to see.'

As soon as Lefebvre was away, Paul rose and dressed. He wrapped a robe around his clothes and draped it over his head in the local style, so that he would not be recognised. Cairo's streets were a labyrinth, but he had made careful notes the day before. With only a few false turns, he soon found himself back at Abasi's house.

This time, her mother escorted him inside. There were only two rooms, partitioned by a curtain. Abasi was waiting in one of them, while her family – a great many children, aunts and uncles – crowded into the other. Abasi wore a plain blue dress, with a scarf tied demurely over her head.

Paul seated himself on a cushion opposite Abasi. Her mother withdrew. An awkward silence fell on the room. Not a sound came from the other side of the curtain: Paul could feel the whole family listening intently. But what could he say?

Paul gazed at Abasi.

'You are beautiful,' he said impulsively.

Abasi stared uncomprehendingly. She had painted her eyelids black, making her young eyes seem rounder, more innocent.

'Beautiful,' Paul repeated.

Frustration crept into his voice; Abasi heard it and took it for anger. She shrank away.

Almost without thinking, Paul pulled out his sketchbook and started to draw. A sinuous line captured Abasi's profile, from the angle of her cheek through the contours of her neck and shoulders, her waist, her hips and down to her feet. A second line added the flow of her hair.

He showed it to Abasi and she gasped. Only two lines, yet it captured her beauty and energy better than any oil painting.

'Do you like it?' he asked.

Again, she did not understand. He pointed to the picture, then to her. He made a smile, then a frown, then a quizzical face.

She smiled. She took the paper from his hands and studied it, delight flooding her face. She turned the paper over to the blank side and tapped it, miming drawing with a pencil.

'You want me to draw you again?'

She nodded.

This time, Paul took his time. He drew her eyes first, wide open, staring boldly off the page. He shaded in her eyelids, and the dimples in her cheeks. He sketched her full lips with their slight pout, the wisp of her hair that tucked out from behind her ear. Although he drew her clothed, he shaded the folds of her dress so subtly that it seemed to reveal her figure beneath. It was almost more shocking than if he had drawn her naked.

He was lost in the moment. He felt as if, in tracing her shape with his pencil, he was running his own hands over her. He did not notice the time pass. She stayed motionless and never once complained.

When he had finished, he passed her the drawing. She stared at it for a long time, then clasped it to her chest, gazing at Paul with her wide-open eyes.

Paul wished she could express that look in words. He wished he could say everything that was in his heart. But . . .

The curtains swished as her mother entered with coffee on a tray. Their private time was up. She banged the cups down, then took up position in the corner like a sphinx guarding a temple.

Abasi rolled up the drawing and slipped it inside her dress before her mother saw it. Paul stood and bowed.

'Thank you for your hospitality,' he said.

He was not naive. He could see why Abasi's mother allowed him into her home. France was the power in Cairo, and if Abasi had a French protector, then she would be safer from the predations of the occupiers. He didn't care. He visited her every day. He spent hours with her, sketching her from every angle, making love to her with his eyes. She was like cool flowing water, answering a thirst he could never slake.

Weeks passed. From headquarters, a string of bold edicts proclaimed the great success of the French regime. On the streets, and in the bazaars, the army knew matters were not nearly so rosy. Murad Bey, the Mameluke commander who had escaped after the Battle of the Pyramids, was still at large somewhere to the south with the rump of his army. In his absence, he had become a hero to the Egyptians. Every night, his name would appear daubed on mosques and public buildings in black paint. However often the French effaced it, the next morning it would appear again.

Then news of a terrible defeat came to Cairo, that Admiral Nelson had fallen upon the French fleet at the mouth of the Nile and destroyed it utterly. Of fourteen ships of the line, only two had escaped; more than four thousand men had been killed or captured. At the height of the battle, Bonaparte's great flagship, the *Orient*, had caught fire. Her hold had stored enough powder to conquer India. When it lit, the explosion blew the ship to pieces. The force of it sent debris flying up to half a mile away.

Paul remembered the beautiful ship he had sketched in Toulon harbour, and was sad for the loss. Then he thought of the degradations Lefebvre had inflicted on him below her decks and was secretly glad that she had been expunged from the Earth.

After the battle, the name 'Courtney' was on everybody's lips, spoken with a mix of dread and admiration. It was the English captain's heroics which had broken the French line and made the victory possible. Again, Paul felt the strange resonance of the name. In the mess, he had to put up with any number of jokes and teasing. He absorbed it the same way he took all indignities, enduring what he must.

Whatever dreams Bonaparte had harboured of marching to India, they had died that night in Aboukir bay under Captain Courtney and Admiral Nelson's guns. The challenge for the French army now was how they would even get back to France. The only man who did not see the danger was Bonaparte. To retreat would be to shatter the myth of invincibility which he had cultivated so assiduously. Weeks turned to months. The men lapsed into a stupor, miserable with boredom and homesick, while the locals sharpened their knives and bided their time. Egypt had seen many would-be conquerors over the centuries. Her people knew how to wait them out.

One of the few men immune to the malaise was Paul. All he could think about was Abasi. Cairo was still not safe for a woman on her own, so he visited often. She was teaching him Arabic. He would sit beside her with his sketchbook and draw: he would say the French word, then she would repeat it in Arabic. He wrote down the words she said phonetically, lying awake late in the nights, reciting them until he knew them by heart.

It was a chaste affair. Abasi's mother saw to that. When they sat in her house, Paul could always hear her washing pots or grinding meal behind the thin curtain. Sometimes she allowed Paul to escort Abasi to the market, or to take a walk by the river, but there was always one of Abasi's younger siblings scampering behind them. Every time he came, Paul brought gifts – tobacco, or cloth, or food he had purloined from the battalion stores. Abasi's mother accepted them with a nod of thanks – and still kept her guard.

At first, he did not mind. Simply being with Abasi was enough, the glow he got from her shy smile and her beauty. But as the weeks wore on, a frustration began to mount inside him. He wanted more. When her hand brushed his, it was like a flint hitting steel and striking sparks of desire inside him. At night, with Lefebvre's sweaty body on top of him, he was shocked to find himself thinking about Abasi. She was so pure and good, what sort of man was he to think of her in such a vile moment?

Did she feel the same way? Most of the time, with her demure expression and downcast eyes, it was impossible to tell. But sometimes, if he had been concentrating for a time on his drawing, he would look up and catch her gaze darting away like a startled bird vanishing into a bush. When they sat side by side, her leg seemed to squeeze against his with more pressure than was necessitated by the width of the seat.

Not knowing how she felt about him drove him almost out of his wits. Hoping she might reciprocate his affections was almost too much to bear. For days, Paul racked his brains for a way he could be alone with Abasi. His schemes grew wilder and wilder, each one conceived in hope and discarded in despair. His moods swung from heights of joy to black depression.

He neglected his work for the Commission. Leaving Cairo meant risking ambush or death, but Lefebvre was a hard task-master who would not let him stay idle. Paul used every excuse he could think of. He feigned illness, and came back with tales of lost sketches and paints that had dried out. Once, he gave himself a black eye to convince Lefebvre he had been attacked and robbed of his work. But Lefebvre grew suspicious.

One day, Paul and Lefebvre were in the market when Lefebvre knocked into an orange-seller, spilling his fruit. The orange-seller was furious. He would have attacked Lefebvre, but Paul managed to slip between them and calm the man down.

'He is a general, very important,' Paul explained in his halting Arabic. 'If you hit him, they will shoot you. Think of your family,' he pleaded.

The man backed down, muttering words under his breath that Paul had never learned.

'I did not know you could speak their language,' Lefebvre remarked afterwards. 'I wonder who you have been learning from.'

'I picked it up,' Paul mumbled.

'You always were a quick learner.' Lefebvre cocked his head and gave Paul a penetrating look. 'Do not forget, you are my creature. I am not willing to share you with anyone.'

Paul had to get away from Lefebvre. He had to be with Abasi. When they went out that evening, walking along the Nile's banks with one of Abasi's sisters trailing behind them, he was in a black and sullen mood. Abasi could feel the frustration shimmering off him. She moved away, putting careful space between them, which made Paul even more miserable.

They bought figs from a vendor, their purple skins bulging with ripeness. Abasi slit them with her long fingernail and peeled them back to reveal the fruit inside. She pressed them to her mouth, prying off every last piece of the flesh. Paul took a bite, but his senses were numb: it was like paper on his tongue. He tossed the half-eaten fruit away.

Suddenly Abasi turned and ran back. Paul felt a twinge of despair, but she only went about ten paces. She kneeled down in front of the sister who had been following them, gave her a fig and whispered urgently to her. The girl ran off.

Abasi returned, a strange shy look on her face. She took Paul's hand and led him around the corner of a crumbling old grain warehouse that overlooked the river. Beetles scattered out of their path.

'What are you doing?'

Abasi put his face in her hands. She stared up at him, her kohl-rimmed eyes so wide he thought he could fall into them. The smell of jasmine enveloped him, and he realised she was wearing perfume. Her lips glistened sticky red from the figs she had eaten.

Delicately, she leaned up and kissed him.

A shock went through Paul's body like a bolt of lightning. Her mouth tasted of cloves and sugar. Her tongue was soft and moist. He wanted it to last forever.

The moment she pulled back, Paul's need for her rose even stronger. Tasting her had not sated the need inside him, but only made him desire more.

'I love you,' said Paul, and though they were not words he had taught her, he could see she understood. 'I want to be with you forever. You.'

He put Abasi's hand in his and pressed it to his heart. She nodded, then lifted it away and cupped his hand against her breast.

'You,' she repeated. 'Me . . . love you.'

The touch of her breast under his hand made Paul unsteady. He could feel the heat through the thin fabric, the softness. He leaned to kiss her again, his hands reaching inside her dress.

Abasi drew back.

'I cannot,' she gasped, though the heat of her body said otherwise. 'Not . . .'

She twined her index fingers around each other, making a knot.

'Married?'

'Married. We not married.'

'Then marry me,' he urged.

It seemed the most obvious thing in the world. A priest, an imam, an army chaplain – he did not care. He wanted to be with her for the rest of his life.

Abasi squirmed and wouldn't meet his eye.

'You go,' she said.

'You want me to go?'

Paul felt he'd been stabbed in the heart. He pulled away, but Abasi held him fast. She pointed to the river, where the great Nile flowed into a distant haze.

'You go.'

'You mean I will go back to France?'

'Yes.'

They stared into each other's eyes, filled with love and longing. Down by the river, a fisherman watched them embrace. Otherwise, they were in their own private world.

'I will not go.'

Bonaparte had lost the war. When his army departed, they would not notice a few soldiers who fell by the wayside. Paul could desert, be free of Lefebvre and the army, and live in Cairo. For the first time in years he would have a home. He could see his future in Egypt as clear as if he had painted it.

'You . . . here?'

'Yes. A thousand times yes.' He stroked her cheek. The black humour that had festered all these weeks suddenly transmuted to golden light overflowing inside him. 'Will you marry me?'

She hugged him tight. 'Yes. Yes.'

Pressed against her, Paul felt a change come over her body. A quivering beneath her dress that he had not felt before. He felt his own body responding, rising to meet her.

This time she did not back away. Instinct overtook them both, urgent and irresistible. Abasi pressed her mouth against Paul's with renewed passion.

'We cannot do it here.'

'Where can we go?'

'My house,' said Paul.

He had never dared take her there. But Abasi's sister had gone, and Lefebvre would be working in the headquarters until late in the evening.

Abasi's cheeks were flushed, and her scarf had slid back, leaving a dark lock of hair falling over her face.

'Yes.'

They ran through the streets like children, heedless of the gazes they attracted. Into the house – the servants might gossip, but Paul did not care – and upstairs. Abasi was as eager as Paul. The moment they were in his room, she undid his shirt, almost ripping the buttons in her haste. She stepped out of her dress and stood naked before him. Paul drank in her beauty: her pouting lips; her firm young breasts with the nipples like two dark rose-buds; her slender legs and smooth thighs.

He pushed her onto the bed. She spread her thighs willingly, drawing him down on top of her. Paul buried his face in her breasts. When he slid himself into her, he almost climaxed at once, but he forced himself to hold back. He never wanted this moment to end.

It was so different from what Lefebvre did to him. The moment he had the thought he banished it, angry with himself for allowing Lefebvre to sully the purity of the moment. Abasi saw the flash of anger on his face and shrank under him.

'You do not like it?'

He stroked her hair from her cheek and kissed her face to reassure her.

'This is all I ever want.'

She relaxed again. She wrapped her arms around him and pulled him down, deeper inside her. Her movements became rhythmic, drawing him on. He could feel the sap rising inside him, desire bursting to get out. He wanted to pour himself into her, like the floodwaters of the Nile breaking its banks and surging eternally towards the sea.

Lost in bliss, senses stupefied by the taste of Abasi on his lips and her soft moans in his ear, he didn't hear the footsteps on the stairs. He did not notice the door open. He could feel his climax coming, surging on, on . . .

Abasi screamed. Paul's eyes opened. Abasi sat up, dislodging Paul just as he came. His seed disgorged over her naked stomach and down her thighs.

Lefebvre stood in the doorway with a pistol in his hand.

'So this is what you have been doing,' he hissed.

His face was white with fury, as angry as Paul had ever seen him.

'I . . .'

Paul stood, still naked. He snatched his breeches and pulled them on. On the bed behind him, Abasi whimpered and covered herself with the sheet.

'To betray me, after everything I have done for you . . .' Lefebvre's eyes blazed at Paul. He had hardly looked at Abasi. 'You are *my* creature.'

His finger curled around the trigger. Paul wanted to hurl himself at Lefebvre, disarm him and blow his brains out. But if he moved he would be dead before he had gone two paces.

'I told you I would not share you,' said Lefebvre.

The pistol shot thundered around the room. A hot breath blew across Paul's naked torso. His body jerked instinctively, before his brain could register that he was unhurt.

On the bed, Abasi toppled over without a sound, her dead hand still clutching the sheet to her chest.

Paul felt a hole open in his heart, as if the bullet had passed through him as well.

'You murdered her.'

'*Ca n'importe rien.*' A fly was buzzing around Lefebvre's head. He flicked it away with the smoking pistol barrel, catching it mid-flight and sending it crashing into the wall. 'What will you do? Report me for killing a local who broke into my home?'

Paul simply gaped at him. Abasi's blood flooded across the bedsheet, but what he saw was his mother's golden hair lying amid the splattered blood on the scaffold in Paris. He could not breathe. The silent scream that had been trapped inside him that day was still in his lungs. He wanted to attack Lefebvre and smash his face to pieces, but when he tried to step towards him, his legs would not move.

Flee, screamed a voice inside him. *Flee*.

He had to be away. He had to get out of there, or he would explode like Bonaparte's flagship.

He took three paces back from Lefebvre and hurled himself out of the open window.

NATIVITY BAY, 1806

R ob lay on the table in the *Valiant*'s cabin. With his ashen skin, he looked like a corpse that had already been embalmed.

'He has suffered apoplexy,' said the surgeon. 'Paralysis caused by stroke. I have taken some blood to release the pressure. There is little else I can do for now.'

'Will he recover?' Adam asked, almost choking with emotion.

'It is not impossible . . . with time.' The surgeon would not meet his eye. 'But I caution you, there may be damage to the nervous system, or a palsy that will not heal.'

Adam had to fight back his tears. He had never feared either hardship or danger – but the thought of his father living life as a cripple made him a little boy again.

Angus was giving him an inscrutable look.

'What?'

'Your father wouldn'ae want you sitting by his bedside like a wee girl.'

'He may wake at any moment. What else can I do?'

Angus pointed through the cabin windows, to the ruins of Fort Auspice.

'That didn'ae happen by accident. Some'un came here to kill the Courtneys.'

'You think I do not know that?' Adam blurted out. His voice was loud, but Rob did not move. 'It happened years ago. I cannot change it.'

'No more you could,' Angus agreed. 'But you doon'ae have to change summat to make it right.'

'What can I do?'

'That's for you to answer.' Angus rose. 'But I do ken if your father was awake, he'd say, "Let's find them and make 'em pay."'

Searching through the rubble was the most agonising hour of Adam's life. In the depths of the African wilderness, the Courtneys had kept an immaculate home, filled with treasures and mementoes of their adventures. Now everything was ruin.

Adam felt the grief opening in his heart ready to swallow him. Grief for the family he had never properly known, grief for the father he might already have lost. He forced it back. It would do his family no good if he succumbed to despair.

Instead, he drew strength from thoughts of revenge. Again and again he asked himself the same question. *Who did this?*

The marks on the walls caught his eye again. There were many. Some were mould or damp; some were scorch marks where the attackers had tried to burn the house down; others were blood. He stayed away from those. But the mark he was looking at now was different from all of them.

'Do you remember those Spanish frigates off Havana?' he asked Scipio.

The memory brought a rare smile from Scipio. Adam had been a midshipman, only thirteen years old; Scipio had been a boatswain. Their ship, the *Phoenix*, had met a Spanish frigate before sundown and engaged her. In the heat of the action, and with night falling, they had not realised there was a second ship approaching. The *Phoenix* had grappled her enemy; most of her crew had boarded her. Adam, as the junior midshipman, had been left behind with a handful of men to keep watch on their own ship.

The second frigate had come up on the *Phoenix*'s other side. Adam did not have enough men to resist her boarding party. Instead, he had hidden below, letting the Spanish think the *Phoenix* was deserted. He had led his men through the gunports onto the second frigate's lower deck, surprising her crew from the rear. He could still feel the claustrophobia of it: squeezing through the gunport, the low ceilings, the night lit only by slow matches and linstocks. A Spanish lieutenant had surprised them. Adam had not hesitated. He had raised his pistol and shot the man.

It was the first time he had killed anyone. He still remembered the awful echo of the gun in that confined space. The way the lieutenant's eyes dilated as the life left him. And the starburst residue that the black powder, fired at such close quarters, left on the bulkhead.

'It was a good day,' said Scipio proudly.

Adam's surprise counter-attack had caused chaos aboard the Spanish frigate. The confusion had given the *Phoenix*'s crew time to meet the new threat. When the smoke cleared, it was the red ensign that flew over all three vessels.

Adam scratched the black starburst on the wall. The smell had faded long ago, but he could still pick out the individual grains of gunpowder embedded in the plaster.

'This was not the work of a local tribe,' he said. 'They were well armed.' He moved down the corridor, pointing out similar patches. 'See here . . . and here . . .'

The more he looked, the more signs of battle he found. Musket and pistol balls, loose on the floor or dug into the walls. There was an ebony walking cane that had been cut in two by a sharp blade. A discarded pistol that had misfired, and the tip of a sword that had snapped. Adam collected them all in the dining room.

'It must have been quite a battle,' he said, eyeing the number of spent bullets.

'The Courtneys do not surrender easily,' said Scipio.

'No.' But something bothered Adam. In the entire compound, only the outer walls had been left intact. 'Why were they fighting in the house? It is almost as if they did not bother to defend the walls.'

'They left the gates open?'

'My grandfather was a cautious man. It would have been unlike him.'

'If only the bones could talk,' said Scipio.

The most gruesome sight of all was the bones that littered the house. Jackals and hyenas, vultures and blowflies had stripped off every scrap of flesh, jointed the carcasses and scattered the bones among all the wreckage in the house. It was impossible to step anywhere without crushing or stumbling on bones under-foot. Some of the larger remnants testified to the violence that had befallen them. In a corner, among fragments of a broken vase, they found a skull with a bullet hole punched through its forehead.

'Let us hope my family sold their lives dearly.'

Adam hoped the bones were those of the attackers, though he guessed others must have been the Courtneys' servants. They would have fought as warriors of Africa, fearless and loyal to the end.

Suddenly, something caught the corner of Adam's eye. He went to it. It was a fragment of paper, almost buried under the rubble. He dug it out with care, not wanting to damage it, and blew off the dust so he would not smudge it. It was a portrait of a young woman, so beautiful she could hardly have been real, but so vividly drawn that surely no imagination could have invented her. She looked as if she had recently grown to womanhood, her long hair falling around her shoulders, and her eyes wide with the innocence of someone who did not yet know her own beauty.

Adam turned it over. On the back was pencilled in tiny letters, 'Mary Jansen, 11 October 1803.'

Adam remembered her. She had been his cousin – Adam's aunt, Susan, Rob's sister, had married a Dutchman named Jansen. The Mary in the picture was much grown from the young girl Adam remembered from his childhood visit to Fort Auspice. They had spent all their days having adventures together from dawn to dusk, climbing trees, finding birds' nests and feeding monkeys with nuts. They had read game spoor, argued about its freshness and followed the tracks far into the wilderness. One time, they had found a herd of grazing elephants; there were so many of the magnificent beasts that Adam gave up counting. He was transfixed in awe of their power, their dignity and rugged beauty.

Now most likely Mary's lovely face was a skull buried outside.

Adam folded the paper and tucked it inside his shirt. He could not show it to Rob yet.

He wondered who had drawn it. Courtneys were not known for their artistic ability and this was clearly the work of a master. Perhaps an artist had visited Fort Auspice?

He moved back to the main living room. The sun had come around. It shone through the broken roof on to the far wall, which had previously been in shadow.

Adam stared. A creeper had grown up the wall, covering it with leaves: but underneath, picked out in the shafts of sunlight, was faded writing. Large letters, daubed in dark brown fluid that might have been paint, or blood. It was still readable under the bright natural sunlight.

'*J'aura mon revanche.*'

Adam had learned French almost as soon as he learned English, from a French clerk named Pottier his father had captured. After the battle, it emerged that the man had been press-ganged and had no love for the revolution. He had been happy to swap sides and served as Rob's secretary.

'If you understand your enemy's language, you understand how he thinks,' Rob had told Adam.

It had been no consolation to Adam, who had spent hours in the cabin with Pottier – whom he'd nicknamed 'Potty' – learning verbs when he would rather have been running up the rigging.

Later, he was grateful for it. And now it meant he could read the writing as fluently as his native tongue, though it gave him no comfort.

'What does it mean?' said Scipio.

'"I will have my revenge,"' said Adam.

Terrible as it was, it also perplexed him.

Who had written it? Did it mean he would avenge the slaughter of the Courtneys – or had the murder of the family been his act of revenge?

Probably the latter, Adam thought grimly. *But revenge for what?*

'Cap'n Courtney,' Angus called. Even now he could not shake the discipline of a lifetime. 'I got summat.'

Adam found Angus in the room that had once been the estate office. An iron lock lay on the floor in a heap of splinters where it had been prised off a strongbox. The box was empty. Someone had pulled out the papers and tried to set them alight, but they must have been interrupted at their work because some of the papers had survived.

Angus was holding a leather-bound ledger. He spread it open on the remains of a mahogany desk and showed Adam the contents: ruled columns filled with names and numbers in a neat hand.

'Any use?'

Adam glanced down the columns.

'It is a logbook. All the ships that called at Nativity Bay, their captains and their cargoes.'

He turned the pages. Just past halfway, the entries ended in a page covered with soot and spots of blood. It must have been lying open when the attackers burst in.

'*Thursday 13th October, 1803*,' was the date. Two days after the date on the portrait. '*Seven Sisters, ex Calcutta bound London. Captain Talbot. Cottons, tea etc.*'

'An Indiaman, by the sounds of her. That may explain the tiger-handled knife we found.'

'They must'ae come as friends,' said Angus pensively. 'Nowt in the logbook to say different.'

Adam scanned the rest of the page. There were no names he recognised. No French ships or pirates. No clues.

He was still staring at it when Phoebe walked in. She was out of breath from running, her dark skin flushed. One glance at her made Adam fear the worst.

'What has happened?'

'Your father is awake.'

Rob sat up in the cabin, propped up by cushions on the bench across the stern windows. He kept his head turned to the left, so that the others could not see the petrified cheek on the side of his face. He was a proud man.

Adam talked him through his discoveries – the logbook, the writing on the wall and the evidence of the battle inside the house. The drawing of Mary was the only item he held back.

'"*J'aura mon revanche*," Rob repeated. '"I will have my revenge." But revenge for what? And why in French?'

'Is there a Frenchman with a grudge against the Courtneys?' Adam wondered.

Angus snorted.

'Every Froggie that ever sailed the high seas, for a start. Leastways, every one that ever crossed swords with Sir Robert Courtney.'

Rob shrugged his one good shoulder. The pages of the *Naval Gazette* were filled with the names of Frenchmen he had bested in battle. Many had been epic duels. But none he could remember that would have left this kind of lasting hatred.

'The French are often in these waters,' he allowed. 'Their privateers use Île de France as a raiding base.'

'Perhaps they thought they could hurt you by hurting your family.'

'But how'd they know this was Admiral Courtney's home?' Angus pointed out. 'And there's no mention of any Frenchie ship in the logbook.'

'Perhaps slave traders?' said Phoebe. 'Robert's fight against their evil trade has cost them a prodigious amount of money.'

Angus shook his head. 'The way they tore the house apart? This was summat deep and personal.'

'What about the *Seven Sisters*?' Adam asked. He showed Rob the logbook. 'She was the last ship to call. Could she have been a Frenchman, or a pirate sailing under false colours.'

'No.' Rob shook his head, frowning. 'I have heard of her.' He had a sailor's memory for ships, even ones he had only seen in port. 'She is an Indiaman.' His speech was slow, every word an effort. 'I have seen her name . . .'

He stared out of the cabin window. Even that effort made him wince. Adam wanted to tell him to stop, to recuperate – but he was desperate to know.

'*Where* have you seen her name, Father?'

'Cape Town.' Another agonising pause. 'The convoy.'

'The supply convoy?' Adam knew the operation to retake the Cape had been planned in two phases. First, Rob's fleet would capture the town. A few weeks later, the East India convoy would call en route to India to resupply the new garrison to India. 'So the *Seven Sisters* is sailing to Cape Town?'

Rob nodded.

'Then that is one small stroke of fortune on this desolate day,' said Adam. Even if Captain Talbot no longer commanded her, there must surely be some members of the crew who had been aboard when she came to Nativity Bay. They might be able to shed light on what had happened in those fateful days. 'We will sail at once.'

Adam walked for the door, ready to give the orders to weigh anchor.

'Wait.'

Rob's voice, heavy with effort but with the power to command. Adam halted and turned.

'What is it?'

Rob pointed to the sea chest in the corner of the cabin. It had been a gift from Phoebe when he earned his first command, and he had kept it with him ever since. It was made from Burmese teak, carved with elaborate knotwork and bound with brass bands.

Without having to be told, Scipio fetched the key and unlocked it. He delved inside, lifting out Rob's most precious possessions until he reached the bottom.

He withdrew a blue velvet bundle and laid it on the table. He unfolded the cloth, revealing gold, sapphire and steel. They gleamed in the cabin light, almost blinding in their intensity.

'The Neptune sword,' Adam breathed.

The greatest of his family's heirlooms, more than two hundred years old and still as sharp as the day it was made. A flawless masterpiece.

Except for one aspect. Thirteen inches down from the hilt, the blade ended in a jagged stump. The rest of it, down to the point, lay beside it on the cloth, two fragments nestled together. A bullet had struck it – a chance in a thousand – and snapped it in two. It had been thirty years since that day, and Rob had never found a swordsmith he could trust to remake it.

'Curse the bullet that did that,' Adam said.

'You forget your father was holding the sword at the time,' Phoebe reminded him. 'If it had not hit the blade, it would have hit him.'

It was a well-known story and briefly it reminded them of happier times they had had.

'It is yours now,' Rob said simply.

Adam was astounded.

'Mine?'

'I will never wield it again, even if it could be remade. You are my heir, the heir to all the Courtneys who ever carried the Neptune sword.'

Scipio lifted the sword by its blade and presented it, hilt first. Adam felt a jolt of electricity run through his fingers as his hand closed around it.

A fierce anger smouldered in Rob's one good eye, a determined force of the old fury that had carried him through so many battles.

'Now find the men who murdered our family and kill them.'

CAIRO, 1798

Paul hurled himself through the bedroom window. He did not fall far: there was a flat roof outside, covering the walkway that overlooked the garden. He ran to its edge, dangled off it by his arms and dropped into the soft earth below. He could hear Lefebvre shouting after him – maybe he was reloading his pistol – but Paul sprinted for the gate, past the astonished servants and sentries, and out into the street before Lefebvre could stop him.

At first, he had no thought but to get away – from Lefebvre, from Abasi's corpse, from his mother, from all the calamitous events of his life. He could feel them at his heels, like a pack of dogs that would rip him apart in their jaws if they caught him. All he could do was run.

But he could not run forever. A stabbing pain spread through his chest: months of long, lazy sitting in Cairo had sapped too much of his strength. He slowed, and as he did, he began to notice the strange looks passers-by were giving him: a shoeless, half-naked Frenchman with tears streaming down his face, running reckless through the streets of Cairo.

He had to think. His mind was still numb with disbelief at what had happened to Abasi, still unable to comprehend her death, but he understood the weight of danger he was in. If Lefebvre caught him, he would surely torture and kill him. There was only one power in Egypt who could stop Lefebvre.

Paul slowed and studied his surroundings. With Abasi, he had wandered widely around the city, and he had memorised certain landmarks. He knew where he was – and where he needed to go.

Endure anything. You will survive.

The French headquarters was in a former Mameluke barracks on the southern edge of the city. Everything was a bustle of activity, with junior officers and aides hurrying about shouting orders at one another. Even so, Paul attracted some startled looks as he ran across the courtyard, barefoot and bare-chested.

'I must see General Bonaparte,' he gasped to the clerk sitting by the door, a corporal with a fine walrus moustache.

The corporal shared a look with the sergeant sitting at the next table.

'The general is elsewhere.'

'Who is in command?'

'Colonel Quenot.'

'I must speak to him urgently, please.'

The corporal eyed him suspiciously.

If he sends me away I will murder him, Paul thought.

He would, too, and the knowledge gave him a chill satisfaction that cooled some of the fever in his mind.

'I have an urgent message concerning General Lefebvre.'

Paul had hoped Lefebvre's name would open the door. But the corporal was not convinced. He valued his job in headquarters, and he had no desire to be assigned a patrol in the desert because he had allowed a lunatic to see his colonel. He folded his arms.

'I regret – *sir* – the colonel is engaged with important affairs.'

Paul stared at him. His biceps twitched; his head seemed to shake; his eyes rolled in their sockets. He wished he had his pistol, so he could force the corporal to obey him as he had the sergeant in the alley when he met Abasi . . .

The painful memory felt like a knife twisting in his heart.

He looked around wildly for a weapon – a letter opener, a bayonet, even a paperweight he could use to smash the man's skull.

What he might have done to the corporal – and what would have happened to him subsequently – he never found out. At that moment, an inner door burst open and a group of men hurried out. In their centre was a silver-haired man with heavy gold-fringed epaulettes on his shoulder.

'Colonel Quenot?' Paul called. The man turned. 'Colonel, I must speak to you. It concerns General Lefebvre. I have news concerning his conduct that . . .'

The colonel stared in astonishment at the half-naked madman who had invaded his headquarters. Two of his aides were already heading for Paul, firm intent in their eyes. But the mention of

Lefebvre's name registered something with the colonel. He held up his hand.

'It is best we speak of this in private.'

Quenot led him back through the door, into an office with a plush sofa and a magnificently carved table. Intricate tile-work decorated the walls. Quenot shut the door, so that he and Paul were alone.

'What is it?'

Paul steadied himself. 'Monsieur Colonel, I have come to report a terrible crime committed by General Lefebvre. He . . .'

He killed the woman I loved, Paul wanted to say. But Lefebvre had been right when he taunted Paul: no Frenchman would care about a dead Egyptian girl. Lefebvre could explain it any way he wanted: a thief, an assassin, a jilted lover. Paul would get no justice for her that way.

'General Lefebvre is a sodomite.'

The colonel had spent years in the army; he was a hard man to shock. He took the news impassively.

'That is a grave charge to lay against any man. Let alone a general of France.'

'It is true.'

'How do you know?'

'He has . . . misused me.' Paul blushed scarlet to confess it. Was he confessing his guilt to the same crime?

Quenot studied Paul carefully. The anguish on Paul's face must have convinced him he was telling the truth.

'You did the right thing coming to me. I am sure it was not easy.'

'Lefebvre is a wicked, dangerous man.' Now that Paul had broken his silence, the words came flooding out. 'What he has done . . . What he made me do . . . He would kill me if he knew I was here.'

'You are safe now,' Quenot assured him. He rose. 'I will see to it personally.'

'But where can I go?'

'I will keep you here at headquarters until we have apprehended Lefebvre.'

Quenot was as good as his word. He had Paul shown to a small room, with a bed and clean sheets. An orderly brought him a plate of food, though Paul had no appetite. He lay there trembling uncontrollably, so hard he almost shook the bed frame apart.

It was one of the longest nights of his life. Maybe he would not have survived it – maybe the guards would have found him hanging next morning with the sheet knotted around his neck – if he hadn't had the promise of vengeance on Lefebvre to cling to. Sodomy was a capital offence. A firing squad would make him pay for what he had done to Paul. Abasi would have justice.

Endure what you must to survive, his mother's voice whispered in the night. But was survival enough?

He lay awake all night, and finally fell asleep just before a soldier came in to wake him up. The man carried a knapsack, which he tossed onto the floor beside Paul.

'Your things. Be ready.'

He left before Paul could ask what he meant. Unbuckling the bag, Paul found all his clothes from the house neatly folded, and his sketching portfolio tucked down the side. Quenot must have retrieved them from the house when he went to arrest Lefebvre.

Outside, in the courtyard, he heard the bray of camels, the shouts of drivers and officers, and the rattle of equipment. It sounded as if the regiment was preparing to ride out on campaign. Paul's stomach rumbled, and he wondered if anyone would bring him breakfast.

He rested the sketchbook on his lap. Part of him wanted to burn it – to avoid the pain of looking at all those pictures of Abasi he had drawn – but a greater part was drawn to it like a child putting his finger in a candle flame. Knowing it would hurt, wanting to feel it.

As he opened the book, a loose piece of paper that had been tucked inside the cover slipped out. On it were a few short words, written in Lefebvre's familiar geometrical handwriting.

You will die in the desert.

Where had it come from? What did it mean? Paul was still staring at it when the door opened again. This time it was the corporal with the walrus moustache he had seen the day before, who beckoned impatiently.

'Come.'

Lefebvre's words swam in front of Paul's eyes.

'What is happening?'

'You are leaving. And take that,' the corporal added, pointing to the rucksack. 'You will need it.'

Confounded with terror, Paul grabbed his pack and the sketch-book and followed him out. The courtyard looked for a moment as if the Mamelukes had returned to occupy it: it was filled with soldiers mounted on dromedaries. It took a second glance for Paul to realise they were Frenchmen. They wore turbans instead of forage caps, and white *jellabiyas* over their uniforms.

The corporal handed Paul a folded paper packet.

'This should make everything clear.'

The orders were sealed with the insignia of the Commission. Paul snapped the red wax and unfolded the paper.

The Commission of the Arts and Sciences orders Lieutenant (honorary) Paul Courtenay to join General Desaix's division ascending the upper reaches of the Nile in order to kill or appre-hend the notorious rebel Murad Bey. Lieutenant Courtenay will fully record the expedition, and any sites of antiquity discov-ered on the march. For the glory of the French republic and the advancement of civilisation.
 Given this day in Cairo,
 General Patrice Lefebvre

Paul went numb. He stared at the paper until the writing blurred on the page, as if he could rearrange the words to change their meaning. They stayed obstinately unmoved.

In the corner of the courtyard, Colonel Quenot was briefing a group of officers. Paul went to him, but before he could inter-rupt, Quenot saw him and broke away.

'What have you done?' Paul's voice was so loud that even in the hubbub of the courtyard, men stared. 'What have you done?'

Quenot eyed him coldly. 'You have your orders.'

'But Lefebvre. I told you what he did to me. I—'

Quenot grabbed Paul's arm and pulled him close.

'If you value your life, you will never mention those monstrous accusations again,' he hissed. 'You are lucky General Lefebvre is a personal friend of mine, so I was able to discuss this with him discreetly. It is only thanks to his mercy that you are not in front of the firing squad.'

Paul reeled. 'His *mercy?*'

He had heard terrible tales from men who had scouted out the southern desert: desolate wastelands, burning sand, and wild tribes ready to prey on any man who entered their territory.

'He was adamant – though I tried to dissuade him – that you should not be punished for your claims. He said all this time away from France had addled your wits. My friend thought some time back with your regiment might aid your recovery.'

'My regiment?'

Paul was a hollow drum; all he could do was echo back what was said to him.

A gust of hot wind blew through the courtyard, lifting the white fabric that wrapped the soldiers. With a shock, Paul saw that the uniforms underneath were those of his old regiment, the 91st.

A man walked towards them. The turban he was wearing shaded his face, but there was something horribly familiar about his slow, arrogant pace.

'It will be good to be back with your old comrades, *non?*' said Quenot.

The newcomer tipped back his head and smiled broadly, showing his rotting teeth. Sergeant Bastiat. He stared at Paul with the same poisonous look he had given that day on the dock at Toulon, and his gaze seemed to speak the same words as on Lefebvre's note.

You will die in the desert.

CAPE TOWN, 1806

As soon as they anchored in Table Bay, Adam visited the harbour master's office and examined all the logbooks. The *Seven Sisters* had called at Cape Town four times in the past three years, twice bound for India, and then on her return voyages to London.

'October 1803.' Adam pointed. 'She came here straight from Nativity Bay. And back again a year later. Regular as a mail coach.'

'And here again soon,' said the harbour master. 'A sloop has just arrived from England with the bill of lading for the India convoy.' He showed them the document which was on his desk, the Admiralty seal freshly broken. 'The *Seven Sisters*.'

'And is Captain Talbot still her master?' Adam asked casually.

'Aye. He owns a share in her – won't trust her to any other man.' The harbour master scratched his whiskers and squinted. Adam could not hide his eagerness to know more. 'You know him, sir?'

'We sailed together off the Coromandel,' Adam lied. 'I would relish the chance to swap yarns with him again.'

'Then with a fair wind, you'll have your chance inside a fortnight.'

In fact, the wind was better than fair. Two days later, a gun fired from the blockhouse on Devil's Peak announced the convoy had been sighted. By nightfall, twenty-seven more ships lay at anchor in Table Bay.

'An' look at the flagship,' said Angus. 'She flies a broad pennant.'

'Thank God,' said Adam.

A broad pennant signified a commodore, not an admiral. It meant that Rob remained the ranking officer in Cape Town.

Adam had spent all afternoon glued to his telescope, scanning each ship as she entered the bay. He identified the *Seven Sisters* instantly. She was a handsome vessel, well ordered despite her months at sea. It was the mark of a captain who did not let things slide. Adam picked him out through the glass, a portly figure on the quarterdeck with sandy hair and a ruddy face. Unusually for an officer, he had a full beard.

What did you see at Nativity Bay? he asked himself, studying Talbot through the telescope.

Angus already had the gig waiting at the bottom of the ladder. They rowed through the maze of anchored ships until they came under the tumblehome of the *Seven Sisters*. Like most Indiamen, she was firmly built, and wide at the stern to support the great cabins and wheelhouse where her passengers berthed. Her sides were painted with a chequerboard pattern, so that from a distance a hostile ship could not tell if she was a merchantman or a two-decked man of war.

'She's a bonny ship,' said Angus. 'Shall I put us alongside?'

'No,' Adam decided. 'I do not wish to raise Talbot's suspicions. I will have my chance this evening.'

By longstanding tradition, a dinner was held at the castle that night to celebrate the convoy's arrival. Adam attended in his full dress uniform. The opulent Grand Rooms were bright and airy, lit by the thousands of handmade candles that sparkled from the chandeliers. Bird of paradise flowers, the newly cultivated *Strelitzia*, decorated the room majestically; a string quartet played; and black footmen spread a sumptuous, never-ending feast on the table. There were kudu steaks and venison pies cooked with Cape springbok, polished silver pots filled with Cape Malay curry, exotic fruits from the Dutch East India Company gardens, sweetmeats, a jelly in the shape of the castle – and all washed down with copious amounts of the finest liquor and wines.

Adam hardly tasted the offerings. He was watching Captain Talbot intensely. They were seated on opposite sides of the table, too far away to engage in conversation, but near enough that Adam could study his quarry. Talbot seemed pleasant enough, not haughty or dour, like some of the other captains. He ate and drank freely, laughed heartily, joked with his companions and gave the impression of a jolly man enjoying himself.

Had he sat in the dining room at Fort Auspice, laughing and drinking in the same way with the Courtneys? Or had he gone there with a darker purpose?

In the midst of those thoughts, Adam found his gaze wandering to the woman seated next to Talbot. There were few ladies at the table, and those mostly garrison wives. But the girl next to Talbot looked to be barely eighteen. Her honey-coloured hair was piled up in ringlets, showing off her long neck and high cheekbones, a face that was alive with wit and intelligence. Her creamy skin blushed with the heat, and small droplets of sweat shone like diamonds on her forehead. She fanned herself with a paper fan decorated with an exotic peacock.

Her eyes caught Adam's looking at her. They were deep blue, the same colour as the sapphire in the Neptune sword. Adam knew he should look away, that he was staring rudely – but he could not stop. Nor, it seemed, could she. She held his gaze like a long-lost friend she had not expected to see again. Had they met before? That was impossible: he would never have forgotten such a face.

The fan had stopped moving. Her mouth opened, lips glistening with wine, as if she were about to say something.

'Your father?'

Adam blinked. He'd been so intent on the girl, he had not realised his neighbour was trying to make conversation.

'I beg your pardon?'

'Your father? He is recovering?'

The man who spoke wore a full captain's uniform, with the twin epaulettes that denoted three years' seniority. He'd introduced himself at the start of the meal, though Adam hadn't been paying attention. Was his name Verrier? He had a high forehead and a long nose, which he seemed always to be looking down even when he was trying to be agreeable.

All Adam wished for at that instant was another look at the girl. But when he managed a glance, she had turned away and was deep in conversation with Talbot.

'My father is mending tolerably well,' Adam allowed.

It was probably the twentieth time he had answered the question that evening: every officer in the room was concerned for Rob's health.

'I heard he had suffered a fit of apoplexy. That he had been left a cripple.'

'My father is a strong man,' said Adam tightly. 'Remember that we would not be dining in this castle tonight if he had not taken a bullet in the operation to capture it, so let us honour his triumph.'

Verrier stiffened. 'You misread me, sir. I have always considered Sir Robert the greatest sea captain of our age. Saving Lord Nelson, of course.'

'I would say "before Nelson".'

'No doubt you would.' Verrier gave a condescending laugh. 'It must have been most advantageous, growing up as Sir Robert Courtney's son. Preferment and opportunities that humbler men could only dream of.'

'In my experience, it meant there was always someone trying to knock me off my perch,' said Adam. This also was a conversation he had had before, with jealous officers who noted his age, his rank and his surname, and drew spiteful conclusions. He nodded to Verrier's pair of epaulettes. 'Which ship do you command?'

'The *Diamond*.'

Adam could not hide a twinge of jealousy. The *Diamond* was the finest frigate in the fleet. Fast, manoeuvrable and well armed, she was the sort of ship every young captain dreamed of: a ticket to action, prize money and glory. Adam had watched her longingly at anchor in the harbour.

'Then evidently you have not been held back by your lack of breeding. I mean to say, family connections,' he added, enjoying seeing the colour rise in Verrier's ice-cold cheeks.

'You will soon find that naval life is a great deal harder when the admiral is not your father. You know Admiral Bolt arrives to take command of the fleet?'

Adam was caught off guard. 'But the convoy was commanded by a commodore. I presumed . . .'

Verrier looked down the full length of his nose. 'Admiral Bolt was delayed two days when we called in at Rio de Janeiro. He will be here on the morrow, or perhaps the day after.' He tossed back the rest of his wine. 'It must be a great relief to you, now that you are aware of the new arrangements, that your father will be able to return to England to continue his convalescence.'

He saw Adam's discomfort and gave a cruel smile, though he did not guess the real reason. The new admiral might order

Adam anywhere in the Indian Ocean – or even back to England. Without Rob's authority, he would not have the freedom to seek out the men who had murdered his family.

As soon as the meal ended, the ladies retired to the drawing room while the men remained behind for confidential talk and cigars. Adam found Talbot and introduced himself.

'Courtney?' Talbot scratched his nose. 'Not the gallant admiral, surely? You are too young.'

'His son.'

Talbot pumped his hand. He was a large man, with a firm handshake.

'Damn pleased to meet you, sir. I have followed your exploits in the *Naval Gazette*. The apple does not fall far from the tree, eh? But I have heard your father has been wounded?'

He was impossible not to like, full of good cheer and warmth. The only blemish, which Adam had not seen until now, was a livid scar which ran down one cheek from Talbot's ear to his chin. The beard covered it, but the fair hair was too sparse to hide it completely.

How did you get that? Adam wondered.

'My father was wounded twice,' said Adam. 'He took a musket ball in his ribs during the landing at Losperd's Bay. Later, he suffered a fit of apoplexy when he returned to his childhood home at Nativity Bay.' Adam locked his eyes on Talbot's, watching for any sign of recognition. 'I believe you have visited our family there before.'

Talbot's eyes looked anxiously about the room. Sweat beaded on his brow. He lowered his voice.

'Not so loud, I beg you. My calls at Fort Auspice were strictly a private affair, on my own account. I would not want my masters in Leadenhall Street to gain a contrary impression.'

In other words, you were trading for your own profit and do not want the East India Company to know about it, thought Adam.

'Did you know my grandfather?'

'Indeed. And his family. His granddaughter, Mary, was quite a beauty. Half my officers were swooning like lovestruck loons the last time we departed.'

He was so jovial, it was impossible to believe he could have witnessed the horror at Fort Auspice.

'So my family were well when you left them?'

'Of course – why should they not have been?'

Adam leaned in closer. 'When we paid a visit two weeks ago, the house was in ruins. All my family were dead.'

Talbot stared at him. His hand crept to his cheek, scratching at the scar, which was throbbing red.

'That is a tragedy. I . . .' He was at a loss for words. 'Was it a fever?'

'They had been attacked and murdered.'

'But by whom? Natives?'

'From the evidence we found, it looked to be the work of European arms.'

Adam extracted the page he had torn from the ledger.

'This was my grandfather's logbook. As you can see, your ship was the last to call at Nativity Bay before the attack.'

Talbot took out his handkerchief and mopped his brow.

'Dear God,' he murmured. 'If only we had known. If we had stayed longer, perhaps we might have done some good.'

'Was there anything that struck you as suspicious. Anything that might identify the men who did this?'

'It was years ago.'

'Could I see your logbook from that period? There might be something, however small, that would give me a clue.'

'Alas, our logbooks are deposited in Leadenhall Street at the end of each voyage.' Talbot drained his glass of brandy and summoned a footman for another. 'Wait. Now I recall. There was a French privateer, the *Requin*.'

'"The Shark",' Adam translated.

'Aptly named. Every merchantman in the Indian Ocean feared her bite. She was prowling the waters south of Madagascar at that time. We'd sighted her, but a gale blew up and we made our escape. We put in at Nativity Bay, to lie low for a few days.'

Talbot took out his snuffbox and offered it to Adam. Adam stared. He was not interested in the snuff, but the box transfixed him. It was made of blue enamel, trimmed with gold leaf, and decorated with pouncing tigers in vivid colour.

Talbot took a pinch of snuff and gave a sneeze that rattled the crystal in the chandeliers.

'For my nerves, you understand. If it was our going to Nativity Bay that led the *Requin* to your family, I would never forgive myself.'

'Where did you get that snuffbox?' Adam asked.

Talbot looked surprised. 'In India. A gift from the Maharajah of Holkar.'

'I found a dagger at Fort Auspice, very similar. A jewelled hilt in the form of a tiger. Was that yours?'

Talbot's eyes were watery from the snuff.

'I have never owned such a dagger. And with the *Requin* in the vicinity, you may be sure that I would not have dropped it if I had.'

It was probably a coincidence, Adam decided. The tiger was a common motif, and every ship that called at Fort Auspice would have called in India. The dagger could have been left by anyone.

'Did my grandfather have any inkling that the French were nearby?'

Talbot shrugged. 'It was so long ago, I cannot rightly recall. I am certain I must have mentioned the reason for our coming. You know your grandfather – he was a vigilant man.'

'That was his reputation,' Adam agreed.

He knew that was why Rob had run away to sea at the age of seventeen – to escape his father's stifling caution. Adam couldn't judge him for that, yet now it filled him with sadness.

'If the *Requin* was such a notorious privateer, my grandfather would surely have been on his guard,' he mused.

'Indeed he should have been,' said a voice from over Adam's shoulder.

Adam turned, to see Captain Verrier, the man he'd been next to at dinner, looking down his long nose. He must have been eavesdropping on their conversation.

'You know the *Requin*?'

'I confess I do not.' Adam spoke sharply, angry that they had been overheard.

'The most notorious ship east of the Cape. Her captain, Jean Lesaut, is an utter villain. He has captured or sunk more than forty of our ships.'

Adam said nothing. He was remembering the writing at Fort Auspice, covered by creepers but still livid like a scar on the wall. *J'aura mon revanche*: I will have my revenge. He remembered the question he had asked – *Is there a Frenchman with a grudge against the Courtneys?* – and Angus's reply: *Every Froggie that ever sailed the high seas, for a start. Leastways, every one that ever crossed swords with Sir Robert Courtney.*

He had not heard his father mention Lesaut. So far as Adam knew, they had never fought. But the man might have had a brother in the navy, or a cousin – someone who had come off worst against Rob. Who knew how far a man might carry a grudge?

Verrier was looking at Adam, waiting for him to respond to something.

'I beg your pardon?'

'Captain Verrier was recounting Lesaut's history,' Talbot explained. 'Apparently he was the son of a nobleman who ran away to sea. After the revolution, the Jacobins in Paris took against his aristocratic lineage and sent a group of commissioners to arrest him in Marseilles.'

Verrier took up the story. 'The commissioners assumed that the crew would support the revolution. They did not reckon on the men's loyalty to their captain. Lesaut allowed the commissioners on to his ship, but as soon as they were aboard his men fell upon them. All were butchered – save one. Lesaut sent the survivor back to Paris with a warning, and an offer.'

'The warning was that the same fate would befall any man who came to take his ship,' said Talbot. 'The offer was that if they left him his ship and his rank, he would serve the revolution as loyally as he had served old King Louis.'

'Needless to say, they accepted the offer,' said Verrier drily.

Adam had little interest in history. All he wanted to know was, 'Where can I find Lesaut?'

Verrier looked surprised. 'His ship is based in Île de France.'

There was a chart of the Indian Ocean on the wall. Verrier pointed to the island, a tiny speck several hundred miles east of Madagascar. The chart had belonged to the Dutch East India Company, and it still showed the island's former Dutch name: Mauritius.

'I thought we kept a blockade of Île de France.'

'Indeed.' Verrier grimaced. 'I myself have spent months on that station. But Lesaut has the Devil's own luck. He slips in and out of that harbour like a rat.'

'I would not have waited for him to come out,' said Adam. 'I would have fought my way into that harbour and taken his ship from under him.'

'Indeed, I am sure you would.' Verrier's cheeks flushed a pale rose. 'Your reputation for intemperance and recklessness is almost as great as your father's.'

'The harbour at Port Louis is quite impregnable,' Talbot put in, trying to defuse the tension. 'The narrow approach is guarded by a battery on one side, and a citadel on the other. Even if you managed to force the entrance, you would never get out again.'

'I am not afraid of danger,' Adam retorted. 'I will find Lesaut wherever he is.'

'Ha.' Verrier's voice was touched with scorn. 'It does not take great heroics to find him. Ten to one, if you venture into the Indian Ocean he will find you. You know what he does to the crews he captures? He brands them with the letter *L*. That is their warning. If they are ever impertinent enough to be caught fighting him a second time, and he sees that mark, he cuts off their hands and throws the men in the ocean. It is very hard to swim without hands,' he added.

That gave Adam pause. Risking his life, even his ship, he would do without thinking. But risking his crew was a different proposition. It was a lesson his father had drummed into him from his earliest days: *The mightiest ship is only wood and cordage without the men who sail her.*

There was no alternative.

'If you will forgive me,' Adam excused himself, 'I must return to my ship.'

'A pity,' said Talbot, rising to his feet along with every other man in the room. 'It is time to join the ladies.'

The doors to the drawing room had been thrown open. Among the stately womenfolk of Cape Town, the girl with the peacock fan stood out like a hummingbird among a flock of hens. Adam looked at her, but her eyes had already found him.

She held back in the doorway, playing with her fan, so that she dropped behind the main group of ladies who had come to greet the gentlemen. Then, hurrying to catch up, she seemed to trip on the smooth floorboards just as Adam was passing. He put out his arm and caught her easily, cushioning her against his chest. She clung on for a moment to regain her balance.

'I am so clumsy,' she exclaimed. 'The ground seems to wobble beneath me. Perhaps it is the heat. Or the wine,' she added, with a grin.

'Sea legs,' said Adam. 'It shows you are a true sailor.'

He held her hand as she straightened. He could feel the room's attention on them, but he didn't care.

'Adam Courtney,' he introduced himself.

'Lizzie March.'

He let go of her hand. She looked as if she was waiting for him to speak, and indeed there were a thousand things he wanted to say – but the need to get back to his father weighed on him. With a new admiral coming, they had no time to lose.

His duty was to his family.

'I was just departing.'

She looked crestfallen. 'So soon?' She stepped away, putting up her fan like a shield between them. 'I am sorry we did not have more time for conversation.'

'The loss is mine,' Adam replied, and though the words were formulaic, he felt it more keenly than he had any right to – the sense of being pulled out of a dream he did not want to end.

He went down the stairs without looking back.

You are a fool, he told himself angrily.

She was a pretty girl, and he had been weeks at sea: that was all. His duty was to avenge his family; nothing else mattered. What sort of a son was he, having his head turned by frivolity at a moment like this?

As he walked out of the castle gates into the warm night, he could not resist one last look up at the windows. If he had been able to see behind the coloured glass, glowing with the light and laughter inside, he might have seen a face returning his wistful gaze.

He went straight to his father's room and relayed in detail what he had learned from the evening. The news kindled sparks of the old fire in Rob's eyes.

'I have heard of this privateer Lesaut, though I do not recall crossing swords with him. A dangerous man.'

'He will be hard to find, in the expanse of oceans,' Adam cautioned.

For all his bravado with Verrier the night before, he did not have any illusions about the scale of his task.

'If you want to hunt a shark, go where the fish are. He will be lurking near the trade routes to India.'

'Agreed. But my *Valiant* is too small to take on Lesaut in battle. And your successor, Admiral Bolt, is due any hour.'

'Then there is no time to lose. While I am still admiral of this fleet, I can dispose my ships as I will.' Rob nodded to his bureau. 'Fetch me a pen and paper.'

Adam obeyed his father's request.

'Write this. I, Admiral Sir Robert Courtney, Vice Admiral of the Red, etc., do order Captain Adam Courtney to assume command of His Majesty's Ship *Diamond*, to patrol the waters of the Indian Ocean, and to do everything in his power to bring to battle the notorious French privateer *Requin*.'

He paused. Adam had not written a word.

'Did I not make myself clear?'

'The *Diamond* . . .' Adam looked bewildered. 'But she is under Captain Verrier.'

'I am giving her to you. I will assign Verrier a new command. *Write it*,' he ordered, seeing Adam was still motionless.

Adam started writing. Conflicting emotions fought within him. It was the ship of his dreams, but in circumstances out of a nightmare.

When Adam had finished, Rob took the pen. He scrawled his name at the bottom of the order, then affixed his seal. He settled into his pillows, the light fading from his eye.

'Go,' he said. 'Before the new admiral arrives and countermands my order. Catch this Lesaut, take his ship, and find out what he knows. Do whatever is required.' His voice had risen; even his petrified cheek was quivering with emotion. 'We must have our revenge.'

Adam embraced his father, leaning over the bed and furling his arms around him. His father's unshaven stubble scratched his cheeks, as it had when he was a boy. He experienced a terrible pang at parting, the fear he might never see Rob again.

'I will not let you down, Father.'

*

Adam and Angus went aboard the *Diamond* next morning. When he read Adam's orders, Captain Verrier looked as if he had swallowed poison. He packed his belongings in furious silence, and departed within the hour.

'What a joy it must be to enjoy the admiral's favour,' he said acidly as he descended the ladder. 'I wonder what you will do when he is gone.'

To be deprived of a command, especially a ship as fine as the *Diamond*, would break any officer's heart. Adam felt no sympathy for Verrier.

'My father will still be giving orders when you are back in England on the half-pay list,' he assured Verrier. 'And I will obey him.'

They sailed on the afternoon tide. Leaving Table Bay, they saw another ship bearing down fast out of the north-east, a two-decker with an admiral's pennant at her masthead. She altered course, intending to hail the *Diamond*, but Adam set more sail and the swift frigate soon outpaced her.

'That was cutting it fine,' Angus muttered. 'We cannae turn back now.'

The *Diamond* was the biggest ship Adam had ever commanded, a thirty-two gun frigate with a crew of over two hundred men. Verrier had kept her in immaculate condition: the rigging taut and gleaming with tar, the decks scrubbed, and no blemish on the paintwork. Not a single gun carriage squeaked.

Adam immediately set about ruining her. He had his carpenters erect bulwarks along the side that made it look as if she sat higher in the water. He set a crew to seal her gunports and paint them to match the hull. Then they painted false gunports on the new bulwark, but so badly rendered that they were obviously fake.

'A wolf in sheep's clothing, dressed up like a wolf,' said Angus.

Adam ordered the sailmakers to pull a spare set of sails from the hold. To their horror, he had them cut and tear the pristine canvas, patch them and rip them again, until they were little more than rags. These he had slung from special spars that he rigged under the main yards, loosely brailed so they could be set quickly. The frigate now carried two sets of canvas: one clean, and one to make her look as if she had been mauled in a storm.

Below the waterline was a different story. Adam moored the ship in a deep bay beyond the Cape and shifted all her ballast and heavy guns to the starboard side, so she heeled over like a drunkard. His men scrubbed the weed and barnacles from her exposed hull until the copper gleamed bright as new. Then they shifted the weight to port and repeated it on the other side.

'Faster than careening her,' said Angus, 'An' worth a few knots.'

Last of all, Adam took down the red ensign and hoisted the red and white striped flag of the Honourable East India Company.

'If an Indiaman can disguise herself as a man-of-war, why should we not do the reverse?'

Angus nodded. 'That Frenchie shark will get a fair surprise if she tries tae take a bite o' this morsel.'

Adam drilled his crew every morning and afternoon. Looking in the *Diamond*'s log, he was horrified to see how Verrier had treated his crew. Almost every day recorded floggings for the most trivial offences, sometimes as many as three or four dozen lashes at a time. Instead, Adam offered grog or golden guineas to the fastest gun crew, the most accurate gunner, the quickest topmen. The crew responded to his new regime with enthusiasm. Within a week, Adam had the men working like the finest Fleet Street clockwork. In a fortnight, they were as sharp as any crew in the Royal Navy.

'We will need all our skill, and Neptune's luck, to see off the *Requin*,' he warned.

From his enquiries in Cape Town, he knew she would be a formidable enemy. Forty guns, larger than any British frigate in the Indian Ocean, with a captain who had won so many victories that more than one underwriter in London had been driven to suicide.

'He is little better than a pirate,' he told Angus. 'But he has not survived twenty years in this ocean by being a fool.'

Adam steered a course past the southern tip of Madagascar, and on east-north-east. Most merchant ships would not dare come so far towards the equator. They would drop down to lower latitudes for the run to India, then turn northwards when they were well past the twin French bases of Île de France and Île Bourbon. With his set of ragged sails, Adam hoped to convince the privateer he had been driven off course by a storm and would be easy pickings.

Adam drove his crew hard by day. At night, he barely slept. Angus, who slept outside the door like a guard dog, would see the lamp in the cabin burning late through the early hours of the middle watch. If he peered in, he would see Adam sitting at his desk, staring into the fathomless blue depths of the sapphire on the broken Neptune sword, turning over the tiger dagger, or gazing at the sketch of his cousin Mary. Sometimes he would have fallen asleep still clutching one of his artefacts. Angus could see Adam's cares taking their toll: he had dark bags under his eyes; his skin had dulled; his clothes had become baggy as his body shrank in on itself. Angus said nothing. He knew the only cure for his captain would be revenge.

It was the season between the monsoons. The winds were inconstant and skittish, forcing the men to work constantly to keep the ship on her bearing. It sapped their strength and their morale. Adam kept up the drills every day, but the crew grew slower. They were restless and sullen. Adam had to flog a man for insubordination.

Grey clouds massed in the sky, covering the sun. They threatened rain, but it never came.

'I almost wish there would be a storm,' said Adam one night. 'It would end this terrible waiting.'

'Aye,' said Angus. 'But sometimes the waiting's better than the getting.'

It was the middle of the dogwatch when the shout came from the masthead.

'Sail ho!'

The men forgot their torpor in an instant. The wind seemed to feel the urgency, plucking at the rigging with a low hum. Adam snatched a spyglass from the rack and raced up the shrouds, nimble as a topman. The lookout at the masthead almost fell off the crosstrees when he saw his captain appear.

'Never used to see Cap'n Verrier aloft,' he muttered.

'I am not Verrier.'

Adam steadied the telescope against the roll of the waves and found the spot on the horizon. Even magnified through the glass, the ship was barely visible, so Adam could not tell if it was the ship he had been looking for.

Then a gust of wind snapped the colours out from her stern, and he saw the bands of blue, white and red billowing in front of the grey sky. The *tricolore* of France.

Adam slid down the back stay to the deck, burning the skin off his palms. His men looked at him admiringly: there were not many officers who would risk their dignity doing that.

'Change the sails,' he ordered.

The men knew the drill. In less than five minutes, the ship's true canvas had been furled away and the false sails set. The ship slowed, barely moving despite the stiff easterly breeze.

'The trap is baited,' Adam murmured. 'Now let us see if they bite.'

The men swiftly cleared the decks for action. Normally, they would have rigged nets above to catch any falling spars and wreckage, but Adam could not risk showing the privateer any sign that they were prepared. He knew he was taking a risk. When they engaged, the men on deck would have no protection.

The French ship was still on the horizon. But although her sails were set full, while the *Diamond* carried little more than bare poles, she was no closer.

'Why does she not gain on us?' Adam fretted.

'Wind's rising,' said the sailing master.

It was true. Even in the time it had taken them to clear for action, the breeze had stiffened. It blew the lines taut and tugged at their makeshift sails. With a snap, one of them split down the seam and carried away.

'Much more of this and we will not have to pretend we lost our canvas,' fretted the first lieutenant.

'Frenchie's taking in a reef,' called Angus. 'She kens we're for heavy weather.'

He pointed astern. As if from nowhere, the clouds that had stifled them for weeks had suddenly coalesced into towering black columns that darkened the ocean.

'She's changing tack,' said Angus. 'Putting her stern to us.'

'She'll be making for Île de France, and safe harbour,' said the master.

The first lieutenant looked to Adam. 'Should we follow?'

Adam looked through the telescope again. The French ship heeled over as she took the brunt of the wind. Tiny black dots moved like ants along her yards to shorten their sail.

He knew the sensible course was to do the same, to reduce his canvas and batten down against the storm. The clouds loomed large; the storm would be terrible. Even if he abandoned the chase now, it would a battle just to save his ship.

But his family's murderer was almost certainly aboard the privateer. Adam could not let her go.

He gazed down the decks, at the eager gun crews waiting by their weapons. All they wanted was a chance to fight.

'Set every scrap of canvas we can bear,' he ordered. 'We must overhaul her before the storm breaks.'

'You will lose any hope of surprise,' warned the first lieutenant.

'Then we will fight twice as hard.' Adam's voice brooked no argument. 'Otherwise we will lose her altogether.'

'An' pray the storm doesn'ae sink us first,' muttered Angus.

But he spoke quietly, and the wind whipped his words away before anyone heard.

The false canvas was taken down, and her true sails set once more. They bulged, straining on their yards like dogs on a leash. The *Diamond* coursed forward, crashing through the rising sea. The work they had done cleaning her copper repaid them as her smooth hull cut through the water like a dolphin.

The French ship was more conservative. Her captain had read the conditions and kept her mainsails double reefed. Even then, the wind was so strong it fairly shot her along. The *Diamond* gained on her, but slowly.

And all the time the storm grew stronger. Across the vast expanse of ocean, Adam saw flickers of lightning on the horizon. It looked impossibly distant, so far off that he almost believed it would never reach them. But the howling wind said otherwise.

He was trapped in a three-way race with the French ship and the weather. He had to catch her before the storm hit the *Diamond*. If he misjudged the timing, if he overreached himself, then the *Diamond* would be left at the storm's mercy.

They reeled the French ship in. She showed no desire to turn and fight, but kept ploughing her furrow. Through the telescope, Adam could read the name painted in white letters across her transom. At first, the letters were so small that Adam was unsure if he was just seeing what he wanted to see, but as the gap between the ships narrowed there could be no doubt. She was the *Requin*.

'Set the royals.'

The sailing master looked at him, aghast. 'Sir?'

'That was an order, damn you.'

'Aye, sir.'

With the extra canvas, soon they were close enough that he could make out the name without the aid of the telescope. Figures scuttled about her poop deck, pointing and staring at the chasing frigate.

Which one of you is Lesaut? Adam wondered.

The thought of meeting his adversary, of killing the man who had murdered his family, warmed his blood.

'Load bow chasers,' he ordered.

The two forward guns were loaded and run out. The gun captains elevated them for maximum range.

'Fire.'

Two explosions sounded as the cannons sent their iron balls chasing after the fleeing privateer. But almost at once another crack came, from overhead. Whether it was the vibration of the guns, or simply the driving force of the wind, the sails could not take the strain any more. With a report almost as loud as the cannons', the foresail split open. In seconds the ship wallowed over to leeward, so far over the water foamed across her gunwales.

As the men cut the broken sail loose, the ship righted herself. But she was barely moving. Adam had gambled – and lost. He looked to the *Requin* to see if she would take advantage of the *Diamond*'s misfortune. Her captain must have seen what had happened, but he did nothing to change course. The *Requin* hurried on, flying towards the safe harbour of Île de France.

A spray of rain dashed against Adam's face. The wind roared at a higher pitch. He had no chance of catching the *Requin* now. If he did not act immediately, he might lose a mast, or the whole ship and her crew.

He had to give up – this time. With a heavy heart, he gave the orders.

'All hands aloft. Down royal masts and topgallant yards,' he ordered. 'Reef mainsails.'

Ahead, the *Requin* vanished into the deepest, blackest clouds he had ever seen.

The storm lasted for four days. Each day, Adam did not think it could get any worse, and each day he was proved wrong. The seas rose; the wind reached new heights of violence. The deck was buried beneath the waves that surged over it. The ship wallowed and rolled. It thundered with the noise of stores, cargo, bulkheads and cannons breaking loose and being tossed against the hull.

On the first night, a gust of wind struck the ship so hard it turned her on her beam ends, her deck perpendicular to the water. It hung at that angle for what seemed an eternity, a terrifying moment. Every man aboard clung to whatever he could, and waited with dread to see if the ship would capsize.

The mainmast gave way first. It ripped free of the keelson and fell into the surging sea. It carried with it the mizzen yard, the quarter galley, hen coops, part of the quarterdeck, and three sailors. All were lost. Adam had his men cut the wreckage loose – it would have dragged the ship down otherwise – and cast it on the waves. Above the boiling storm, they could hear the screams of the men who had been pitched adrift.

On the second day, the foremast snapped off short at the deck and went overboard, along with the jib-boom and the bowsprit. Now the ship was moving under bare poles on a single mast, barely enough to maintain steerage through the mountainous waves that surged over her deck. They had battened down the ship's hatches as swiftly as they could in those horrendous conditions, but gallons of water poured through the hole where the mast had been, flooding the area belowdecks. The men worked the chain pumps tirelessly every hour of the day, but all they could do was slow the torrent.

On the third night, Adam was standing on deck, wrapped in his fear-naught coat. A safety rope lashed him to the bulwark; he held a lantern cradled to his chest, trying to protect the flame against the wind so he could read the binnacle. Suddenly, a flash of lightning split the sky above him – only for a moment, but the image seared itself onto his eyeballs. The *Diamond* sat in the bottom of a deep valley, a trough between waves so high they towered over her like mountains. Adam rubbed the rain from his eyes to look again, wondering if he was hallucinating, but the lightning had passed and the sea was dark again.

Half a second later, he realised what would come next.

'Belay yourselves!' he screamed.

The great wave broke over the ship. Such a weight of water, it was like a boulder had slammed down on her. The *Diamond* was driven underwater. Adam had time to gulp half a mouthful of air before he was drowning.

The rope around his waist was no longer a lifeline. It was a noose that would drag him to the bottom with his ship, if he could not free himself. He fumbled with the knot, but the wet rope was too tight. He had lost his knife days ago.

Then there was a rush of water beneath his feet. The ship's buoyancy was bringing her to the surface. Adam thrashed about, touched something solid and clung to it for his life.

The ship broached the surface like a whale rising from the deep. Adam was thrown in the air – though in the maelstrom of wind and water, there was hardly any difference between the ocean, the air or the sky.

He landed on the hard deck. The ship had survived, but the angry ocean had not finished with her. Lightning flashed again, giving him a glimpse of more waves rising to strike.

He lunged for the ship's wheel. Angus joined him. Hanging off the spokes, using all their weight, they wrenched it over. Astonishingly, the rudder still answered. The ship slewed around, nosing into the waves so that she caught them bow-on. They rode them like a bucking monster, each one threatening destruction but none quite able to deliver the final blow.

Dawn brought no relief. The wind had eased, but the sea was running so high that every wave threatened to break the ship in two. The daylight was foreboding and grey. Worse, it let him see the damage the *Diamond* had taken. Of her three masts, only the stump of the mizzen remained. Her foc'sle had been swept away, along with half her guns and her rigging.

'I've seen Deptford hulks more seaworthy,' said Angus.

Eventually the wind dropped. An oily calm settled over the sea. Adam set work parties to patch up the worst of the damage to the hull. The pumps at last began to win their battle against the water in the hold.

The lower decks had been wrecked. Adam stood in the doorway to what had once been his cabin and surveyed what remained of it. The windows had been blown out, and the furniture washed away. Everything he owned was lost.

'The Neptune sword!' he cried.

He imagined the sapphire in the pommel, plummeting through the depths until the blue faded to black. The wrecking of his ship; the lost lives of the crew; letting the *Requin* slip through his fingers; almost dying himself: they were nothing compared to losing the Neptune sword. He went cold. He felt as if all the gods were cursing him.

'Lookin' for this, sir?' Angus was behind him, carrying a long bundle wrapped in an oilskin cloth. 'I put it in the sail locker when the storm hit. A wee bit damp, but none the worse for it.'

Adam seized the bundle, almost tearing the cloth as he unwrapped it. There was the Neptune sword, and the tiger dagger and the sketch of Mary.

He embraced Angus.

'I feel as if you have saved my life.'

'Aye.'

But Angus did not smile. Saving the Neptune sword was only right. He would have dived to Davy Jones's locker to fetch it, if need be. But as for the dagger and the sketch, he was not so sure. Perhaps they would have been better left at the bottom of the ocean.

A warm breeze blew through the open cabin.

'Where now?' said Angus.

Adam didn't answer. He knew his best hope was to return to Table Bay under whatever sail he could jury-rig for his ship.

It felt almost as much a failure as losing the Neptune sword would have been.

'If we go back to Cape Town, the new admiral will give me fresh orders. Who knows where he will send us? We will have lost our chance to capture the *Requin*.'

Angus gestured to the shattered ship.

'With respect, sir, we haven'ae chance anyway. If she holds together to see us home it'll be more'n a miracle.'

'Then let's hope the carpenter and the sailmaker are miracle workers.'

It took a day and a half to clear the wreckage, rig a mast from one of the spare spars in the hold, and fit a single sail. Adam was impatient for progress, but also dreading the moment when he would have to make a decision.

'What course?' the sailing master asked at last.

All eyes turned to Adam. They knew they were lucky to have survived: they had lost shipmates in the storm. Superstitious men, they did not believe in tempting fate further.

But Adam was the captain.

He had tucked the tiger dagger into his belt. He thumbed it now, feeling the cold metal and the sharp points of the tiger's fangs digging into his flesh. The spur of revenge. He could not let that go.

'Set your heading—' he began.

A shout from the bow cut him short.

'Sir! Ship off the starboard beam!'

Every man rushed to the side. The *Diamond* had no lookout at the masthead – she had no mastheads – so the other ship had been able to sail close before anyone noticed her. Adam did not need a telescope. She carried full sail, snapping from her yards as crisp and white as a starched shirt. The contrast with the *Diamond* could not have been greater.

'Is she one of ours?'

The Royal Navy kept ships patrolling off Île de France to try and catch the privateers. It was possible one of them had managed to avoid the storm. If so, she would have spare masts, spars – everything the *Diamond* needed to make repairs.

She bore down on them. From head on, Adam struggled to make out her lines. Her figurehead was hidden in the shadows under her bowsprit.

She hoisted her ensign. At the same time, she paid off a point to leeward. The sun caught the carved figure under her bow, a lunging shark with silver-painted teeth that gleamed in the light.

Adam had barely slept in a week. He was exhausted, hollowed out from working the *Diamond* against the storm for so long. He looked at his ship and broke out into deranged laughter. His plan had worked almost perfectly. The *Requin* had found them, a dismasted and storm-battered hulk, a juicy prize too easy to resist.

Except it was no illusion. He was utterly helpless.

The injustice of it almost made him weep. How had she escaped the storm unscathed, while his own ship was smashed to pieces? They must have reached Île de France before the worst of the storm hit. That, or Lesaut was the Devil himself.

'We could still give her a bloody nose,' said one of the men, optimistically.

It was not in Adam's nature to surrender. But looking down the length of his ship, her mangled rigging and shattered timbers, he knew it was hopeless. They could not move. If they did not strike their colours, the *Requin* could stand off and blast them apart at her leisure. He would throw away his crew's lives for nothing.

And if he surrendered, he would be taken aboard the privateer. He would get what he craved above all else, the ultimate object of his mission: to meet her captain face to face.

'Sir?' said Angus. 'Should we clear for action?'

Adam's throat was so tight he had to force the words out.

'Run up our colours.'

A few of the men cheered.

'Then strike them.'

EGYPT, 1799

The column departed Cairo on a cloudless December day. The men gave three cheers for the republic and three cheers for General Bonaparte. Their commander, General Desaix, reminded them they had beaten the Mamelukes twice already, at Alexandria and at Cairo. He promised that in a short while they would add a third and final victory to the roll of honour. Everyone marched out singing in high spirits. Everyone except Paul.

They kept close to the Nile. In Egypt, the river was life itself, a great artery running through the kingdom. To their left, where the floodwaters irrigated the ground, the soil was dark and the land was green. Thick stands of palms shaded the fields, and the river-banks were lush with reeds and grass. On their right, past the high water mark of the floods, the desert stretched featureless and bare to the horizon.

Paul hated the desert. He tried not to look at it. But he could feel its presence, like a vast mouth waiting to devour him. From the corner of his eye he sometimes sensed movements of shadow, as if the desert had come to life and was riding along beside him. Of course, there was nothing there. But when he turned to his left, there was Sergeant Bastiat, trotting along on his camel. There was no escape.

Bastiat was a model soldier. He saluted Paul punctiliously, called him 'sir', and ensured his camel was saddled and ready every morning. Even Colonel Quenot noticed it.

'You are a lucky man, to have such a devoted ally.'

'Yes, sir.'

It made Paul sick to have to agree. Every moment of the march was torment; every second in the camel's uncomfortable saddle, all he could think of was Abasi.

I loved her. And because I loved her, she died.

Of course, Lefebvre had shot her. But he would not have done it if Paul had not brought her to the house. Paul had endless hours in his own company to rake his conscience ragged with guilt.

He longed to be away. But with the desert on one side, and Bastiat dogging his every move, it was impossible to escape. During the first night out of Cairo, Paul determined to walk back, but when he went to the edge of the camp Bastiat came gliding out of the darkness, asking Paul if he needed anything, with the same predatory look as a cobra circling a mouse.

Each night after that, Paul lay awake, a pistol at his side and a knife under the portfolio he used for a pillow. All he heard were the cries of jackals, and the Arabs who stalked the army, and Lefebvre's parting words echoing in his soul. *You will die in the desert.* He knew it was no idle wish or threat. Quenot and Bastiat surely had orders to see that Paul did not survive the campaign. They might leave him alive long enough to see if thirst, or disease, or the Mamelukes did their work for them. If not, they would kill him when no one was watching and blame it on an assassin. No one would mourn him.

Why not do their work for them? Sometimes in the night, Paul's right hand would creep across the sand to the pistol, warmed by sand. He could end his misery with a single shot. But every time, Constance came to him and made him repeat her final words, mumbling them over and over like a prayer.

Endure what you must to survive.

The column straggled on. The landscape looked flat and featureless, but it was an illusion. Empty riverbeds constantly interrupted their path, steep gullies that had to be scrambled up and down in clouds of dust and curses. Fingers were crushed and bones broken in the effort to move the cannons across them. And half a mile later, they would have to do it again.

Paul's best hope was that they would catch Murad Bey quickly. In the confusion of battle, he might escape unnoticed and return to Cairo, where he could hide. But the most they saw of Murad Bey was a spire of dust in the distance kicked up by his army. Sometimes, it seemed so close that the colonel sent his cavalry galloping out to chase it, but they always returned hours later, camels lamed, to report all they had found were old campfires and hoof prints.

'We are like the Israelites in the Bible, chasing a column of smoke across the desert,' Paul said one night.

He generally kept apart from the others in camp, but he had made one friend: a young surgeon called Marcel. They often spoke in the evenings, when the rest of the army was sleeping or idling.

'If only we could reach the Promised Land, *non?*' Marcel poked at the fire.

With no wood, they had to use dry camel dung for fuel. The smell of the smoke was revolting.

'Why do we not turn back?' Paul said. 'Surely we have driven Murad Bey far enough into the wilderness that he is no threat any more.'

Marcel lowered his voice. 'It is not so easy. General Desaix is caught in an elegant trap. As long as he advances, Murad Bey will retreat. The moment we turn for home, Murad will be able to fall on our rear. And the further we go, the longer our retreat will be.'

'But that is madness.' Paul imagined marching for ever through the barren country. 'Where does it stop?'

'Who can say? This godforsaken continent must end somewhere.'

They were deep in upper Egypt now, approaching the white space at the edge of the map. The ribbon of green cultivation that bordered the Nile grew steadily thinner, squeezed between the vast deserts on either side. The villages grew fewer. The ships that were supposed to have come upriver to resupply them did not appear. And every day, their scouts reported that Murad Bey and his army had retreated further south.

It felt as if they were walking through a land of gods and giants. One afternoon, they came across an ancient road running across the desert. The surface was beaten hard, the sides lined with blocks of stone covered in impenetrable signs. They followed it for several hours, until it disappeared as suddenly as they had found it. Another time, they stumbled upon the remains of a quarry carved out of a granite hillside. The hard stone had preserved the chisel marks so perfectly, you could imagine the masons had downed tools that very morning. Colossal outlines spoke of the blocks that had been cut away, each one taller than a man. Across the naked rock face, the ancients had inscribed a line of hieroglyphs, commemorating their achievement. Now there was no way of knowing what they meant.

After six weeks, the flat desert rose towards a plateau of granite hills. The placid Nile grew agitated. Boulders strewed its way, pink and black granite polished like glass. Flecks of white rippled the surface as the river flowed through a ravine of red granite that glowed in the sunlight. Further up, imposing ruins overlooked the river from an island in the middle of the stream.

'The First Cataract,' said Quenot.

There was no sign of Murad Bey. He had gone past the falls and into the great desert beyond.

'Does that mean we can go home?' Paul asked.

Quenot gave him a sour look.

'I am surprised at you, *monsieur*. Bonaparte's orders were clear – we must bring Murad Bey to battle. The ancients may have stopped here but the French march on. General Desaix has charged me personally with leading a detachment into the wilds of Nubia to scout out the enemy's dispositions.' He jabbed a finger at Paul's chest. 'Naturally, I will require you to accompany us.'

'Naturally.'

Above the cataract, the land changed. The river could not hold back the desert. Rock and sand came up to the shore; there was nothing to forage except palm nuts, and whatever waterfowl they could shoot. But after three days, even that was taken from them. The Nile turned in a wide bend, but the tracks of Murad's army carried straight on, away from the river and into the void of the desert.

'What do we do?' said Paul.

Quenot stared at him like a cretin.

'What would Bonaparte do?'

'With respect, Colonel,' said Bastiat, 'it may be a trap.'

Quenot coloured. 'The Mamelukes do not have the wit for such cunning. They are fleeing, like the craven imbeciles they are. But we will run them to ground.'

They went to the Nile and filled every goatskin, flask and barrel they had. The operation was punctuated by the rattle of musketry as sentries fired to scare off the crocodiles which lurked close to shore. By the time they were ready to leave, every man was on edge.

The landscape was so desolate, Paul could not summon the will to draw it. Orange sand stretched as far as he could see, broken by low, conical hills that erupted from the desert like pustules.

Round stones littered the plain like spent cannonballs. They were hollow, and when broken, contained pockets of sand. They made for treacherous going. One of the camels tripped and lamed itself and had to be shot.

At first Quenot marched them through the heat of the day. 'If we move by night, Murad's army may slip by us,' he reasoned.

After one day of marching under the relentless desert sun, when the soldiers were flayed alive and several had collapsed with exhaustion, Quenot reconsidered his plan. From then on they travelled like the Arabs, marching by night and into the morning, then resting in any scraps of shade they could find during the noon heat. It made the journey even more unreal. Dreams and nightmares and the unceasing suffering of being awake blended into one. Even Bastiat was too exhausted to torment Paul, though Paul never forgot about him. He could feel the sergeant's malevolent presence at the back of the column, like a wolf biding his time. Every time Paul went to sleep he was convinced that Quenot must give up the quest. Then, the bugle call woke them for more marching.

Six days into the march, Paul was riding with the advance party at dawn when he saw two peaks break the lonely horizon. He studied them through his spyglass. They were so regular they must be man-made, but too thin to be pyramids and too wide to be obelisks. At that distance, with the desert behind them, it was hard to establish a sense of scale.

'I would like to investigate,' he told Colonel Quenot.

'Out of the question. Our mission is to hunt down Murad Bey.'

'My mission is to explore and document the treasures of antiquity.'

Paul brandished Lefebvre's commission, though his skin crawled to touch the document that had condemned him.

'For the glory of the French Republic,' he added sardonically.

Quenot grunted. The ramrod martinet Paul had met in Cairo was no more. He hadn't shaved in a week. Tufts of beard sprouted through the sunburned blisters on his cheeks; his eyes were sunk and glazed by the sun.

'You know what the Bishareen will do to you if they catch you.'

Paul's buttocks clenched. The Bishareen were the Arabs who lived in the desert – brigands and robbers. They were not loyal to Murad Bey, or anyone else, but scavenged off any travellers foolish enough to pass by. Two days ago, Paul had watched them swoop in on horseback, snatch a straggler from the back of the line and carry him away, like birds of prey grabbing a vulnerable animal. They had stripped the poor soldier naked and gang-raped him in full view of the column. Then they had beheaded him. Not a single man had dared try to rescue the unfortunate victim, for fear of suffering a similar fate.

'I am willing to take the risk. Of course,' Paul hurried on, 'I could not ask anyone else to hazard his life in an archaeological excursion. Sergeant Bastiat and his men should stay in the safety of the column.'

'The column will not wait for you,' Quenot warned. 'If you do not return before we set out, we will continue our march. If you do not catch us up, we will consider you lost to the desert.'

Paul nodded. Had Quenot forgotten his instructions from Lefebvre? Or was he calculating that this far out in the wilderness, he could rely on the desert to execute his murderous task for him?

'I will take my chances. *Pour la France.*'

As soon as the column had made camp for the day, Paul mounted his camel and rode out. He had hoarded his rations and packed as much food as he could into his haversack. He strung two large waterskins from his saddle, bursting at the seams. He knew the water would go quickly. In his sketchbook, he had kept a detailed map of each day's march, noting every well and watering hole. He thought it would be enough to get him back to Cairo.

And then what?

Without Abasi, Cairo had nothing to offer him. But where should he go? He had no family, no friends, no place in the world. No home.

If you think like that, you may as well give up now, he told himself.

All he could do was survive one day, then another, and see where it led him.

He rode towards the strange formations he had seen, trying to keep up his lie as long as possible while he was still in sight of the column. The formations were nearer than Paul had thought, though with the sun in his eyes he could not make them out clearly. They were too solid for buildings, but with a symmetry that could only have come from human hands. Maybe the supports for a lost arch?

Then he realised what they were. Figures, but so vast his eyes hadn't comprehended them. They sat on stone thrones, hands resting on their laps, eyes staring imperiously over their domains, their headdresses draped over their shoulders like lion's manes. Even in the warm morning light, their faces were cold and unyielding.

'They must be gods,' Paul murmured.

For a moment, their grandeur made him forget his plans for escape: everyday concerns seemed irredeemably trivial in the shadow of those colossal statues.

He opened his saddlebag and took out his pencil and portfolio. If anyone was watching Paul, they would see him sketching the antiquities, as he had promised. But a compulsion had seized him. He wanted to comprehend the statues, but his mind was too small. The only way was to draw them.

He had to turn the sketchbook sideways to fit in their full height. Even then, he could not capture their real-life proportions. He drew a tiny figure a distance away from the base, head tipped back in awe, a dark smudge smothered by the long shadows the statues cast.

The heat on his face returned him to his surroundings. The sun had risen blisteringly high while he was sketching, and his cheeks had started to burn. Behind him, the column would have settled down to sleep. Surely even Bastiat would not be watching. If Paul wanted to live, now was the time to brave the desert.

He mounted the camel and climbed the rise behind the statues, moving slowly in the heat. He took a deep draught from his water skin, then regretted it. How could he make it last the journey home if he drank it all now? He hooked the water skin back onto the pommel of his camel's saddle – and as he did, he made an unpleasant discovery.

The holster that hung over his camel's flank was empty. He had forgotten his carbine. In his haste to be away, terrified of being challenged or stopped, he had left the gun in camp.

Idiot, he berated himself.

He thought of going back, but he had already delayed too long. If he returned to camp now, he might never have the chance to escape again.

Could he survive the desert, and the long journey back, with no way of hunting or defending himself? He was still wondering about it, half tempted to abandon the whole scheme, when he reached the top of the rise. He had come to the mouth of a shallow valley, though for a moment he didn't look at it properly. Then he did, and forgot everything except what was in front of him.

A huge complex of ancient buildings stood at its head, as proud as the day they were built. It was almost as big as a city. Rose-granite obelisks thrust up to the sky. Fat columns held up blocks of stone so huge they must have been lifted by giants. Slanted walls buttressed vast buildings. Stone lions crouched low, like swimmers in the sand.

'What is this place?' he wondered aloud, though the only living creatures to hear him were his camel, and the birds circling above.

The ruined city throbbed in his vision, shimmering in the heat haze. It felt like a mirage, except it was too fantastical to be a trick of the eye. The massive stones were so physical he could almost feel their gravity pulling him in.

Paul started towards it. The ground was rough and uneven; he had to dismount and lead his camel, kicking up whirlwinds of dust and dislodging loose rocks. Like the statues, the buildings were so gigantic they distorted his sense of scale. They looked to be a few hundred feet away, but Paul must have walked nearly a mile before he reached them.

Two obelisks flanked a monumental gate. Paul stepped under it, gazing nervously at the massive lintel. If one of those blocks fell . . . And they were not even at their full height. Desert sand had blown in over the centuries, accumulating in great drifts between the sheltered walls.

Leading the camel, he walked through the gate and into the abandoned city, half-striding, half-swimming through the deep sand. It was like a dream, but more unreal than any dream he'd ever had. He moved between rows of columns taller than the masts of ships, through doorways that could have accommodated whole houses. He felt himself shrinking in their presence, no bigger than one of the grains of sand blowing around his feet. It dawned on him that this could not have been a city: no human being could have lived in these buildings. They must be temples, for only a god could inhabit such a space. He had never felt so utterly alone.

But maybe he was not alone. In the wind-smoothed sand, he sometimes saw small impressions. Some were round – probably jackals or wild dogs – but others looked like human footprints. Paul glanced about him, his gaze jumping from shadow to shadow, wondering what might lie within the ruins. There were a million places to hide. If the Bishareen were here, they could take their time with Paul: hours, maybe days. The French soldiers would never come, even if they heard his screams.

He wanted to flee, but his feet kept moving forward, as though an invisible power was pulling him deeper into the city. Though the ground was buried, Paul sensed he was following a road that ran through the heart of the complex. The geography of the place seemed pregnant with indecipherable meaning. He understood – he didn't know how – that the buildings were not individual structures but part of a greater whole, like many trees growing from a single, deep-buried root.

The road culminated in a temple that dwarfed everything that had gone before. Sphinxes and lions adorned the roof, while a statue of a bird-headed man with a long, sharp beak guarded a door waist-deep in sand.

This was the heart of the complex. Paul could feel the power throbbing from it, dormant but not dead. All routes led to this place. Even the winds could go no further. They had filled the temple with sand, a mountain of it that climbed to the lofty roof.

The shadows at the top were ink-black. The wind blew between the columns, a mournful sound like dead spirits. He felt certain there must be something terrible up there.

He had never been a brave man, but curiosity compelled him to discover what it was. He tethered the camel to a fallen column and started to climb.

It was just past noon. The sun flayed his back like a whip. Its rays reflected off the sand, stinging his eyes. He had to keep them almost shut, but grit found its way between his eyelids and chafed his eyes raw. With every step, sand cascaded away underfoot, sucking him backwards. The effort to keep going was immense. He collapsed on to his hands and knees, crawling like a dog: he could hardly push himself on. The sand shifted beneath him; at any moment it might collapse completely and carry him back to the bottom.

He came under the shadow of the portico. At least now he had the sun off his back. He worked his way across to the wall, finding handholds in the stone to steady himself and drag himself up. His arms ached with the effort. His fingernails started to bleed. He did not know why he continued onwards. It had become a battle of wills, and he would not give up.

Suddenly he put his hand out and felt cool stone. The sand levelled into a narrow shelf. He had reached the top.

Paul wiped the tears from his weeping eyes, waiting to adjust to the dim light. When he could look without flinching, he examined his surroundings.

It was awe-inspiring, as befitted the house of a god. Every inch of the walls was decorated. The grooves on the walls that he had used as handholds were in fact images, chiselled into the sandstone blocks, then coloured with paint. In the shade, enough light penetrated that Paul could see the ancient paint, thousands of years old, still vivid and bright. The dry climate had preserved it almost perfectly. The predominant colour was blue – the blue of the Nile, the blue of the sky, of fish scales and desert orchids and the evening sky – complemented by reds and yellows that spoke of the warmth of the sun.

It was a far cry from the desolate landscape outside. Had the men who did it painted it from memory – or had the Nile flowed near here in ancient times, making the desert a green and lush place? In the pictures, it was beautiful – but it was a terrible beauty, the beauty of a naked blade or a flower about to wither. The more Paul observed, the more he saw one particular character – the sharp-beaked, bird-headed god whose statue he had seen outside – stalking through the scenes like an angel of death. In one panel, the god stood holding a pair of scales. A disembodied heart lay on one side, a single feather on the other. There was nothing to explain it, but Paul understood through the alchemy of the art that if the impurities of the heart weighed more than the feather, then judgement would be swift. A terrible monster, with the front quarters of a leopard and the head of a crocodile, waited to devour the unworthy man.

Paul pulled out his sketch pad. He was swooning on the richness of the imagery around him, yet seized with the fear he could not possibly remember it all. He knew he ought to be making good his escape, but these pictures held some awful mystery, and he felt if he could only decipher it then he would possess some great and terrible power.

He was exhausted. He had not eaten since sunrise, and he had left his water with the camel. Parched and famished, he descended into a sort of trance. He filled page after page of his portfolio with dense, intricate drawings. He wore his pencils down to the nub. When those ran out, he used his tinderbox to make a small fire and blackened some sticks to make charcoal. Drawing became an act of worship, of transubstantiation. He consumed the pictures, allowing their magic to enter him.

His trance became a dream. In the great hall, he did not know if he was awake or asleep; if the images he could see were in front of his eyes or behind them. The bird-headed god came alive and walked within him. The heart on the scales was his own.

Pain beat inside his head, but as he listened, he realised it was the bird-headed god speaking to him.

I will raise you up, the god said.

Paul felt a presence growing inside his soul, like a butterfly taking flight from its chrysalis. The ancient gods of Egypt gazed down at him from the walls.

Justice comes to every man. For everything you suffer, you will have your reward.

Paul stood. The mountain of sand was so high he could touch the stars that decorated the temple ceiling. He was walking among planets, taking his place with the gods. Bestriding the universe, floating in space, untethered to the ground.

To master life, you must hold it as light as a feather.

Paul realised he was falling. His eyes opened. It wasn't a dream. In his trance, he had wandered to the edge of the slope. The precarious sand had given way, cascading down in a torrent. Paul flung out his arms, but there was nothing to hold on to, nothing to stand on except the ever-receding sand.

Sand filled his eyes, his ears, his nose and mouth and clothes. It carried him down the high mountain, flinging him about like a rag doll. The best he could do was curl into a ball and hope he didn't break his neck.

He fell for longer than he had thought possible and came to a halt with a bone-crunching jolt. Sand rushed over him, mounding on top of him, and he realised with horror that if he lay still he would be buried alive. He pushed himself up, flailing to scoop the sand away. As fast as he removed it, more flooded down. Somehow, he managed to claw himself upright. Kicking his legs like a swimmer, he lifted himself out.

As the last flow of sand trickled around him, Paul stood sunk up to his waist. The bird-headed god statue stared at him from a distance, likewise half-buried. Paul spat out a mouthful of sand and tried to clear his eyes. He rubbed his limbs, wondering if anything had broken.

Suddenly, he remembered his portfolio. He had been holding it when he fell, but he must have let it go. If it had been swallowed by the sand, he would never see it again. He looked around desperately.

Thankfully, it was only a few feet away from him, battered and filthy but intact. But suddenly, that didn't matter. He wasn't alone. A small Arab girl in a filthy dress squatted on the ground, staring at him from under a fringe of matted hair. She had picked up the sketchbook and was clutching it to her chest.

Paul, waist-deep in sand, stretched out his arm towards her.

'Pull me out?' he asked in Arabic.

His throat was dry, his mouth caked with sand. His voice sounded more like clashing stones than words.

The girl's eyes widened. She stood.

'Please,' gasped Paul.

The girl turned and ran. Paul swore. He needed the pictures in the portfolio to remind him of what the god had said. Frantically, he squirmed and dug with his hands, until he managed to wrench himself free. Her track wasn't hard to follow – clear footprints in the sand – but his bruised legs stumbled and splayed as he ran after her. He chased her up a slope, around a building and between two vast columns of a colonnade.

Then she vanished. Her tracks ended suddenly at the foot of a stone wall, each massive block taller than Paul. He blinked. Had she been a ghost?

A ghost could not have picked up his sketchbook and run off with it.

The slither of loose sand drew his eye to the foot of the wall. There was a gap between the stones: not much bigger than a fox-hole, but wide enough for a malnourished girl to squeeze into. Big enough for a man? Paul decided to take the risk. He flung himself down, worming head first into the hole. It narrowed around his shoulders, eased a little, then tightened more. How thick was the wall? What if he ended up trapped here, unable to move?

Panic gave him strength. He sucked in his breath, tensed his muscles, then heaved himself forward, shredding the ragged shirt and the skin on his arms beneath. The rock pressed him back. Then, grazed and bleeding, he was through.

He was in a small square room. Shafts of sunlight filtered through the cracks between the bare stone blocks, illuminating the dust and flies in the air. It stank. Even with sand in his nostrils, Paul could smell the rancid air. The girl cowered in one corner, holding the portfolio like a shield. A gaunt woman sat slumped against the wall beside her, unmoving. She was the source of the stench – and the flies.

'I will not hurt you,' said Paul in Arabic.

The girl shrank back. It was hard to guess her age. Her body was still a child's, but her face had a maturity that was ageless. It might have been a pretty face, if it wasn't screwed up in a feral snarl.

'I only want my book,' Paul said.

The smell and the close air made him want to vomit. He had to restrain himself not to snatch the book, or beat her until she gave it up. He was bigger than her, and he still had some of the god's strength coursing through him.

But she was helpless. Her arms and legs were so thin he could have snapped them like twigs. Whatever family she might have had, clearly she had no one now except the corpse festering beside her.

He pointed to the body.

'Your mother?'

The girl nodded.

'What about your father? Any family?'

She shook her head.

An orphan, Paul thought, *like me*.

He needed to get out of the room, away from the flies and the stink of death. He needed water. But he could not leave the girl here.

He pointed to himself.

'Paul.'

She nodded.

'Your name?'

She thought carefully before answering.

'Sana.'

He smiled. His lips were chapped and bleeding; he looked ghastly. But under the long fringe, he thought he saw a twitch of response.

'Come with me.'

He wriggled back out, grateful for the fresh air. He thought she might not come, but a few seconds later she emerged, pushing the sketchbook in front of her. She gave it to him.

'Thank you,' said Paul.

He took her hand. She flinched, but did not let go. They walked together like lost children, down the monumental avenue of ruined temples, colonnades and statues. Paul clutched the portfolio under his arm, thinking of the pictures within. He felt like a thief who had stolen treasure from a giant's palace. He could sense the eyes of forty centuries upon him, but he didn't dare look back. He thought that if he did, they might turn him to stone.

The enormous gate rose in front of them. With a shock, as if waking from a dream, Paul remembered why he had come in the first place. His escape. Everything that had happened in the ruins had driven it from his mind. But what about Sana? Where could he leave her? He could not afford another mouth to feed on his trek through the desert. But he had seen no villages or settlements nearby, no clue where she might have come from.

Sana stumbled. Instinctively, her small hand tightened around Paul's. She steadied herself and glanced up at him. The sort of look a child would give a parent.

In that moment, Paul knew he could not leave her. She had nothing. He would have to make the food last as best he could, and pray she knew of wells where they could replenish their water.

No one has ever helped you, said a voice in his head. A voice he had never heard before: the bird-god's voice. *Why should you help her?*

Because I know what it is to be helpless.

You do not even know who she is. A wild beast. She will slow your escape – you will be caught. Or you will die of hunger. Or she will cut your throat in your sleep and steal everything you have.

I will not leave her here to die.

He would not be like the Jacobins who had murdered his mother for politics; not like Lefebvre who had killed Abasi. He was better than them.

'Get up.'

He cupped his hands to help her mount the camel. She was so light, the beast could carry both of them. They left the city, and climbed out of the valley. From the ridge, the desert stretched as far as he could see.

'Is your home near here?'

She pointed south-eastwards. At first Paul saw nothing, but if he shaded his eyes and squinted, he could make out a dark line in the smooth desert that was too even to be natural. A house, perhaps? Surely nobody could live out there.

Where else could he go? He could not bear to spend the night in the ruined city, and nor did he want to strike out in a direction where he might intersect with Quenot's forces again.

'That is where we will go, then.'

The line Paul had seen turned out to be a squat mud-brick wall. Not a village, not even a house: only a square pen around what had once been a waterhole. But the water had dried up, and a patch of mud was all that remained.

A gunshot echoed across the desert behind them. Paul whipped around. A man was riding out of the desert on a camel. Paul thought of ducking behind the wall, but it was too late. The rider had seen him. He raised his arm and trotted towards Paul. Two more camels fanned out behind him. Were they Bishareen?

Paul had no time to run – and nowhere in the open desert he could flee to. The day had gone darker: clouds had boiled up, though they did nothing to cool the temperature. If anything, it felt more oppressive.

'Who are they?' said Sana.

Paul shook his head. If he was lucky, they would be merchants or traders. If not . . . Wind-blown sand made the air hazy, so he could not make out the riders until they had almost reached him. Even then, all three wore the desert dress of the locals, long white *jellabiyas* that covered their faces. Paul could only wait and watch them approach. He cursed himself for forgetting his carbine.

They halted in front of the little compound. The lead rider unwound the cloth that covered his face.

'Imagine finding you here, *Couillon*.'

Paul felt his insides turn to liquid. It was Sergeant Bastiat, with two men Paul remembered from his platoon: a Breton nicknamed Coquille, and a man from Tours whose face was always such a mess of shaving cuts that the men called him Razor. Paul would have felt safer with the Bishareen.

What have I done to deserve this?

Bastiat studied Paul with mock concern.

'When you did not return to the column, we thought you must have died in the desert. I said we should leave you, but Colonel Quenot said we had to be sure. He said the general in Cairo would not want any doubt as to what had happened to you.'

Paul licked his lips, though the rising wind dried them almost before his tongue was back in his mouth. To be caught alone in the desert with Bastiat was what he had dreaded ever since they left Cairo.

'As you see, I am perfectly safe.'

'Safe, yes.' Bastiat jumped down from his camel. 'But a long way from your regiment. You know the penalty for desertion.'

'I went to sketch the ruins. I lost my bearings when I tried to go back.'

Rote protestations, barely worth the effort. Paul knew Bastiat would not believe him. He had to keep the sergeant talking, endure as long as he could and hope for a miracle to save him.

I will raise you up, the god from the temple whispered to him. *For everything you suffer, you will have your reward.*

Empty words.

'I am in your debt. I might have wandered in the desert for days.'

'Then it is lucky we found you.' Bastiat gave a sadistic laugh, which trailed off as he caught sight of Sana. 'Who is this?'

A new terror trickled through Paul's heart.

'I found her. Her mother had died.'

Bastiat ran his eyes over Sana's frame, the bare skin showing through the scraps of her dress.

'She is a little young for my tastes.'

Paul flushed, furious. 'Not that.'

He wanted to hit Bastiat. Even the suggestion of such a violation felt like a crime.

Sana couldn't understand what the soldiers were saying. But she saw the looks the soldiers were giving her – hungry and pitiless. She shrank against Paul, pressing herself to him. The soldiers thought it was hilarious.

'That's where you want her.'

'She'll keep you warm at night.'

Coquille licked his lips. 'While we're here, we might as well have some entertainment.'

A slow smile spread over Razor's lumpen face.

'I haven't had any *foufoune* since we left Cairo.'

'You've never had any pussy in your life,' Coquille retorted.

'She's a child,' Paul protested.

'Then imagine how tight she'll be.'

Paul edged back, pulling Sana away. But the compound walls surrounded him on every side: there was nowhere he could go.

'Sergeant?' he said to Bastiat. 'You must stop this.'

Bastiat gave a shrug. 'Do I care what they do to your little Arab bitch? Maybe when they're finished, I'll let them have a go at you, eh?'

He grabbed Paul's shirt front and threw him aside. Sana made to run, but Coquille caught her in a second. She bit him; he yelped, but didn't let her go. He struck her face so hard it sent her sprawling onto the sand. Before she could move, Razor had pinned her arms. Bastiat slit open her dress with his knife and tore it away. Paul lunged towards them, but Coquille tackled him and pushed him against the wall. Over his shoulder, Paul could see Sana's head twisted around, staring at him with eyes that pierced like daggers.

'What the devil is that?'

Coquille pointed between Sana's thighs. Paul had averted his eyes in shame, but the surprise in Coquille's voice drew his eyes unwillingly. With horror, he saw a small line of stitches running up her hairless cleft. Someone had sewn her shut, leaving the tiniest holes for her bodily functions.

Sana blushed and writhed. Bastiat laughed.

'I have seen it before,' he said. 'These Egyptian mothers, they would rather mutilate their daughters than see them screwed by a Frenchman.' He puckered his lips and made an exaggerated thrusting motion with his hips. 'You think they would be grateful for some prime French cock.'

'I saw a girl who died of it,' said Razor. 'The mother made sure that nothing could get in, nothing could get out either. Her bowels ruptured and she died.'

'Then we'd better open her up.' Leering at Sana, Bastiat took his bayonet from his belt and ran his thumb down the blade. Paul had seen him grinding it against the whetstone so many times in camp, he knew how sharp the edge was. 'I will do the honours.'

Sana understood what was happening. Her jaw was clenched, her eyes blazing furiously. She squirmed and kicked, mouthing curses that no one could understand.

Bastiat sauntered towards her with the bayonet.

'She is a child!' Paul raged.

He struggled against Coquille, but the Breton was a big man, and Paul was weak from the march through the desert. Once again, he was powerless.

'Don't think I've forgotten you,' Bastiat assured him. 'I will take care of you, after I have made you watch what we do to her.'

The blowing sand hid the sun and made its light a smoky red. It felt like sunset, but it could have been any time. Paul couldn't watch. He raised his eyes to the horizon and . . .

'What's that?'

Something was moving in the clouds of sand. Like a man, but unfeasibly tall, with stick-like legs and a long snout. Paul stared. He knew that figure. It was the bird-headed god from the temple, born from the fragments of Paul's visions and nightmares.

The figure halted. Paul blinked. His head cleared and he saw it was only a camel and rider – of course. With his face shrouded against the flying sand, there was no way of telling if the man was friend or foe.

Coquille realised Paul had stopped struggling. He glanced back and saw the figure.

'Sergeant!' he called.

Bastiat, who had the Devil's gift for sensing danger, was already rising. With his trousers around his ankles, he snatched up his musket and levelled it at the new arrival.

'*Qui va?*' he shouted, voice rasping with the sand in his throat.

The rider did not reply. He swung his arm in a kind of salute, and as he did so he released an object from his hand. It flew over the wall and landed in the centre of their enclosure, a few feet from where Sana lay.

Paul looked at it long enough to know he would never forget the sight. It was a severed human head. Quenot's gaunt eyes stared out of his sun-scarred face, a picture of horror. Fresh blood dripped from the remains of his neck, making Paul wonder if some feeble pulse of life still beat in his brain.

A musket fired. Hooves drummed on the hard desert floor. The lone rider had become a company, scores of men mounted on camels who flitted through the haze around them. They circled the enclosure like sharks homing in on a wounded fish, hollering their eerie battle cry.

'*Mamelukes.*'

Bastiat, Razor and Coquille ran into the compound and kneeled behind the mud-brick wall with their muskets. Paul lifted Sana to her feet. A livid bruise was forming on her face where Coquille had hit her, and there were more bruises on her wrists and legs where Bastiat and Razor had held her. But she was unbowed. She picked up the bayonet Bastiat had dropped and took a step towards the Frenchman.

'Leave him,' said Paul.

Sana ignored him. The wind howled around them. Even sheltered by the enclosure, Paul could hardly stand upright.

Bastiat's musket flashed fire as he took aim at the riders. One of them went down. Bastiat hunched over his musket to reload, struggling to keep the wind from scattering his powder. He did not notice Sana approaching behind him.

Paul told himself afterwards she could not have known what she was doing. She was a child, after all, her arms so thin they looked as if they might snap. Bastiat could have knocked her away with a swat of his fist.

But Bastiat didn't see her.

Sana drove the bayonet into Bastiat's side, under the ribs and up into the vital organs. His body convulsed. He dropped the musket and jerked back, head up, staring in astonished horror at his unlikely nemesis.

Sana spat in his face.

Bastiat keeled over, knocking into Razor beside him. Before Sana could retrieve the blade, Razor saw what had happened. He raised the butt of his rifle to club her brains out.

That was unwise. He had put his head above the parapet, and the Mameluke riders with their long jezails needed no second chance. A bullet opened his skull and threw him to the ground.

Now only Coquille was left. He gazed at Sana, an imp standing straight-backed and remorseless. He had a musket; she was unarmed. Yet it was the Breton who looked frightened.

A spear flew over the wall and stuck quivering in the sand two feet from Sana. Paul took her hand.

'Leave him,' he said. 'He is dead already.'

He lifted Sana over the mud-brick wall and scrambled after her. On the other side, the sand had drifted so high there was hardly any distance to drop. They rolled to the foot of the slope, picked themselves up, and were immediately knocked flat again by the wind.

Lightning flashed. The wind raised clouds of sand so high they blotted out the sky. The burning sun was reduced to a dim moon. Head down, eyes almost closed, Paul crawled forward. Sana came after him, gripping his ankle. If they were separated now, they would lose each other for ever.

The ground shook: maybe a gust of wind, or a lightning bolt hitting the earth. Paul risked a glance – and froze. They had been seen. A rider was coming towards them, robes flapping around him and lance raised for the kill.

Paul flung himself over Sana. At least his body might stop the lance going through her. The rider was so close Paul could smell the camel, and he had time to feel an irrational burst of anger that this was the last sensation he would feel.

The rider towered over him, arm back, spear point aimed at Paul's chest.

A gust of wind hit them, stronger than anything Paul had felt before. Through the raging sand, Paul saw the rider blown out of his saddle and carried away like a sheet of paper. Then, as if an invisible fist had let go, the man fell to the ground.

The fall had concussed him. Before he could move, Paul was on him. Every Mameluke carried a beautifully wrought dagger with a curved blade in his belt. Paul found it and cut the man's throat. Blood spilled out, but sand clogged the wound so quickly Paul worried the man might live after all. He stuck him through the heart to be sure.

Sana came out of the storm, leading the camel by its bridle. There was no question of riding, and no chance of going back to the enclosure. They could worry about escaping if they survived the next ten minutes.

Paul had no compass. He could not see the sun; he could barely stand upright and could hardly breathe. Sand clogged his nostrils, but if he opened his mouth sand was forced down his throat. All he had to keep him alive was fear.

It would have to be enough. Head down, he chose a direction at random and set off through the sandstorm.

Paul woke alone. He was lying against the camel's flank, with Sana curled up in the crook of his elbow. But when he stood, in a shower of sand, the desert horizon was empty of life.

He had escaped. From Bastiat, from the army, from the Mamelukes. A bubble of elation rose through his chest. He was free.

Then he remembered where he was. Miles from the river, and hundreds of miles from any town or city. Without water, without food, without hope of rescue.

Sana woke. She spat sand out of her mouth and frowned at him. The camel grunted.

'Where are we?' Paul wondered aloud.

They could not have gone far in the storm, yet there was no sign of the mud walls at the oasis. The sand must have covered it. And where were the Mamelukes? Had they been wiped out, too?

Sana shrugged.

Paul knew the river was west. In Cairo, he had seen maps that showed the Red Sea coast running down the east side of the continent. He supposed he would find villages there, too, ships that could take him . . . *where?*

He was an enemy of the revolution, a deserter from the army, an invader in a foreign land, and an infidel among the heathen. Where could he go?

The elation he had felt when he woke turned in on itself, shrinking to a black hole of despair. He was an outcast. There was not a place on earth he could be accepted.

Sana's cool gaze restored his senses. Self-pity could come later; it would do him no good if he did not find water and food. He pointed west.

'River.' Then east. 'Sea.' Then spread both arms wide. 'Which?'

Sana squinted, then pointed south.

'Gondar.'

'What is Gondar?'

'Kingdom. Rich.'

Paul looked the way she had indicated. The desert seemed to stretch to the limits of the world, red sand and grey hills.

'How do you know this?'

'Caravans come. Slaves. Gold.'

'Across the desert?'

She nodded.

'Far?'

She shrugged.

'Is there water?'

She nodded, eagerly this time.

'The mother of rivers.'

Her words conjured a vision of green trees, still waters and soft rain. Paul's mouth puckered at the thought – but it was probably a fairy tale, he told himself, something Sana's mother had told her. He could not trust his life to that. As for the other options, west meant the Nile and a way back to Cairo. Back to Lefebvre.

He weighed his future, with nothing but the ramblings of a child to guide him.

He pointed east, to the sea.

'That way.'

They rummaged through the food bags tied to the camel's saddle and laid out what they found: dates, two stale flatbreads, and a handful of nuts. There was a flask with barely enough water inside to fill the cup that came with it. That was all. The look on Sana's face was almost as heartbreaking as the sight of what little they had.

'It will have to do.'

For Sana's sake, Paul tried to stay cheerful. With his clothes torn to rags by the storm, his skin scoured like a leper and his voice thorny dry, he probably looked and sounded demented. Sana gave him a glance and said nothing.

She was still naked. He tried not to stare at the gruesome stitches between her legs, but now that he had seen them it was impossible to look at anything else. What sort of mother could do that to her daughter? Or how terrible must the French seem, that sewing a person shut seemed like the better alternative?

He could not leave her like that. Razor's words preyed on him: what if she died of a ruptured bladder, or something burst inside her?

He took out the Mameluke's knife and tested the blade. Lethally sharp, its point honed fine as a needle. Sana watched him warily.

'I can undo you.'

Undo? He did not know the right word in Arabic, or perhaps it did not exist. He pointed between her legs, flushing with embarrassment that flared even brighter as she shrank away, baring her teeth.

'No. Not that. I am not like the others. I will not force you.' He spread his arms in innocence.

Her eyes locked on to his, brimming with an anger that verged on madness. How long had she spent in that city with her dead mother? What other tragedies had she suffered – even before Bastiat tried to rape her?

No wonder she does not trust me.

'I will protect you,' he promised.

If it was the sincerity in his voice, or the prospect of release, or if she saw something in his face that she believed: his words seemed to convince her. She lay on the ground and spread her thin legs. Paul knelt beside her.

'Hold still.'

He took a deep breath. He had never thought of himself as dex-
trous, and he was squeamish when it came to blood. Any mistake
would inflict horrible pain on her, maybe permanent mutilation.
He gripped the knife like a pencil and tried to imagine he was
drawing on the finest tissue paper. Even an ounce too much pressure would ruin everything. He moved slowly, tiny flicks of the
blade, as if he were sketching in shadows. He cut each stitch one
thread at a time. When the tip of the knife nicked her soft skin and
drew a bead of blood, Sana hissed, but did not move.

At last he was finished. Sana examined herself, then gave Paul
an indecipherable look. Gratitude, perhaps, but so fierce he had
to turn away. He wondered when was the last time anyone had
shown her a kindness – if you could call it that.

He wished he had a fire, and water to boil, so he could wash
the wound and soothe some of the pain. The only thing he had to
offer was a rag torn from a piece of his shirt. Sana pressed it against
herself, covering her modesty, while Paul cut the saddle cloth into
a rough tunic for her to wear, belted with a length of the reins.

'We will have to guide the camel without a bridle.'

He picked up the saddle to replace it on the camel's back.

The animal had other ideas. Separated from its master and
freed of its tack, it decided to take its chance. It bolted. Paul
lunged, but only managed to grab the tip of its tail. It tugged free;
he was left holding the saddle in one hand, and a clump of camel
hair in the other, as the camel receded towards the horizon.

He dropped the useless saddle and kicked it in frustration.

Paul thought he had plumbed every torment of trekking through
the desert. He was wrong. Marching with Quenot and the men
had been miserable – he had hated every one of them – but at
least they had had strength in numbers. Now, he and Sana were
alone against the immensity of the desert.

Step by step, the impossibility of the task was hammered into
him. Even if they took the merest sips, their water wouldn't last
two days. He was already dizzy with thirst and faint with hunger.
When he tripped, which was often, he did not have the strength
to regain his balance, but flopped face forward onto the ground.

Each time, it took him longer to rise. He told himself he had to keep going for Sana's sake, but more often it was she who helped him up. The heat and hunger affected her less; in her short life, she had grown used to it. But even she could not last indefinitely. Every hour her pace slowed, and her head drooped lower.

They had reached a rocky part of the desert, sharp stones underfoot which lacerated Paul's shoes. When the shoes were gone, the rocks tore into his feet. Every step became such agony that Paul didn't notice the camel until he almost walked into it.

It was dead. If not for the flies, it would have looked like a lump in the ground.

Sana sniffed it.

'It died recently,' she pronounced.

'Is it ours? The one that ran away?'

Sana showed him the embroidery on the bridle.

'Bishareen.'

A cold prickle of fear went down Paul's back.

'You're certain?'

'I have seen it.'

Her words carried a weight of knowledge that made Paul wonder what other things her young eyes had seen. He looked around the empty landscape, as desolate as the craters of the moon. No sign of any living thing.

'It must have wandered off from a caravan and got lost,' he said.

That earned him another inscrutable look from Sana.

'Bishareen do not travel alone.'

'Well, I cannot see any.'

'You do not see them in the desert. Not until they want.'

Paul kicked the camel's corpse.

'If it was still alive, it might be some use to us.'

Sana squatted beside the camel and took out Bastiat's knife. She put the point against its belly, then folded both hands over the pommel of the knife and pushed hard. Blood and bile spilled out of the hole she had made. The smell made Paul want to vomit, but he clenched his teeth. There was so little fluid in his stomach, he could not afford to lose a drop.

With deft motions, Sana sawed open the camel's underside. A bloody mass of guts slithered into the sand. Sana plunged her arms in to the elbows. She found the stomach and cut a hole in it, then reached in with the cup from the flask and scooped out the contents.

She gave Paul the cup.

'Drink.'

It contained a green, fibrous liquid. The smell was indescribable. The taste was worse, like drinking out of a latrine pit, he imagined. Paul swallowed it as if it were clear spring water. The sensation of moisture in his mouth and throat was sheer bliss. He thrust his arm into the stomach and scooped out another cup of the stuff.

They spent much of the morning dissecting the camel. Paul had thought that the hump was where the beast stored its water, but when he cut it open he found fatty tissue. He cut strips of meat off its flanks, which Sana stretched out to dry in the sun. They continued on their journey.

The desert had become a maze of rocky hills and gullies, which made it impossible to keep a straight course. Each route looked the same. Paul's sense of direction deserted him; he began to feel certain he had seen places before. He tried to change course, but the landscape never varied and the feeling of going in circles grew more oppressive.

His vision started to fail. One eye had grown infected, weeping a yellow pus that dried and crusted the eyelid shut. The other was half-blind from the glare. The world was a place of shapes and vague outlines, half-glimpsed like a dream.

He was convinced they were not alone. He could sense a presence beside him, a shadow on the sand that vanished every time he looked. Sometimes it spoke to him, though it used different voices to confuse him. He thought it was the bird-headed god, or perhaps Abasi, or his mother.

'Do you hear that?' he mumbled. 'It says there is water over the next hill.'

Sana gave him a dark look. 'The desert is stealing your mind.'

The liquid he'd drunk from the camel's stomach tormented him. The refreshment had lasted as long as it took to swallow, but the taste remained in his mouth and throat like a festering sewer. It roiled his intestines and shot agonising cramps through his body. When he tried to eat a piece of the dried camel meat, he could feel it sitting in his belly like a lump of poison.

By the second morning, Paul knew they wouldn't survive. It wasn't a sudden realisation. It had crept up on him as they trudged through the darkness, seeping into his soul like mist. Morning brought the final proof. Before sunset, he had marked their position by a conical hill in the distance. He had walked all night, but when the sun rose the hill was as distant as it had ever been.

Strength left him. He dropped to the ground and sprawled out as flat as a corpse. He told himself it was only for a few hours, then they would resume the march – that there might be a well, or even the coast, a few miles distant – but he knew it was a lie. This was where he would die. Perhaps in a thousand years some traveller would find his bones, as ancient as the pharaohs. Perhaps no one ever would. His vision blurred to darkness, and his last thought was that death would be a blessed release.

The pain in his belly woke him. The camel fluid had spread like fire through his guts, burning agony shooting through him.

I must be alive, he thought, *otherwise I couldn't wish I was dead.*

Or perhaps he *was* dead, and his body had started to rot from the inside.

He rolled over and tried to vomit. His stomach heaved until he thought the muscles had burst, but nothing emerged. He rolled and writhed like a demented animal. He came to rest a few inches from Sana.

A fly crawled over her eyelid. Her face was still, peaceful; he was certain she was dead. Then she breathed. She was sleeping the sleep of an exhausted child. Her eyes fluttered open. She saw Paul and her smile was guileless but fearful.

Paul could not let her die in the desert. Not while a breath remained in his body. He forced himself to stand.

'Come on.'

They had been walking for an hour when Paul stepped in a soft and yielding substance, utterly alien on that flinty ground.

It was a heap of camel dung. Sana was studying it.

'This is recent. And look . . .'

His eyes hurt too much to glance at the sun to orientate himself. He had no idea where the tracks led.

It hardly mattered. Whoever had travelled this way would surely have water and food – a way out of the interminable desert.

Not a mile further, the tracks went over the lip of a hill into a round crater. The floor was strewn with boulders, so large Paul wondered how they could have got there. Then he saw the well. Not the mud hole where Bastiat had died, but a well with a stone rim, a wooden frame and a canvas bucket tied to a rope.

Paul stumbled down the slope, tripping on the loose stone and cackling like a hyena. Sana followed. Paul dropped to his knees beside the well and threw in the bucket. He felt it go taut as water flooded into the container. He began to heave, but he was so weak he could barely manage the weight. Sana joined him. Even with both their strength, they struggled. The well was deep. At last, Paul saw the gleam of sunlight on water as the bucket rose to the rim.

On the far side of the well, one of the boulders moved. The surface of the stone rippled and rose.

The boulder turned into a man. Then another, and another, until the field of stones had spawned a dozen men.

The rocks were camels, hobbled and covered with tawny cloth awnings to disguise them and shade them and their riders from the sun.

Paul let go of the rope. The bucket of water slithered down the well and splashed to the bottom.

The men were Bishareen Arabs: lean, strong and well armed, with dark skin and long black beards. They used their captives with brusque practicality. They raped Paul, and he suffered it, and afterwards he thought he should be grateful to Lefebvre for teaching him to endure such pains. Then they gave him water from the well, and set Sana to help the wizened old woman who prepared their food. When evening came, they bound Paul and prepared to set out.

'Where are we going?' Paul asked his captor.

The Bishareen Arab tightened the rope around Paul's wrists. He fastened the loose end to his camel's saddle, so that Paul would have to trot along behind. Sana was put on a shorter halter fixed to Paul.

'We go to Gondar.'

INDIAN OCEAN, 1806

As the *Requin* came alongside the *Diamond*, Adam only had eyes for the man on her quarterdeck, the man he had crossed an ocean and braved a hurricane to find: Jean Lesaut.

It was not hard to identify him. He was dressed in extraordinary fashion, like a French courtier from the previous century. He wore a curled white wig, a long purple coat that appeared to be made of silk, and a cocked hat fringed with white feathers that ruffled in the breeze. His shoes sported ostentatious silver buckles. A sky-blue sash stretched across his chest, and a star of silver lace gleamed on his left breast. If you had met him in the gardens of Versailles, before the revolution, you would have thought he was overdressed.

But though he looked like a fop, he was no fool. With the *Diamond* dismasted and battered, Lesaut did not drop his guard. His ship was cleared for action. His men crouched by their guns, stripped to the waist. Adam could smell the smoke from the slow matches, and the tang of powder in the air.

The *Diamond* shuddered as the other ship bumped against her hull. Ropes were thrown and made fast. Whooping and cheering, the French sailors swarmed over the side. They herded the *Diamond*'s crew into the ship's waist, brandishing pikes and boarding axes.

A tanned lieutenant accepted Adam's surrender. He said little, but confiscated Adam's sword and led him aboard the *Requin* to the great cabin. Two sentries in red uniform coats stayed to watch him.

He studied the cabin, searching for any clue that might link its occupant with the slaughter at Nativity Bay. Adam had spent half his life in ships' cabins, but never one like this. The walls were hung with paintings in lavish gilded frames. Lesaut's tastes in art ran to hunting scenes and nudes. The hunts were visceral and bloody, with hounds ripping open a fox's throat or sinking their claws into a deer's hide. The nudes were voluptuous women, lounging on beds with legs spread and leaving nothing to the imagination.

The door opened. Lesaut entered briskly, carrying an oil-skin bundle that he tipped onto the table. The Neptune sword, together with the dagger and the sketch of Mary. Adam rose from his seat at the sight, but a warning glare from the sentry pushed him back.

A steward took Lesaut's hat and coat. Lesaut settled himself into a chair behind the desk and called for wine. He had a craggy face, deep-lined by years on the quarterdeck, and eyes that sparkled with dark purpose. He must be nearly old enough to be Adam's grandfather, but he was still handsome enough to attract looks from women half his age. He smelled of rose water.

'You must forgive my delay,' he said in perfect English. 'I was making arrangements for your crew.'

'Thank you for your concern,' said Adam in perfect French.

Lesaut's mouth twitched, as if indulging a private joke.

'You prefer we speak in French or in English?'

'You are the victor. When I have you captive aboard my ship, we will speak my language.'

'A shame. I always enjoy the chance to practise.' Lesaut studied his captive. 'Adam Courtney. I have heard of you. Son of the great Admiral Sir Robert Courtney?'

There was no point denying it.

Lesaut held the Neptune sword up to the light, studying his reflection in the pommel.

'A beautiful weapon – though now, maybe, it is not so useful.' He pointed to the fractured stump and gave a thin smile. 'Like your ship, *non*?'

Adam didn't answer.

'This sword belonged to your father?'

'It has been in my family for eight generations.'

Adam sat motionless, his gaze boring into Lesaut's face as if he might read the secrets hidden inside.

'And this?' Lesaut held up the sketch. 'Your wife?'

'My cousin.'

'She is very beautiful.'

'She is dead. She was killed at her home in Nativity Bay, on the east coast of Africa.' Adam held Lesaut's gaze. 'I believe you know it.'

Adam could see every pore in the man's face. At the mention of Nativity Bay, Lesaut flinched; the restlessness in his eyes skipped a beat, a sudden stillness before he remembered himself.

'I have been to Nativity Bay,' Lesaut allowed.

'And what did you do?'

Lesaut gave him a keen, appraising stare. He looked as if he was wrestling with something on his mind.

'You say it was your family who lived there?'

'Did you kill them?'

'*Non.*'

Lesaut was about to continue when a cry from the deck above came through the open skylight. It was the scream of a man in pain.

'What is that?'

All Adam's senses were alive at once. Had his crew decided to fight? Had they managed to throw off their captors and seize weapons? If not, it would be a massacre.

But the chaotic noise of battle did not erupt – only one man in absolute agony. A tendril of smoke spiralled through the skylight, bringing the noxious smell of burned flesh.

Adam remembered what Captain Verrier had said at dinner in Cape Town:

'*You know what he does to the crews he captures? He brands them.*'

Adam sprang to his feet. On the table, the Neptune sword was in easy reach. The jagged point of the broken blade was more than sharp enough to ram through Lesaut's chest.

Lesaut sat back in his chair, unconcerned. Adam knew that if he grabbed for the Neptune sword, the guards would shoot him dead before he touched it. Even then, he might have risked it. But to kill Lesaut would be to destroy his only hope of finding the truth of what had happened at Nativity Bay.

'This is not the law of war,' Adam snarled.

'Indeed,' Lesaut agreed. 'It is purely business. You know how much it costs me, each time I have to repair my ship after battle? If your seamen encounter me again, they will think twice before they decide to fight.'

Another scream sounded from the deck. Adam's crew were stout men, and none would want to show weakness in front of the French. Adam could only imagine how much pain they must be suffering.

'But I am an honourable man.' Lesaut turned the sword so that the hilt pointed towards Adam. 'If you give me your parole, your promise not to attempt escape, I will give your sword back. You will have a cabin, and every courtesy that is due your rank.'

The sword lay on the table between them, the sapphire aimed at Adam's heart. The facets of the gem reflected his face a hundred times over.

Adam reached for it. His fingers touched the hilt, that so many Courtneys before him had held. The familiar electric current ran up his arm.

He spun it round so it pointed back towards Lesaut.

'I will not make a promise I have no intention of keeping.'

Lesaut did not look surprised. 'I admire your honour. But . . .' He gave an airy wave through the cabin windows at the expanse of empty ocean around them. 'Your ship is a wreck. Your crew are captive. What will you do?'

'Whatever I can.'

Lesaut shrugged. 'As you wish. *Ça ne fait rien.* I will lock you away like a common prisoner.' He ran his fingers along the sword blade, a connoisseur admiring a masterpiece. 'And I will keep the sword.' He pried at the sapphire with a long fingernail. 'This jewel alone is worth more than your entire ship.'

On deck, another man screamed as the hot branding iron was plunged into his skin. Adam felt the anger surge inside him. For all Lesaut's manners and aristocratic dress, he was little better than a pirate.

'The difference between you and me,' Adam said, 'is that you fight for money, while I fight for my country's honour.'

Lesaut shrugged. One of the guards stepped forward with a pair of manacles.

'A man fights for what he does not have.'

Adam had many hours to regret his decision. Lesaut locked him in the brig like a lowly prisoner, wrists shackled, guarded day and night. In deference to Adam's rank, the Frenchman did not brand him – but the ordeal of listening to his men being disfigured was almost worse punishment. It lasted longer than he thought he could endure. Adam would rather have endured the pain himself a thousand times than make his crew suffer for his folly.

He had no hope of escape. He had lost his ship, his crew and his sword. The thought of the Neptune sword in Lesaut's hands, the gems being prised out and the gold melted down, made him almost burst with frustration.

Sometimes, in the pitch-black night of the hold, the darkest thoughts crept from the deepest recesses of his soul. Adam held them back. He had to bide his time – and save his strength for the next battle.

He did not know what course they were steering. But he had lived all his life afloat; he could feel a ship's rhythms in the creak of every plank. After five days, he sensed a new urgency in her handling, and guessed she was coming into port. An hour later, he felt the splash of her anchor vibrate through the hull.

There were only two ports in the Indian Ocean she could have reached in that time: Île de France, or Île Bourbon. He guessed the former. As the guards led him onto the deck, he was greeted with the most picturesque harbour he had ever laid eyes on, a paradise. Every cloud had been scrubbed from an azure blue sky. The air was pure and wholesome. Around the broad harbour, whitewashed houses with green verandas and trellised windows lined the slopes of the basalt blue mountains that ringed the bay. One of the mountains rose almost sheer to a rounded summit, like a giant thumb thrust out of the earth. The slopes were lush with vegetation, running with streams that cascaded down the rugged rocky precipices.

Adam barely noticed. His attention was on the *Diamond*, coming in behind them under a jury-rigged sail – and on the harbour's defences. Two batteries guarded the mouth of the bay, while a citadel on the eastern shore commanded the approach with her cannon. He remembered Captain Talbot's verdict: *The harbour at Port Louis is quite impregnable.* Even if Adam could escape his prison, if he could somehow commandeer a ship, he would never get out past those guns.

Lesaut's men took him ashore in chains, up the hill to a plaza in front of a square-turreted cathedral. Opposite, the Government

House looked as if someone had transplanted a Loire château to this tropical island. The reception rooms were no doubt airy and graceful, lavishly furnished and blessed with the finest French wines. The basement was none of those. The guards locked him in a cell in a dank, low-vaulted cellar, and left him.

Ten minutes later they returned with Angus.

'I told 'em I was your valet,' Angus explained, when they had gone. 'Even in jail, a Frenchie wouldn'ae deprive a gentleman of his manservant.'

Adam embraced him. Angus winced where the flesh was still livid with the *L* that Lesaut had branded into it. Guilt and fury boiled in Adam's heart.

'I am sorry for what you suffered.'

'Not as sorry as that Frenchie'll be, when I get a crack at him.'

His stoic calm cheered Adam.

'I do not suppose you chanced to bring a key?'

'Must'ae lost it in the storm.'

From above, the sounds of music and laughter filtered through the metal grating that was their only light.

'It sounds as if they are holding an assembly or a banquet,' said Adam.

'You should'ae given your parole. You'd be up there now eating like a lord, not locked in this coop.'

'You know my honour would never let me do that.'

'Aye. But what use is honour to an empty stomach?'

'I do not intend to have to choose.'

After days of solitude in the brig, Angus's presence filled Adam with hope again. Plans and schemes poured out of him, while Angus listened patiently.

'I was across the table from Lesaut,' said Adam. 'When I told him about Nativity Bay, he knew what I was talking about. He is hiding something. If I could have five minutes with him alone, I would make him give up everything he knows.'

'Aye. An' if prison bars were sausages, we could get out of this cage and fill our bellies at the same time.'

They waited. The shadows coming through the window grille lengthened, then faded as dusk fell. A cannon boomed from the harbour.

'A rescue?'

Adam was on his feet in an instant. He grabbed the bars and hoisted himself up so he could peer through the window. Angus stayed on his mattress.

'Signal gun. Ship arriving.'

It seemed he was right. There was no more cannon fire. Adam sat down again.

But something had changed. Soon, footsteps came running up the steep road from the harbour. He heard shouts, surprise that turned to delight.

Angus opened an eye. 'What're they saying?'

'I cannot make it out.'

Everything was hubbub and confusion. Adam pulled himself up and looked through the window again. He saw lanterns being strung up across the square. A band appeared and began to play rousing French war songs, *La Marseillaise* and the *Chant de Départ*. The smell of gunpowder filled the air, but not from battle. They were letting off fireworks.

'What has happened?' Adam was desperate to know. 'They are celebrating as if the war is over.'

Tables were erected. Bowls of punch and casks of beer were served out. Men and women mingled freely, dancing and flirting. Adam saw several disappear, giggling, into the bushes.

'It is a complete debauch. Do they do this every night?'

'You ken what the Frenchies are like.'

The smell of the food reminded Adam how ravenous he was. He banged on the bars of the high outside window to get attention, hoping one of the revellers would feed him a morsel of news – or at least of food. No one noticed him. The fireworks, the music and the chatter were too loud, the ladies too enchanting.

'Get down from there!' said a French voice behind him.

Adam let go of the bars and dropped to the floor. A guard had appeared in the corridor, a gun in one hand and a glass of wine in the other. He gestured at Adam with his bayonet to keep back.

'Why all the celebrations?' Adam asked in French.

The guard didn't answer. He was a private, no more than a teenager, with wisps of a moustache on his upper lip. Too young and raw to think of disobeying instructions. He had been ordered not to speak to the prisoners, and normally that would have been final.

But this news was too good not to share.

'A ship has come from France,' he confided. 'She has brought dispatches. There has been a great sea battle. Your Admiral Nelson, curse his name, is dead.'

Adam froze in disbelief. He stared at the guard, open-mouthed.

'Dead?'

'*Oui.*'

No wonder the islanders were celebrating so raucously.

'And the battle?'

'The report says it was a glorious victory for France,' said the private proudly. 'The English fleet is utterly destroyed. Now the Emperor Napoleon is invincible. Perhaps already he has invaded England, eh?'

'Where was this battle?'

'The coast of Spain. A place called Cape Trafalgar.' He raised his glass in a mock toast, then drained it in one gulp. 'The Battle of Trafalgar. A name that will live forever to the glory of France.'

Adam wanted to scream at the walls. But he had the guard's attention. This might be his only chance.

'I sailed with Nelson once,' he said.

Angus opened one eye in surprise, then closed it again.

The sentry looked impressed.

'*Vraiment?*'

'He gave me a gold medallion. I have carried it with me ever since.'

The sentry's eyes widened. 'You have it here?'

'Of course – it is my most treasured possession. I hid it from Lesaut when he captured me.'

'I would very much like to see it.'

Adam recoiled from the bars. 'You would steal it, to show to your friends so they could crow over their victory.'

'Never, *monsieur*. I wish only to see it as a memory of the great admiral. He was a *cornard*, true, but a great man, also.'

The private was already thinking of the look on his sergeant's face when he showed him the medallion. If it was truly gold, he would receive a fine price for it. Enough to buy some memorable nights in the brothels of Port Louis.

Adam sensed the private's greed. He smelled the wine on the youth's breath and thought how the alcohol would spur his desire. Adam reached inside his shirt. He balled his hand and held it out to the guard.

'Take it.'

The guard had the wineglass in one and his musket in the other. He laid the weapon against the wall and opened Adam's hand.

'There is nothing there,' he said.

Adam grabbed the guard's collar and jerked him forward. The youth's face struck the bars so hard he was almost knocked unconscious. Angus snaked an arm around his neck and held him there. The guard's eyes bulged; his lips stretched open in a soundless cry. He tried to struggle, but Angus and Adam held him firm against the cell bars until his body sagged and he passed out.

Angus lowered him to the floor.

'His keys.'

Through the bars, Angus frisked the body. Metal jangled as he extracted a ring of keys. One key undid their manacles; a second opened the cell door. A moment later, Adam and Angus were outside the cell, and the unconscious guard had been stripped naked and locked inside.

'D'ye think it's true what he said, about Cape Trafalgar and Lord Nelson?' said Angus.

There were more cheers and shouts.

'They seem sure of it.' Yet even in disaster, there were seeds of hope. 'Every Frenchman in the garrison will be drunk as a Plymouth doxy tonight. This is our chance.'

'It's a long sail to Cape Town, for two men.'

'You forget, the rest of our crew are somewhere on this island.' Adam knew that was the beginning of their difficulties, but he put it out of his mind for the moment. He finished dressing in the French guard's uniform. 'The only matter that remains is to find Lesaut.'

Angus stared at him. 'Beggin' yer pardon, sir?'

'I need to find out what he knows. My father entrusted me with this task. I have lost my ship, my freedom, and too many men to turn tail when I have him in my reach.'

'But be careful that your reach doesn'ae exceed your grasp.'

Both men knew Angus was arguing for the sake of it. They were already moving. Angus wore the manacles loose around his wrists; Adam, dressed as the lieutenant, was behind him.

'Where are the rest of our crew?' Adam whispered.

'I saw 'em took to the wee fort by the harbour.'

'By "wee fort", I take it you mean the fortress defended with three batteries and no doubt garrisoned by at least five hundred men?'

'Aye.'

'We will be noticed if we break in there.' Adam thought quickly. 'I will find Lesaut. You reconnoitre the fort and see if you can find a way in.'

'Aye, sir.'

'Wait for my arrival. Do not do anything rash without me.'

'Wouldn'ae dream of it.'

'And wipe that smirk off your face. Have you forgotten you're supposed to be a prisoner?'

But there was no one to see them. The guards had abandoned their posts to join the revels, which had spilled into the streets surrounding the square. No one challenged them as they left the building. Angus slipped off the manacles and dropped them in a flower bed, then set off towards the harbour, edging inconspicuously through the crowds.

Adam found a French sailor with a glass of punch in one hand, the other clutching a woman in a low-cut dress.

'*Vive l'Empereur!*' Adam shouted.

'*Mort à Nelson,*' the sailor toasted him back.

'Captain Lesaut – you know where he is?'

Adam knew his French accent was imperfect. A sober man would have seen through it in seconds. But the sailor was blind drunk, and too preoccupied fondling his companion.

'In the governor's house, at the banquet. You know he captured an English admiral's son. Maybe we kill them both. *Mort à Nelson! Mort à Courtney!*'

Adam imagined sticking his bayonet into the sailor's stomach and watching his guts slither out. He resisted.

'*Mort à Courtney,*' he repeated.

He crossed the gardens to a grand door at the head of a carriage drive. Fires burned high in the braziers that flanked the door. A trio of ladies in fine dresses had dismounted their coach, and were being escorted into the building by a group of officers in uniforms that groaned with gold braid and medals. Adam quickened his pace and fell in behind them, as natural as a footman or an equerry. Nobody challenged him.

As soon as he was inside, he branched off down a corridor. None of the doors was locked. The first room he came to was a clerk's office, with an inkstand on the desk and paper across the surface. Adam scrawled a quick note on a blank sheet.

Captain Lesaut—
I have vital intelligence concerning the disposition of the British fleet. I am willing to reveal it to you in exchange for my freedom, but you must come now.

He signed it with his own name and folded it, then returned to the main hall. From the clinking of glasses and chime of cutlery on china upstairs, it sounded as though the banquet was in full swing. Adam knew this was madness – to have escaped his cell, only to push deeper into the heart of the French headquarters. He had to trust that hardly anyone ashore had seen him. If he was recognised, the charade would be over before it had begun.

He carried on. He had to get to Lesaut.

A grand staircase led to the ballroom on the first floor. It was unguarded, but as Adam reached the top, his luck ran out. A footman – a black man in a gold-trimmed blue livery coat and a white powdered wig – emerged from the dining room, carrying a tray of glasses. He saw Adam and stopped, blocking his path.

'*Oui?*' said the footman.

He might only be a servant, but a great part of his job was ensuring that his master was not troubled by undesirable guests. In those lavish surroundings, Adam's grubby uniform stood out like a coal smudge on a bedsheet.

Adam thrust out the piece of paper.

'*Pour Capitaine Lesaut,*' he said, slurring his words like a drunkard to disguise his accent. '*Maintenant! Tout de suite!*'

The footman took the paper irritably. As he reached forward, the velvet sleeve of his coat was tugged up. Adam saw a deep black weal in the skin around his wrist.

There was only one thing that could make a mark like that. An iron shackle, locked so tight and worn so long that it rubbed away the skin and through to the bone. A slave's chains.

Adam studied the footman more closely. He might have come from Madagascar, or Mozambique, yet something in his colouring and his bearing looked more familiar. Slavers shunned the dangerous coast around Nativity Bay, but he knew from his father that raiding parties sometimes came from the Portuguese settlements further north.

'You hate the French?' Adam said quietly – not in French, or English, but in the language of the Qwabe that had been his mother's native tongue. It was years since Phoebe had taught it to him, but he had never forgotten it.

The footman's eyes widened. He glanced anxiously over his shoulder, but everyone else was busy with the banquet.

'Who are you?' he asked, in the same language.

'A friend in need of help. And perhaps I can help you, too.' He pointed to the note. 'Give that to Captain Lesaut and tell him he must go to the jail immediately. When he comes, follow him.'

Adam saw in the man's eyes that he was tempted. But Adam was a stranger, and even a slave still had plenty more to lose.

'Why should I?'

'This island is a prison for me as much as you. If you come with me, there is a chance we will both escape.'

The hope in his eyes was almost too much to bear, yet still caution.

'How do I know I can trust you?'

'My name is Adam Courtney.' It was a high risk, revealing his true identity, but it was the only way he could think of to earn the man's trust. 'I am a British officer and I have escaped from the prison. And now I am entirely in your power.'

The footman gazed at Adam, his eyes boring into his soul. Whatever he read there, it was in a language beyond words. He nodded, and as he did, he seemed to grow two inches taller. He put the tray of drinks aside.

'I will bring Lesaut to the prison.'

He took the note and turned to go, but Adam called him back. 'What is your name? Your real name.'

'Bheka,' said the man. Pride entered his voice, maybe for the first time in years.

'Then pray to my god and yours that we both escape this island together.'

Adam ran across the gardens to the jail. Nobody stopped him, and no one seemed to have come to find the captured guard. Adam hid himself in the shadows and waited.

A few minutes later, he heard Lesaut's voice calling his name down the stairs.

'Courtney? If you are wasting my time, I can make you suffer worse than you have already.' He came to the cell and looked in. 'Courtney?'

Too late, he saw that the man in the cell was not Adam Courtney. He was a French private, naked except for his drawers, moaning through the gag that covered his mouth.

The point of a bayonet pricked against the small of Lesaut's back.

Lesaut turned slowly. His face darkened to rage as he saw Adam pointing the musket at him, all the greater for the fact he could do nothing about it.

'I told you I would do everything I could to escape,' said Adam.

Lesaut was a man accustomed to being in control. To lose it was intolerable.

'What can you do?' he sneered. 'You are a thousand miles from hope.'

'Then I will need a fast ship.'

Adam did not want to linger in the jail. He twisted the bayonet off the musket, then passed it to Bheka, who had followed Lesaut.

'Who is he?' shouted Lesaut, pointing at Bheka.

'Another man who has tired of your hospitality.'

'A confounded turncoat. I'll have him flogged and quartered, then I will eat his heart.'

Bheka blinked once and smiled.

'You go first,' he said to Lesaut.

'All it will take to reveal you is one word,' Lesaut warned him.

'You would be dead the second you said it,' said Adam.

'If you have your negro shoot me, you will bring every soldier on the island down on you.'

Adam slid the bayonet into his sleeve. The shirt hid it, but if he dropped his arm he would have it in his hand in an instant.

'That is why I will stay close enough to kill you silently.'

'You think you could kill me and no one would notice?'

'I fight for my country,' Adam reminded him. 'To die honourably would be my privilege. Whereas you . . .' He tapped Lesaut's back with the bayonet and felt the captain flinch. 'You need to stay alive if you want to enjoy the riches you have accumulated.'

The look on Lesaut's face told him he had judged his man correctly. With Lesaut leading the way, and Bheka flanking them with the musket, the three men hurried out of the jail towards the harbour.

Revellers crowded the streets. It needed deft use of Adam's elbows to keep within bayonet range of Lesaut. He had no doubt the privateer captain would betray him in an instant if he thought he could survive it. Down by the docks, smoke drifted through the air where the sailors, unable to get hold of fireworks, had let off their cannon instead. Every tavern overflowed with soldiers, sailors, stevedores and whores joining the celebrations.

A road led around the arm of the bay to the citadel on the eastern shore. It was an area of warehouses and chandleries, squat buildings shut up for the night. Away from the lights of the town, all was dark. Adam kept watch for Angus, knowing he must be somewhere near, but there was no sign of him. What if he had been captured? What if the French had learned of Adam's escape, and even now were setting a trap for him?

'Your next move?' said Lesaut, reading Adam's concerns. 'The three of you will steal a ship and sail her away?'

'Fortunately, I already have a crew in this port.'

Lesaut looked at the citadel across the water.

'You think you can free them from there?'

'I do.'

The Frenchman snorted. 'I would like to see it.'

'Alas, you will not.'

Adam nodded to Bheka. Without warning, he reversed the musket and clubbed the back of Lesaut's head. The French captain dropped soundlessly to the ground.

'We will need all our strength to get into the castle,' Adam explained. 'And we could not risk him giving us away.'

'Then why bring him at all?'

'Because once I have freed my crew and escaped, I intend to have a long talk with him.'

A figure appeared, hurrying down the road. Adam stiffened, fearing someone had seen his assault on Lesaut. But it was Angus.

'Is there a way in to the citadel?'

'She's near impregnable, sir.'

Adam would have been disheartened. But he detected a gleam in Angus's eye that belied his words.

'What did you find?'

'Everyone has an arsehole.'

'What do you mean?'

'I'll show ye.'

They left the road and skirted the bay along the shore, where sea grass and palm trees hid their approach. The moon had risen. As they drew near, Adam saw that the citadel was built on a point of land that had been cut off by a canal, making it an island. A narrow drawbridge was the only way across. The bridge was down, but the gates were locked shut.

'There,' said Angus.

The castle walls went down to the water. The moon shone off the sea, fringing the base of the walls with a ring of silver light. But in one place, where Angus was pointing, a shadow broke the brightness.

'Culvert,' said Angus. 'I reckon it's where the latrines feed out.'

Adam stared at him. 'And you want us to swim up there?'

'Only one of us. You're a better swimmer'n me.'

Adam stripped off his shirt. 'And when I get there?'

Angus chuckled. 'Pray there isn'ae a Frenchie taking a shit.'

The sea was calm, with enough breeze to raise small wavelets that broke up Adam's silhouette. He swam slowly, trying not to make a sound and hoping that any guards would be too busy watching the fireworks over the town to notice.

His nose told him when he was close to the culvert. Angus had been right. It must carry out the effluent of all the latrines in the castle. Five hundred men, Angus had said, plus the two hundred from the *Diamond*. Even the rise and fall of the tide could not scrub away the stink.

The culvert opened into a low-roofed tunnel that carried the seawater under the castle. Inside, the stench was ten times worse. Adam swam in, holding his breath and pursing his lips tight so that the foul water would not enter his mouth. Slime-spattered holes in the walls brought the effluent down from the latrines, but they were too small for Adam to climb through.

He swam on. His lungs started to burn. Little moonlight penetrated this far; the tunnel closed in darkness around him. But there was a light ahead. Slivers of yellow light in the ceiling, filtering through a grille. Treading water, he reached up and grabbed the bars. They were set into the stone: as hard as Adam heaved and shook them, they would not lift.

Adam gripped the iron bars, hanging half out of the water. At least he could breathe without risk of swallowing a floating turd. There was no way in. He would have to swim back and tell Angus it had been for nothing.

The grille had been installed when the citadel was built. For decades, it had been exposed to salt water and the fetid tropical air. Acidic urine had spattered over it, further eating into the metal. It had corroded until the corners that were set into the stone were as thin as paper. Adam's weight, hanging from the bars, was its breaking point.

The bars snapped. Adam dropped into the water. The grille hit his head, but he had the wit to close his mouth before he took in a mouthful of sewage. When he surfaced, the light above was brighter. The hole yawned open. He reached up, gripped the groove where the grille had rested, and hauled himself out of the water into the shaft. The stone was slick with mould and excrement – there were no handholds – but the shaft was so narrow Adam was able to brace himself against the walls with his shoulders. He wriggled up.

Soon he was covered in the black slime that smeared the walls. The climb seemed to go on forever. Gradually, though, the light grew brighter. Craning his neck, he could see a square of lamplight coming nearer. Another grating covered it, but this one was made of wood. When his head bumped into it, it lifted away.

He scrambled out and fell onto the floor of a low-vaulted room. Stone benches with wooden seats lined both sides. It was the latrine.

'*Mais qu'est ce qui se passe alors?*'

A French soldier stood in the doorway. He was carrying his musket; he must have come in from guard duty. Maybe he had fallen asleep. He rubbed his bleary eyes, staring at Adam as if he'd been caught dreaming. Then, realising he was awake, he aimed his musket.

If he fired, the whole castle would know he was there. Adam sprang off the floor and lunged for the soldier. His muscles, aching from the ascent, responded slowly; his wet feet skidded on the stone floor. He was too slow.

In the low vaulted room, the sound of the musket's explosion was like being trapped in the barrel of a cannon. Smoke and noise filled the chamber, deafening and blinding both men. The bullet passed over Adam's head and smashed into the back wall with a spray of stone chips.

Adam collided with the soldier's legs. Both men went down. They wrestled on the ground, barely able to see each other. The soldier had his hands around Adam's throat. Flexing his neck muscles, Adam let his head sag back and then brought it forward with all his strength. He smashed his forehead into the Frenchman's face and felt the nose crack. Blood gushed on Adam; the grip loosened. Before the man could retaliate, Adam threw him aside. His hand went to his belt and closed around the letter opener he had taken from the desk at Government House. He pulled it out and stabbed the Frenchman through the eye. The man jerked like a hooked fish, then went still.

There was not much time. The gunshot would have alerted every soldier in the garrison. Adam stripped the guard of his weapons and dumped the corpse down the shaft. He wished he could swap shirts with the man – better to be soaked with blood than covered in shit – but there was no time. He slung the ammunition pouch and powder horn over his shoulder, reloaded the musket, and headed out.

The door led him into a corridor with a spiral staircase at the end.

Up or down?

The sound of footsteps hurrying from above decided it for him. He went downwards, around the twist of the stair and out of sight. He waited, musket ready for anyone following him.

The footsteps paused. Two men, by the sound of it. They saw the musket smoke billowing from the latrine door and went to investigate. Adam edged up the stairs, to listen. Urgent, bewildered voices told him they had found the bloodstains on the floor, but no sign of victim or killer.

One spoke to the other.

'You tell the commandant. I will check on the prisoners.'

The men returned to the staircase. One started to climb; the other descended. Adam backed away, using the curve of the staircase to keep out of sight and beyond the light from the oncoming Frenchman's lantern. The sentry's boots echoed in the stairwell, while Adam's bare feet made no sound.

The stairs ended in a wooden door, studded with nails and fastened with an enormous lock. Adam was trapped. The spiral of the staircase tapered to a dark recess behind him. He hid, just as the sentry came around the final corner. The man did not see Adam lurking in the shadows.

The guard took a large key from his belt and unlocked the door. He was about to step through, when he felt the tip of Adam's musket poking between his shoulder blades.

'Is this where all the English prisoners are kept?' Adam asked in French.

The soldier gulped and nodded.

'Show me. And if I even think you are calling for help, I will put a bullet through your backbone.'

The guard opened the door slowly. They were in the deepest level of the castle, low brick vaults built on a bare stone floor. An iron cage kept anyone from approaching the door from the inside. Beyond it, lumpen objects like sacks of peas or flour strewed the floor.

As light from the guard's lamp flooded in, the lumps started to unfurl themselves into the shapes of men. Adam's hopes soared as he recognised them: Hurrell the boatswain, O'Brien the sail-maker, and many others. The French guard unlocked the inner gate, and they flooded out.

'I's told'ee Cap'n Courtney'd not forsake 'is crew,' Hurrell declared.

'Never,' Adam agreed.

'But by God almighty, you stink!' said Hurrell.

They declined Adam's proffered handshake, and he met their grins with smiles of his own – but inside, he was in turmoil. He had been separated from them since he surrendered the *Diamond*, so he had not seen Lesaut's handiwork. He saw the full barbarity of what Lesaut had done to them. On their bare chests and arms, each man sported the imprint of a letter *L* seared into his flesh.

'I will kill the man who did this to you,' Adam promised. 'But first we must escape this place.'

Sounds of alarm drifted down the stair shaft. Adam's men were free, but they were outnumbered, with only two muskets between them.

'Follow me.'

He led them back up the stairs. The noise from the garrison grew louder. At the next level, he pointed down the corridor to the latrine.

'There's a hole on the other side of that door that leads out to the sea. Just follow the smell. Any man who can swim, get out that way. You'll find Angus waiting for you on shore.'

'What about the rest of us?' asked the boatswain.

He knew some of the crew would be able to swim, but more than half could not.

'We will fight our way out.'

He turned to the captive French guard they had dragged with them.

'What is your name?'

'P-Pierre,' the youth stammered. He had a shock of red hair, and a freckled face that the tropical sun had not treated kindly.

'Where is the armoury?'

Pierre hesitated; Adam put the bayonet against his cheek, so that the sharp edge drew a line of blood.

'If we get out alive, you will live. If we die, you die first.'

Pierre understood. He pointed up the stairs and babbled directions.

'Show me.'

Pushing Pierre in front, Adam led the remaining men up the stairs. It ended in a guardroom, whose window overlooked the interior of the fort. Pierre pointed across the courtyard, to a squat building guarded by two sentries. The windows were narrow slits, and no light burned inside.

'The armoury.'

Adam swore. To reach it, they would have to cross the open courtyard in full view of the sentries and any men on the ramparts.

'Is there no other way?'

'*Non.*'

The moon had slipped below the walls, but its light still flooded the courtyard. There was nowhere to hide. Adam gripped Pierre.

'Go over there and tell the sentries you have found an intruder. Tell them they must go at once.'

'They are under orders never to leave their post.'

'Then you had better—'

A shot from the guardhouse drowned whatever Adam was about to say. The alarm had been raised; soldiers were issuing from the barracks. Adam had run out of time.

'We need those muskets.'

There was no alternative – no clever stratagem or ruse he could use now. Adam simply ran. Out of the guardhouse, across the moonlit courtyard in full view of the French soldiers coming out of the barracks.

The sheer boldness of it got him halfway there. One stride, then another and another, each one taking him closer to the armoury. The soldiers hesitated, uncertain what they were seeing, wary of opening fire on one of their own.

Perhaps one of them had better eyesight; perhaps he was simply more nervous. A single musket fired, and though the shot went wide, the flash of the muzzle was like a spark to a powder keg. The whole courtyard erupted in gunfire. Musket balls hammered the ground around Adam; all he could rely on to protect himself was their lack of accuracy, and his own speed. He raced across, making straight for the armoury.

With a huzzah, his men charged after him, fanning across the courtyard. That gave the French more targets – but too many. Some sailors were hit, but more managed to climb on to the ramparts. They began a furious hand-to-hand battle with the French garrison. Soldiers were thrown down from the walls, or spitted on the bayonets that had been wrested out of their hands.

Adam reached the armoury. The two guards still stood there, rooted in shock. Adam shot one, bayoneted the other, and took his keys to unlock the door. As the *Diamond*'s crew reached him, he began pulling weapons from their racks, handing them to the men as fast as he could. There were muskets, but also pikes and swords, which suited the sailors better. He took them all.

Now the battle was more evenly matched. But it was also chaos, a melee all around the castle yard. Fighting at close quarters, there was no time to reload, and musket flashes no longer illuminated the scene. Men fought by moonlight and in shadows, with only luck to stop them running through their own comrades.

Adam's crew fought with desperate courage. But they were outnumbered. As soon as the French regained their order, discipline and numbers would surely tell. Adam had to escape with his men as soon as possible.

In his journey through the castle, and now the confusion of battle, he had lost all sense of direction. He could see a squat tower to his right, and a heavy gate set into it. That would be the way out – if the French had not raised the drawbridge.

'On me!' he called. '*Diamond*, on me!'

This was the moment of greatest danger. As the men abandoned their individual battles to rally around Adam, the French had their chance to regroup. Over the fray, Adam heard sergeants barking orders, the rattle of ramrods as muskets were reloaded. If he could not get the gate open, the fight would become a mass execution.

'Back!' Adam cried.

He led his men at a run towards the gate. It was smaller than it had looked when he reconnoitred it from the outside, but it was stout, fastened with heavy bolts. The men with muskets made a semicircle in front of the gate, shooting at any Frenchman who presented himself, while the rest wrestled back the bolts.

'Aim for the men on the walls!' Adam shouted.

The French were using the cover of the barracks to form up in line – but Adam had seen a new danger. Up on the ramparts opposite, a gun crew were using spikes to lever one of the cannons around, towards Adam and his men. Loaded with grapeshot, a single blast would turn them to bloody chaff.

The drumbeat of musket fire intensified as his men responded to the danger. Two of the French gunners went down, but the rest continued their work. Adam saw their movements in the flashes of gunfire. A man loading the bag of grape. The rammer ramming it down. The gun captain tamping the charge.

The last bolt shot free. The press of men against the gate pushed it open with a bang so loud Adam thought the cannon must have fired. The *Diamond*'s crew poured out under the walls, desperate to flee the French artillery. Adam screamed with jubilation. They had escaped.

The shout died on his lips. The men on the other side of the gate had stopped short. Beyond them was not the drawbridge and the island, as they had expected, but the silver expanse of the bay.

Disorientated by the battle and the unfamiliar geography, Adam had gone the wrong way. This was the watergate, facing seaward on to a small dock where boats could unload supplies for the castle. The *Diamond*'s crew were now crammed on to the wharf, trapped between the French artillery at their backs and the sea facing them.

Some leaped into the water, even though they couldn't swim. Others were pushed in by the relentless press of the men still trapped in the courtyard, who had not seen that their escape was a dead end. Adam cursed himself. He had offered them hope and led them to disaster.

Across the water, he saw a frigate nosing towards them. He recognised her at once, for there was only one frigate in Port Louis. The *Requin* had weighed anchor and was sailing close under furled topsails to cut off escape by sea. The *coup de grâce*.

He heard the rumble of trucks as her gunports lifted and her starboard battery ran out. Whoever was commanding her in Lesaut's absence was a fine seaman. Unless Lesaut had escaped as well. That would be the final insult.

A sudden pause came over the battlefield. The men on the wharf stopped jostling and stood still, finally accepting the inevitable. Behind them, the *Requin*'s guns waited like a row of teeth. Ahead, the castle garrison made a crisp double line across the courtyard, blocking them in. On the opposite rampart, a gunner's linstock smouldered in the grey early morning, lest any man think of trying his luck.

I have failed, Adam thought bitterly. *My crew, my father, my family – everyone I hold dear.*

He hoped Angus had been able to escape. Perhaps with some of the men who had swum out of the castle, he might take refuge in the mountains inland and avoid capture. It was a faint hope.

A man in a major's uniform strode forward from the line of soldiers. He was furious. He had been called from the governor's ball at this ungodly hour of the night, just when he was on the verge of persuading an exceptionally beautiful young planter's daughter to take him to her bed. The temptation to order his men to open fire was immense. He could always say the English had died trying to escape.

No. Better to get them back in his dungeon, where his torturers could exact revenge at leisure. He knew who his adversary was – the young Captain Courtney. He had been at the governor's house when a naked private had crashed into the ballroom, belatedly announcing that Courtney had fled.

He will not escape this time, the major promised himself. He had grown up in the revolution, and did not approve of the way Lesaut pandered to rank. *I will treat Courtney the same as his men.*

He raised his sword. The line of soldiers readied their muskets. 'Surrender! Otherwise . . .'

Adam hesitated. He could see the intent in the major's eyes. He was not bluffing. If Adam did not surrender now, his crew would be massacred.

The silence over the courtyard was so profound, you could hear the sparks hissing off the gunner's linstock.

And then the *Requin* fired. A full broadside, every gun brought to bear, that broke the silence like a thunderclap. Yet, though the timing was in perfect unison, the aim was curiously awry. The balls shrieked over the heads of the *Diamond*'s crew on the wharf. Some dipped into the line of French infantry in the courtyard; others went higher and slammed into the gunners on the rampart. One scored a direct hit on the cannon, throwing it off its carriage.

'What is going on?' screamed the major. His moment of victory had turned to carnage. 'Cease firing!'

The *Requin* fired again. She had adjusted her aim: her broadside went lower this time, but it did the French no good. The *Diamond*'s sailors on the wharf had dropped to the ground, so the balls passed over them again. The full weight of the broadside slammed into the French infantry. Lined up, they made an unmissable target.

Adam did not understand what was happening, but this was his chance. Gathering his men around the edge of the gateway, he set up a barrage of musket fire against the French soldiers. Twice that night, the garrison had suffered a surprise attack. They did not have the strength to fight any more. They broke ranks and ran.

'After them!' Adam called. 'We must find the land gate.'

'Wait!'

Hurrell, the boatswain, grabbed his sleeve and pointed back. Three longboats had set off from the *Requin* and were pulling towards the wharf. They moved swiftly, the men on the oars bending their backs to speed them on.

Adam paused. The *Requin*'s guns had fallen silent. And in the stern of the lead boat, standing by the tiller, he saw a familiar figure silhouetted against the silvered sea.

'Dock ahoy!' came Angus' voice. 'Would you be needing a way out of the castle?'

Adam could hardly believe it, but as the longboats glided out of the darkness towards the wharf, there could be no doubt. The *Diamond*'s men scrambled down into the boats, reunited with their comrades who had earlier escaped by swimming through the sewer.

Adam was the last to leave. There was barely space in the boats for all the men: some had to go in the water and hang on to the gunwales. But they made room for Adam, and soon the boats were hurrying towards the *Requin*.

'You are a miracle worker,' Adam told Angus.

'I have my wee ways,' Angus agreed.

'How did you do it?'

'I had a feeling you'd mebbe need a route out of the castle,' said Angus. 'Young Bheka here's a handy fellow, knows how to handle a boat. Together we cut out a small ketch. Then when some of the lads started popping up in the water, we thought we'd need summat a wee bit bigger. So we took the ketch and paid a call on the Frenchie frigate. There was a skeleton crew – the rest'd gone ashore. They gave us nae bother.'

'And Lesaut?'

'Safe and sound in his own brig. I picked him up after you'd given him that whack on the head.'

The longboats came alongside the *Requin*. The men scrambled aboard and up the rigging to prepare the sails.

'I fear we have outstayed our welcome.'

On shore, Adam could see soldiers hurrying about the town, riders galloping between the castle and the governor's house. It would not take them long to piece together what had happened.

'Take us out to sea.'

'An' the *Diamond*?'

Adam looked across the water. The *Diamond* lay at anchor where Lesaut had towed her, a dismasted hulk. Even if they could board, they would never sail her out of the harbour.

'Leave her.'

He ached to abandon his command. But the *Requin* was a fair compensation, bigger and more heavily armed. Adam could feel the power in her timbers, matched with speed as the *Diamond*'s crew loosened her sails and caught the night breeze.

'Put men on the guns,' Adam ordered.

They were not out of harm's way: there were two batteries guarding the mouth of the bay. A few well-aimed shots with heated cannonballs could end their escape.

The *Requin* gathered pace. Adam held his breath. He could see the gunners on the batteries watching them, their faces lit in the glow of lanterns and slow matches.

But the news that night had been confused; the gun crews could not be sure of anything. The *Requin* was Lesaut's command, and they knew his reputation too well. To open fire on his ship would be to risk court martial, or worse. Besides, she was flying the *tricolore*.

So they let the *Requin* pass out into the ocean. Only when he was well out of range did Adam strike the *tricolore* and raise the Union Jack he had found in Lesaut's flag locker. It was the *Diamond*'s old ensign, which Lesaut had taken as the spoils of victory. The men cheered to see it flying over their prize.

They were not the only things Lesaut had kept. In his cabin, Adam found the oilskin bundle with the Neptune sword, the tiger dagger and the sketch of Mary. He felt the familiar tingle run through his wrist and up his arm as he held the sword, and tried to forget the men who had died in the storm and at the castle in the cause of his revenge.

They had escaped. That was enough.

By next morning, Île de France was a speck on the far horizon. Adam scanned the sea behind them, but there was no sign of pursuit. That did not surprise him. He had seen few ships in Port Louis that could outpace the frigate, and none that could bring her to battle.

When Adam was satisfied that his crew had had their injuries tended, and been fed, he fetched Lesaut to the cabin. The French captain was a sorry spectacle. He had lost his wig, leaving only a bare scalp covered in grey stubble. His cheeks sported a day's ragged beard, and the lace cuffs of his shirt were torn.

Adam showed him the Neptune sword.

'I am taking this back,' he said. 'As for your sword, I will not offer you parole. I know you too well.'

Lesaut shrugged. 'I did not expect it. But . . .' Unbidden, he settled into a chair upholstered in fuchsia silk. 'I am willing to buy my freedom.'

Adam pretended to consider the offer seriously.

'With what? I have your ship, your crew, everything you own.'

His men had searched the hold and found five strongboxes. It had taken Angus and three other men two hours to break them open with boarding axes, but it had been worth the effort. They contained a small fortune in gold, gems and coins.

Lesaut took a pinch of snuff from a box on the table.

'A farmer does not keep all his chickens in one henhouse, and Jean Lesaut does not keep all his riches on his ship. I have treasure hidden in secret places everywhere around this ocean.' He sneezed prodigiously. 'A fine ransom, *non?*'

'Ransom?' Adam spat the word back at him. 'I did not bring you here to ransom you.'

'*Pourquoi, alors?*'

'Nativity Bay. Where you called, three years ago. I want to know what you really did.'

A glint came into Lesaut's eyes, the look of a merchant scenting a bargain to be struck.

'You wish to know what happened to your family.'

'I want to know why you killed them.'

'I assure you, *monsieur*, I am guilty of many things. But not that.'

'Why did you leave that message on the wall? *"J'aura mon revanche."* Revenge for what? What was your quarrel with the Courtneys?'

'I did not write those words.'

'What other Frenchman was there? Who else could have written it?' Adam leaned forward. 'If you do not tell me, you will not live to care.'

The threat made no impact.

'You cannot kill me. I am too valuable.'

Their eyes locked. Lesaut yielded nothing. He might dress like a fop, Adam reminded himself, but he was a merciless killer who had sent countless men to their deaths. It would take more than empty threats to break his confidence.

'What you forget,' said Adam, 'is that I do not fight for money. I am not interested in your value as a hostage.'

He beckoned the sentries forward.

'Lash him to the bow chaser.'

Before Lesaut could protest, the sentries grabbed his arms and dragged him from the cabin. By the time Adam had followed them on deck, Lesaut was trussed like a chicken. One of the long thirty-two pounders in the bow had been hauled in on her tackles.

Lesaut was stretched over the barrel like a prisoner on a rack, his hands tied to one of the trucks and his feet to the other, with the muzzle pressing against his belly. In the tropical sun, the metal was hot enough to scald off his skin.

'Is the gun loaded?'

The gun captain knuckled his forehead.

'Aye, sir.'

The gun crew stood around, leaning on their ramrods and worming irons. The rest of the crew gathered behind to watch. Every one of them bore the mark he had branded into them. None felt a crumb of sympathy for him now.

'Tell me what happened at Nativity Bay,' said Adam.

Lesaut gritted his teeth against the pain of the burning iron.

'Not until you free me.'

'You know I will not do that until you speak the truth.'

'Then we are at an impasse.'

If Adam hadn't been so desperate to know the fate of his family, he would have admired Lesaut's coolness. Instead, he felt a wave of frustration.

'Fetch a light,' he ordered.

Smoke coloured the air as the gun captain lit the wick of his linstock. Lesaut's face twisted with pain, but the defiance in his eyes remained unbroken.

'You cannot kill me.'

'Light the match.'

The gun captain grinned. He touched the linstock to the end of the match-cord that led into the gun's touch hole. The cord began to smoulder.

'If you do this, you will never know what I could have told you,' said Lesaut.

His words dug into Adam's mind. What Lesaut said was fact, and now they were locked in this battle of wills, he could not back down.

If he spared Lesaut, the Frenchman would know all Adam's threats were empty.

The match-cord fizzed sparks onto the deck and turned the air blue with smoke. The gun captain, knowing Adam's intention, had rigged a good length, but it had already burned more than halfway down.

Adam and Lesaut stared at each other, unblinking.

'Maybe your gun is not loaded?' said Lesaut.

'You will find out when it puts a hole in your belly,' said Adam tightly.

The match burned down, seemingly faster every second.

'Wait.'

The voice cut through the tension that gripped the deck, sudden and unexpected. It was Angus, hurrying up the companionway with a book in his hand. One of the midshipmen was beside him, panting from running up to the deck.

'We don't need him to tell us. We've found it.'

The flame was vanishing into the touch hole. Adam stepped forward and pinched it out. Belatedly, he saw the sweat streaming off Lesaut's face.

Angus spread the book on the capstan drum. It was a logbook, filled with columns of numbers for bearings, positions, dates and weather observations, and all the other happenings of her voyages. All the entries were in French – but some facts were the same in any language. Angus pointed to a string of numbers on the page.

'That is the position of Nativity Bay.'

Adam knew the numbers by heart. But that was not all. On the line above, written in capital letters and underlined so there would be no mistaking it, was a name that Adam had seen before. SEVEN SISTERS.

'This was when they sighted her?' said Adam.

'Aye.'

'I did not know you could read French.'

'No more I can, sir. But Mr Enstone' – he pointed to the midshipman he had brought – 'he reads it like a Froggie.'

'Then tell me, for God's sake.'

Adam could have worked out what the French meant, but his head was too full of rage and impatience.

Enstone stepped forward, swallowing hard. He was barely thirteen, his body a collection of gangly parts bundled up in his midshipman's uniform, his face cratered with acne. But he was bright and hard-working, Adam knew, a clerk's son determined to make his way in the Royal Navy.

'"We encountered the East India ship *Seven Sisters*, bound for Cape Town and London. From her we bought five hogsheads of peas and three casks of brandy."'

'That cannot be right,' Adam snapped. 'Talbot said he fled the *Requin*. That is why he put into Nativity Bay.'

'It is not what the log says, sir,' said Enstone.

'But the *Seven Sisters* was an Indiaman, fully laden on her return voyage with valuable goods. A man like Lesaut would never let such a rich prize slip through his fingers.

He glanced at Lesaut, still bound to the cannon. His face was set rigid, but the corners of his lips twitched.

'The date, sir,' said Angus softly.

Adam read it. '*23 Vendémiaire An XII.*'

It was written in the new format that the French had adopted during the revolution. The revolution aries had been so thorough, they had tried to revolutionise time itself. The old calendar, with its irregular months and irrational timings, filled with archaic saints' days, had been abolished. Instead, the revolutionaries had decreed a new order. Every month would be three weeks, every week ten days, and every day should be ten hours of one hundred minutes each. The months would have new, literal names that reflected the character of the seasons, rather than old gods and emperors. Rational time, for a new rational French republic.

Adam was not familiar with the new format, how the dates translated into the proper months and years the English calendar used.

Enstone, however, knew it by heart. 'The years begin on the autumn equinox, and are numbered from 1792,' he explained. 'That would make year twelve 1803.'

He saw Adam's look of surprise.

'My father worked for a wine merchant who imported French wines. Even in the midst of war, his clients never stopped demanding the wares he brought across the Channel. I used to help him with the books. We had to learn the calendar, otherwise we would not know when our shipments were due.'

'Go on,' Adam said impatiently.

'*Vendémiaire* is the grape harvest month, the first month after the equinox,' Enstone continued. 'So the twenty-first of *Vendémi-*

aire . . .' He counted on his fingers. 'Round about the sixteenth of October.'

'Just after the *Seven Sisters* had quit Nativity Bay.'

The events in the logbook were backwards. Had the *Requin* met the *Seven Sisters* before or after she visited Nativity Bay? Had she attacked Fort Auspice, or traded?

'What was the date again?' Adam asked.

'The sixteenth of October, 1803.'

'We were not at war.'

The realisation stunned him. Britain and France had been fighting for so long, it was easy to forget there had been a brief pause to the hostilities. Only for a year, and then only so that the two nations could repair their ships and replenish their armouries for another round of war. But there had been peace, while it lasted.

He rounded on Lesaut with fury.

'You met them during the Peace of Amiens.' Even a privateer needed war to give her piracy the fig-leaf of legality. 'That is why you did not attack her.'

Lesaut's expression had not changed. But he could not deny it. All the details were there in the logbook.

'So why did Captain Talbot say he was fleeing from you? That you threatened his ship and you did not meet?'

Again, the answer was so obvious it did not need to be said.

Talbot had been lying.

'It appears, *monsieur*, that your efforts to find the real villains have been wasted,' said Lesaut.

Adam was furious with himself for being tricked. He grieved the crew who had been lost in the storm and the battle because he had not seen through Talbot's lie. He would have to make sure they had not died for nothing.

Angus had followed his train of thought.

'Back to Cape Town, sir?'

'Talbot will have sailed by now,' said Adam. 'There is nothing to gain patrolling the sea lanes, we would never find her. But there was another chance, and they had to pursue it. 'When I last spoke to Talbot he said the *Seven Sisters* was bound for Calcutta. We will have to follow her there.'

A thousand thoughts crowded Adam's mind. But in his tumult, he noticed Midshipman Enstone trying to say something.

'What?'

'There is more about Nativity Bay in the logbook.'

'Then tell me, damn you.'

The midshipman flinched at the curse.

'Yes . . . yes, sir. Two days after she met the *Seven Sisters* – "We anchored in a sheltered bay to replenish our fresh water supply. The place was formerly inhabited, but no longer when we arrived. The house had been attacked, the evidence of the violence on every inch of the homestead. We found five graves – and many dead."'

He paused, looking uncertainly at Adam.

'Keep reading,' said Adam.

'"The corpses were recently dead, not yet decomposed. We took what we needed for our ship and left quickly."'

Adam looked balefully towards Lesaut.

'You knew all along. This information was no use to you. Why didn't you tell me?'

'Information is valuable. I do not give it away.'

'You thought you could make me buy it from you? That it was one more commodity to be traded?'

Adam took the linstock from the gun captain, still burning.

'What you will never comprehend,' he went on, 'is that some causes are worth more than any sum of money.'

Adam put the linstock to the touch hole. The fuse had burned so low, Lesaut had no time to scream. His face began to twist in horror; then his body was blasted in two by a thirty-two-pound cannonball passing through at point-blank range. A spray of blood and smoke and powder grains fanned over the water. Lesaut's legs and his upper body, still bound by the ropes but no longer attached to each other, flopped lifeless to the deck.

'Throw the remains overboard for the sharks, and see that you swab the deck,' said Adam.

He snatched the logbook from Enstone and turned to go back to his cabin, when a shout from the masthead stopped him.

'Deck there! Sail off the starboard bow!' Then, a moment later, 'Three sails. No, five.'

In the confusion that followed, even the splash of Lesaut's remains dropping into the sea went unnoticed.

'If that is the French, we will have a devil of a fight on our hands,' muttered Adam.

'Good sport,' said Angus.

Even though they were outnumbered, it did not cross Adam's mind to surrender.

Every man on deck waited for a further command. Adam clenched the halyard tight.

'Clear for action?' pressed Angus.

As the *Requin* was still an unfamiliar ship to them, it would take more time even for his skilled crew to make it ready for battle, but Adam did not give the order yet. He was seized with the hope that one of the vessels ahead of them could be the *Seven Sisters*. Then he could confront Talbot that very afternoon. Perhaps the Fates were smiling on him at last.

He swung himself into the rigging and hared up the shrouds like the nimble boy he had once been.

'Can you make out who they are?' he asked the astonished lookout as he hauled himself onto the crosstrees.

'They've seen us.' The sailor pointed to the horizon.

What had been five ships were now a dozen: far off, but already altering course.

'The French do not have that many ships in this ocean,' said Adam confidently. 'It must be the India fleet.'

As if to prove his words, the ships chose that moment to hoist their colours. Eleven of the red-and-white striped banners of the East India Company billowed from their sterns, while the twelfth sported the red ensign of the Royal Navy.

'What ship is that?'

'*Indomitable*, sir,' the lookout answered. 'She was in Cape Town when we sailed.'

Adam scanned the other ships in the convoy. He could not make out the *Seven Sisters* at that distance, but he knew she must be there somewhere.

He descended back to the deck.

'Signal the *Indomitable* that I wish to confer with her captain,' he ordered Midshipman Enstone. He looked to the bows, where some of Lesaut's entrails had splattered over the ship's timbers. 'And scrub away that mess.'

ABYSSINIA, 1800

The caravan wound its way through the grassy valley. Birds sang from the acacia trees that shaded the road, while the sun shone from a perfect blue sky. The desert was far behind. The Bishareen had swapped their camels for horses; rocks and dust had given way to long grass and foliage.

Paul shuffled along towards the back of the column. Head down, arms tugged forward by the rope that linked him to the next person in line, one foot in front of another until the drivers called a halt.

He had lost count of the dreadful days they had marched. Weeks, certainly; maybe months. Possibly years, for all he knew. A lifetime in the desert, then a flat plain that seemed to stretch to eternity. At least there had been water and game there. After that, a salt lake, days walking over a white crust that was as brittle as ice and as sharp as diamonds. Then mountains, passes where eagles flew and cliffs grew so steep that if one slave had lost his footing, he would have dragged the whole coffle to their deaths. And now this mysterious kingdom, which he had heard mentioned numerous times: Gondar.

It was a strange kingdom, like something out of a fairy tale or a geographer's fantasy. They passed neat villages, round huts with conical roofs, with eggs as large as melons set as a capstone (later Paul learned they were ostrich eggs). It was the first place he'd seen since leaving Cairo that looked like a civilisation. Inexplicably, it seemed to be a Christian country. Every village had a church, round like the huts, but decorated with crosses and pictures of saints. Sometimes he heard the low chanting of hymns being sung as they passed.

Paul did not understand how this could be. Maybe he had died in the desert after all. Perhaps the long march had been the struggle through Purgatory, and now he had arrived in a version of Heaven. But if that was the case, why was he still bound and lashed by the overseers? Why was he so hungry? His needs were so real, it did not feel like Heaven.

His body had changed. In the desert, the Bishareen had given him food and drink to keep him alive, but no more. They were testing him. If he survived, they could make use of him; if he didn't, no great loss. Paul had woken every day believing he would die. It would have been a mercy. Every step, he imagined the cool release of death in intricate, loving detail, until he could no longer tell if it was a dream or a memory.

Sana kept him alive. She was the reason he didn't give up, didn't strangle himself with his own bonds. There was not much he could do for her, except offer a few drops of his water when the guards were not looking. But he could not leave her alone. She was yoked behind him, the last in the column, as always.

Not all the prisoners in the caravan survived the march through the desert. Every day the captives left bodies by the wayside, festering among the bones of those who had died before them. But Paul and Sana had survived. As they left the desert behind, the Bishareen took a greater interest in their well-being. Their rations were increased; their wasted bodies began to grow again. By the time they reached the mountainous kingdom of Gondar, Paul had been whittled down to a hundred and forty pounds of pure muscle. If the Bishareen meant to sell him, as he supposed they did, he would fetch a good price.

He heard a commotion from the front of the line. He didn't look up. He had learned, painfully, to keep his eyes on the ground – nothing but the next step. Whatever was coming would arrive. He had long since stopped anticipating any good thing happening to him.

But this was different. The Bishareen guards rode down the column, herding the coffle into the grass at the side of the road. Paul heard drums and trumpets, the clash of cymbals and the disciplined tramp of many feet moving as one.

'The king is coming!' the slave driver shouted. 'Make way for the king!' He took up position at the end of the line. 'If I see you move, I will flay you alive. Unless the king sees you first, and then you will *wish* I had flayed you.'

Paul stood ramrod-straight and kept his eyes downcast. Sana, curious to see a king, peered out and looked up the road. The slave driver cuffed her angrily. Sana drew back, enough to satisfy the overseer but still able to see the royal procession as it approached.

First came the trumpeters, followed by the drummers beating huge kettledrums. Then the army. Each regiment carried a standard of a long pole topped with a silver sphere. Their battle flags were made of brightly striped cloth, blazoned with images of lions and stars.

Something prickled on Paul's skin. A huge wasp had settled on his wrist and was crawling up his forearm. He could see every detail: its stick-like legs, bulbous eyes and a stinger as long and sharp as a thorn sticking out from its belly.

Paul shook his arm, hoping to dislodge the insect. The wasp didn't move. The overseer growled threateningly. Paul forced himself to keep still.

The army was magnificent, though its variety and inconsistency would have made Bonaparte weep. It was as if it had been assembled by a child from a toy box, thrown together with whatever came to hand. Men with spears and shields, straight out of the pages of chivalry, were followed by lancers who rode with the flair of French dragoons. Archers with bows and arrows rubbed shoulders with musketeers whose weapons seemed to have been made in the previous century. Their uniforms – if you could call them that – were a riot of brightly coloured cloth and wild animal skins. Proud heads held high on their long necks, clothing flashing with silver. Each man had close-cropped hair and deep brown skin, much darker than the people of Egypt.

The wasp clambered over Paul's bicep and disappeared inside the sleeve of his tunic. Paul gritted his teeth with pain.

At the head of each regiment rode a man in a silver breastplate, with a silver circlet across his forehead that sported a sharp spike, like a unicorn horn. Then came priests, wearing turbans like the imams of Egypt, but carrying icons and gilded crosses. They seemed to hurry on to keep clear of the next man, who rode alone. He wore a simple blue robe and a conical hat, with gold bangles on his wrists. It was hard to tell what his purpose was: he did not carry any religious relics, and he was unarmed except for two leather nooses hanging from his saddle.

After him, again at a safe distance, two men rode side by side on black horses. One was tall with a noble face, the other shorter and stouter, with puffy lips and small eyes. Both wore long black cloaks fringed with silver tassels, and silver crowns on their heads. They must be princes, Paul guessed.

And after all that, surrounded by a phalanx of guards, came a man on a white horse under a fluttering awning.

'The king,' whispered Sana.

Paul had never seen her impressed by anything, but she seemed excited to be in the presence of royalty.

The wasp crawled up Paul's back slowly.

The king rode a spotless white horse, draped in a shimmering sheet of gold. The saddle-cloth was a leopard skin, and the saddle was gilded and set with jewels. The king sat erect in his seat, perfectly still. He wore a gold cross over his chest, and a broad-brimmed golden helmet hung with a curtain of silver chains that veiled his face. Four riders rode about him, carrying the poles that supported the canopy that shaded him.

The wasp had found the opening of Paul's tunic. It came out into the sunshine and worked its way up the back of his neck.

The king was almost level with them. The tramping soldiers and horses kicked up dust from the road that billowed out in clouds and rose up Paul's nose.

He sneezed.

His body convulsed. The wasp responded in the only way it knew. Paul felt as if someone had jabbed a hot needle into the side of his neck. He jerked forward, knocking into one of the guards marching alongside the king. The soldier was a big man, but Paul had caught him by surprise. As the men collapsed on top of each other, the guard flung out his spear arm for balance. The point of his lance pricked the flank of the king's horse. Blood welled out across the golden cloth.

Goaded by pain and surprise, the horse reared up. The king had not been holding the reins. He flew out of the saddle and landed heavily on the road in front of Paul. The helmet slipped off, and the chain veil was torn away. Dust stained the king's face grey; his golden brown eyes stared, unmoving. Blood dribbled from his nose.

I have killed the king.

A scrum of bodies surrounded the king and hid him from Paul's sight. Rough hands lifted Paul. A knife cut the rope that had yoked him to the rest of the slaves, so he could be dragged away. Through the throng, he saw the tall prince in the black cloak kneeling beside the king. The fatter prince stayed on his black horse, his face expressionless.

The king rose unsteadily to his feet. He had a stout belly and a face bloated with power. The rolls of fat in his neck quivered with rage, and his eyes blazed.

He bellowed angry commands, and the men around him drew back to open a path before him. The guard Paul had knocked over, whose spear had pricked the king's horse, was brought to the open ground in front of the king. Over his shoulder, Paul could see the leader of the slave caravan twisting his hands in terror.

The king made an impatient gesture. One of his bodyguards shouted, 'Kitzera!' It seemed to be the name of the man Paul had seen earlier, riding alone in front of the royal party. He dismounted and walked forward, carrying the two leather thongs. He smiled, baring a mouth of misshapen teeth. He made a loop in the leather rope and put it around the guard's neck, then threw the loose end over a branch of the tree. Sweat prickled the guard's face; his eyes were white with fear, but he did nothing to resist. When the executioner hoisted him into the air, the only sound that came from his body was a throttled gurgle.

His struggles shook the tree, disturbing a stork that had perched in its upper branches. It flew up, squawking in protest. Paul saw its broad wings and its long, pointed beak piercing the sky.

Bright light flashed in his mind. Paul knew with the certainty of revelation that the stork was a sign. The bird-headed god was there. As rough hands pulled Paul to face the executioner, he clung to that thought.

To master life, you must hold it as light as a feather.

The guards had moved aside to give the executioner room. Kitzera grinned. Paul smelled something foul on his breath, like rotting meat, while from behind him came the stink of urine and faeces as the hanged man emptied his bowels for the last time.

Kitzera reached up to put his noose around Paul's neck. And as he did so, Paul dropped to his knees. Too surprised to move, Kitzera stood holding his noose around thin air.

When you are a slave, you are accustomed to gazing down. You always know what is at your feet. There was an egg-shaped rock on the ground, and Paul's hand found it without looking. It fitted his fist perfectly, as he had known it would. The bird-headed god had left it there for him to find in that moment.

Slowly, Kitzera's eyes followed Paul down. Paul had already started to rise. The power of the god coursed through his veins. He extended his arm and, without hesitating, smashed the fist that held the rock hard into the executioner's face.

Kitzera collapsed, blood flowing from the mess of broken skin and cracked bone Paul had made. Paul spun around, arm raised to strike again. Spattered with blood, his face stretched in a mask of divine fury, he looked so terrifying that even the armed guards shrank back.

One man was not cowed. The king pushed the guards aside and marched up to Paul. Paul could have dashed his brains out. But the power that the god had given him was already ebbing away. The blood disgusted him; the stone in his hand felt like an abomination. His arm seemed to wither under the king's haughty stare. What did Paul think he could do? He might kill one man, but he was surrounded by thousands more. He had probably only earned himself worse punishment.

The king spoke rapidly, spraying spittle over Paul's face. He sounded furious. The two princes Paul had seen earlier had come up beside him. They must be his sons, though they could not have looked more different. The fat one eyed Paul with cold disdain. The tall one looked as if he wanted to rip Paul apart with his bare hands.

Paul shrank away. The king seemed to be waiting for Paul to answer – but he could not reply. What did the king want? Guilt? An apology? For Paul to drop to his knees and beg for his life?

Paul's silence drove the king into an even greater rage. When he realised Paul could not understand, there was much shouting and agitation as the guards tried to find someone to translate. They found the slave-driver, who had been hiding behind a thorn bush, and hauled him forward. The wretched man could barely stammer the words out.

'He says, why you try to kill him?'

'I fell over. A wasp stung me.' Paul turned to show the spot on his neck where a livid red bump had swollen as big as a quail's egg. 'It was an accident.'

The king grunted and kicked the body of the executioner on the ground. The shadow of the hanged man spun lazily over him.

'And him? You think you can escape if you kill him?'

'I did not want to die.'

It was the simple truth, but the king reacted as though it was a splendid joke. He laughed uproariously.

'He says you are a brave, crazy man,' the slave-driver translated.

The king snapped an order to one of his guards. The man picked up the rawhide noose that the executioner had dropped and passed it to the king with a bow. Paul stiffened. He tensed the arm that held the rock, but the king only laughed again.

'Not today, little lion,' he said. 'The almighty Lord has spared my life. Now I will spare yours.'

He pointed at the executioner on the ground. The blood flowing from his temple had slowed to a trickle, and his eyes had blinked open. He stared up at Paul, trying to focus, to understand what had happened.

The king spoke again. He never stopped smiling, but his voice had become lethal.

'He says he cannot have an executioner who does not execute people,' said the translator. 'This man, his servant, has failed. You are to take his place.'

The king held out the noose. It hung like a hole in the air, a window to a different life. Paul could only stare. A moment ago he had been willing to beat the executioner to death, but that was with the god's fire coursing through him. To kill a man in cold blood . . . And through the roaring in his ears and the poor translation, he realised at that moment that if he went through that window, it would be the beginning of a new life. Paul would become the executioner.

Voices from the past whispered in his head.

To master life, you must hold it as light as a feather.

Do whatever you must, endure anything, say anything, become anything. But promise you will survive.

On the ground, the executioner began to struggle. He pushed himself up with an effort, fighting through his agonised daze.

Annoyance flitted over the king's face. He was not used to being kept waiting, and he wanted his spectacle. He stepped back, holding the noose equidistant between the two men. Now it was a straight contest. Whoever took the noose first would save his own life and condemn the other man.

Kitzera rose. He was panting, sweat dripping from his face; the blow had left him unsteady, but his eyes were wide awake and filled with rage. He could see the noose inches away, and beyond that, the chance to take revenge on the man who had nearly killed him. He lunged forward and snatched at the leather cord like a drowning man grasping a lifeline.

His fingers closed on empty space. He lost his balance, stumbled forward and only just managed to pull himself up short in front of the king.

Two feet away, Paul held up the noose.

The three men looked at one another: Kitzera imploring the king; the king waiting for Paul; Paul gazing at the man he had to kill.

The king said something curt and final.

'Use it,' the translator said to Paul.

Paul scanned the sky for the stork, praying for a sign from the bird-headed god. His limbs had turned to lead. He did not want to move. But the king was losing patience. Paul could see hope flaring on Kitzera's face. If he did not do this now, his life would end right there.

A small hand pressed against his back and pushed him forwards – Sana. The impulse seemed to unlock something inside Paul. He threw the noose around Kitzera's neck and drew it tight. In his panic, he tugged too hard. Kitzera's eyes bulged from his head. His tongue lolled out of his mouth. He staggered towards Paul, but Paul slung the end of the cord over the branch and pulled for all his might. No one came to help him. He hauled Kitzera's weight off the ground by himself, inch by agonising inch. Two thousand men watched in silence.

Kitzera had not given up. He kicked and clawed the air, swinging on the rope end. His nails scraped deep welts down Paul's cheek, nearly ripping out his eyeball. The pain made Paul lose his grip on the rope. It slipped through his fingers; Kitzera's toes touched the ground. With the noose still hanging from him like a leash, he launched himself at Paul.

A circle formed around them. The king wore a broad smile on his face, delighted at seeing them fighting for their lives. Like a cockfight, he did not care who won: he simply loved the blood sport. The watching soldiers started shouting and chanting. Paul guessed they weren't cheering for him. He grappled with the executioner, trying to fend him off, but his enemy had the energy of a man who has cheated death. He threw punches at Paul, until Paul was beaten down to the ground.

Kitzera stood over him. He still had the thong around his neck, its end trailing over the branch where Paul had thrown it. Kitzera kicked Paul and spat on his face. He thumped his chest repeatedly, and bellowed a victory cry that was taken up by the soldiers around him. The executioner made a beckoning gesture. He reached for the noose.

Paul acted on instinct, without weighing his chances. He lunged upwards and grabbed the end of the leather rope before it could slither over the tree branch. As he caught it, he kicked out and swept Kitzera's feet from under him.

The rope went taut. Kitzera stopped abruptly as the noose brought him up sharp. He slumped towards the ground, a man caught in the act of falling. Paul began to haul him up again, then realised it was a waste of effort. The fall had broken the executioner's neck.

Delight spread across the king's face. He laughed like a madman.

Paul sank to his knees and vomited out everything in his stomach. That only made the king laugh harder. The spectators joined in, while the king pointed to Paul. Though the words were foreign the meaning was clear.

'You are the executioner now.'

INDIAN OCEAN, 1806

Two hours after the *Requin* had sighted the *Indomitable*, the *Requin*'s boat was alongside the British frigate and Adam was climbing aboard. He remembered the ship from Cape Town, though he had not been much interested in her then. She was one of an older generation of frigates, which lacked speed and still sailed with an outdated armament. Nothing to excite a young captain, or make him want to command her: a ship that was suited to convoy duty, but not much else. It was fortunate she had never come up against the *Requin* in anger.

A crisply dressed lieutenant with a pronounced overbite and a stutter welcomed Adam aboard and escorted him to the stern cabin. He was obviously curious to learn how Adam had ended up in command of the most notorious privateer in the Indian Ocean, but he was too well bred to show it. Instead, he mostly talked about the weather as he led Adam down the companionway.

'A t-terrible storm,' he stuttered. 'If the c-captain had not brought us into the lee of M-Madagascar, we would have been quite r-ruined.'

'Indeed,' said Adam. The memory of the men he had lost weighed on him. 'But what of the *Seven Sisters*? Did she survive the storm?'

All afternoon he had examined every ship in the convoy; the *Seven Sisters* was not there.

The lieutenant looked surprised.

'The S-S-Seven S-S-Sisters?'

But before he could say more, they reached the cabin. The marine sentry saluted and opened the door, revealing the captain rising from behind his desk, where he had been writing. Against the bright stern windows it was hard to see his features, but the long nose and high forehead made a striking silhouette.

Adam had only met him once, and never thought he would see him again. But you do not forget the man whose ship you have taken, wrecked and lost.

'Captain Verrier,' he said weakly.

'Captain Courtney.' If Adam had had any hope that Verrier might not bear a grudge, those two words dispelled it. Every syllable was whetted with bitterness. 'What have you done with the *Diamond*?'

'Lesaut took her.'

Verrier's face was ice-cold. 'I trust you have an explanation.'

It took nearly an hour for Adam to give his account. Verrier made him stand the whole time, without any refreshment. Despite the Indian Ocean heat, Verrier wore his full uniform coat. He must have seen Adam approaching in the boat and put it on especially. Now his hand crept to his shoulder, touching the tassels on the gold epaulette.

'A remarkable tale,' he said when Adam had finished. 'You have lost one ship and gained another. I do not know whether the Admiralty will promote you or have you drummed out of the Royal Navy.'

Adam bowed his head. Any captain who lost his ship would face a court martial. Even if he was blameless, it could blight his career. At the moment, it was the least of his concerns.

'Are we still at war?' he asked. 'While we were held captive in Port Louis, news came of a great French naval victory. Nelson is dead, and the fleet sunk.'

Verrier looked at him as if he had lost his mind.

'Where was this great French victory presumed to have happened?'

'Off the coast of Spain. Cape Trafalgar, I believe.'

Verrier gave a barking laugh. 'Then I can disabuse you. The news was false. There was a battle at Trafalgar, and Lord Nelson – God rest his soul – did indeed perish. But it was a glorious victory. The combined French and Spanish fleets were smashed, more than twenty ships sunk or captured. Our children will be old men before the French can contest the seas again.'

'You are sure of it?'

'A sloop brought the news to Cape Town after you sailed.'

'Thank God,' said Adam.

After all his suffering, the news of the navy's victory at Trafalgar came as cause for cheer. He smiled as he thought of the French garrison at Port Louis, whose sore heads would hurt even more when they found that they had been celebrating a British victory.

'On the subject of fallen sailors, what happened to that villain Lesaut?' Verrier pressed.

'He died during our escape, sir.'

It was a necessary lie. Summarily executing a French officer, even a privateer captain, by blasting him from a gun, would not be condoned within the protocols and regulations of the Royal Navy. But the Admiralty would never know. Every one of Adam's crew would swear Lesaut had died in battle.

'No great loss,' sniffed Verrier. 'The man was little better than a common pirate.'

'My thoughts precisely.'

'He was rumoured to have amassed a great treasure, killing honest sailors and capturing their ships.' Verrier leaned forward keenly. 'Did you find any trace of it?'

'I fear, sir, he must have hidden it ashore. He was careful with his fortune. He would not have risked it aboard a ship that might be sunk or captured.'

Verrier looked disappointed. 'I suppose it will never be heard of again.'

'I suspect not, sir.'

Adam remembered what Lesaut had said: *I have treasure hidden in secret places everywhere around this ocean.* Those locations had gone with him to his grave: men would be seeking the treasure for the next hundred years. But there was no need for Verrier to know about the strongboxes Adam's men had found in the *Requin*'s hold. That, too, was something the crew would keep perfectly secret.

Verrier changed tack. 'It was a bold action to try and tempt Lesaut to battle on your own. Especially during hurricane season.'

'Those were my father's orders.'

It was the wrong response. Verrier flushed.

'Do not think I have forgotten it. They were the same orders that removed me from the *Diamond* and gave me this lamentable wreck to command. Do you know what I have had to do to get some semblance of discipline in the men?'

Adam remembered the punishment log aboard the *Diamond*. He could imagine too well how Verrier would have taken out his frustrations on the crew. But that was not his concern now.

'I need to find a ship called the *Seven Sisters.*' He had been waiting to ask it since he came aboard. 'She was at Cape Town – but I do not see her in your convoy.'

'She sailed for Calcutta in advance of the main fleet. Captain Talbot was eager to be away.'

No doubt he was, Adam thought grimly, *knowing that the son of the family he murdered was anchored next to him.*

'Then I must follow her to Calcutta.' Verrier started to object, but Adam went on, 'Those were my father's orders.'

A cold smile spread over Verrier's face. He tipped back his head, his eyes almost shut as he looked down his long nose at Adam.

'That will not be necessary. I have new orders for you.'

'But my father—'

'Your father has sailed for England – his orders are void. Admiral Bolt commands the Indian Ocean squadron now. And, in his absence here, I am the senior officer. You will do as I please.'

He slid a piece of paper across the table – the sheet he had been writing before Adam arrived.

'I did not think it likely I should find you. But now that I have . . .'

Adam scanned the page. What he read made him sick to his stomach.

'I am to join the squadron blockading Île de France.'

He knew what that meant. Months keeping station on a small pocket of ocean, fighting the wind and currents and weather just to go nowhere. Watching the ship wear out and tempers fray from boredom. For any frigate captain, it would be like being chained to a rock. For Adam, desperate to catch Talbot, it was like a death sentence.

'My father was most insistent I should rendezvous with Captain Talbot.'

'Your loyalty to your father is touching.' Verrier's voice dripped sarcasm. 'But your duty is to your commanding officer – and that is *me*. Is that plain?'

Adam looked out through the stern windows, thinking desperately.

'How about the convoy? They are making for Bengal. Let me go with them as an escort.'

Verrier shook his head. He was enjoying stamping his authority on Adam.

'Even with Lesaut gone, the greatest threat to that convoy is the French fleet in Port Louis. I need my best ships – and yours is the finest I have. Even the wretched *Indomitable* will be more than adequate for protecting the Indiamen from Malabar pirates and Coromandel corsairs.'

'But, sir—'

'Enough!' A dangerous light had come into Verrier's eyes. 'I trust, sir, I do not have to remind you of your duty. There are already too many questions to be asked over your conduct in the loss of the *Diamond*.'

Adam's jaw tightened. 'Yes, sir.'

'Your father had no right to give you that ship – *my* ship. You can be sure I will be writing to their lordships in the Admiralty with a full account of Sir Robert's reckless actions. You may think that your family's fame gives you licence to act as you choose, but you will find that the name of Courtney is not so much protection as you thought.'

Adam could not bear to be there a moment longer. He turned to go, without waiting to be dismissed. But Verrier had not finished.

'I regret that we do not have the officers here to relieve you of your command at once. You may be sure, as soon as we return to Cape Town I will have Admiral Bolt convene a court martial. Until then, you will keep this station or suffer the consequences.'

He tapped the piece of paper which Adam had left on the desk.

'Do not forget your orders.'

As soon as he was in the jollyboat, Adam crushed the paper into a ball and hurled it into the sea. Angus, sitting in the stern, noted the look in his eyes and said nothing. He had served long enough with Adam to recognise a storm brewing inside his captain.

Back on his own quarterdeck, Adam became obsessive about inspections. Nothing satisfied him. The bell had to be polished, the rigging parcelled and served to replenish the tar that kept it watertight. He put men to work sanding down the deck and retouching it. He ordered all the ship's boats to be lowered and put out to tow behind, so that the crew could oil and paint the davits. A platform was hung behind the stern, and men sent down with a pot of paint to erase the ship's name and write on a new name. Adam rechristened her *Nemesis*.

'This is a Royal Navy ship now, not a poxy French privateer,' he growled. 'Lesaut may have kept his ship like a brothel. I will not tolerate any negligence.'

The men jumped to his orders. Adam was a fair man, and they held him in high regard; but he was still a captain and when he was in a bad mood and his temper was hot, they knew to obey orders expeditiously and keep their heads down.

After supper that evening, he announced that he was feeling unwell. He retired to his cabin, locked the door and gave orders that no one was to disturb him.

'Not even you,' he told Angus.

He lay in his cot, trying to get some sleep. It didn't come. He tossed restlessly, turning over in his mind the idea that had come to him in Verrier's cabin. His whole life had been dedicated to the Royal Navy, since the day his mother birthed him in a frigate's cabin. The ship's surgeon had been the midwife, and the chaplain had baptised him with water drawn from the sea. His first solid food had been ship's biscuit dipped in milk, from the goat that Rob had kept for that purpose. The rigging had been his nursery, belaying pins were his toys and the deck was his playground. Sailors served as his uncles and elder brothers, the Articles of War were his catechism, and the navigation primer was his schoolbook. The proudest moments of his life had been receiving his sword from Rob when he passed his lieutenant's exam; and then stepping aboard his first command with a commander's epaulette shining like the sun on his shoulder.

If he disobeyed Verrier's orders, he would lose everything. He would be a deserter, a fugitive and a traitor. If he ever set foot on a Royal Navy ship again, it would be to face a court martial and the hangman's noose.

But if he followed his orders, he would fail his father, his grandfather, and all the generations of Courtneys who had ever held the Neptune sword.

He climbed out of bed and lit the lamp. He unwrapped the sword and held it, staring into the sapphire. Shadows flitted across its deepest facets every time he moved it, like ghosts of the past. If only it could show him his future.

He took the sketch of his cousin Mary, rolled it up tightly and slid it into an empty bottle. He corked it and sealed it with wax. He laid it beside the Neptune sword and the tiger dagger, together with a brace of pistols and his own sword. A change of clothes completed the bundle. He wrapped everything in an oilskin cloth, and tied it securely with a rope, leaving a loop that would fit over his shoulder.

Beyond the stern windows he could see the navigation lights of the convoy spread across the ocean, a constellation brighter than the stars above. Below, the ship's boats made dark shadows on the water, fringed with silver from their bow waves.

He took a last look around the cabin. He felt he ought to say goodbye to his former life, but there was nothing here he was attached to. Everything belonged to the dead Lesaut.

He opened the stern window and hoisted himself onto the sill. He looped the oilcloth bundle over his shoulder, making sure the knots were tight. He readied himself for the drop.

'Funny time for a swim, sir.'

Adam almost fell into the water in surprise. He caught himself on the window frame and pulled back in. He swung around, flushed with anger. Angus stood in the cabin doorway.

'I forbade you to disturb me,' Adam snapped.

He had deliberately avoided telling Angus anything, partly to protect his loyal friend, but mostly because he could not bear the goodbye.

Angus observed the scene in the cabin. If he was surprised to find his captain halfway out of the window in the middle of the night, his meagre possessions bundled over his shoulder like a burglar, his face did not show it.

'Also,' Adam continued, 'I am certain the door was locked.'

'I found a spare key.'

'You do not understand my predicament.'

'Mebbe not. But if I had to guess, I'd say you've a mind to stow away aboard one of the Indiamen and take passage to Calcutta.'

'You should keep your thoughts to yourself until I ask for them.'

'As my ma often said,' Angus agreed. 'Only if that's what you mean to do, you'll need a friend with you, someone who might be useful to save your arse one day.'

Adam could not be angry any longer. He crossed the cabin and held Angus's arm, filled with sadness.

'Don't you think that I would want you to follow me if it was possible? I have considered it a thousand times, but you cannot. It is a hundred to one against my plan succeeding. But with two of us trying to prowl around the Indiaman's hold, it would be impossible. We have fought together many times. But this task I must do alone.'

'I cannae let you do that.'

Adam gripped Angus's arm tighter. 'You must. If I am lucky, they will find the empty cabin and the open window, and think that I fell overboard, either by suicide or misadventure. If I am unlucky, they will notice the missing boat and realise I have disobeyed orders and deserted my command. Either way, if my father hears of it, the shock will kill him. You must go back to England and tell him what I intend to do.'

'And what is that?'

'That I am obeying the charge he gave me. That I will prove myself worthy of his trust.'

'A letter could say the same.'

'But who would deliver it?' Adam stared into Angus's eyes, willing him to understand. 'You are the only man I can trust, and the only man my father will believe. Please do this – for him, and for the sacred memory of my family, if not for me.'

Angus bowed his head. A tear escaped his eye and ran down his cheek, the first time Adam had ever seen him cry.

'If you do it, you'll never come back to the navy,' Angus warned.

'I know.'

Adam embraced him, clinging on to the big man like a young boy again.

'You had best go,' he said at last. 'Leave your key so you are not suspected of anything.'

They parted hurriedly, each afraid of embarrassing himself with more tears. As soon as Angus left the cabin, Adam locked the door from the inside and crossed to the stern. This time, he did not hesitate. He climbed through the open window, balanced on the balls of his feet, and sprang out. He dropped into the calm water, barely making any splash.

He surfaced almost immediately, touching his shoulder to be sure the bundle was safe. The ship's stern rose out of the water above him, the paint on the transom still wet where her new name had been inscribed that afternoon. The white letters glowed in the starlight: *Nemesis*.

Cables stretched overhead to the boats being pulled behind. Adam swam to a small gig, and hauled himself in. He sawed through the tow rope with his knife. Each cut felt like severing another link to his former life.

In a few minutes the boat floated free. The rechristened *Nemesis* drew away, became a receding shadow in the darkness, then dimmed to nothing but a figment in his mind.

He waited until there was a good distance between them, in case any lookout was watching. Then he stepped the little boat's mast, unfurled her sail and sheeted it home. The wind filled the canvas, an old sail of dark brown cloth that blended with the night.

Adam was alone.

Bobbing on the starlit sea, a tiny speck among the great Indiamen, a memory came back to him of when he was at Nativity Bay, visiting with his father. His cousin Mary had come to his room one night. Without a word, she had led him outside and through the trees to an open stretch of grassland. It was a moonless night, but the stars were so clear they lit up the savannah almost as bright as day.

A herd of elephants had come down to drink from the river. They grazed across the plain, gliding like a fleet of galleons through the long, rippling grass. Adam had counted more than a hundred of them before he gave up. He had stood there, holding hands with Mary, the dewy soil damp between his toes, while the stars turned in the heavens and the great beasts made their stately progress. He had felt small, dwarfed by the immense grandeur of the world.

He had never forgotten the wonder of that night. He felt an echo of it now. The boat hurried forward eagerly, urged on by the steady breeze, unaware this short journey would be her last. Adam cradled the tiller in one hand, keeping the main sheet tight in the other.

All afternoon, while he was terrorising his crew with chores, he had studied the other ships in the convoy. He had marked which were smartly kept, and which had tears in the sails or scars in the woodwork that had not been repaired. Unobserved, he watched how the crews carried themselves: those who moved briskly with good discipline, and those who slouched about their tasks. One ship, the *Mornington*, had stood out above all the others. Her sails were threadbare, and set so badly the ship was constantly spilling wind and falling behind. Her sailors did little, and her officers were nowhere in sight. Of all the ships, Adam decided, she would be the least likely to keep a vigilant watch at night. As a bonus, it would be easy to pick her out at the back of the convoy.

He could see her now, a dark silhouette against the starlit sky. He adjusted course, computing in his head how the wind and current would bring the two vessels together. He could not risk getting this endeavour wrong.

The gig closed with the hulking Indiaman. This was the most dangerous part of Adam's plan, requiring precise movements. To grapple the *Mornington*, he would have to stand in the bows ready to let fly the grappling hook. But that would leave the boat without steerage way. If he had misjudged the course and speed even a little, or if a wave knocked him forward, he would be crushed under her bows.

He loosened the halyard and let the sail drop. Now he was entirely at the mercy of the sea. He slung the bundle with the Neptune sword over his shoulder, grabbed the coiled rope and sprang forward to the front of the boat. He crouched, whirling the grapnel in a circle as he watched the Indiaman bear down on him.

He had judged it almost perfectly. In the dead of night, he had brought his boat to intersect with a moving target on the exact same spot of open ocean. It was an extraordinary feat of seamanship, with only the tiniest margin of error.

But in the open waters of the oceans, even a small margin of error could cost your life. Whether the gig had slowed faster than he had expected, or if the *Mornington*'s helmsman could not steer a straight course, there was still nearly twenty feet of clear water between the two vessels.

There would be no second chance. In a moment, the *Mornington* would be past him. Even a slow sailor like the Indiaman would easily outpace the gig. Adam would be left behind the convoy, adrift and abandoned to his fate. Without food or fresh water, he would certainly die before he could ever reach land.

The *Mornington* ploughed on. What had seemed like stately progress from a distance was a storm of violent motion close up. Her towering bow rose and crashed over the waves, throwing up sheets of spray that drenched Adam. Her deck rolled and heaved.

Adam whirled the grapnel until it was a blur of motion, then let fly. He felt time freeze as he watched it sail through the air, the rope paying out behind it. It was impossible to gauge the distance in the dark. The grapnel rose, then started to fall back towards the sea. Had he misjudged it?

The rope stretched taut. The grapnel's prongs caught the bowsprit and bit into the wood. Adam's aim had been true. But he had no time for relief. As the *Mornington* surged on, the rope was almost snatched out of Adam's hands. He tightened his grip, turning it around his wrist just as the rope jerked him over the edge of the boat and into the sea.

The shock of this unexpected manoeuvre and the cold water almost made him let go of the rope, but he clung on to it, hauling himself up the wet, slippery rope, one hand over the other. The ship dragged him forward and forced water into his face. He could hardly breathe.

The *Mornington*'s hull hit his shoulder hard, numbing it instantly. The barnacles that crusted it cut open his shirt and tore his skin. It was like being pulled over a bed of razors. He would be ripped apart and, if he survived, blood in the water would bring a shiver of sharks in an instant.

Adam kicked off the timbers in a frenzy, using his feet to propel himself. As he got closer to the end of the rope, he started to rise out of the water. He breasted the tumblehome where the hull swelled outwards. If any sailor on deck had peered over the gunwale, he would have seen the most extraordinary sight: Adam attached to the rope, walking himself almost horizontally across the ship's side, like a spider on a thread.

He was almost high enough to touch the gunwale. He reached up, fingers scrabbling on the planking for a handhold. Another two inches and . . .

A heavy wave hit the ship on her opposite side. She heeled over. Adam's feet slipped off the slick surface as it rolled away. With nothing to steady him, the rope swung him under the bows. He dangled under the bowsprit, kicking and jerking like a hanged man.

The grapnel had held, but for how much longer? Every swing of the rope threatened to dislodge it. Adam's hands were already chafed bloody raw from hauling himself along the wet rope; blood was pouring from his arm where the barnacles had scraped it. His sodden clothes weighed on him, dragging him into the sea.

Something moved in the water below him. It might have been a ripple, but to Adam's heightened senses it looked more like a shark's fin knifing the surface. He gritted his teeth and forced himself to climb. Hand over hand, ignoring the agony in his shoulder and his burning palms, bleeding arms, he inched higher up the swaying rope.

Then he raised his hand and felt solid wood. He grabbed on. Like a fish being brought over the side, he slithered over the prow and collapsed in a heap on the platform behind the figurehead.

He was aboard the ship.

He gave himself a few minutes to catch his breath. He tore a strip off his ragged shirt and bound his bleeding arm the best he could. It would do no good to leave a trail of fresh blood around the ship. He pulled out the grapnel and let it drop into the sea. Then he raised his head to peer on to the deck.

There were few men on watch, and those mostly clustered around the wheel towards the stern. They had not noticed Adam's arrival. Nor did they notice as he crept past the wooden crates on the foredeck and towards the for'ard hatch, which had been left open to let in the night air.

Suddenly an indignant squawk shrieked into the night; Adam dropped to the deck noiselessly, hoping he had not alerted the watch. What he had thought were crates was actually the hen coop.

The hens huffed and preened their feathers. The sailors paid them no attention. Adam waited until the birds went quiet, then crept on and slipped down the hatch.

Below decks, the ship was pitch dark. Men slept in hammocks slung from every beam; Adam had to feel his way between them. In the cramped space, it was surely impossible to remain unnoticed. He moved as carefully as possible, relying on darkness and the men's exhaustion. He hoped no one would notice the trail of water his sodden clothes dripped along the deck.

A bulkhead divided the cabins from the crew's quarters. Adam had expected to find a ladder leading down to the hold, but the Indiaman's owners were no fools. They had put the entrance further aft, away from the temptations of the crew's idle hands and light fingers. Adam would have to run the gauntlet of the officers' and passengers' quarters to reach it.

On a man-of-war, a marine sentry would have guarded the aft section. On the merchantman, there was no one. Trusting his luck would hold, Adam pushed into the narrow corridor between the flimsy partition walls. He hurried on, imagining Verrier's triumph if Adam was caught and hauled before him.

At the end of the corridor, the binnacle lantern shone through a grating into the mess room. Beneath it, Adam saw a ladder descending to the lower decks. He quickened his pace.

'Who the bloody hell are you?' said a voice.

Adam realised the mess room wasn't empty. The light was not the binnacle lantern, but a lamp on the table, where a man in a uniform coat sat poring over an account book. It was probably the purser. Sitting in a corner, he had been hidden until Adam was almost in the room.

Adam turned to run away. But the only place to go was back through the forecastle, a blind obstacle course of hammocks and sleeping men. He would surely wake half the crew.

The purser was approaching, and he was bringing a light. But for half a second more, the corridor was in darkness and Adam was invisible.

Most of the doors had names pinned on them, but one was blank. Adam pushed inside and closed the door. A moment later, he heard the purser's footsteps hurrying down the corridor. He blundered past the cabin and into the forecastle.

The cabin was dark, but an unused gunport was tied open for air. Moonlit shone in. As Adam's eyes adjusted, he made out the basic fittings: a washstand, a mirror hung on a nail, a chest of clothes and a tiny cot suspended from ropes in the ceiling.

If the purser came, there would be nowhere to hide. Even the space under the cot was barely big enough for a cat. Adam kneeled to see if he could squeeze under it.

A snore sounded from the cot. Adam jerked up, knocking the cot with his shoulder and setting it rocking. Looking down, he saw a woman asleep, almost hidden in its high-sided shadows. She lay on her side, her legs crooked to fit into the narrow cot. She seemed to be naked.

Adam froze. These were temporary cabins, tiny hutches partitioned with curtains. If she made a sound, it would raise the alarm on the whole ship. Further forward, he could hear a commotion as the purser rousted the crew from their hammocks.

She stirred and stretched her arm up to her cheek. She might wake at any moment. Adam could not stay. But where could he go?

The gunport. It was the only way out. He would have to clamber through, and hope he could cling on to the outside of the hull and find some other open porthole to climb back into the ship. He put his head out. It would be tight: his shoulders would barely fit. Perhaps if he took his shirt off . . .

'Who are you?'

The woman was sitting up, clutching a sheet to cover herself as she stared at Adam. Waking in the night with a strange man in her cabin: there was only one conclusion.

She was about to scream. He moved to stop her, but he was too late.

But she did not scream. Instead, she said in an astonished voice, 'Captain Courtney?'

Adam stopped dead. He studied her more closely. And for the second time that day, he found himself looking at a familiar face in the most unexpected place and circumstances.

He had every excuse not to remember her. He had met her once, and briefly. So much had happened in the meantime that the memory should have been driven from his mind. Yet her face felt as familiar as his own reflection, and her name rose effortlessly to his lips as if he had known it all his life. She was the girl with the peacock fan at the governor's dinner in Cape Town.

'Lizzie March.'

'What in God's name are you doing on this ship? And in my cabin?'

Adam glimpsed himself in the small mirror Lizzie had hung on the wall. His face was bruised and streaked with tar from the planking. His shirt was missing both sleeves, one torn away by the barnacles and the other turned into a makeshift bandage, which was now soaked with blood. His trousers had been cut to ribbons by the ordeal of coming aboard. One broad tear started at the button of his breeches and ran diagonally down across his pelvis to his thigh, leaving little to the imagination. Lizzie was staring at it.

Adam covered himself with his hand.

'My apologies, Miss March. I know this is . . . irregular—'

'It is quite scandalous.' Though the words were sharp, her tone sounded more bemused than angry. 'But you still have not answered my question. How did you come to be here?'

Before Adam could reply, footsteps sounded from the passage and stopped outside the door.

Adam's eyes met Lizzie's. 'Please,' he mouthed.

There was a knock at the door, but the handle was already turning. There was no lock. Adam dived behind the door before it was flung open.

In the mirror on the wall, Adam saw the purser framed in the doorway. Another step would take him into the middle of the cabin, where he could hardly avoid seeing Adam cowering in the corner. Or maybe the purser had seen him already. If Adam could see him in the glass, then surely Adam's reflection would be visible.

But the purser was not looking in the mirror. He was staring at Lizzie. The sheet she had wrapped around herself had fallen away, and she stood stark naked in the centre of the cabin.

Lizzie screamed. The sound shocked the purser into remembering his decency. He stepped back into the passage and shut the cabin door so hard it shivered the ship's timbers.

Adam, crammed in the corner, could only stare at Lizzie in admiration.

'Beggin' your pardon, miss,' said the purser from the other side of the door. 'I thought I saw an intruder aboard.'

'An intruder?' said Lizzie, incredulously. 'We are in the middle of the Indian Ocean. Where could such a person possibly have come from?'

'Ah . . .' the man stumbled. 'See, there's a trail of wet footprints leading to your door.'

Lizzie put her foot on the discarded sheet and wiped it across the floor, mopping up the water Adam had dripped.

'Do you think a *merman* has crept aboard?'

'Well, no, miss. But there are . . . ah . . . French privateers in these waters.'

'Have you seen one?'

'No.'

'Then do you think, sir, that this is justification for bursting in on a solitary young lady, in the most *intimate* state of undress, in the privacy of her cabin?'

A grunt from outside conceded he did not.

'You may be sure I will inform the captain of this,' Lizzie continued. 'And my fiancé will hear of it when we reach Calcutta. Can a lady not travel in a ship of the *Honourable* East India Company without fear of molestation?'

'Just trying to keep you safe,' muttered the purser nervously.

Lizzie had done nothing to cover herself but stood there unashamed, splendid in her nakedness.

'If you are so certain there is an intruder aboard ship, then allow me a little time to make myself presentable. I should be delighted for you to search my cabin presently.'

Adam's jaw dropped. Surely she had gone too far. He tried to catch her eye, gesturing her to stop. If the purser came in again . . .

'That won't be necessary, miss,' he muttered. 'Apologies for disturbing your good self.'

His footsteps shuffled off down the passage.

'How did you do that?' said Adam.

Lizzie brushed a stray lock of hair from her face. Belatedly, it seemed to occur to her she was naked, in a tiny cabin, with a man she hardly knew.

'Avert your eyes,' she said briskly. 'Do not think you are safe yet. If you try anything improper, I will call the purser and tell him you held a knife at my throat.'

'Nothing improper, I give you my word,' Adam promised.

He turned and faced the corner while she pulled on a nightdress.

'Do you always sleep that way?' Adam asked.

'It was the heat,' she said. 'This cabin is stifling. And I did not expect I would be receiving so many uninvited callers in the middle of the night,' she added tartly. 'You may turn around now, Captain.'

Lizzie sat up in the cot, wearing a plain white nightdress and a lace shawl wrapped around her shoulders. She fixed him with a firm gaze.

'You still have not answered my question. What are you doing here, and how did you get aboard this ship?'

'It is a long story.'

'Then you are fortunate that I have plenty of time to listen.' She folded up her legs and put her arms around her knees. 'Tell me.'

Adam sat on the floor facing her and started talking. He began his story with the assault on Cape Town and Rob's grave injury – but he realised that was not the beginning, only the latest chapter in a story that had been written over centuries. So he went back to his great-great-grandfather Tom Courtney, who had fled to Africa from England after mistakenly killing his murderous older brother Black Billy, who had attacked him in disguise at London's docks. Adam told her about Tom's brother Dorian, who had been captured by a Muslim pirate ship on the high seas, and later became Caliph of the Omani in Muscat.

'How could that be?' Lizzie asked.

'The Caliph Abd Muhammad al-Malik adopted him. Dorian had red hair, and he had spoken Arabic fluently since childhood. His captors thought he was a descendant of the Prophet Muhammed, fulfilling an ancient prophecy.'

Adam continued the story with his great-grandfather Jim, who married a convict girl who had been transported from Holland. Her name was Louisa, convicted unlawfully, but Adam's great-grandfather Jim had rescued her from a shipwreck and escaped with her from the soldiers who pursued them. They had settled at Nativity Bay, where Adam's grandfather George grew up and, in time, fathered Rob.

Last of all, Adam spoke of his own father, who had fled the safe haven of Nativity Bay for a life of adventure. He had gone to England and, after a series of misfortunes in London, ended up in the Royal Navy. He had fought against the rebellious colonists in America, in the Caribbean, and then all over the world.

Adam barely knew Lizzie, but speaking to her came naturally. The words flowed, memories came alive again, and she listened eagerly. Adam told her how Rob had rescued Phoebe from slavery, how they had raised Adam aboard ship – and how they had made their fateful return to Fort Auspice.

He took the oilskin bundle and showed her the broken Neptune sword, the tiger dagger and the sketch of Mary.

'I swore to my father I would find the men who did it.'

He told her of his interview with Talbot, his pursuit of the *Requin* and his escape from Île de France, and finally his confrontation with Verrier.

'And now I am here. At your mercy.'

Lizzie had listened to the tale in wonder.

'That is why you were in such a hurry to leave the night we met in Cape Town,' she said. 'I feared I had somehow insulted you.'

'I feared I had insulted you.'

'And you think you will find this Captain Talbot in Calcutta?'

'That is where he was bound. Unless he lied about that as well.'

'Then I will help you get there,' said Lizzie, with a warm smile.

Adam was grateful to the fate that had brought him to her, but also alarmed for her safety. When he had first seen her tucked up in the cot, she had looked so young. It would be an evil act to drag her into his revenge.

'I could not ask that of you. I am on a deadly quest.'

'You did not ask it. I will do it freely, because I believe in the justice of your cause.'

Her face was fixed with forceful determination, but she spoke so softly her words were almost lost in the hiss of the ocean outside the hull. Adam had to lean forward to hear. A wave rocked the boat and swung the cot towards him. In the tight confines of the cabin, their faces were almost touching. Her perfume enveloped him with the scent of an English garden. A silky curl of her hair tickled his cheek. Her lips parted.

On deck, the watch sounded seven bells. The sound rang through the whole ship, tolling for morning and the end of sleep. Adam felt he was being pulled away from a dream that he could not bear to end.

A gust of warm air blew into the cabin through the gunport. The spell had been broken; the moment passed. Lizzie threw off the shawl and climbed out of bed.

'There is no room for you in this cabin. You had best hide yourself in the hold with the cargo. I will save some food and drink from my meals and bring it to you at night.'

'But please . . . think of the risk to your reputation if you were found out as a party to my plan.' He remembered what she had said to the purser. 'What would your fiancé say?'

'I am not married yet. And he need never know.' The strange warm light kindled in her eyes again. 'No doubt it would scandalise him, and ruin his fine reputation, to know that I was harbouring a fugitive and a deserter from the Royal Navy aboard this ship, so I rely on you to have the good sense not to get caught.' She peeked into the passageway to make sure the corridor was clear of sailors, then ushered him out. 'Come here tomorrow night, Adam. I am sure you have more stories of your brave forefathers to tell. You can repay me for your passage by recounting them to me in detail.'

The door closed, leaving nothing but the scent of roses to prove it had not been an extraordinary dream.

Adam had spent all his life at sea. He had navigated Cape Horn and the Cape of Good Hope, and survived storms on three oceans. But the weeks sailing to Calcutta were the hardest voyage he had ever endured. He lived in perpetual darkness, trapped in solitude. For long hours of each day he was trapped in the hold, with only the faintest slivers of light through the cracks in the deck's planking. Rats infested the hold, filling it with their stench and scrabbling over him in the darkness. In heavy seas, water slopped out of the bilges and drenched him. He had never been seasick, but the smells of rancid pork, mouldering ship's biscuit and rat faeces that filled the air left him constantly nauseous.

The days passed in grim silence. Like his father, and all his Courtney ancestors, he had never been good at keeping still or being idle. Boredom started to weigh on him like a boulder on his heart. Sometimes it brought him to the edge of despair. Then a rat brushing against his toes would bring his mind back to riddle of Nativity Bay, and the twisting path his vengeance had taken so far. Angus's last words played in his head again and again. *If you do it, you'll never come back to the navy.*

He thought about his unknown future. The darkness could not douse his hope of avenging his murdered family. But as the days passed, he found that thoughts of Fort Auspice receded. Instead, he found himself thinking more and more about Lizzie.

Every night, in the middle watch, he lifted the hatch and crept silently to Lizzie's cabin. They talked through the short remaining hours of the night, their voices low so as not to be heard through the partitions. Adam told her more stories of his experiences at sea, and of his family's illustrious history – tales of pirates, ancestral sibling feuds, Tom and Guy Courtney, Indian rajahs, Arabian princes, and the wide expanses and savannas of Africa where few white men had ever set foot. Fortunes had been won and lost, loves gained and betrayed. They were histories he had heard from his father many times, handed down through the generations as each successive Courtney added his own.

What stories will my children tell about me? Adam wondered. *Will they live up to my forefathers' deeds?*

He found he had a talent for storytelling. He began timing them by the ship's bell, so that just as he reached the climax of the action, he would have to depart.

'You are my Scheherazade,' Lizzie complained. 'Coming to my chamber every night to tell me the most fantastical stories, and then breaking off at the most exciting part.'

Adam looked shocked. 'You know the Arabian Nights?'

'Of course. My mother read them to me as a child. They were captivating.'

'No doubt.'

Adam had read them as a child, too. Later, he had discovered that his great-uncle Dorian, who had spoken Arabic fluently, had made his own translation of the Arabian Nights from a manuscript he had bought in a Cairo bazaar. Adam had found the translation one day in the Courtney family library, during his visit to Fort Auspice – full of details that the prudish English publication omitted. The carnal uncensored tales had opened his pubescent mind to all manner of possibilities he had never imagined. It had also given him a new respect for his great-great-uncle.

Unlike the Arabian Nights, Adam's evenings with Lizzie were chaste affairs. She sat on her bed, and he on the floor. The moment that first night when their lips almost touched, when he had felt their bodies drawn to each other like two magnets, was never repeated.

There was little distance between them when they were together. It would have been easy to lean across the cabin and kiss her. Every night, Adam felt the desire building inside him, sometimes so powerful he could not concentrate on what she was saying. But then he was ashamed of himself. She had prospects, a husband-to-be waiting for her in Calcutta. To seduce her now would be to endanger the only hope she had for a prosperous future. She had already risked her reputation to save Adam, whom she barely knew. To take advantage of her kind nature would be the worst sort of lechery.

And, as he learned, she had suffered enough calamities in her life already.

'My father was in the army. He died in Holland during the invasion.'

Adam remembered the campaign: a short-lived attempt by Britain and Russia to invade the Netherlands. They had been defeated and forced to surrender, with nearly half the force killed or wounded – a bloodbath that achieved nothing.

'I was ten years old,' said Lizzie. 'My father had married for love and his family did not approve of the match. I think they were glad he died – it relieved them of an embarrassment. My mother and I went to London to beg their charity, and they pretended we did not exist.

'My mother became a seamstress, but she did not earn enough to keep us. She sought a new husband, but all the men she met could sense her desperation. Some took pity, and some took advantage, but none took us in. The things my mother tried to win their affections . . .' She shuddered. 'Each failure only debased her further.

'She became very sick, and because we could not afford a doctor, she died. Perhaps that was the best thing that could have happened to me.' She glanced at Adam. 'Do you think I am callous?'

'You loved your mother.' He could see it in her eyes, glossy with unspent tears. 'It was not your fault she died.'

'I sometimes wonder.' Her voice cracked. A tear ran down her cheek. 'Perhaps I should have run away. If my mother had not had me to worry about, she might have taken better care of herself.'

'You would only have broken her heart.'

Adam could not bear to see her so desolate. He reached forward and took her hand, stroking it gently.

Lizzie shook away the tear and sat up.

'In any event, her death saved me. An aunt – my father's older sister – took me in. By now I was sixteen, and she saw that the best way to secure my future was to marry me off.'

'I should have thought with your beauty you would have had the pick of every bachelor in England.'

Lizzie ignored the compliment. 'After my mother's decline, there was no one in society who viewed me as a good match. Eventually my aunt wrote to an old comrade of my father's, a major from his regiment, who had taken up a posting in India. He was willing. Everything was arranged by return of post.'

'I hope he is a dashing and gallant young officer,' said Adam, pretending he meant it.

'I am told he is kind. His letters show a man of feeling.' She rummaged in her travelling chest and pulled out a book. 'This is what he sent me as a gift to mark our engagement.'

Adam read the title: A GRAMMAR AND EXERCISER OF THE HINDUSTANI LANGUAGE.

'My betrothed thought I should learn the language, so that I am able to command my servants. He is worried I am not used to managing such a large household.'

'I hope he will care for you as much as I would.'

Adam had spoken without thinking. He only realised what he had said when he felt Lizzie's hand tighten around his. Her eyes fixed on him, burning with a question he did not dare to answer.

'I m-meant,' he stammered, 'that all anyone could wish is your happiness.'

'I see.' Lizzie pulled her hand from his and folded it in her lap. 'Then I am grateful for your good wishes.'

After that night, Adam borrowed Lizzie's grammar book and a candle, and whiled away the hours in the hold teaching himself Hindustani. It relieved some of the monotony as the voyage passed. Adam saw nothing of the ship's progress, but he read it in the rhythms of the timbers and the pitch of the water under the keel. He felt the heavy ocean swell soften as they rounded Cape Coromandel and passed Ceylon; the snapping waves off Madras that kept the ship wallowing for days; then the glassy stillness that indicated they had reached the Bay of Bengal.

They entered the Hooghly, the great river that led to Calcutta. Even in the depths of the ship's hold, the aroma of the new continent penetrated over the stench of rotten provisions and bilge water. It was dust and spices and dank vegetation. The ship's progress slowed as she navigated the endless shoals and bends of the river's course. Sometimes he heard her keel slithering over a sandbank beneath him, and braced himself for disaster.

Adam was glad at the prospect of ending the voyage. He took out the Neptune sword and the tiger dagger again, drawing strength from them and reminding himself why he had come. The thought of escaping his world of permanent night, into sunlight and air, was like the promise of salvation.

But even after so many weeks, part of him did not want it to end. Arriving in Calcutta meant saying farewell to Lizzie. There would be no more long nights telling stories, or counting the hours until the moment he could creep up to her door. She would join her appointed husband, and her life would diverge from Adam's as suddenly and completely as they had come together. Probably, he would never see her again.

Those last few days the air was heavy, charged with storms that refused to break. The ship seemed to sweat moisture and tar. Even sitting motionless in the hold, Adam's shirt was drenched with sweat. The weather seemed to affect Lizzie's mood. When he went to her at night, she had become sullen and listless. Before, there was never enough time for everything they wanted to say; now long, awkward silences punctuated their conversations. Adam wondered if she had grown bored of him. Perhaps now she was so close to her future husband, she regretted the intimacy she had shown him.

The last night before they reached Calcutta, he almost didn't go to her cabin. He did not want his last memories of her to be uncomfortable. He was afraid – if he was honest – that she would be glad to be free of him.

But he had to see her one last time. He could not let her go without saying goodbye. When the bell sounded the middle watch, he clambered out of the hold and stole through the ship to Lizzie's cabin. By now, he could have done it blindfolded.

'The other passengers swear there is a ghost aboard,' Lizzie had told him. 'They hear the most irregular bumps in the night. One swore she saw you two nights ago. She said you had cockle shells for eyes and black seaweed for hair.'

Lizzie was in her bed, the sheet pulled up to her neck. Despite the sultry heat, she seemed to be shivering. Her cheeks were flushed red and glossy with perspiration. Adam wondered if she was ill.

'I came to say goodbye.' The words came out flat, more brusquely than he'd meant them to sound. 'Thank you for everything. You saved my life, and for that I will always be grateful.'

Lizzie said nothing. Her silence weighed on Adam; in the stifling cabin he could not breathe. Hardly knowing what he was doing, he turned to go. He put his hand on the door when . . .

'Wait.'

All the hours they had spent together, she had never raised her voice above a whisper for fear that someone might hear them through the cabin's canvas walls. But now her voice was firm and unafraid. Adam turned.

'There is something I want of you.'

She threw off the sheet. Underneath, she was as naked as the first night he found her. Her skin glowed; her thighs were parted slightly to reveal the shadow between.

For a long moment Adam stared, gazing at her beauty. Then something gave inside him – a release of pent-up emotion. His clothes dropped to the floor. His body pressed on hers. She gasped, clutching him closer. She planted his face with kisses.

He knew it was wrong – that somewhere close, Lizzie's future husband would be sleeping in his Calcutta mansion, dreaming of his bride-to-be. Adam could not stop himself, and nor could Lizzie.

She put him between her legs and pulled him into her. He felt a moment of resistance; she whimpered, and he remembered this must be her first time. He made himself move slowly, but she was too eager. She put her hands on his buttocks and pulled him in deeper. Their slick bodies glided against each other without resistance.

The cot, suspended from the ceiling, rocked gently. The only sound was the squeak of its ropes. If anyone had heard it, they might have wondered why it was moving so much on the perfect calm of the Hooghly river. But no one interrupted them. They climaxed together, bodies shuddering in unison. Adam pressed his mouth on hers, so that even their cries of ecstasy entered each other.

They lay there for a long time afterwards. The cot came to rest. Lizzie wriggled around so she lay on top of Adam, her head resting in the crook of his arm and her hair fanned across his chest.

'Would you think me very unladylike if I said I had wanted to do that since the first time we met?' she asked

'When I burst into your cabin?'

'In the castle at Cape Town.' She giggled. 'Even then, you made me quite moist with desire.'

'I wish we had done it that night.'

They lapsed into silence. Both knew this was their last time together. They could feel the night draining away, each stroke of the bell hastening the moment.

At last the waiting became too much. Adam pulled away, but Lizzie would not let him go. She opened her legs and wrapped them around him, pulling him against her.

'Take me with you,' she said suddenly.

'Where to?'

'Wherever you go. Anywhere, everywhere . . .'

'But . . . your husband.'

Saying the word was a mistake, breaking the spell. Lizzie stiffened.

'He is not my husband,' she said vehemently. 'He is some man I have never met, who is willing to take a wife on the strength of my aunt's correspondence.'

Adam had no answer.

'I know more about you than I will ever know about him. We have done everything that husbands and wives do. Why should we not make it legitimate – or illegitimate, I do not care – if only we can be together?'

'I cannot.'

'Is there a wife you have not told me about?'

'No.' Adam was horrified. 'You know everything about me – even more than my own father.'

'Why, then? Do you not love me?'

'I . . .' Adam floundered. Commanding a ship in a sea battle was a trifle compared to this onslaught. 'I do love you.'

'Then marry me.'

'I cannot.' He wanted to push her off him, but the narrow cot was so tight there was nowhere to move. 'I am a fugitive. A deserter. Perhaps it sounds romantic, but I promise you the reality is different. There is nowhere in the world I can be safe.'

She would not let him go.

'Do you think I was deaf all those nights you came and spoke to me. I know exactly what you are. I do not care about safety. My major would be *safe*, and I would die of boredom before the year is out.'

'You would die a lot sooner with me,' Adam warned her. 'And a horrible death. The men I am looking for performed unspeakable cruelties upon my family. When they learn I have come for them, they will try to do worse to me.'

'I am not afraid.'

'But I am.'

He told himself he feared for what might happen to her, that his enemies might use her to hurt him. But even then he was not being entirely honest with himself. What frightened him most was that if he went with her now, then happiness would make him forget his quest. He would fail his father and his family.

He rolled her over and pushed himself out of bed. The cot swung wildly as he searched for his discarded clothes on the floor.

'Please go to your major,' he said, more assertively than he meant to. 'You said he seemed a good and kind man. Take the life that was meant for you, and forget I ever existed. It is for the best.' Still he made no impression. 'Think of your father. He married for love, and it brought nothing but misery.'

Lizzie sat up in bed, naked and imperious like the night he met her, a goddess in her wrath. When she spoke, her voice was a whisper, but hissing with the venom of a thousand snakes.

'How dare you try to turn my own history against me? If my father had not married my mother, I would never have been born.'

'I only meant—'

'On her deathbed, I begged my mother's forgiveness for the grief I had caused her. Do you know what she said in reply? That my father and I had been her greatest joys – that she would not have traded one day more of her own life for one day less with us.'

'I did not mean . . .' Adam felt he had been pitched off the highest topmast and was falling towards a hard landing – everything a blur, nothing to cling to. 'But I have my duty to my family.'

'If you choose hate over love, what do you have left?'

Adam did not know what to say. Her words struck home. He stared at Lizzie: her flawless body, her intelligent face and the hurt in her eyes. He felt a void inside. Perhaps she was right: perhaps he had no answer because there was none.

Except, of course, he did. He had known it all along, since he found the wreckage of the house at Nativity Bay.

'I will have my revenge.'

KINGDOM OF GONDAR, 1800

'**K** itzera.'

Paul was walking in a garden. Sweet-smelling roses burst from the flower beds, while the tree branches above drooped their fruit low. The air was pink with clouds of blossom.

A young woman walked beside him. Her long golden hair hung loose over her shoulders; her hand slipped easily into Paul's. He couldn't see her face, but he knew she was beautiful. She plucked a pear from one of the trees and fed him the sweet fruit.

'Kitzera!'

The word changed the garden like an evil enchantment. The roses turned to brambles; the orchard withered into thorn trees. As they shed their leaves, Paul saw a body dangling from one of the branches on a leather cord. The head had swollen to twice its normal size. A fat tongue stuck out between black lips, while the empty eye sockets stared mercilessly at Paul. The woman had vanished.

Paul woke from his dream on a warm stone floor, the edge of the coverlet tickling his face. He must have rolled out of bed. The rising sun shone through the window, making a square of light. And in the middle of it, like a button-faced angel looking down on him, was Sana.

'Kitzera,' she said again. 'It is time for the king.'

Paul had learned many things in the last month. One, that Kitzera was not the name of the executioner he had killed: it was his title. Now the title belonged to Paul, and he hated it.

He washed in the bowl of water Sana brought, and ate a quick breakfast of yoghurt and fruit she had prepared. He opened a chest and took out the tarades, the long bull-hide thongs that were the symbol and tool of his office. He wound them tight, one around his left wrist and another around his right.

'It will be a busy day,' said Sana.

Paul crossed the courtyard towards the palace. The palace complex was as grand as anything in France, limestone walls four storeys high and capped with whimsical battlements. The round towers were shaped like windmills or pepper pots, and surmounted with domes that reminded Paul of Cairo. The doors and windows were framed with red tufa stone, with lions and crosses decorating the walls.

But from a different angle, its appearance changed. You could see the scorch marks on the walls where the main tower had been gutted by fire. A cedar tree grew out of the roof of the east wing, where the roof had fallen in. Behind the lofty walls, only the ground level was occupied. The higher floors were crumbling, shedding roof tiles and riddled with holes like a moth-eaten blanket. Stones sometimes came loose and fell without warning. Paul had seen one courtier struck on the head during a royal audience and drop dead instantly. The king had continued as if he had not noticed, while flies buzzed around the unattended corpse.

It was a fairy tale kingdom in ruins.

Paul took his place in the hall just in time. Trumpets sounded, and the doors were thrown open. A line of priests filed in, followed by the king riding on a donkey. He did not dismount at the entrance, but rode up the palace steps and the length of the audience chamber to the throne at the far end.

The first time Paul had seen it, he had almost burst out laughing. The king cut a ridiculous figure, waddling through the palace on the tiny animal. But it was a serious ritual. The king would not let his feet touch the floor, but dismounted onto a silk footstool placed by a servant, and then straight onto his throne.

The donkey was led away. The king's advisers fanned out either side of the throne, with his two sons in the positions of honour. They were the princes Paul had seen the day he encountered the king's army. Their names were Yostos and Goshu. Goshu, the elder, was the shorter and quieter of the pair. He had his father's searching eyes, and pouting lips that made him look constantly dissatisfied. His brother, Yostos, was taller and more strongly built. He had a warrior's musculature, and an open face that had not yet learned to hide its emotions. He was just older than Paul, but carried himself with the confidence of decades. Paul had been surprised to learn he was the younger son.

A purple curtain was raised in front of the king, part of the ritual of Gondarian justice. The king should not see the men he was judging. The first pair of disputants were brought before the throne. They looked nervous. Justice in Gondar was as brutal and decisive as combat in the Roman colosseum.

Paul had learned the rudiments of Amharic, the language of Gondar, but not enough to follow what was said. He followed the trial in the body language of the two men, in the voices of the ministers who quizzed them, and in the faces of the watching courtiers. Sometimes one of the litigants would glance anxiously at Paul. When a man did that, Paul knew the trial was not going well for him.

This morning, it was a complicated case. The arguments went back and forth. The king stayed hidden, but his sons joined the debate with enthusiasm. They seemed to have taken opposite sides. Goshu made his points with cold precision and small, jabbing motions of his hands; Yostos spoke passionately, his voice ringing with authority. The exchanges between the brothers grew heated and angry. The men on trial were forgotten: they hardly spoke. They had become proxies in the two princes' argument, and the only question was which of them would win.

The room fell silent. The chamberlain scuttled behind the curtain to receive the king's verdict. When he returned, his face was solemn. He pointed to the man on the left.

'Kitzera.'

The man went pale. He looked as if he was about to faint, but before he could fall, two guards grabbed his arms and dragged him out of the chamber. Goshu's pouting mouth widened in a smile; Yostos's face was murderous. Paul hurried after the condemned man.

Notwithstanding its other deficiencies, Gondarian justice was at least swift. The guards tied the prisoner to a stone pillar in the courtyard. Paul unwrapped the tarade from his wrist. The prisoner gibbered and cried; he pleaded for his life. But Paul could not understand his pleas, and he had learned not to listen. He made a noose, and slipped it over both the prisoner's head and the pillar, so that the man's throat was held fast. Then he inserted a stick in the band and twisted it, tightening the loop until he heard the windpipe snap and smelled the familiar ammonia stench of a dead man's bladder.

This was the forty-first man he had executed. He had counted every one.

He heard footsteps behind him and turned slowly. You always moved cautiously at the court; otherwise, people might think you were frightened, that you had something to hide. If you were frightened, you must be guilty. If you were guilty, there was only one sentence.

It was Goshu, the king's elder son, flanked by half a dozen of his guards. That did not put Paul at his ease.

Goshu studied the dead man with an anatomist's curiosity.

'You know what his crime was?'

He spoke Arabic so Paul could understand. It was the language of the traders and merchants in Gondar.

'No, lord,' said Paul.

'He owns an estate, out towards Agara. My father was riding past it. This traitor' – he prodded the dead man's belly – 'had not trimmed the trees that overhung the road. A thorn scratched my father.'

Paul waited for the rest of the story. But that was it – there was no more. Goshu had moved on, walking slowly around the stone pillar. He tugged at the bull-hide thong that Paul had used, testing the tightness of the knot.

'You are good at your work.'

'I serve the king, lord.'

Goshu turned suddenly. His small eyes fixed Paul like two pins.

'Do you know what is the most important quality for an executioner?'

'No, lord.'

'It is not brute strength, or cunning, or a delight in pain – though these are all necessary. It is loyalty.'

Goshu moved closer. He took Paul's arm and unwrapped the other tarade bound around his left wrist.

'My father had an executioner once, one of your predecessors. A very able man. One day, he boasted to my father he would kill any person in the kingdom if my father commanded it. So my father tested him. He ordered him to execute himself.'

Goshu made a loop in the tarade and fastened it with a slipknot. He put it over Paul's neck, as if decorating him with a garland. Paul's body went rigid.

Goshu leaned close, whispering in Paul's ear.

'That Kitzera tied the noose himself. He strung it from a rafter in the palace, and then he hanged himself. *That* is the true meaning of loyalty.'

As he spoke, he had been slowly pulling the cord tight until it pressed up so snug against Paul's throat his windpipe was cut off.

'That is what the king demands of the Kitzera above all else.'

Paul nodded as much as he could with a noose around his neck.

Goshu jerked his thumb at the dead man tied to the post.

'Did he say anything before he died?'

'No, lord.'

That displeased Goshu. 'You were too quick. You must learn to prolong their deaths, tease them out as long as you can. Let them think you might relent. That way, they will tell you anything you ask.' He kicked the corpse. 'My father has many enemies who wish to take his kingdom and see his rightful heir deposed.' He paused, so that Paul could appreciate the significance of his words. 'There are men in that hall, some within touching distance of the throne, who would betray my father. They must be rooted out.'

Paul said nothing. The cord was so tight he couldn't open his mouth.

'You know of whom I speak?'

Paul grunted. *Within touching distance of the throne* could only mean the younger brother, Yostos.

'Has he spoken to you? Has he asked you to spy on me, to extort false confessions from the men in your care? To spread lies about me?'

Paul tried to shake his head, though with the tarade around his neck he could only make an infinitesimal movement. Goshu held the cord with both hands: one on the knot, one on the loose end like a leash. A single firm tug would break Paul's windpipe. His eyes drilled into Paul's.

'Do I have your loyalty?'

He relaxed the knot just enough for Paul to speak.

'I promise, lord,' he choked out – almost unintelligible, but enough for Goshu.

The prince let go so suddenly, Paul almost collapsed.

'Now take that corpse away before he starts to rot.'

When Paul returned to his apartments that evening, Sana was in a sulky mood. She banged the pots so hard she cracked one in half. Stew spilled into the grate, where it hissed and fizzled.

'Your visitor is in the bedroom,' she said.

Paul froze. No one ever called on him in his quarters. To the rest of the court, he was untouchable. He put his finger to the welt that still throbbed around his neck. Had Goshu changed his mind? Had he sent his guards to test Paul's loyalty still further? What if they went for Sana?

'Danger?' he mouthed.

Sana gave him an inscrutable look. 'No.'

Paul went through to the bedroom – and stopped. The visitor was not Goshu, or one of his henchmen. She was a young woman, maybe seventeen, with long legs and wide sparkling eyes. She wore a white cotton tunic tied over one shoulder, with a necklace of bright red coral.

'Who are you?'

She gave a smile. She did not speak Arabic, or apparently any language that Paul knew. By way of an answer, she shrugged the robe off her shoulder and let it drop to the floor. She was naked underneath. Her skin was light brown, her breasts firm and full. An evening breeze blew across her body, making her nipples harden.

Paul stared at her, like a teenage boy on his first visit to a brothel. His mind raced.

'Did Goshu send you?'

She must have recognised Goshu's name, but all she did was smile. A shallow smile, not enough to mask the nerves underneath. Her gaze darted about the room and fell on a niche in the wall above the bed, where a carved wooden figurine stood.

It was the bird-headed god. Paul had drawn it from memory, and taken it to one of the wood-carvers in the market outside the palace. The woodcarver was a talented artist: he had captured the subtle terror of the god perfectly. The beak was sharp enough to pierce skin, while the god's posture – even at eight inches high – had the power of cold command.

The girl tore her eyes away, remembering what she had come there to do. Recovering her smile, she stepped close to Paul and put her hands on his belt. It came away, followed by his tunic. Still smiling, she kneeled in front of him and took him in her mouth. Her tongue was warm and moist.

It hardly mattered who had sent her – whether she was a reward, an inducement, a spy. If he refused her, it would be taken as a sign of his disloyalty. And Goshu had made clear the price of disloyalty.

He sank back on his bed. He had no control over his fate. All he could do was enjoy the moment.

Since his first days at the palace, Paul had been aware of the struggle between Yostos and Goshu. Now it was plain to see. It infected the court like a poison cloud. Every grant of land or privilege, every marriage that was approved, every child that was born and every criminal Paul put to death – they all weighed on the balance of the brothers' rivalry.

The only man who seemed oblivious to it was the king. When he emerged from behind the purple curtain, his face was serene. At feasts, he ate and drank without noticing the glowering sons beside him. It was only after weeks of observation that Paul began to see the patterns in his behaviour. If a man whom Yostos favoured won a promotion, then the next week one of Goshu's loyalists would gain a command. If a judgement displeased Goshu, then it was inevitable that soon Paul would be fitting his noose around the neck of one of Yostos's faction. It was artfully done; even the brothers could never be sure it was intentional.

'The king is not the king,' said Sana one evening.

Paul thrust his hand over her mouth.

'What are you saying?' he hissed. 'Even to *think* that . . . If anyone heard, they would kill us both.'

'All the servants say it,' said Sana calmly.

'When do you speak to them?'

'At the river, while we do our laundry.'

'And what do they say?'

'That he is hostage to his sons.'

Paul was astonished.

'Why do they say that?' he whispered.

'The sons want to kill him.'

'Goshu is loyal. It is Yostos who conspires against his father.'

'That is not what the servants believe,' said Sana darkly. She thought for a moment, twisting a lock of hair around her finger. 'If I was the king, I would not let anyone tell me what to do. Not even my own children.'

'How would you do that?'

She fixed him with a child's gaze, full of serious intent.

'I would order you to kill them both.'

One day, the king went hunting with Yostos. This was unusual. If he rode out from the palace, it was with both sons, or with neither. While he kept them together, they acted as natural checks on each other.

But this time, Goshu had been sent north to put down a rebellion in the province of Tigré. The hunting party assembled in the palace courtyard. Paul rode near the front with the captain of the guards.

Yostos was displeased to see him.

'Why has he come?' he asked in a surly voice.

'The Kitzera always accompanies the king,' came the bland response.

They rode east into the mountains, climbing a succession of ever-higher valleys. The land grew greener as they went up. The ubiquitous thorn bushes gave way to wizened juniper trees, wild yellow roses and blood-red thistles.

Paul had hunted before. His father had taken him to the forests around their château when he was eight years old. He still remembered the rush of excitement, the baying of the hounds and the thrill of the big horse under him. They had brought the stag to bay, and Paul had shot it. He still remembered the expression on his father's face: the only time he had ever seen his father look proud of him. Then Paul saw the blood leaking out of the deer and burst into tears. His father had ridden off in disgust. His mother had refused to serve the venison at her table, and given the carcass to the gamekeepers instead.

How did that squeamish boy become an executioner? he wondered, as he rode.

It was not that he was immune to his victims' suffering. The twist of the noose, the crack of the windpipe – these were things that still had the capacity to fill him with horror. But horror would not keep him alive. He felt his soul had been divided, like an old house cut up into tenements. Any feelings of remorse or anguish he had, he kept them locked deep out of sight.

Endure anything, say anything, become anything.

Was this what she had meant?

Paul did not have high hopes for the sport that day. He rode through the grass, paying more attention to the scenery than to the game. His presence was ceremonial. Normally he would have kept close to the king, but Yostos's glowering figure made it clear he was not wanted there. He drifted away, keeping the royal standard in sight through the trees but otherwise left on his own.

It was a hot afternoon. He dismounted and tethered his horse so he could walk in the shade under the atwat trees that lined the river gorge. It was the first time he had left the palace in weeks, away from its stifled world of plots and terror. The sense of freedom disoriented him.

Down in the gorge, an ibis flew low over the river. Paul saw its silhouette against the sparkling water, its feet tucked back and the long, curving bill. A tremor went through him. Was it an omen from the god? What did it signify?

Then he saw the blood.

It was a drop at first, smeared on a leaf. Then he saw another, and another – dark streaks on the earth. He followed the trail, noting the bent grass and broken sticks where something heavy had been dragged along the ground. The trail ended after about twenty paces in a patch of long grass amid a thicket of trees.

The king was not the only hunter in the valley that day. Someone – or something – had killed a young nyala. It must have been surprised when it went to the river to drink, then been brought to the clearing.

Flies swarmed around it, darting between the vultures who were feeding greedily. The nyala could not have been dead long, but already there were white bones showing through the gore and torn flesh.

One of the vultures saw Paul's shadow and lifted its head. Its face was smeared with blood, and a string of sinew hung from its beak. Its beady eyes watched him jealously, one scavenger regarding another.

Paul was about to leave when something made him hesitate. A sensation he knew well: the feeling of danger. Living in the palace, a whim away from death at any moment, had made him acutely sensitive to it. Slowly, he turned his head in a wide arc.

Adrenaline heightened his senses. His eyes caught every leaf and blade of grass around him. Even then, he almost missed the predator. It lay stretched out on the branch of a juniper tree, its mottled coat almost impossible to tell apart from the dappled shadow of the leaves.

It was a leopard. Paul had never seen one in the wild, but the king had their skins all over his palace. It was a noble animal. Stretched out on its branch, it looked to be more than six feet long. It must be strong to have dragged the nyala from the river gorge. Now it was asleep, sated from its meal.

Paul was only a few dozen yards away. He had his gun: he could easily have shot it that moment, claimed a noble animal. But that would have been his death warrant. Only the king could hunt this majestic game.

If Paul brought the king to it, he might be rewarded. But he was now a long distance from the main hunting party. Sound echoed off the cliffs that hemmed them in, and made it hard to tell where they were. Most likely, they had ridden further up the valley, on the far side of the river gorge.

The ravine was steep and treacherous. It would take Paul the best part of an hour to reach its head. If he managed to cross it, he might be in time to find the king before the leopard woke.

A warm breeze rustled the grass. Dry branches chattered; the sheregrig birds screeched their crow-like cries. And in the woods beyond the clearing, something chimed like a bell.

It would have been so easy to ignore it. A stone falling, an unknown bird call; maybe something he'd imagined. But again, Paul's instincts were alerted. He dropped low in the grass and crawled behind a bush. He lifted his head and peered through the foliage.

For a few moments, nothing happened. Then the leaves rippled, and a large beast pushed through the long grass. Not the leopard, nor a lion nor an elephant – it was a jet-black horse, shod and bridled, with a rider in the saddle. He was followed by another, then a large column of men.

They were soldiers, but not any of the king's men that Paul had ever seen. Each man carried a long, leaf-headed spear and a square oxhide shield. They wore hats made of grey colobus monkey skins, with the tails hanging down their backs. Their horses' hooves had cloths tied around them, and they rode with rope bridles that would not jingle.

They had not seen Paul. If they had, he would surely be dead already. But they were heading for the bush where he was hiding. If he broke cover, they would see him at once. If he stayed where he was, they would ride right past him.

Paul had seconds to decide. There was only one explanation for why the men were here: they had come to kill the king. They would probably succeed. The king had twenty men with him; Paul counted at least a hundred soldiers approaching him. They handled their weapons with the easy confidence of practised killers.

Paul was not loyal to the king. He would happily have abandoned the monarch, if it saved his own life. But what if the king survived the ambush? Or if he did not, and the soldiers captured Paul – he was the king's own executioner. He knew what they would do to him.

A shout sounded from the head of the column. They must have seen him. Hiding was futile now. If Paul showed himself, perhaps he could at least hope for a quick death.

But as he rose, he realised none of the soldiers were looking his way. He had forgotten the leopard. The smell of the horses had woken the big cat. It leaped down from the branch where it had been sleeping and confronted the column, legs splayed, hackles back. It growled.

The sound terrified the horses. One reared up, nearly throwing its rider. Another shied away and knocked into its neighbour. Down the line, men fought to control their mounts. Some horses veered into thorn trees, foaming with pain as the long spikes drew blood.

The leopard bolted and vanished into the grass. Paul did the same. Keeping as low as he could, he scuttled across the open ground and into the trees at the edge of the ravine. No one saw him. As soon as the trees screened him, he picked himself up and ran.

He edged around a bend in the gully, where a rock outcrop hid him, and paused for breath. The trees muffled the sound of the horses, but he could hear the riders wrestling them under control. Soon they would be moving again.

The ravine was too steep for horses to manage. To reach the king, they would have to ride around the end of it.

Again, Paul felt the weight of his own life hanging on his decision. If the king died, no one would look for Paul. He could slip away, forgotten. He knew from the merchants who visited court that there was an ocean somewhere to the east. If he could find it, he might yet return to civilisation.

But Paul had already lived through one revolution. He knew what happened when you killed a king. It would unleash a terrible slaughter, a reign of terror, and the palace would be its epicentre. Sana would be trapped in a bloodbath.

Paul would not leave Sana to die like his mother, like Abasi. To save her, he would have to save the king.

He plunged down the steep bank, slipping on the dry earth and tearing his clothes on thorns. In this season, the river was only a trickle. He stepped across and started to climb the far bank. This was steeper. He had to scrabble at tree roots and vines to haul himself up.

He found the king and Yostos in a clearing half a mile further up the valley. The king had brought down a kudu and was examining the carcass with delight. The chief huntsman had cut out the beast's heart for the king to eat, which had left a bloody ring smeared around his lips. It reminded Paul of the vultures he had seen.

'Your Majesty,' Paul gasped. His clothes were torn, his face streaked with earth. 'There are soldiers coming this way. I have seen them.'

He had spoken in Arabic. But before his words had been translated for the king, Yostos reacted.

'You lie,' he snarled. 'No one knows the king was coming to this place.' He turned to his father. 'The Kitzera is trying to provoke you into a trap.'

'If I lie, let the vultures devour my entrails,' said Paul, using the traditional formula.

'If you lie, I will cut out your guts and feed them to the vultures while you watch,' said Yostos.

He turned to his father and spoke urgently in Amharic.

The king remained so calm, Paul wondered if his warning had been translated correctly. But then: 'How many of these soldiers are there?'

'A hundred.'

As Paul described them, the suspicion on Yostos's face turned more serious.

'They are men of Tigré. My brother Goshu was supposed to have crushed them in battle.'

'Some must have got past him.'

'Perhaps.' Yostos's voice was brittle. 'The question is, what do we do?'

'Maybe Goshu will rescue us,' said Paul. 'If he has pursued them, he could fall upon their rear.'

'Goshu is certainly many miles away.' Yostos gave him an indecipherable look. 'We must look to the king's safety at once.'

Paul examined the terrain. On both sides of the valley, steep-sided cliffs rose high and sheer.

'Is there a pass at the head of the valley we can leave by?'

'There is no way out. The end of the valley closes like a sack.'

Suddenly it dawned on Paul that this was the perfect place for an ambush. Rather than saving himself by warning the king, he had walked deeper into the trap.

'How far away are they?'

Paul shrugged. 'I am surprised they are not here already.'

Yostos barked commands. The king's guard mounted up and began to form a line.

'What are you doing?' said Paul.

'Preparing for battle.'

'They will massacre you.'

They were on flat, open ground with nowhere to hide. The Tigréan cavalry could surround them and butcher them from every angle.

'Then we shall die a glorious death,' said Yostos.

Paul looked the prince in the eye. 'Is that what you want? A glorious death?'

'Do you have an alternative?'

Paul's mind was racing. The flat terrain brought back memories: outnumbered infantrymen facing a horde of superbly trained cavalry. He had seen this battle fought before, and by the greatest military genius of the age.

'Have your men dismount. Send the horses away.'

He hadn't expected the reaction he received. With a blur of motion, Yostos had a sword at his throat.

'Speak one more word of this treachery, and I will ensure you are the first to die. Is that why the Tigréans sent you ahead?'

'No!'

How to make him understand?

'Listen to me, if you want to live the next hour.' Paul spoke quickly. 'The Tigréans have horses, but they do not have guns. You do. I have seen the finest cavalry in the world charge an infantry square. It was like throwing grass in a fire.'

The soldiers had gathered around with their weapons levelled at Paul. Behind them, the king sat on his horse, immovable as stone. In the distance, Paul could see a plume of dust rising up on the edge of the forest. The ground started to tremble underfoot.

'They are coming. Do we fight among ourselves – or against them?'

Yostos stared at him. His pride ached to take military advice from this insolent, foreign, white-skinned slave.

But the younger sons of kings do not grow to adulthood without a will to survive. And though he had never left Gondar, he had an interest in the affairs of the world. He had heard stories from Arab traders of the white men, of their mighty ships and enormous armies that no man could withstand.

'If you are lying. If you fail—'

Paul laughed.

'You think because I am a slave, I do not value my life?'

The ground shook harder. The vibrations ran up his legs and into his body. Through the scrub, he could see the tips of spears shining bright in the sun.

Urgently, Paul gave his orders. When Yostos repeated them to the men, he thought they might mutiny. What he was suggesting was heresy to the proud warriors.

But they were disciplined men who had learned to obey their prince. They dismounted and sent their horses away. On Paul's orders, they formed a tight square two ranks deep, the front rank kneeling and the rear standing. The king stood in their midst with the royal standard. Compared with the squares Paul had seen at the Battle of the Pyramids, each a battalion strong, it was a feeble formation. It would have to be enough.

The first Tigréan riders burst out of the trees, the tails of their monkey-skin hats flying out behind them. Their captain was an enormous man, wrapped in a black ape skin so large it completely covered him. The animal's head was pulled over his helmet, with two giant canine teeth protruding down his face so that his head looked like a huge gaping jaw.

The captain paused when he saw the band of the king's men, knotted together on the open ground. Why had they dismounted? Surely it was a trap? Then his keen eyes picked out the king in the middle of the square. He opened his mouth, and let out a booming roar that echoed off the valley walls. His men dropped their reins, beat their spears against their shields, and shouted taunts and battle cries. This would be an easy victory.

The captain kicked his horse and charged forward. His men followed. The hard-baked earth shook like silk in a breeze under their hooves. Paul felt his teeth rattle inside his head. He scanned the sky for an ibis – any bird, some sign that the bird-headed god was watching him. But the sky was empty.

The riders swept towards them.

'Wait until they are in range,' Paul warned.

Yostos repeated the order.

The Tigréan cavalry lowered their spears. They were so close, Paul could see each face individually, fringed with monkey fur. Their line bunched together as they veered towards the narrow target.

'Fire.'

The front rank fired their muskets. At that range, even the Gondarians' antique weapons could not miss. Five horses collapsed in a spray of earth, causing chaos in the tight-packed line. Other horses were tripped or knocked down. Some screamed with the agony of snapped bones; others tried to get back up, and collided with the horses coming in behind.

They could afford the losses. The remaining riders knew the musketeers would not be able to reload in time. They kicked their horses harder and leaned forward, closing the gaps in the line.

It made an easier target for the second rank of musketeers. They fired on Paul's command, punching another hole in the cavalry line. The same bloody pantomime of tumbling men and horses played out a second time.

Now was the moment of reckoning. In Bonaparte's army, there would have been a third rank of men to sustain the barrage of fire, while those in the front rank reloaded. If the cavalry pushed home now, the king's men would be pulped under their hooves and spears.

The cavalry baulked. Paul's men were a far cry from the well-drilled machine of Bonaparte's army, but the Tigréan warriors had never faced such disciplined fire. The second volley had cut the heart out of their line. The survivors had a split second to decide which way to go. Instinct took over. They veered away from the infantry square, dividing around it like a river round a rock.

It seemed the safer option, a chance to regroup and come at the infantry from behind. They had never fought an enemy who formed up facing both ways before. As soon as they were past the square, they came into the line of fire of the men formed up to the rear. Two volleys crashed out, and another half a dozen riders went down before they saw who had shot them. The men panicked, galloping away until they were beyond the reach of the Gondarian bullets. By then the king's men had reloaded.

Clouds of dust and powder smoke swirled around the battlefield. Through it, Paul saw the Tigréan captain angrily rallying his men. Paul made a rough count, and his heart sank. The Gondarians had brought down twenty horses and riders, for not a single loss. A miraculous performance, but it still left them badly outnumbered. If one horse breached their line, it would open them up to be massacred.

Paul had never been a good soldier. He had spent Bonaparte's campaigns puking out his guts with terror. But he had absorbed more than he knew, and now, in the heat of battle, it came out like a piece of steel from the forge. Scanning the battlefield, a plan came into his head.

He explained it to Yostos, who passed the commands on to the men. There was no time for debate. The Tigréan cavalry had formed up again, this time in three compact lines. The captain left clear space between them, so that the men in the ranks behind would not be brought down by falling horses in front.

He means to use his men as a battering ram, Paul thought. *It does not matter how many die.*

The captain would sacrifice half his men, letting them soak up the musket volleys, if it meant a dozen got through.

From inside the shadow of his helmet, the captain barked the order to advance. It wasn't the calibrated manoeuvre of European cavalry, rising from a trot to a canter to a gallop: they came at full tilt from the moment they started moving. The riders howled their war cries and sat up in their saddles, aiming for the heart of the square. They would not deviate this time.

Wreathed in dust and screaming their blood-curdling cries, they made a terrifying sight. The stoutest soldier's nerve might have failed. The men of Gondar broke ranks and fled.

Paul ran with them, keeping close to the king. All was chaos and motion. The ground shook; the air swirled with sand; a cacophony of drumming hooves, shouts and screams filled his ears.

Paul glanced back through the dust. At the sight of the fleeing soldiers, the cavalry had lost their discipline. The rear lines spurred forward, not wanting to miss the slaughter. That forced the front row apart, until the squadron was stretched in a single ragged line across the battlefield.

Through the tumult, Paul found Yostos.

'Now!' he shouted in his ear.

'Now!' Yostos repeated it in Amharic. He had been raised to command since the day he was born; his voice cut through the din of battle so that every man heard it.

As one – just as Paul had prepared them to do – the Gondarian soldiers turned.

Probably, no army in Gondar had ever executed such a move. But Paul's tactical square had shown them how infantry could withstand cavalry, and that gave them confidence to follow his hastily given instructions now. The prospect of certain death if they failed did the rest. What had looked like a rout suddenly became a double line of armed men facing the onrushing cavalry.

The horsemen were so close the infantry didn't have to wait.

'Fire.'

The first row crashed out their shots.

'Fire.'

The second row did the same.

'Fire.'

Paul's heart sat still in his chest. Through the choking gun-smoke, he could see the shapes of horsemen still coming at them. If the soldiers could not reload in time . . .

A third volley of musket fire crashed along the line, less concerted – some of the men were slower than others – but no less deadly. The cavalry's spears and oxhide shields were no protection.

'Advance!' Paul shouted. The old commands came back to him as if he was breathing them through the clouds of gunpowder. 'Five paces and fire.'

Again, Yostos relayed the order above the battle noise. A spear flew out of the smoke and skewered the man beside him, but the prince didn't flinch. His shoulders were set apart, his head raised proud as he faced the oncoming enemy.

The soldiers advanced, fired and advanced again. Deeper into the battlefield, they could not hold their line; they had to step around the dying men and horses they had brought down. Paul saw one soldier knocked unconscious by a kick from a horse, lying on its back and flailing its legs on the ground. More gaps opened in the line, and he began to see how foolhardy the advance had been. Tight formation was all that had saved them from the cavalry so far; they had lost that advantage. Even after the slaughter, the Tigréans had the numbers to overwhelm the king's guard with one final charge.

But they were broken. The bravest men, in the front, had been cut down. The rest were disorientated. Faced with soldiers who advanced when they should be fleeing, they began to fall back. The captain raged and bellowed, but they were in the grip of panic. There was nothing he could do. If he stayed any longer, he would be alone and exposed.

With a howl of despair, he turned his horse and spurred away down the valley. Paul watched him go, the black animal skin flying out behind him like wings.

Paul had won.

While the soldiers looted the corpses of the fallen, Paul found the king. His aloofness had not survived the battle. When he saw Paul, he threw his arms around him, kissed his cheeks, and spoke at him in a stream of earnest, heartfelt words.

'He says he did not know that the Kitzera was a mighty general,' Yostos translated. For the first time, Paul saw respect in the prince's eyes. 'I did not know that either.'

All his life, Paul had wanted to avoid attention. Often, his survival had depended on it. He had downplayed any achievement, shunned praise. But he knew modesty would not serve him well now.

'I fought with the greatest Frankish general in history.'

He did not have to say anything else. The proof of what he claimed was in the dying men around them. The respect in Yostos's eyes deepened.

'It was God's will you were here today.' He looked as if he was about to say more, then changed his mind. 'We will speak further when we return to the palace.'

Something soft and wet struck Paul's cheek. When he touched his face, his hand came away smeared with blood. Had he been hurt? But there was no wound.

He looked down to see what had hit him. It was a piece of flesh, about the shape and length of a finger, oozing blood into the ground from the stump where it had been hacked off.

It was too thick to be a finger.

Another one struck him, then another. The soldiers had gathered around and were throwing body parts at him like flower petals. They rained down on Paul, Yostos and the king, leaving bloody marks on their skin and clothes.

They were the penises and testicles of the enemies who had been killed – or, judging by the screams, enemies who were not yet dead. The victorious soldiers had hacked them off as trophies and showered them over their king. Paul felt a familiar churning in his stomach. Something was rising in his gorge; he tried to hold it in, but it was impossible.

It burst out: a rolling laugh so loud it stopped the soldiers from their butchery. He couldn't stop. The scene was obscenely ridiculous, there was no other response. Yostos caught his eye, and then the king, and soon all three of them were crying tears of mirth.

Many of the Tigréan cavalry had died in the fighting. Those who survived the battle didn't survive the aftermath. By the time the Gondarians had taken their trophies, only one man on the battlefield remained alive. They bound his hands and feet and threw him over the saddle of a dead man's horse. Then, smeared in the blood of dead men's genitals, the victorious hunting party bounded away.

The king had hunting lodges and estates nearby where they could have rested, but he insisted on riding hard back to Gondar. When the sun set, they made torches from dry branches to light their way. Sap boiled out of the wood and spat burning gobs of resin that scalded their hands and faces.

They reached the palace after midnight. Normally it would have been dark, only a sentry's lamp in the gatehouse, but that night it was ablaze with lights and the bustle of men and horses camped in the imperial compound. The palace, in the centre, looked like a building under siege.

'I do not like this,' said Yostos. 'We should withdraw.'

'A ruler does not fear his own subjects.' The king shook his head emphatically. 'Rumours run faster than the leopard. The men must see their king is alive, or who knows what they may believe.'

Yostos looked grim-faced as they rode through the city to the castle. He was more disconsolate when they found the great gates locked against them. Before the column had halted, two guards appeared on the gatehouse. Light from their torches coloured the battlements orange, and reflected angrily on the barrels of the muskets they carried.

'Is he dead?' they called. And then, recognition dawning, 'Who are you?'

'This is King Salomon of Gondar,' said Yostos angrily. 'Open the gates.'

Urgent whispers drifted down from the wall. With the creak of a windlass, the gates swung open. A guard captain, summoned in haste and still buckling on his armour, saluted them.

'What is happening?' Yostos asked him. 'What is this army?'

'Prince Goshu, your brother, has returned from his campaign earlier than expected.' The captain swallowed. 'There was a rumour . . .'

'What rumour?'

'That the king had died in a hunting accident.'

'As you can see, he is very much alive. Praise God.'

'Praise God.'

They passed through the gates. Paul wanted to slip back to his room, to wash and eat and sleep. The aftermath of the battle had left him an empty husk. But a stern look from Yostos said he was not excused yet. He followed the company as the king rode his horse to the palace building, up the steps and into the throne room.

Goshu was standing by the throne, surrounded by a knot of his men. The cushion on the throne was indented, as if someone had been sitting on it only a moment earlier.

'Thank God you are alive, Father.' His voice was warm with emotion. 'We heard terrible rumours.' His eyes flickered across to Yostos. 'And my brother, I rejoice you are unhurt.'

A servant came running with a footstool so the king could dismount. Another servant hastened to his side and fanned him with an ostrich feather. The king lounged back in his throne.

'How did you fare in your campaign against Tigré?' He asked it as casually as enquiring about the weather.

'A glorious victory.' Goshu gave a tight smile. 'Actually, it was not so glorious. The men of Tigré are cowards, they folded almost the moment they saw my army.'

He laughed at his own joke. The king did not share it.

'Not all the men of Tigré are such cowards. A company of them ambushed me on the hunt and nearly killed us all.'

The sweat on Goshu's face shone gold in the torchlight.

'Praise be to God that you survived. But, my father, I swear to you that none of the men of Tigré could have escaped the trap I set them. They must have come from elsewhere.'

'See for yourself.'

On the king's command, two guards brought forward the man they had taken captive. He still wore his armour, and the colobus monkey skin on his head. After riding so far with his private parts amputated, it was a miracle he had not bled to death.

Goshu's eyes widened. 'This was one of the men who attacked you?'

Yostos threw the man to the ground. He pulled off the monkey skin hat and held him up by his long hair.

'Tell the king who sent you.'

The man never answered. In a single blurred movement, quick as a striking adder, Goshu drew his sword and swept it in a lethal arc. Paul's brain was still processing what it had seen when the prisoner's body toppled sideways and slumped to the floor. The severed head dangled from Yostos's hand like an apple from a tree. Goshu's blade must have come within a hair's breadth of his brother, yet there was not even a nick in his robes.

'Let this be a warning to any man who attacks my father!' shouted Goshu.

'You should have left him for the Kitzera,' said the king mildly. 'There is much he might have told us.'

Yostos hurled the head away. It bounced and rolled down the steps. The blood spouting from the corpse's neck puddled around the prince's feet, but he did not move.

'To fight off a company of Tigréan cavalry with only a hunting party is no easy feat,' said Goshu. 'May I ask how you accomplished this miracle?'

'The Kitzera. He organised our men in the Frankish way, a way the cavalry could not defeat.'

'Indeed?'

Goshu's searching gaze found Paul in the shadows where he had been hiding. It was not the look of a grateful son, but a serpent sizing up a mouse. The naked sword dripped blood on the floor.

'We will speak more of this tomorrow.'

His tone said Paul would not enjoy the conversation.

Paul's misgivings only rose when a chamberlain came next morning and summoned him to the palace. The audience chamber was empty; the court had not assembled. The blood from the night before had been mopped up, but some must have soaked into the floor cracks. Flies buzzed as Paul followed the chamberlain through a door into the east wing of the palace.

'Where are you taking me? Where is the king?'

The chamberlain said nothing, but hurried on. Down a dark passage, up a flight of stairs and to a pair of mahogany doors embossed with golden lions. Paul had never been here, but he knew the design. It was Goshu's emblem.

The door swung open as if by magic. The chamberlain ushered Paul in.

Goshu's apartments were as luxurious as befitted the heir to the empire. The floors were covered in carpets from Arabia, the furniture inlaid with ivory and upholstered with silks. A giant leopard skin draped the biggest bed Paul had ever seen. There was an icon of the Virgin Mary on one wall, and a pair of crossed spears on another.

But it was not Goshu waiting for Paul – it was Yostos. He strode forward and embraced him like a son.

'The hero of the hour!' he exclaimed. 'The man who saved my father's life, and mine.'

'Where is Goshu?'

'My father has sent my brother away from court,' said Yostos, not attempting to hide the triumph in his voice. 'He will be gone some time. As he will not be needing his apartments, my father – in recognition for your service yesterday – has given them for your use.'

'Mine?'

'You have been promoted. You are now a general of his armies. You will teach all his men to fight in the Frankish way. These quarters befit your new rank. I think you will find them comfortable.' He led Paul through a door into a second room. 'And the view is magnificent.'

He winked. It was true that the windows gave a splendid view over the walls, across the valley to the church on the hill opposite – but that wasn't what Paul saw. Ten young female slaves were lined up for his inspection. They wore loosely draped robes which revealed curves and full hips. They giggled and curtsied at Paul.

'They are your servants,' said Yostos. His voice left no doubt as to the services they would perform.

'Why so many?'

The chamberlain had followed them in behind.

'You are important, now,' he said, not without a trace of jealousy. 'A man of your dignity needs many servants.'

'Where is Sana? The girl who served me?'

'It has pleased the king to find her new employment.'

Yostos dismissed it with a wave. A servant girl was beneath his interest, and Paul knew enough about the ways of the palace not to push the question. Here, to care about anyone was to hand your enemies a weapon against you. Showing what Sana meant to him would only put her in danger.

'Does this mean I am no longer the Kitzera?'

The tarades felt like manacles around his wrists, chaining him to his horrific task. He longed to be free.

Yostos smiled. 'No.'

'But—'

'Your role as general is in addition to your responsibilities as the king's executioner.'

'Surely there are others who could serve as Kitzera.'

'Many others. And not a man among them who is not bound either to me, or to my brother.' Yostos touched one of the spears on the wall, testing the point with his thumb. 'If my father appointed a new executioner, he would have to favour one or the other.'

'Am I so important?' Paul wondered.

'The Kitzera is the most powerful man at court. He decides who dies quickly without revealing his secrets, and who lingers until he has told everything he knows. Goshu would not accept my placeman in that position – nor I his.'

Paul thought about that.

'I do not feel powerful.'

Yostos laughed. 'Neither does my father. But men still tremble when he speaks.'

He crooked his head. He seemed to be waiting for Paul to say something, though Paul could not guess what.

'It was lucky you were with us yesterday. Some say a miracle.' Paul started to demur, but Yostos continued in a harder voice, 'Almost too good to be true.'

There was no mistaking his meaning. Paul edged back. He put his hand out to steady himself and touched a sumptuous silk cushion.

'Some men say nobody could have rallied the guards as you did. Nobody could have fought off so many cavalry . . . unless he knew they were coming.'

'How could I have known?'

'Perhaps my brother Goshu arranged everything. Perhaps he wanted you to rise higher in the king's favour.'

'Why would he want that?'

'Everyone knows you are my brother's man.'

Paul shook his head. 'I serve . . . I serve the king.'

Yostos gripped his shoulders and looked deep into his eyes, searching for any sign of deceit. Paul had felt the same helpless terror when Goshu put the noose around his neck. His life was out of his hands.

'I believe you,' said Yostos. 'I saw the terror in your eyes in the battle. But Goshu has spoken to you?'

Paul nodded.

'He told you that I wish to usurp the crown?'

Paul couldn't deny it. To his surprise, Yostos burst out laughing.

'How could I betray the king? Even if I did not love him as my own life, my father is the only man who protects me from Goshu's jealousy. The moment he dies, Goshu will be king. Then he will summon you, Kitzera, to put your bull-hide cord around my neck.'

Paul saw the sense in what he was saying.

'Then why did your brother tell me . . .?'

'Because being the heir is not enough for him.' Yostos gave a grim smile. 'A month after I was born, my nurse found me asleep with a scorpion crawling over my face. She removed it, but the next day, she found another. Day after day, similar *accidents* – it was only by the grace of God I did not die a dozen times. At last she found out why. My brother was trapping them in the garden and dropping them in my cradle. He was two years old.

'Since the day I was born, he has seen me as a threat. He fears that my father will one day prefer me over him. He does everything he can to destroy me.'

Yostos stretched his arm out and took a spear down from the wall.

'But that is not his true aim. Who do you think sent those Tigréan warriors yesterday? Who had his army ready to seize the kingdom? He was already taking his seat on the throne when we returned.' He turned suddenly. 'He told you I wanted to kill the king? Maybe he even believes it. But the thought comes so easily to him because that is what he intends himself.'

'But now his treachery has been revealed,' said Paul. 'The king has banished him.'

'For now. Goshu's lies have poisoned our father's mind too deeply. He does not trust Goshu, but he does not trust me either. He will not send Goshu far. But you . . .' He jabbed the spear towards Paul. 'You he trusts absolutely. You must watch closely for any sign that Goshu is moving against him again. In the meantime, you will train the king's armies in your Frankish way of fighting – so that when Goshu strikes again, as he assuredly will, we are ready for him.'

He held the spear level, its point aimed at Paul's belly.

'Do I have your loyalty? For the king's sake?'

What else could Paul say?

'Of course.'

After Yostos had gone, Paul dismissed the servants and lay on the bed. He wrapped himself in the leopard skin to feel the animal's strength around him. He remembered the animal on the hunt. If he had not seen it, he would almost certainly be dead.

All the luxury of his surroundings could not hide the fact that this was a cage. He was trapped with three fearsome predators – Goshu, Yostos and the king.

And I have sworn loyalty to all of them, he thought miserably.

He worried for Sana, but could not think how to find her without raising suspicion. Inevitably, she found him first. He didn't hear the door open, but suddenly she was there on the bed, playing with one of the leopard skin paws.

'How did you get here?' He sat up. 'Where did you go?'

Sana looked around. 'I like your new room. It's bigger.'

'I preferred the old one. And where have you been?'

Sana slid off the bed and started examining the icon on the wall.

'The royal nursery. For the king's children,' she added, when she saw Paul didn't understand. 'I play with them. He has a very fat baby.'

'A baby?'

'Did you think the king has only two sons?' Sana wrinkled her nose, condescending as only a child could be. 'He has many children.'

'How many?'

Sana shrugged. 'Very many.' Numbers were a vague concept for her. 'They used to live on a mountain,' she volunteered. 'Now he keeps them in a castle. Over the hill.'

'I have never seen them. Why do they never come to the palace?'

'Because they are in the castle.' Again, she was impatient that he did not understand. 'Like a prison,' she added. 'They cannot go out.'

Paul felt a pang of compassion. He was not the only one in a cage. What must it be like for those children? Their lives were nothing, no better than spare candles, to be locked in a cupboard unless they were needed.

'I do not think the king likes his children,' said Sana.

Paul looked at Goshu's monogram carved into the bedstead. He wondered what would happen if the owner returned and found that his younger brother had installed Paul in his apartments.

'Who can blame the king?' he murmured.

But Sana was peering into the dead leopard's mouth and didn't hear him.

*

After the day of the hunt, the court changed. It had always been a harsh place: now it was brutal. It reminded Paul of Paris in the Terror, blood in the air and the threat of violence rumbling constantly like a thunderhead. It could strike at any moment. Paul was worked harder than ever – so many executions that his dreams could not hold the ghosts of all the men he had killed.

Another fact he learned: there was no sensation so extreme or terrible that repetition would not dull it eventually. He finally understood the words the god had whispered to him in the temple. *To master life, you must hold it as light as a feather.* In the depths of the night, when the alcohol had worn off and the girls had gone and the cellar doors in his soul creaked with all the ghosts inside hammering to be let out, he repeated it to himself like an incantation. Trying to convince himself that what he did was the god's work.

He was glad Sana was not there to see what he had become.

The rest of his time, he was kept busy on the parade ground. He had been given a shirt of gilded chain mail, a lion-skin cloak and a helmet capped with ostrich plumes. He looked foolish and felt more so: the feeblest private in Bonaparte's army drilling a thousand men at a time. He wondered what Sergeant Bastiat would say if he could see him.

At first the power frightened him. Then he got used to it, and that was almost more frightening: a life of unrestrained authority, brutal violence and sensual pleasure. Once, a memory came back to him: the alley in Cairo, aiming the pistol at the soldiers who meant to rape Abasi. He remembered the intoxicating rush of power, of being able to bend a man to his will or end his life.

This was nothing like that. Even if he had revelled in his work, even if he had not simply been a slave to the king, there was still a fear he could not shake: Goshu. Paul had taken more than the exiled prince's rooms; he had taken his life. His legions, his authority, even his chair beside the king at dinner. But Goshu was still alive. As much as Paul tried to convince himself otherwise, deep down he knew the prodigal son would return eventually. The court's iron law of gravity demanded it. One son could not fall without the other rising, and the king would not accept Yostos becoming too powerful. Paul was a placeholder, keeping Goshu's bed warm. He had no illusions what Goshu would do to him when he returned.

The question gnawed at Paul until it consumed him. Every day, he watched the king's mood, saw how he became irritable and difficult with Yostos. Every day brought Goshu's return one day closer.

Yostos had noticed it, too. He came to Paul's apartments one afternoon, alone and unannounced.

'The king is uneasy,' he said. 'The attendants in his bedchamber say he does not sleep well.'

Paul knew that. He had bribed the king's servants for news as well.

'A ruler needs his sleep,' Yostos continued. 'It is in our dreams that the Lord speaks to us. If a king does not hear the voice of God, how can he rule wisely?'

Paul looked into the distance and kept quiet. Yostos took out a small leather pouch filled with dried herbs.

'I got these from a wise woman. She says they will help my father sleep. You must give them to him.'

He held out the bag. Paul could smell the scent wafting out of it, bitter and dark. He knew he could not reject an order from the prince. Even so, he did not rush to take the bag. His arm felt as if he was reaching for a snake.

'I have begged my father to take a draught to help him sleep, but he refuses. At dinner tonight, you must sprinkle these on his food when no one is looking.'

'Why me, lord?'

Yostos looked sad. 'I fear he does not trust me as much as he once did. If he caught his son adding unknown herbs to his food, he would take it . . . badly. But you, he does not suspect.'

Paul understood perfectly well. If the king caught him, Yostos would deny all knowledge and Paul would meet the fate he had given so many others.

He took the bag, praying he would not get caught.

'Just to help him sleep?' he repeated.

'Just to help him sleep.'

The banquet that night was a celebration – Paul didn't know of what. The hall was brightly lit with many fires. Warrior shields were mounted on the wall, with their plumes hanging down. Low round tables had been set about the hall like beads on a necklace. At each table, a man and a woman sat in a pair. The woman's role was to feed the man.

The meal was raw beef – so raw, in fact, that Paul could see the muscle fibres still twitching in it. The butchers cut it from the cow while it was still living, a custom Paul could not get used to. The woman at his side used a thin knife to cut the steak into strips, then crossways to make small cubes. She wrapped it in a piece of flatbread, and powdered it with salt and fiery red pepper, then wrapped the bread into a roll and fed it to Paul in a single mouthful.

It was succulent, but Paul hardly tasted it. His hand kept going to the little bag under his tunic. He felt its presence like a hot coal against his skin.

'Just to help him sleep,' he repeated to himself.

Under all his finery and his diadem, the king looked haggard. Goshu's exile had not reduced the factions at court – if anything, it had intensified them.

Paul took another roll in his mouth and made a sour face.

'This meat is no good,' he complained. 'Go and tell the servants only to cut it from the tenderest flank.'

The woman scurried to obey. As soon as she was gone, Paul reached inside his tunic, pretending he was scratching an itch. When his hand came out, the little bag was invisible within it. He sprinkled it quickly over the next piece of flatbread, then hastily hid the bag under the table.

He knew he should not catch anyone's eye, but still he kept looking around the room. If anyone had seen him, this was the moment they would challenge him. However innocent the powder, what he had done would taint him with unshakeable suspicion.

But no one had seen him. The king was deep in conversation with Yostos; the other courtiers were busy devouring their meals or fondling the serving girls. On the flatbread, the finely ground powder was almost invisible among the pepper.

The girl returned with a fresh piece of meat dripping blood. Paul watched while she diced it and spread it over the bread.

'Take that to the king, with my compliments.'

The woman flushed. This was an honour. Paul watched her cross the hall and bow to the king. She presented him with the roll. The king glanced over to Paul and said something that made the woman laugh, a joke of some kind.

She popped the roll into his mouth. The king, well used to these affairs, swallowed it almost whole.

'He is pleased with you,' the woman told Paul when she returned. 'He says he will give you estates by Lake Tana.'

She began to prepare another roll for Paul. Paul glanced at Yostos, sitting on the king's far side. But he was talking to the man on his left, and gave no sign he had noticed Paul.

'Here,' said the woman, feeding Paul another roll.

He bit into it. Blood oozed out of the fresh meat and dribbled down his chin onto his hands.

Paul ate and drank. He took the girl to his room and used her until he was bored. He lay awake; he thought about calling the girl back but could not muster the desire. He wished he had some of the herbs he had given the king to help him sleep, but he had burned the bag.

At last he fell asleep. In his dream, he was drawing the noose around the king's neck, but however hard he pulled, the king would not die. Yostos and Goshu urged him on, surrounded by the ghosts of all the men he had killed. Their eyes had become hunks of raw beef, bleeding down their cheeks. A sharp-billed ibis flew overhead.

Suddenly Paul was being shaken awake. His hand was reaching for the knife under his pillow when he recognised Yostos's face, eyes and teeth gleaming white in the darkness.

'What–?'

'My father is dead.'

Paul stared at him, uncomprehending. Was this still part of his dream?

'He died in his sleep.'

Cold terror gripped Paul's soul.

'You do not think . . . the herbs . . .?'

He already knew the answer. He had known it since Yostos handed him the bag, though he had refused to admit it to himself.

Yostos knew it, too. He leaped on Paul, seized him by the throat and pressed him against the bed.

'Never speak of that again,' he hissed. 'If anyone found out you had doctored the king's food the night that he died, you know what they would do to you? They would strip your skin off your body, inch by inch while you were still alive, then stuff it with straw and hang it from a tree as a warning. Shall I let them?'

His hands were so tight around Paul's neck he could hardly gasp out the answer.

'No, Lord.'

'Good.' Yostos let go and swung himself off the bed. His body quivered with coiled energy, like a big cat preparing to pounce. 'Do not forget it.'

Paul tasted blood in his throat. 'What happens now?'

'As he lay dying, my father whispered in my ear that he wished me to succeed him. He said my brother Goshu is not worthy to be king. Will you aid me in fulfilling my father's dying wish?'

The words were clearly rehearsed. Probably, Yostos had already said them more than once that evening. He did not wait for Paul to reply.

'My brother believes he is the heir, and he has many allies. As soon as he hears the news, he will rush to the palace to claim the throne. You know what he will do to you if that happens.'

Paul felt his skin crawl.

'Our only hope is to act quickly. I must proclaim my kingship, secure the succession and ensure there are no traitors who would betray me to my brother. There is a task you must do for me.'

'Anything,' said Paul.

Yostos pointed out of the window. 'On the far side of that hill, there is a fortress surrounded by acacia trees. Go to it.'

'I know it.'

It was where Sana lived, taking care of the children in the royal nursery.

'Kill everyone you find there.'

Paul stumbled out of bed and dressed quickly. Out of habit, he picked up the tarades to wrap around his wrists – then dropped them like burning irons as he imagined putting them around the necks of the children in the castle.

If he did not go, Yostos would kill him. The prince would send other men to the castle, and they would murder everyone, Sana included.

If he went, he would be a mass murderer of children. Even in his busy career as Kitzera, that was one atrocity he had avoided.

He glanced wildly around the room. His gaze alighted on the carved ibis, watching him down its beak from a shelf by the window. *To master life, you must hold it as light as a feather.*

He knew what he had to do. He went to the stables and saddled a horse. The imperial compound was dark, but he could hear scuttling and whispering, punctuated by the occasional scream, as if the palace had been infested with rats. Probably even now, men were being dragged from their beds and butchered – anyone who was suspected of disloyalty to the new regime.

The gates were barred and guarded by over a hundred men from one of Yostos's companies. They let Paul through without a challenge. He heard hoof beats and, turning back, saw that four riders had followed him out. They fell in behind him, neither closing nor falling back, but always there, like shadows.

Even with his escort, there was relief in being out of the claustrophobic palace, in the cool of the night. The horse was a comfort, the familiar smell and the steady rhythm rising and falling beneath him. Until he remembered where it was taking him: then the clop of its hooves sounded like the drums beating victims to the guillotine.

Some of the children were only babies; most were younger than Sana. Could he really put the noose around their necks and pull it tight?

He could not answer the question. Not because it was so abhorrent, but because – in his heart of hearts – he did not dare admit the sickening truth.

But what then? He began to understand the remorseless logic of Yostos's plan. Yostos had used Paul to kill his father, and now to murder any other claimant to the throne. Paul was the only living witness to his crimes, and that made him a threat.

He knew how Yostos dealt with threats to his power.

A lion roared in the night. Hyenas cackled, knowing that when the lions hunted they would not go hungry. An owl, perched in the dry branches of an acacia tree, watched Paul pass with its wide feathered eyes.

If Paul disobeyed his orders, Yostos would kill him. And if he carried them out, Yostos would kill him.

He had run out of time. He came around the hill to a fork in the road and there, off to the left, was the castle. Its turrets rose from a thicket of trees, silhouetted against the starlit sky. From one of the windows, he heard the wailing of a sleepless baby, and the soft song of a nursemaid lulling it back to sleep.

There was a gatehouse, but the guards were absent and the gate was unlocked. Was that carelessness, or had they been warned? Paul tethered his horse to a ring in the wall and slipped through. The four horsemen followed him. The baby had stopped crying; a hush had descended on the palace.

Paul crossed the threshold into a square courtyard ringed with a colonnade.

'Sana?'

A shadow uncurled itself by one of the pillars and rose. It was not Sana but an old man, hair white against his dark skin and no teeth. He shrank back, eyes wide, when he saw Paul and the men who accompanied him.

'Sana?' Paul repeated.

The old man nodded. He limped away and did not return. Probably, he was hiding under a bed and hoping whatever was about to happen would pass over him. But a moment later, Sana emerged silently from the darkness.

'Kitzera?' It was what she always called him, even when they were alone.

'Wake the household. I want every person, even the youngest, out here in this courtyard.'

It seemed to take forever for the household to assemble. Tousle-haired children clutching blankets; babies suckling their nurses' breasts or cradled in their mothers' arms. There was a stoop-backed old man whose blank eyes told of a lifetime in captivity. He seemed familiar, until with a jolt Paul realised he looked like the dead king. Maybe a brother? There were adolescent boys with spindly limbs who would never lead an army into battle, and young women in the full ripeness of youth who would never marry or bear children. Almost forty in all, the widespread branches of a family tree that now needed brutal pruning.

What sort of lives had they lived, forever confined in this castle? Perhaps death would be a mercy for them.

'Tell them that the king is dead,' he said to Sana.

He saw the fear flare in their eyes. The knot of people shrank, huddling together like a herd of antelope scenting the lion. Children who were old enough to know what it meant began to cry, while those who were too young to understand clutched their siblings' hands.

'Yostos is the king. He has given me a message for each of them. I will see them one by one to deliver it.'

He found a small room off the courtyard, empty except for a chest and two stools. Without being told, two of the soldiers came in with him, while two others stayed outside to guard the gate.

Sana came, too. As soon as the door was shut, the two guards grabbed her and pinned her down to the chair. She shrieked and tried to bite them, but one of the guards struck her across the face, leaving a bloody welt on her lip.

'No!' shouted Paul. 'I need her to translate for me. She dies last.'

He didn't know how much the guards understood his pidgin Amharic, but he got his meaning across. The guards released Sana.

'There was a young man in there, about eighteen,' said Paul. 'I will start with him.'

Sana, who had taken herself to huddle in a corner, translated. The guards nodded at the sense of his suggestion. One left to bring in the first victim; the other stayed. They must have had orders never to let Paul out of their sight.

Sana sat in the corner. Her eyes blazed at Paul.

'You remember Sergeant Bastiat?' Paul said to her in Arabic.

The door opened and closed. The guard dragged in the youth Paul had seen, a skinny frame with light brown skin and bushy hair. He would have been handsome, if not for the fear disfiguring his face. He was carrying a small child, perhaps a younger brother or cousin. Paul frowned. That would not make it any easier.

The guards pushed the prince onto the stool and held his arms. Sana took the child he had been holding. Paul could see the prince trying to keep up his courage – he was a royal child, after all – but his lip trembled and a tear escaped down his cheek.

Paul stood behind the prisoner and unwound the tarade. He flexed the bull-hide, snapping it so loudly that the young prince gave an involuntary cry. The little boy began wailing piteously from the corner where Sana had put him. Paul wished Sana would quiet him, but she was standing with her fists clenched at her side, her gaze fixed on Paul. Paul shut her out. This was already hard enough.

'Get on with it,' said the guard. 'We will be here all night.'

Paul nodded.

My star is already falling.

A day earlier, the guard would have been straight on the execution block if he had spoken to the Kitzera with so little respect.

Paul fed the tail of the tarade through the loop in the end to make a noose. He wanted to say sorry for what he was about to do, but he was long past apologising.

'In the name of the king,' he murmured.

The tarade had grown so familiar over the past months, the hide was almost an extension of his arm. With a casual flick of his wrist, the noose sailed through the air and settled around the guard's neck. Paul yanked the cord tight with such expert technique that the man's windpipe snapped.

'What—?'

The second guard was holding the prince down with both hands. That cost precious moments before he could reach the knife he wore. By the time his hand touched his belt, the knife was not there. It was buried in his side, with Sana's hand on the hilt. The guard stared at the knife, at Sana, and at the blood spilling out of him. Then, with a roar of pain and a spurt of fresh blood, he tugged the knife out and lunged at her.

He never reached her. Paul had already whipped the noose off the dead man and flung it over the bleeding guard's head. It brought him up short, out of reach of Sana. Before the guard could turn, Paul put his foot against his opponent's back and kicked him forward. At the same time, he yanked back on the tarade. Two powerful and opposing motions worked through the guard's body and met in his neck. His neck snapped and he lolled to the floor.

The child in the corner had stopped whimpering and was gaping at the scene before him with wide-eyed wonder. The young man on the stool looked just as surprised.

'Quick,' said Paul.

They dragged the two guards where they would be hidden behind the door and mopped up some of the blood with the dead men's tunics. The room was so dark the stain was not obvious.

'Get the other two guards. Tell them to bring the next victim,' Paul told Sana.

No one suspected a waif-like slave girl of treachery. The two guards entered the room and quickly met the same fate as their predecessors as Paul wielded the tarade and Sana her knife.

The prince looked at Paul with something like awe.

'Who are you?' he mumbled in Amharic.

'I am the Kitzera.'

And standing over the bodies of four dead men, who could doubt it?

Paul went to the courtyard. The relatives cowered back when they saw him, the tarades in his hand and blood spattered on his tunic. But when the young prince followed Paul, alive and unharmed, they began chattering eagerly.

'King Yostos has ordered you all to die.' Paul waited while Sana translated for the prince, who spoke to the group. 'But I will not kill you. If you want to live, flee this place.'

Forty pairs of eyes stared at him. No one moved.

'Go.' He flapped his hands at them, like shooing chickens. 'Soon Yostos will send others, and they will not be as merciful as me.'

He turned to Sana. 'Are you translating this properly?'

'They do not know where to go.'

Somewhat to his surprise, after all the people he had executed, he felt a pang of pity for the young princes and princesses. They had been raised in royal captivity: what chance did they have of surviving as fugitives in the brutal world beyond the walls?

More chance than if they stayed. Also, if Yostos was looking for several dozen rival claimants to his throne, it would distract him from hunting down his disloyal executioner.

Paul threw open the doors to the courtyard. The smell of sage and dust drifted in, and he saw his audience stir.

'Gondar is that way.' He pointed west. 'You go north.'

In ones and twos, they straggled out of the door. At last, only Paul and Sana were left.

'Are there kitchens?' Paul asked. 'We will need provisions.'

Sana handed him a sack. Inside, Paul found bread, vegetables, salt meat and cheese. There were also two skins of water. He hadn't noticed her slip away.

The dead guards' horses were still tethered outside, saddled and bridled. They took two each, one to ride and one to carry provisions.

'Where are we going?' Sana asked.

Paul felt light-headed. He was no different from the prisoners, stumbling out of captivity to a freedom he could not understand. Above, the Milky Way stretched across the heavens like a river of light. The vast expanse promised unlimited possibilities in the world.

'We will go to the coast. And then . . .' He shrugged. A cloud drifted over and hid the stars. 'First we must escape Yostos.'

They mounted up the two horses. Sana looked tiny on the huge warhorse, but she gripped its flanks with her knees and clutched the reins tightly. Paul led her slowly at first, but she learned quickly and soon they settled in to a steady rhythm.

They rode until dawn, following tracks across the hills that avoided the main roads. Near sunrise, they found shelter behind a giant baobab tree, with a stream to water the horses. They ate a breakfast of bread and cheese.

'At least we are better provisioned than the last time we set out on a long march together,' said Paul, remembering the desert.

Sana nodded quietly. The look in her eyes suggested she had not forgotten how that journey had worked out.

Paul made a bed among the roots of the tree. Sana curled up against him. Then, for the first time in months, he slept without nightmares.

The blast of a horn woke him, though he wasn't sure if he had heard it or dreamed it. He sat up, rubbing his neck, which was stiff from lying on the roots. The sun was high. Their horses cropped the long grass, swishing their tails at the flies. Sana was gone, but that didn't worry him. She would be stealing honey from a bees' nest, or making snares to trap wildfowl, or stalking some quarry she had found.

The horn blew again, and this time Paul knew he had not dreamed it. It was a sound he had heard every day on the parade ground, the deep blaring rams' horns that the king's legions carried. How could it be here, so far out in the wilderness?

Sana's head appeared from behind a bush. She looked worried. 'Come.'

They were high up on the ridge of the hills. Following Sana, Paul saw that to the north, the heights dropped away suddenly into a steep-sided valley. Paul and Sana lay on their bellies and crawled towards the cliff edge so they could look down.

The valley was filled with men. Tens of thousands of them, the lion banners fluttering overhead. The full strength of Yostos' army.

They are for me, Paul thought, his insides turning to water as he imagined the punishment Yostos had waiting for him.

Paul had never imagined the prince would come after him so quickly – and in such force.

Then he saw the second army.

It was the banners that had confused him. Both armies carried the device of the imperial lion, because both claimed the dead king's crown. But looking more closely, he could see one lion was silver, and the other gold. The two armies lined up facing each other, with clear space in between. He could even make out the two brothers, Yostos riding tall on an immense white charger, darting about giving orders; Goshu opposite, sitting still on a black mare under a sun awning.

They had not come for Paul. They were preparing to fight for the kingdom. It seemed extraordinary that both brothers could have put together their armies so quickly, but of course they had been building up to this moment for years. Goshu would not let his brother consolidate power in Gondar, with all the trappings of office and legitimacy; Yostos could not afford to leave Goshu at large to marshal his strength and gain allies. They would decide their contest at once.

The horns sounded again. The armies began to move. Paul knew he should run, but he was transfixed by the sight.

He had witnessed many battles in his life. In Italy, France and Egypt he had seen battles that would live in the history books for centuries, battles dictated by the greatest military genius of the age. The battle for Gondar was none of those. But for sheer, bloodthirsty ferocity, it was the worst he had ever seen.

Yostos had more musketeers, and he packed them in his centre protected by cavalry on the flanks. Goshu had more cavalry, but he would not commit them to battle too soon. He must have heard what the infantry would do, using the formations Paul had taught them. Goshu spread out his pikemen and musketeers in a long line and kept the cavalry back as a reserve.

The kettledrums beat the advance, echoing up the valley. Yostos's regiments marched forward in good order, just as Paul had trained them. He was not sure if he should be proud or afraid.

'Who do you want to win?' Sana asked.

She lay on her stomach, chin resting on her folded hands, watching the battle unfold with interest.

Paul considered it. Whichever brother won, if they caught Paul they would kill him.

'I want them both to lose.'

That looked unlikely. Yostos's troops were advancing smartly, and Goshu didn't have the strength to resist him. If his men stood their ground, they would soon be in range of Yostos's superior firepower. They began to withdraw, back up the slope.

'The silver lion is running away,' said Sana.

Did Goshu have a plan? Perhaps he had underestimated his brother's strength, and was now hoping to escape and regroup until he could bring in more allies. Perhaps he hoped that the narrowing valley would give him a shorter front to fight on, where Yostos's greater numbers could not gain the advantage. Already, Paul could see confusion on Yostos's flanks, where the cavalry was being squeezed against the infantry. But that would not be enough to save Goshu.

The drums beat out, louder and louder until Paul realised they were not drums, but a great peal of thunder. He glanced at the sky. The clouds had closed in solid.

'It will rain,' said Sana.

The first shots sounded from the valley. The threat of rain had added urgency to the battle. Yostos's men fired at will as they followed their enemies up the slope, aiming at any target they could find. Puffs of white smoke blossomed on the hillside.

On the broken ground, discipline was lost. The battle disintegrated into a brawl, every man fighting the nearest enemy he could find. Paul saw units firing into the melee without sight of their targets. They must have killed as many of their own side as the enemy. A squadron of cavalry rode into the smoke cloud and disappeared. He watched two men in matching uniforms lay about each other with pikes until, at the same moment, they ran each other through. Had they not realised they were in the same company, or had they taken opposite sides?

Thunder rumbled again. Paul picked himself off the ground and turned his back on the battle.

'Whoever wins, it will take them a week to recover from it,' he said, wincing as he thought of what the victors would do to the losers.

As he lifted Sana onto her saddle, he felt the first drop of rain fall on his hand.

'By then we will be far away.'

The rain made their journey a torment. Paths became mires, and dry gullies turned to foaming streams. The rain loosened the earth, so that with every step Paul feared he might dislodge the ground he was standing on. In places, landslides had broken up the ground and carved deep scars down the hill. Paul had to dismount and lead the horses through. He could not prevent one from slipping into a crevice between two rocks and breaking its leg. He had to slit its throat so that its screams would not give them away.

When one of the other horses showed signs of going lame, Paul knew they could not go on.

'We have to find shelter!' he shouted to Sana.

He was almost deaf from the incessant hammering of the rain on his ears, half blind from the water running down into his eyes.

Sana nodded. Without asking him, she slipped away on foot and plunged down the hill, skipping between rocks and over fallen trees like a butterfly.

'Careful!' Paul called after her, but she couldn't hear.

He thought about following, but he could not leave the horses in the storm. He waited and fretted, long anxious minutes until he saw the smudge of Sana's sodden dress climbing back up to him.

'I found a house,' she said.

It was not far, but it took almost an hour to negotiate their way off the treacherous ridge with the horses. The building she had found was a traditional round structure – larger than most – with a low-pitched thatched roof that made a conical hat.

'Are there people inside?' Paul asked.

'It is empty. Only pictures.'

He didn't understand. Then he opened the door, and the dusky smell of wax and incense wafted out. It was a church. Beautiful icons of saints and the Holy Family covered the walls, faint in the dim light.

The door was too small to bring in the horses, so he tethered them outside. Paul and Sana huddled together in the church, listening to water drip through the thatch.

'How long do you think the rain will last?'

At court, Paul had heard that in the wet season rain could fall for months at a time.

Sana shrugged: this was not her land. In Egypt, rain had been rare. It still held a wonder for her.

'In my country, it rained often in spring and autumn,' said Paul wistfully. 'Gentle rain that softened the earth for planting and made sweet grass for the cows to chew.'

Sana considered that. 'Even in the deserts?'

'There are no deserts in France.'

She snorted with laughter. 'Everywhere has deserts.'

'Not everywhere.'

'Then what do you do with your camels?'

They lay in the gloom, watched over by the saints, and he told her about the green fields of France, her rivers and vineyards and fields of wheat. He told her about the sea that was as vast as the desert, and the ships that sailed it and the great whales that lived in the depths. He could see she didn't believe him. To her ears, they sounded as fantastic as fairy tales.

Sana's short life had taught her to take nothing on trust. But as her natural suspicion softened, she began to delight in Paul's extravagant stories. Paul started to embroider his tale to see how far he could stretch her credulity. Cities grew in the telling. He talked of carts that could move without horses, and men who could fly on wings like birds.

Seeing the smile light up her face, hearing her giggle, feeling her poke him indignantly when she thought he was enhancing the truth, he felt a rare happiness. He did not know how old she was; maybe she didn't know herself. He suspected she was older than her waiflike body made her seem. But listening to his stories, she was like a young girl.

He stroked her hair, until she fell asleep curled next to him. Looking at her face, peaceful and innocent, it was easy to forget that she had killed men in cold blood.

It was the last time he ever spoke to her.

The rain had ceased when he woke, though he could hear water dripping from the sodden thatch. Sunlight shone through the church windows and made the gold leaf in the icons glow. A dark-skinned angel with bushy African hair held a naked sword aloft, gazing down at Paul with soulful eyes. Was it exhorting Paul to battle, or condemning him to eternal punishment?

Sana had disappeared. Paul felt a flicker of annoyance. They had not travelled far enough from Gondar, and after the battle the countryside would be crawling with bands of soldiers, whichever side had won. They needed an early start to get away.

He ducked through the doorway and stopped.

In the storm the day before, he had been too desperate for shelter to notice any of the church's surroundings. Now he could see that it sat on the outskirts of a village. A series of domed huts, smaller versions of the church, straggled down the valley, surrounded by bleached wood fences. Chickens pecked the dirt, and naked children ground manioc between stones.

The horses were not where he had left them. A group of about a hundred villagers – mostly dirty and raggedly clothed – had crowded around the front of the church. They chattered excitedly when Paul appeared. He guessed they had never seen a white man before.

At the head of the group was a man in a white robe, tied with a richly decorated belt. He wore a crimson cape, a pointed hat and a silver cross around his neck. A deferential teenager stood behind, holding an umbrella. It must be the priest whose church Paul had slept in.

Paul bowed and spoke a greeting in Amharic. He wished Sana was there. Her greedy young mind had picked up the language almost fluently, while Paul could barely stumble through a few phrases. He tried Arabic, but received a blank response.

'God save the king,' Paul said. It was something he had heard often in the palace.

The priest frowned. In a time of civil war, it was a dangerous thing to say.

Paul wanted to offer a gift, but the bags of food they had brought from the castle had vanished with the horses. Paul showed his empty hands and smiled.

'I have nothing.'

The priest misunderstood. With elaborate courtesy, he ushered Paul down the hill into the village. Paul tried to demur, but the villagers crowded round him, jostling and pressing so he was forced to follow. They gave him injera – thin bread like a pancake – and wat stew from a clay pot. Paul wolfed it down. He had not realised how hungry he was.

An awkward silence followed. Paul stood, but the priest waved him to sit, and again the press of people around him was so tight he had no choice. As the minutes passed, his anxiety mounted. There would not be many white men wandering these mountains, and he did not want word getting back to Gondar.

Where was Sana? He didn't dare to ask the villagers in case they harmed her. But if he left without her, how would she ever find him?

The priest seemed to be waiting for something. That worried Paul most of all. He rose again, and this time he did not let the crowd push him back.

'I must go,' he said, summoning up all the authority of the Kitzera. 'Where are my horses?' Incomprehension. 'I had horses. By the church.'

He mimed riding, and the priest's face relaxed in a smile of understanding.

'Horse,' he repeated. 'We bring.'

'I go.'

'You go,' the priest agreed.

A group of men and boys went down towards a pasture by the river. Paul could not see any sign of his horses there. But in a few minutes, he heard the drum of hooves coming up the road.

It was approaching fast, much faster than a horse which had been half-lamed in the storm should be ridden. Not from the pasture, but from the direction of the mountains. And it was not the sound of a single horse, but the hard pounding of many hooves.

He had waited too long. Paul shouldered through the crowd, pushing away the hands that tried to grab him. If he could reach the scrubby slopes above the village, the horsemen would struggle to follow. If he . . .

A company of cavalry galloped out of the trees and reined up in the village square. They carried shields tasselled with fur, hastily painted with the golden lion emblem.

Yostos must have won the battle, Paul thought, though it did not make any difference.

He was caught.

The soldiers bound his hands and tethered him behind one of the horses, so that he had to run to keep up when they set off. They did not take him far. Blundering through the storm, Paul and Sana must have wandered in circles. Between two hills, clouds of vultures came into view as they scavenged the battle-field like sheets of rain. Bodies littered the ground; the ground was spattered with blood.

Further down the valley, a safe distance from the carrion birds, they reached the camp. Paul was taken to a large, gold-trimmed tent with the royal lion standard fluttering outside it. He steeled himself to face Yostos's fury.

The curtain flap lifted. But it was not Yostos who emerged. It was a squat figure, his plump body straining the chain mail he wore as he waddled forward. On his head was the wide-brimmed silver hat of the king, with the silver chains veiling his face. Before he spoke, Paul knew who he was.

'The Kitzera,' Goshu said with mock grandeur. 'The king's loyal executioner.'

Paul said nothing.

Goshu pulled off the veil. His face was smooth and unmarked: he must have kept well out of the fighting.

'I thought of you often during my exile,' Goshu went on. 'How you were lying in my bed. Wearing my clothes. Fucking my slaves. You, who promised me your loyalty. I spent many nights thinking what I would do to you.'

'The king commanded it,' Paul protested.

Goshu's corpulent body quivered with laughter. His mouth split open, white teeth bared in delight.

'And did the king command you to slip poison herbs in his supper?'

'That was your brother.'

Goshu's grin broadened.

'Was it his hand that fed my father the poison? I doubt he had the balls for that. He would have found a willing accomplice to be his executioner.'

'It was Yostos,' Paul insisted.

'And you would swear it in front of him?'

Paul was trapped. He could not back down now.

'I will.'

Goshu led Paul through the camp to an enormous sycamore tree. Its trunk was twisted and gnarled; its bare branches had been festooned with crimson cloths. The ground underneath was carpeted with what looked like pink and red flowers, as if a gust of wind had suddenly made the tree drop all its blossoms. They were the severed testicles of the defeated army.

A man dangled from one of the branches, strung up by a leather tarade. Even by the standards of mutilated corpses, there was something uniquely terrible about this one. His naked body was bloated and deformed, the limbs flabby as if they'd been rolled out of dough. It looked more like a scarecrow than a man, though not enough to scare away the crows who perched on his shoulders and pecked at his lips.

A breath of wind spun the hanged man around so that he was facing Paul. It was barely recognisable as Yostos. His features, once so strong, had somehow been flattened. His commanding jaw and aquiline nose were no more than pimples, while his eyes were ragged sockets.

Paul realised why. It was only his skin. Goshu had flayed him, then stuffed the shell with grass and straw to make a plump effigy. Paul wondered if Goshu had killed Yostos before he did it. He suspected not.

'My poor brother,' Goshu said. 'He put all his faith in your white man's war magic. He forgot that when the rains come, even the greatest musket is no better than a stick.'

Paul could only imagine the horror of the battle, fighting at close quarters in that lancing downpour. Blood flowing so thick that the rain could not wash it away. Yostos's schemes and ambition drowned by something as commonplace as the weather, and a brother's hatred.

'I told you he would bring ruin on the kingdom,' Goshu whispered in Paul's ear. 'I told you to be loyal to me. Instead, you betrayed me. Now you will pay the price.'

'I only ever . . .'

There was no point protesting. Everything was futile. If Yostos had not killed the king, Goshu would have done so. Whoever won, Paul would have been crushed between them like grain under millstones.

Goshu pulled the veil back over his face.

'Your voice is poison to my mind. I never want to hear it again.'

While they had been speaking, a group of guards had formed up around them. They were the same men Paul had fought on the day of the hunt – Tigréan warriors with long colobus monkey skins fixed to their helmets. They seized Paul by the arms. Their captain stepped forward, and again Paul felt the shock of familiarity as he saw the open jaws of the snarling mouth that surmounted his helmet. He wore two leather tarades wrapped around his wrists.

'Greet the new Kitzera,' said Goshu's voice from behind the veil. 'As you know, his first job is to kill his predecessor.'

Paul's eyes went instinctively to the tarades. Goshu shook his head.

'That is too easy a death for a traitor like you. First, he will cut out your tongue. Then he will take you to the wilderness. The hyenas and jackals will eat you alive.'

Paul struggled. He fought and twisted to get free, but the guards were too strong. Two held his legs, and two his arms, while a fifth stood behind him and gripped his skull like a vice.

The executioner drew his knife. He approached Paul until he was so close that Paul could see into the shadows beneath the screaming mask. Paul clenched his teeth, but fingers squirmed between his lips and pried his jaw apart. Paul tried to bite the hands, until suddenly he felt the cold steel of the executioner's blade in his mouth. If he bit down now, he would slice his mouth open.

The executioner lifted his tongue with the point of the knife, like a doctor performing an examination. He started to cut. Paul screamed and screamed, until there was so much blood in his mouth, he could scream no more.

The executioner pulled out Paul's tongue, now a grotesque lump of flesh. He showed it to Paul, then tossed it in the dust. A pair of hunting dogs flew on it. Paul spat out blood, in the executioner's face, but the captain laughed. He licked it off slowly, moving his tongue lasciviously around his lips.

The guards stuffed a rag in Paul's mouth, bound his hands, and took him to the wilderness to die.

CALCUTTA, 1806

The *Mornington*'s anchor dropped into the brown Hooghly river. Adam heard the splash and the gurgle of water as the flukes sank into the mud. There was excited chatter as the passengers boarded boats to row ashore. Adam had not seen the other passengers before, but Lizzie had described them in such mischievous detail, he felt he almost knew them. She had a keen eye for their absurdities and ridiculous mannerisms. Often, during their long nights talking together, she had almost made Adam give himself away by laughing at her impersonations.

He imagined her among the other passengers in her bright dress and sun bonnet, gazing at the continent that was to become her home. He imagined her as he had last seen her, naked and beautiful, and felt an ache inside. She had offered him a life of happiness, and he had spurned it.

He told himself to forget her. All that mattered now was his revenge.

He had to leave the ship unnoticed. He stripped naked, tied his breeches around his waist to make a rough loincloth, and wrapped his shirt in a turban about his head. The dark skin he had inherited from his mother could easily pass as an Indian's. He stooped, so that his height would not mark him out, and hoisted one of the casks onto his back. When the Indian lascars entered the hold to unload it, he slipped in among them unnoticed and carried his load up on deck.

As he climbed the ladder through the main companionway, the light was so bright he cried aloud. It was the first time he had seen the sun in weeks, and his eyes were unprepared for the harsh tropical glare. He screwed them shut, and nearly fell back down the ladder in his blindness.

Tentatively, he squinted, enough to see his way. Dressed as a native, he became invisible to the ship's officers and crew: with so many stevedores swarming aboard, one unfamiliar face was unremarkable. No one challenged him as he carried his load to the ship's side and slithered down the ladder into the waiting boat.

This was his first visit to Calcutta, and in all his voyages nothing had prepared him for it. It was as if imperial Rome had been rebuilt in the middle of the Indian jungle. As far as he could see, the river was lined with palatial villas whose long gardens ran down to the water. Closer to the centre, the bastions of Fort William sprawled over almost a square mile footprint, stamping down the East India Company's military power. It had been built to replace a predecessor fort, which had been sacked by an Indian army some fifty years earlier. The defenders who were captured had been locked in an airless cell, nicknamed the 'Black Hole', on the hottest night of the year. Of the hundred and fifty who were incarcerated, only thirteen had survived.

Beyond the fort stood the administrative centre, where the East India Company ran the commerce and government for the empire they had built. These buildings were white and grand, proud blocks dressed up with pillars and domes and porticoes. The greatest of them was the new Government House, so excessively huge that even the Company had balked at the cost and recalled its architect in disgrace. The Governor-General of India, the first Marquess Wellesley, was sacked for profligacy.

That was the Calcutta the Company wanted to show to the world – a place of imperial authority and power. But there was another city that existed behind the mansions and away from the mighty civic architecture, where rickety bamboo buildings lurched over dark, narrow alleys. This was Black Town, home to hundreds of thousands of Indians who had flocked to the new metropolis to serve as shopkeepers, servants, carriers, stevedores, labourers, whores and thieves – anything to profit from the appetites of their occupiers.

The scene was so overwhelming, it made Adam almost physically sick. After weeks in virtual isolation, he felt like a fasting monk suddenly made to gorge himself on a banquet. Half a million people lived here, and it felt as if he could see every one of them crowded on the waterfronts and the great avenues.

The only clothes he had were the makeshift loincloth and turban he wore, and the one good suit that he had brought in a sack from the *Requin*. He could pass for a native, if no one looked too closely, but he knew little of the language apart from what he had taught himself from Lizzie's grammar book. Nor could he present himself at Government House and announce his real name. Word of his disappearance would have circulated in the convoy. Verrier would have warned all the captains to look out for him. Already, perhaps, Adam's name was being added to the lists of deserters and undesirables that the authorities kept.

He plunged into the city without any destination in mind. For the moment, it was enough to breathe fresh air – even the heavy, fetid air of Calcutta – to stretch his legs, and walk upright. In the crowds, dressed like an Indian, he was at the least risk of discovery since he had dived off the stern of the *Requin*. The British were visible only to each other, oblivious to anyone with brown skin. They floated above the city like clouds in their curtained palanquins and chaises.

'Courtney,' said a voice.

Adam froze. He hesitated for a second, but that would be enough to give himself away. How could someone have recognised him so soon?

'Courtney of India. Greatest hero since Marlborough,' said the voice again.

Were they talking about him? Adam edged away, then turned a little to see who had spoken. Two English officers, with red coats and red faces soaked with sweat, had descended from their palanquins to admire a statue in the middle of the boulevard.

It was an imposing monument. It stood on a marble plinth higher than the men themselves. Atop it, a soldier on horseback stretched out an arm to the horizon. A turbaned Indian warrior lay on the ground, being trampled under the horse's hooves.

Adam read the inscription on the plinth.

GERARD COURTNEY
HERO OF THE DEFENCE OF CALCUTTA, 1756
SURVIVOR OF THE BLACK HOLE
CONQUEROR OF BENGAL
GOVERNOR-GENERAL OF INDIA
HONOUR, COURAGE AND VIRTUE

Adam stared up at the bronze figure, imperious and untouchable. How strange, to encounter his ancestor here. He knew a branch of his family had made their fortunes in India. One of them, Christopher, had entered Parliament and become a high-ranking member of the British government. That side of the family carried an unshakeable grudge against Adam's ancestors, dating back over a hundred years to the two brothers, Tom and Guy. When Rob went to London as a young man, Christopher had ordered his accomplices to murder Rob. Rob had only escaped by joining the Royal Navy as a sailor. Later, when Rob returned to England as an officer and a hero of the American war, he had threatened to expose the treasonous plot Christopher had concocted with the West India sugar planters. Christopher had tried to kill Rob in his chambers in the House of Lords, but Rob had defended himself and killed Christopher instead. Adam had heard the story often: it was Christopher's bullet that had shattered the Neptune sword that day.

Gerard Courtney must have been Christopher's son. Had he been the paragon described on the statue? Adam thought it unlikely. After Calcutta had been captured by a local ruler in alliance with the French, the East India Company and the British army had returned in force to make a brutal example of their enemies. By the time the campaign was over, they had done more than recapture Calcutta: they had grasped almost immeasurable power. The Company's possessions in India had grown tenfold. Britain had gone from a mercantile power to an imperial overlord. And the generals who led it – Lord Clive, Lord Hastings, Gerard Courtney – had made themselves the richest men in the world.

Adam suspected that conquering an empire and winning such a fortune had not been achieved by being over-scrupulous about honour and virtue.

'What are you looking at, you nig-nog?'

Adam started. The officers were talking to him. They had seen him staring at the statue, though they had not seen past the turban and the loincloth.

'Clear off,' said one. 'Don't you have work to do?'

There were many retorts Adam could give, but none that would do his cause any good. As an Indian, a 'nig-nog', he could be thrown in jail for the least reason. He hid his anger, bowed his head and disappeared into the crowd.

He moved more carefully, like sailing in enemy waters. Through a mix of stubbornness and luck, questioning passers-by at random, he at last found himself in front of a large mansion near the river on Manningham Street. It was not so grand as some of the others on the avenue, though in London it would have been considered almost a palace. Its gateposts were decorated with two life-size stone dolphins, and guarded by a fearsome Sikh in a crimson turban.

The Sikh saw Adam approach and assumed he was a beggar come to try his luck. He hefted the big stick which he carried and said a few curt words that were not to be found in Lizzie's *A Grammar and Exerciser of the Hindustani Language*.

Adam straightened and looked the Sikh in the eye.

'Excuse me,' he said in English, summoning all the dignity and presence of a captain in the Royal Navy. 'Is Mr Cornish at home?'

The Sikh stopped and looked Adam up and down. Adam pressed the advantage, and said politely, 'Would you be so kind as to inform him that an old friend of his father's is visiting?'

The Sikh growled something to a servant lurking behind him, who sprinted up the drive and spoke to a doorman. The doorman in turn shouted into the house, presumably to another manservant inside. Adam had never seen so many servants.

The guard glowered at Adam. But he stood his ground, affecting nonchalance.

'And who the devil are you?' boomed a voice that made the dust jump off the trees.

A portly man in a long white tunic and Persian slippers was descending the stairs of the house, puffing and panting. From the neck down he was impeccably Indian, but his sunburned nose and rust-red hair could be nothing but European.

He gave one look at Adam and turned to the guard angrily.

'Don't I pay you to keep the riff-raff away from my door, Harbajan?'

'Is it so long since we played together in the rigging of your father's ship?' Adam called out. He pulled off his makeshift turban, revealing the shock of dark curls. 'Don't you recognise an old friend of yours, John Cornish?'

Cornish peered closer. Even without the turban, Adam was a shadow of himself after the hardships of getting to Calcutta. But there was that ferocious life in his face, the unmistakeable intelligence in his eyes, and a dignity in his bearing, that no changes in clothing or appearance could disguise.

'Adam Court—'

'Indeed.'

Adam did not let him finish the sentence. He did not want his name heard in Calcutta, and Cornish had a mighty pair of lungs.

'How in the name of Jesus did you come here?'

'I will tell you when we are inside,' said Adam. 'It is quite a story.'

Cornish nodded. 'With you Courtneys, it always is.'

Cornish had known the Courtneys all his life. The families had been close friends and loyal allies; they had often fought together at crucial moments in the Courtneys' history. Cornish's grandfather had helped defend Fort Auspice when it was newly built; his father had given Rob passage when he ran away to sea from Nativity Bay.

'I remembered you had come here to make your home on this continent.' Adam gestured to the magnificent house. 'It always puzzled me. Now I see why.'

'It is a pestilential city,' said Cornish. 'The wickedest place in the universe. Most of our race last no more than two monsoons here, and I have survived five, so I am living on credit from the Almighty.'

'You are the only man I know who chose to live here a second longer than he had to,' said Adam. 'Why do you stay?'

Cornish lounged back. He had clearly embraced the customs of his new homeland, for he sat Indian style, cross-legged on a plump pile of cushions. His robe was belted with a black-and-gold chequered cummerbund and fringed with tassels of gold thread on the lapels. Two servants stood behind him, one to fan him with ostrich feathers and the other to tend the shisha pipe that bubbled in a corner.

'It was the usual story,' said Cornish. 'Every sailor's ruin.' He pointed to a large portrait hanging on the wall. 'That's her. Noori.'

The woman in the picture was a striking beauty, with soft features and a full figure wrapped in a wine-red sari that seemed to flow over her body. Underneath, her bodice was sewn from shimmering cloth that puckered tight where it stretched over her breasts. Her eyes were downcast, a demure smile on her lips as if she was embarrassed to have been caught by the painter's eye. Her arms, wrists, neck and ankles were draped with gold jewellery.

'You have not lost your eye,' said Adam. 'She is a beauty.'

Cornish glowed with pride. 'She is indeed. And do not let that chaste little smile fool you. She is a perfect minx in bed.'

Adam spluttered with shocked laughter. He had forgotten how forthright Cornish could be.

'How do you expect me to look her in the eye after that description? Is she here?'

'She has gone up to Chittingbazar to visit her family. She will be back within the week.'

'I look forward to meeting her.'

'You will like her. She is quick and kind, and she knows how to treat an old sailor like me.'

'Will you ever return to England with her?'

'I could not. The way she would be treated in society, an Indian woman . . .' Cornish shook his head. 'I know Rob married your mother, but that was a generation ago. Folk were more tolerant, then.'

The servant handed him the mouthpiece of the hookah pipe. Cornish took a long draw.

'Even here, times are changing. Twenty years ago, we treated the Indians as men. Men to be distrusted, certainly – sometimes to be fought – but men nonetheless. We respected their civilisation. If we found some of their ways were superior to ours, we adopted them gladly.'

He took another draught from the hookah pipe.

'Now we treat them little better than dogs. The quality of a man's character or the richness of his mind count for nothing against the colour of his skin.'

'Why?'

'Because we are no longer merchants. To trade with a man, you may lie to him, and you are almost honour-bound to try and cheat him. But eventually you will shake his hand, and there must be a modicum of trust.

'Now we are conquerors. And to conquer a man's country, to steal his land and property and subjugate him utterly, you cannot allow he had any right to it in the first place. Otherwise you would be little better than a thief. So we deny the Indians' humanity, or at least degrade it, to justify our depredations. And it follows that everything Indian must be inferior and contemptible.'

He gave a rueful smile.

'Listen to me. Here I am talking philosophy, when an old friend has just walked through my door, unannounced and dressed like an itinerant fakir. Tell me your story. And first, tell me, how are your family?'

Adam's face darkened.

'Alas, my family and my purpose are two parts of the same story. And it is not a happy one.'

Cornish put down the pipe.

'Tell me.'

By the time Adam had finished, Cornish's ruddy face had turned white with shock. The coals in the hookah pipe had burned out, and the coffee sat cold on the table.

Cornish leaned forward and gripped Adam's hands in his own.

'Your loss . . . I do not have the words. You know I loved your family.'

'Thank you.'

Telling the story again had brought back all the agonies of the discovery at Fort Auspice. A softer man might have cried – but weeping would not help the dead.

'I must find Captain Talbot and make him tell me everything he hid from me the last time we met. Assuming he is here in Calcutta?'

'There I can help you. The *Seven Sisters* arrived a fortnight ago.' Cornish saw Adam's surprise. 'I may be retired, but I still have a merchant's heart. I receive news of every ship that docks in Diamond Harbour. I will make enquiries to find out where Talbot is lodging.'

'Discreetly, I hope.'

'Of course. Most likely, he will be at the Captains' House, where the Company put up the masters of visiting vessels.' Cornish sniffed. 'In the meantime, my house is at your disposal. And if I am not mistaken, you are in sore need of a bath.' Another thought struck him. 'Six weeks in the hold, you say? Perhaps you need a woman as well.'

Adam tried not to wince as he thought of Lizzie.

'Just the bath.'

Adam washed, dressed and ate. For a man who was supposed to be in hiding, it was a strangely public business. There were seven servants to run his bath, three to shave him, five to help him dress, and a round dozen to bring him a light meal. By the time he had finished, he was unrecognisable from the wretch who had come out of the *Mornington*'s hold. And Cornish had news.

'Talbot is not staying at the Captains' House. He has been given the use of a mansion on Garden Reach. It is the most exclusive part of the city. It appears he has friends in high places.'

Adam swore. 'It will be hard to get in there unnoticed.'

'There is another way.' Cornish gestured to a servant to refill his glass. 'Talbot is a man with appetites, and he is notorious for creeping out into the brothels of Black Town to satisfy them. He goes alone.'

'Then perhaps we can provide him with some company.'

They passed the afternoon yarning and dozing, and as the sun set the servants brought supper. There was no cutlery. Cornish tore a piece of flatbread and used it to scoop up a ball of rice and stew.

Adam copied him. With the first bite, he felt as if a gunpowder cask had exploded in his mouth. He drained his glass, and as soon as a servant had refilled it, he drained it again.

'What is that?'

'Curry,' said Cornish, who was eating it as easily as a bowl of lettuce. 'Is it not to your liking?'

'I cannot say,' gasped Adam. 'It has seared my tongue raw.'

'I can have my cook prepare you something more familiar, if you like. He does a particularly fine omelette.'

Adam forced another bite into his mouth. Tears streamed down his cheeks.

'This will do nicely.'

He forced himself to finish the dish. Afterwards, the servants brought mangoes and coconut, which cooled his mouth. Then they brought a pair of pistols, beautiful weapons with gold chasing and hammers shaped like peacocks. Cornish loaded them carefully and gave them to Adam.

'These are dangerous men you are going against,' he said. 'Be careful.'

He dressed Adam in loose trousers and a flowing tunic, with a turban around his head.

'Anyone who sees you will think you are a Mussulman merchant.'

'Unless they try to talk to me.'

All the hours of studying Lizzie's grammar book had given Adam a fair knowledge of the Hindustani language – but he had never spoken it aloud, and he did not know if he would understand a word if he heard it spoken to him.

Cornish nodded to the enormous Sikh whom Adam had met at the gate.

'Harbajan will accompany you. He will do any talking. Passers-by will think twice about accosting you with him walking in front of you.'

The city had seemed to sleep most of the afternoon. At dusk, it came back to life. Lamps were lit. Ladies promenaded in their finery, while young men with too much money raced their phaetons and gigs down the broad avenues. No one, it seemed, moved without a retinue of at least a dozen servants.

Adam and Harbajan slipped out through the back gate of Cornish's mansion. The streets were busy, but the crowds parted readily before Harbajan's bulk. Adam followed in his wake, keeping his head down, though when he heard a trill of feminine laughter, he could not help looking up, hoping against hope he would see Lizzie.

'Idiot,' he chided himself.

Away from the centre, the graceful streets gave way to narrow lanes crowded between shabby buildings. Mud brick, straw and bamboo replaced the classical columns and gleaming stucco. The houses were built so close together that some had sprouted rickety bamboo bridges connecting them to their neighbours across the street. The air thickened with smoke from dung fires and spice dust blowing off the stalls in the bazaar, scented with the perfume of unseen women.

Harbajan brought Adam to a monumental arch near the bazaar. Once, it must have marked some entrance to Calcutta; now it was marooned as the city expanded.

'This is the way the captain comes,' Harbajan said in guttural English.

They took up position in the shadows near a small shop. Through the slatted window, Adam could see men inside, flopped on straw mattresses, surrounded by long pipes. They lay so still they might as well be dead. Sweet smoke drifted out of the window and made Adam dizzy.

'Opium,' said Harbajan.

Adam turned away, taking shallow breaths to keep the narcotic from his lungs. He needed his wits sharp. He tried to concentrate on the passing traffic.

It was as well he had disguised himself as a local trader. There was hardly a white face to be seen in this part of town. If Talbot came, he would be easy to see.

Will he come?

Adam remembered the man, so bluff and genial. It was hard to imagine him creeping out to a Calcutta brothel. But then, every word he said would appear to have been a lie.

'There.'

Harbajan saw him first. Despite the heat, Talbot wore a long cloak and a hat pulled low over his face. He passed almost within arm's reach of Adam, and plunged into one of the little alleys that led off from the bazaar. Adam followed.

In the maze of tiny streets, Talbot moved with the pace of a man who knew where he was going. The other pedestrians shrank away when they saw him. In the narrowest streets, he always had a bubble of space around him. Adam did not attract a second glance.

Talbot went into a crooked house halfway down a blind alley. Adam hesitated. If this was a trap – if Talbot had noticed him – he would be caught with no way out.

He waited at the mouth of the alley, watching the door to see if Talbot emerged. It stayed closed. After fifteen minutes, Adam grew impatient. He would have to risk it.

'Be ready,' he told Harbajan.

The Sikh nodded. Adam approached the door. A wooden carving of a bare-breasted goddess sitting cross-legged was mounted above it. The windows were covered with wooden screens, with red orchids in window boxes in front of them, and red gauze curtains hung behind them. Moans and squeals drifted through them, leaving little doubt what was happening inside.

The door shot open before Adam could knock, and almost hit him in the face. A mountain of a man, bigger even than Harbajan, filled the entire doorway, so fat that his belly poked out into the street. He wore a black tunic and a black turban, and a black scowl that did not welcome visitors.

He barked a few words. Adam smiled and shook his head, palms up in incomprehension.

'A girl?' he said, in his faltering Hindustani.

The doorman peered at Adam. He had almost no neck, so he had to stoop and lean forward, putting his face six inches from Adam's. His eyes were small and pig-like.

He did not like the man in front of him. Maybe he saw through Adam's disguise, or noticed the bulge of the pistols under the fold of his tunic; maybe he just recognised trouble. But his decision was clear. He was not letting Adam in.

Adam could smell the onions on the man's breath, as the doorman said something curt and final.

Adam smiled. He grabbed the doorman's collar and pulled. At the same time, he grabbed the open door with his other hand and slammed it hard into the doorman's face. The man collapsed into the street, blood gushing from his nose.

Adam did not wait for him to get up. Harbajan was coming; the Sikh would take care of it. Adam drew his pistol and bounded over the prostrate man into the house. Two girls in gauzy saris and gold bangles screamed and fled. Half-dressed men followed them, shouting complaints, but one look at Adam's expression cut them short. They pulled on whatever clothes they had and ran.

Adam hurried from room to room, tearing down the curtains that covered the doors. He interrupted half a dozen couples in various states of coitus, ignoring their shock and frustration long enough to establish that none of them was Talbot.

The brothel was bigger than he thought. Downstairs, he could hear the sound of Harbajan and the doorman in an almighty struggle, while upstairs he had unleashed panic. What if Talbot heard it and took fright? Adam quickened his pace, up another flight of stairs and through more rooms. These were more richly decorated, with proper sheets on the beds and softly burning lamps. They seemed to be for customers willing to pay for more specific tastes. Adam saw one man dressed in a woman's clothes; another being pleasured by two other men; another wearing a mask like an elephant god. He tore off the mask, but it was not Talbot.

He was almost at the top of the house. Had Talbot slipped away through an open window or a back door, he wondered?

There was one more flight of stairs that ended in a trapdoor, probably an attic or the roof. His hopes fading, Adam opened it and looked inside.

It was a long room below the roof timbers. Lamps on the floor threw shadows against the ceiling, which was covered in murals showing naked figures entwined in an array of inconceivably gymnastic positions.

Talbot was suspended spread-eagled from the ceiling beams by ropes tied to his wrists, standing on the balls of his feet. He was naked, except for a blindfold. A woman, also naked, knelt in front of him with his member in her mouth. Another woman stood behind him. She held a cane switch, which she was thrashing energetically against Talbot's buttocks.

She saw Adam first and dropped the cane. The kneeling woman heard the clatter, broke away from Talbot and turned in Adam's direction.

'Don't stop, damn you,' grunted Talbot. 'You have not finished.'

Adam gestured the two women to the door. They noted the pistol in his hand and ran out, their bare feet making no sound on the floorboards.

Talbot's tumescent penis throbbed with frustrated desire.

'What is happening?' he called. 'I will have you thrashed when your mistress hears of this.'

Adam walked behind Talbot, letting his heavy footsteps echo around the room. Talbot sensed a change, but with the blindfold he could not see. He squirmed in his bonds, trying to free his wrists from the knots. But the women were professionals: they had tied them tight. He could not get out.

'Who are you?' he called. 'How dare you interrupt me? I'll have your blackie head mounted on a spike over Government House.'

Adam picked up the cane that the girl had dropped. He gave a couple of practice strokes, letting Talbot hear it hum through the air. Then he lashed it against the back of Talbot's thighs.

Talbot screeched with pain. 'What the devil are you doing? This isn't what I paid for.'

'No,' Adam agreed. 'But you *will* pay.'

He swung the cane again. Whatever pleasure Talbot had taken from being beaten by the girl, he felt none now. He screamed.

'Who are you?' he gasped.

The sound of an English voice, in the last place he expected, had made him realise this was no simple robbery.

'I am the man whose family you murdered.' Another hit, another scream. 'I am the man you lied to, so that more men died on a fruitless quest.' Another hit. Adam walked around and tore off the blindfold. 'You know who I am?'

Talbot's eyes bulged. 'Adam Courtney. But how—?'

'You know why I have come?'

Talbot's silence was confession enough.

'I know what you did at Nativity Bay.'

Seeing Talbot's face, puffy and unrepentant, drove Adam into a rage he did not know he possessed. He slashed at Talbot with the cane, drawing blood on his thighs and his genitals. Talbot contorted in agony. He screamed, but no help was coming. The building had emptied, and the neighbours knew not to interfere.

'You lied to me. Lesaut did not chase you there. You met him in peacetime and sold him food. When he went to Nativity Bay, he found it was already in ruins.'

'No . . .' Talbot was almost sobbing, incoherent. 'No . . .'

Adam struck him across the face with the cane. 'Lie to me again, and I will shove this so far up your arse that it comes out of your mouth.'

'The ship's owner made me do it,' Talbot gabbled.

'Who is the owner?'

Silence. Adam supposed that the ship's owner must be recorded in some sort of registry he could find. But that would take time. The cane was more efficient. He gave another couple of cuts with it, then asked again, 'Who?'

'*Courtney.*'

Babbling and choked with pain, Talbot could hardly get the word out. Adam thought it was another plea for mercy. He raised the cane, but before he could land the blow Talbot screamed again, '*Hugo!*'

Adam stopped mid-swing. He stared at Talbot, the captain's body now a bruised and blood-spattered mess.

'*Who?*'

'Hugo Courtney.'

'Who is he?'

'Gerard Courtney's son.'

Adam stepped back, ignoring Talbot's pleas and whimpers. He remembered the statue he had seen outside Government House. Gerard Courtney: *Honour, courage and virtue.*

Hugo Courtney, who owned the *Seven Sisters* and had given Talbot his orders, was Gerard Courtney's son.

Gerard had been Christopher Courtney's son.

And Christopher Courtney was the man whom Rob had killed so many years ago.

Now Adam understood everything. Hugo Courtney had sailed halfway around the world and massacred an innocent family, to avenge his murderous grandfather.

Now Adam would repay the debt.

He stepped back, gazing at Talbot. The captain dangled like a piece of meat in a butcher's yard, shrivelled and bloody. Adam might have felt sorry for him, but in his mind he was revisiting the bones crunching underfoot at Fort Auspice.

'Tell me everything. From the beginning.'

'Cut me down.'

'No.'

Adam's voice offered no mercy. Talbot's only hope was to keep speaking. He cleared his throat and spat out a gob of blood and spit.

'Gerard Courtney had been looking for Fort Auspice for years – probably before you were born. He knew your family had settled on the south-east coast of Africa. Whenever a ship came in to Calcutta, he would ask the captain what he knew. Twice, he outfitted voyages to scout the African coast and search it out, but they could not find it.

'Then, in Cape Town on an outbound voyage, I was offered a consignment of ivory from a captain bound for London. He'd bought it from a trader who lived in a hidden bay up the coast. He marked its position on my chart.

'I called in. I met George Courtney and his children. They were suspicious of an Indiaman – they knew Christopher and his son had been powerful men in the Company – but I persuaded them I was a friend. I enjoyed their hospitality. I traded with them. And when I got to Calcutta, I went to Gerard Courtney and told him what I had found.'

'No doubt you did not give him the information for nothing. What price did he give you?'

'A half share in the vessel.' Talbot writhed in his bonds. 'It was more than I could earn in a dozen voyages. One more voyage, and I could retire in comfort. You must understand . . . Five years ago my ship struck a reef off the Moluccas and nearly foundered with all hands. Since then, my wife has begged me to retire from the sea. It has ruined her health, worrying for me every day while I am gone. With what Courtney offered me, I could have given her a life of ease and comfort.'

Adam nodded. 'One more voyage.'

'Gerard Courtney sent thirty men aboard my ship. He would have led them himself, but he was on his deathbed and the voyage would have killed him. He sent his son, Hugo, instead.'

'Did he tell you what they meant to do?'

'No.' A prod from the cane made Talbot cry out. 'But I could guess. The men were cut-throats, freebooters scraped from the prisons of Bengal. Hugo loaded twenty stands of arms aboard.'

'Go on.'

'We put in to Nativity Bay, just as we had before. I paid my compliments at the Fort. The Courtneys suspected nothing. Hugo and I even dined with them. Hugo wanted to see his quarry.'

He hung his head.

'That night, I stayed aboard our ship at anchor in the bay while Hugo took his men ashore. I heard it all: shots, then screams. The house caught fire and lit up the night. When Hugo returned, before sunrise, he was horribly burned and covered in blood up to his elbows. Of the thirty men who had gone with him, only seven returned.'

Adam thought of all the bones in the ruins and was glad some had been his enemies. It was a little consolation that the Courtneys had sold their lives so dearly, though even that thought had a bitter edge. They must have come so close to winning.

He remembered the walls around Fort Auspice, unbroken and undamaged. How had the attackers been able to get in?

'Did Hugo say anything about the battle?'

'Not a word. He locked himself in his cabin and did not speak for the entire voyage back to Cape Town. He left us there and took another ship back to Calcutta. I sailed on to London.'

Talbot risked a small glance up.

'I am sorry for what he did to your family. It has haunted me ever since. You must believe me, if I could undo what I did . . . I have prayed to God for nothing else.'

He hung there, his eyes pleading for release but not daring to ask.

'One thing I do not understand.' A detail, but it was easier for Adam to think about details than look into the black void at the heart of Talbot's story. 'You said Gerard promised you enough money to retire from the sea. Yet now you are here in Calcutta again.'

Talbot shifted uncomfortably in his bonds. 'Our hold was filled with luxury cottons and bright calicoes. With the peace, there had been a great demand for it. But by the time we reached London, the war had started again and the fashions had changed. People wanted clothes that were austere and drab. We barely turned six-pence profit on the venture.' He sighed. 'So you see it was all for nothing. We have both lost what we desired.'

Adam took the dagger from his belt – the weapon he had dug from the ground at Fort Auspice. The tiger's ruby eyes glowed.

'I showed you this once before.'

'It was Hugo's dagger,' Talbot confirmed. 'A gift from some local prince where Hugo was stationed. He presented it to George

Courtney. I think it amused him, giving a weapon to the man he intended to kill.'

Adam held it up. The curved blade made a sickle moon in the lamplight.

'Where is Hugo now?'

'I do not know. Not in Calcutta. Most likely he has gone to one of the Company's domains upcountry.'

Adam put the blade against the rope that tied Talbot's wrist. Talbot relaxed – but Adam hesitated. He turned the story over in his mind. Was there anything else Talbot could tell him, any question Adam had forgotten to ask?

No. He had learned what he needed. Finding Hugo was what mattered now.

He reached to cut Talbot down. But his arm rebelled: he could not do it. Talbot had not wielded the weapon that killed the Courtneys, but he had enabled the crime. He had found Nativity Bay, sold the location to Hugo and carried him across the Indian Ocean to deliver his vengeance. He had sat at dinner with the Courtneys, eating their food even as he knew what would happen to them, and given no warning.

We have both lost what we desired.

That Talbot could compare lost profits to a murdered family was monstrous. He had neither guilt nor shame.

Adam lowered the knife. With a vicious jab, he plunged the blade into Talbot's belly. The sharp blade slid into the flesh like a sword into its scabbard.

Talbot's eyes widened. He screamed and jerked, writhing in his bonds, but the dagger was in tight and he could not dislodge it. Blood dribbled from his stomach, but slowly. The dagger acted as a plug on the wound it had made.

'Do not struggle so much,' Adam told him. 'The dagger is all that is keeping you alive. If it comes out, you will bleed to death.'

Talbot's wriggling reduced to a few spasmodic shudders.

'As it is, it will take hours for you to die. Someone will find you before that happens. They will see your wound, but they will also see a gold-hilted dagger set with rubies that is worth more than they earn in a lifetime. If they are merciful, they will call a doctor before they remove it and you will probably survive. If they are greedy, they will take the dagger and leave you to your fate.'

Talbot's cries rose again. Adam put his hand on the hilt of the knife and leaned his weight on it, levering open the wound. The flow of blood increased. Talbot's screeches turned to screams.

'Greed or mercy – the same choice that you had. Be thankful I am leaving your fate to luck.'

Deaf to his screams, Adam turned and walked out of the room.

Harbajan was waiting at the bottom of the stairs. The fat doorman lay at his feet, badly bruised and tied up.

'Did he give you any trouble?' Adam asked.

Harbajan grinned. His lip was split, and he was missing a tooth.

'No trouble.'

They left the brothel and walked out in the warm Calcutta air. Talbot's agonised cries followed them down the alley, fading into the busy night until Adam no longer heard them.

Cornish was waiting for them when they returned, pacing anxiously in his drawing room. He listened to Adam's story in silence. When he heard Hugo's name, he went pale.

'I must warn you, Hugo Courtney is the most dangerous adversary you have faced. His father, Gerard, survived the Black Hole. You know the story?'

'I do.'

'Imagine what sort of man it takes to survive that. He went on to conquer half of India.'

'I saw the statue.'

'When he died, he was the richest man in Calcutta. That branch of your family has controlled the East India Company for generations, each one more ruthless and avaricious than the last. To go against them is to fight the whole power of India.'

'Do I look afraid?'

'I wish you would. You do not understand the danger you are getting yourself into.'

'It would not help if I did. I have no choice. Where can I find Hugo Courtney?'

Cornish went to his hookah pipe and fiddled with the coal until it bloomed red. For a moment, the only sound in the room was the bubble of the smoke as it passed through the water.

'You know I must do this,' Adam said softly. 'For my family. For my father.'

Cornish blew out a long stream of smoke. He sighed.

'After you appeared this morning, I made some enquiries about your relatives. I had a suspicion they would have some part to play in your story. Hugo Courtney has been sent as ambassador to Holkar.'

The name meant nothing to Adam.

'Where is that?'

'It is an independent kingdom, far in the interior.'

'Why would Hugo go there?'

'Because the Maharani of Holkar sits on the richest diamond mines in the world. Those diamonds you see in your Bond Street jewellers in London – every one of them has been dug out of her lands. The Company has eyed that kingdom for a long time. Hugo is there to secure the trade once and for all.'

It fitted perfectly with what Adam knew of Hugo's character.

'To conquer it?'

'They call it a trade mission. They say they have only gone to negotiate.'

'But he will have Company troops with him, I suppose?'

'Probably an army. The Company likes to negotiate from a position of strength.'

'And the full power of the Company at his command?'

'Indeed. They will not let this fail.'

'How long will it take me to get there?'

'Three months.' Cornish saw the expression on Adam's face and burst out laughing. 'You do not understand this country. It is bigger than you can imagine.'

'Then I must go at once.'

Cornish's face turned sombre. 'I cannot go with you. I could spare Harbajan, perhaps, but he has seventeen children here in Calcutta and—'

'I was not asking you to come, or any of your household. I will go alone.'

'Against an army?'

Adam thought of how he had plunged the knife into Talbot's stomach. 'I do not need to beat his army. All I have to do is get within striking distance of him.'

Adam left Cornish the next morning. Low mist hung over the Hooghly river and shrouded the city; the roar of Calcutta's trade was muted like a distant waterfall. The great Indiamen lay still at anchor on the glassy river. If word had got out that one of their captains had been found dangling naked in a Black Town brothel, stabbed through the guts, there was no sign of it.

Adam was dressed as he had been when he first came ashore, in a loincloth and turban, with a blanket thrown over his shoulders against the cool morning. He looked like a ryot, a Hindu labourer. Cornish had made it clear that an Englishman travelling alone would be as inconspicuous as an elephant riding down Pall Mall.

'Every trading factory you passed, every town you called in, your visit would be known before you even arrived. Every Company official would know your business. Hugo would get news of you, and the Company would make sure you did not get within five hundred miles of him.'

'Then why not go as a merchant?' Adam had asked Cornish. 'It served me well enough last night.'

'And this morning all the Company informers in Calcutta will be looking for that man. Also, a merchant attracts more attention. There are many thieves on the roads. A simple labourer will draw less attention.'

Adam could see the logic. Cornish gave him a quick lesson in the basics of Hindu manners.

'Eat with your right hand only, never eat beef, and do not presume to touch any other human being.'

'I was not planning on romantic entanglements,' Adam protested.

'That is not what I meant. The Hindus divide themselves into a labyrinth of castes, and woe betide the man who touches a fellow of greater or lesser rank. Either you defile him, or you defile yourself, and either way it will be remarked upon.

'Lastly, if anyone speaks to you, pretend you are deaf. For the rest, pray no one looks too closely.'

'And if they suspect?'

'Of course they will suspect something!' Cornish roared. 'They are not fools. What matters is that the Company do not guess – and if they see brown skin and a turban, they will not look any closer. They rule this country, but they do not care two figs for its people. All they see is profit to be extorted.' He slapped Adam on the rump. 'Happily, they will see little of that to be had from you.'

The full unlikelihood of what he was attempting dawned on Adam. To travel a thousand miles alone, in an unknown country, while trying to pass as a native, was bordering on impossible. Yet he had to try.

'Thank you,' he said to Cornish. 'I could not have done this without you.'

'You have done nothing yet,' Cornish reminded him. 'Most likely all you will do is get yourself killed.' His face softened. 'But I wish you a safe journey, and Hugo Courtney dead at the end of it.'

Adam stepped into an ungainly boat at the foot of a ghat, the stepped wharves that lined the riverbanks below the warehouses. The boat was a local craft called a budgerow, a flat-bottomed vessel with long cabins at her stern, and an open deck for'ard where the rowers sat. She was attended by three other similar boats: one for baggage, one for horses, and one that served as a kitchen.

The monsoon rains had ended, and the river was running high. The men on the oars had to bend their backs against the current, while another crew on the bank hauled the boat upriver using a track-rope. Even with such slow progress, the surroundings afforded endless changing vistas: drooping bamboo and thickets of trees gave way to tilled fields, which in turn opened to broad expanses of yellow-reeded marshland many miles wide. There were crimson fields of poppies, and cotton plants whose pods were bursting with snow-white wool. At night, they moored near villages, where women brought brass bowls to fill with water, and children splashed in the shallows. Monkeys chattered in the tamarind trees and pelted the decks with fruit. One night Adam saw a herd of elephants come down to drink. It reminded him again of that moonlit night with Mary Jansen in the fields of Africa. If the slow journey had dulled his thoughts of revenge, that was all the reminder he needed.

They passed the battlefield of Plassey, though the river had spread in the last fifty years and it was now slipping into swamp. This was where Lord Clive and Gerard Courtney had defeated the Nawab of Bengal, in the campaign of revenge following the Black Hole of Calcutta. On that field, they had won British mastery over Bengal for generations. As they passed by, the Englishmen on the boat emerged from their cabin and drank a toast to Clive, and Courtney.

'A glorious victory for British arms,' they crowed.

They had forgotten, or did not care, that the battle had mostly been won with an enormous bribe. Despite its historical significance, it was more of a skirmish than a full-scale battle, and Lord Clive's victory had been achieved through the black arts of subterfuge, and a torrential downpour of rain.

Adam hid his face and gave a grim smile. It amused him to think of what they would say if they knew there was another Courtney aboard the boat, and what he intended.

Day by day, he grasped more deeply the ancient power of the country. On a bend in the river, a crop of rocks jutted into the stream. They had been carved into the likenesses of Hindu gods and strung with wreaths of flowers, gently wilting and shedding their petals into the water. The towns they passed sported the high pagodas and temples of the Hindus, but also the onion domes and minarets of Islamic architecture. One afternoon, they passed a city in ruins. The river had burst its banks and flooded it, but the stumps and arching skeletons of magnificent palaces remained, thrusting out of the water like tombstones.

No one could conquer this country, Adam thought.

They might rule it for a time, through fear and power, but in the end they would fail and their works would become more ruins.

At Mirzapore, Adam disembarked to join the great trunk road heading south-west. With the dry season begun, the roads were busy with travellers. The Indians did not travel alone, but in large groups, sometimes two or three hundred strong. With much bowing and gesturing and pretending he could barely speak because of his deafness, Adam attached himself to one of these parties.

There was safety in numbers, but he worried his fellow travellers might begin to suspect him. He was terrified that some accident – a fall, a roll of thunder, a snake in the road – would make him blurt out in English, or somehow reveal that he was not deaf. He kept to himself, but it was impossible to travel for weeks in the same company and remain completely anonymous.

Some of his companions seemed to be growing suspicious. One, a high-caste Brahmin in a silver-embroidered coat, kept staring at Adam. He appeared to be a wealthy merchant, with a retinue of porters, guards, secretaries and servants. His attentions alarmed Adam: he could not afford to be discovered here, hundreds of miles from any prospect of help. He was relieved when the man took himself to a different part of the column.

Sometimes they encountered Company officials going about their business. The Englishmen travelled in great curtained palanquins, carried by teams of bearers who jogged along, wearing deep ruts in the dusty roads. New teams waited every three or four miles, so their lords could travel indefinitely, hundreds of miles without ever setting foot on the country's soil. Once, when a gust of wind blew the palanquin curtains open, Adam saw one of the passengers: a fat man wearing baggy pantaloons and a silk dressing gown, reclining on cushions and drinking from a cup of sherbet. He might as well have been lying in bed in Grosvenor Square, for all that India intruded on him. Not for the first time, Adam wondered how the Company could govern India, yet remain so aloof from it.

Adam thought enviously how quickly he would reach Holkar if he had the Company's litter-carriers at his disposal. But his slow journey had some consolations. He had started to understand his companions. Weeks on end of keeping silent had left him plenty of time to listen. His ear learned to distinguish individual words from the stream of sounds, then tentatively to apply some of the lessons he remembered from Lizzie's grammar book. He knew he was improving when, one day, he heard a lady asking for her parasol. Adam almost gave it to her, before hastily remembering he was supposed to be deaf.

In the second month, he fell in with three companions. Their names were Ravi, Shrisanth and Sanjit; they seemed to be brothers, though more unalike brothers it was hard to imagine. Ravi had a thin face with a pointed beard; Shrisanth was stout and at least twenty years older, with a head of fleecy white hair; Sanjit had pale, feminine features offset by a prodigious moustache that curled up at the ends. They were travelling from Agra in the north all the way to Hyderabad: they had an aunt, or possibly a niece, who had died and left them an inheritance. They were jolly men who sang all day. In the evenings, they invited Adam to their campfire and shared their food with him.

He was glad of their company. They lifted his spirits and relieved a little of his lonely existence.

The country changed as they went south. Every day was like walking through a battlefield. The ryots whom they saw going out to their fields each morning carried not just mattocks and hoes, but clubs and small shields. Much of the land had been burned; the fields were scorched. The people they met had little food to barter. There were few young men in the villages, but many women and young children. From conversations he overheard, Adam gathered that this had been another front in the East India Company's wars.

One evening, they made camp by a copse of trees, where the ground sloped down from the roadside to a small stream bed. Ravi and Shrisanth spent the afternoon digging a large hole by the stream, near the roots of a neem tree. By the time they were finished, it was so deep that it went up to their necks.

By gesturing, and with a few words of broken Hindi, Adam asked what they were doing. The answering gestures were incomprehensible, and the wide-toothed grins they gave him left him none the wiser. Later, eavesdropping around camp, he gathered that a local ruler was rumoured to have buried his treasure in this place when the Marathas invaded. The brothers had heard that it was marked by a neem tree, and decided to try their luck.

That evening, the brothers were unusually skittish. There was much giggling – not the easy laughter of other nights, but something twitchy and slightly nervous. Even though they believed Adam was deaf and usually spoke freely in front of him, that night they kept whispering to one another, exchanging sly glances when they thought Adam was not looking. He began to wonder if they had actually found the fabled treasure, and wanted to keep it secret. They looked over their shoulders towards where the Brahmin merchant had pitched his tent, as if they were afraid he would discover them.

But after Adam had gone to bed, lying on a blanket on the ground, he heard Shrisanth say quite distinctly, 'We go at midnight. I will lead him there. You two be ready.'

It was a tone of voice Adam had not heard from him before, cold and cruel, hard to match with the smiling and shambling man Adam had walked so many miles of road with. Adam waited, awake, puzzling it over and listening.

The moon rose, the merest sliver like a crack in a door. Insects buzzed, and fireflies flashed in the darkness.

Even forewarned, Adam almost missed them. He had begun to doze off when suddenly he felt a presence, a man kneeling beside him. He was so close Adam could smell the cardamom on his breath. It must be Shrisanth.

A hand reached under the sack Adam used as a pillow. Was Shrisanth stealing from him? But there was nothing in the sack except some old clothes and the sketch of Mary. Adam had left the Neptune sword in Calcutta with Cornish – and the tiger dagger in Talbot's guts. He had nothing else worth stealing.

Adam kept still, his eyes closed, pretending to be asleep.

Shrisanth finished his rummaging and walked away. Adam counted to twenty, then rolled over and put his hand under the sack. He felt cool metal – a cup. When he pulled it out, it gleamed silver. He had never seen Shrisanth or his brothers with such a cup; it looked far too rich for them.

Was that part of the treasure? Had they hidden it there for safekeeping?

Shrisanth had not gone back to his bed. Adam could see his shadow, picking his way through the campsite. Ravi and Sanjit's bedrolls were empty, too.

Adam rose and crept after Shrisanth. Most travellers slept in the open air, but the wealthy Brahmin had a tent which his retainers pitched every night. Shrisanth went there. One of the servants appeared to be sleeping in front of the door, but when Shrisanth spoke a few words in his ear, he jumped up and disappeared.

Shrisanth went in. Adam stole up to the canvas and put his ear to a seam.

'This afternoon we have found something most valuable,' Shrisanth was saying. 'But if we take it now, brigands and robbers will fall upon us. Your master is a great lord. He can send soldiers to protect it and we share the treasure, him and us. And you.'

'What did you find?' The Brahmin's voice, suspicion tempered by sleepiness.

'Treasure, *sahib*. Most valuable. Come and see it.'

Adam heard a rustling as the Brahmin pulled on his robe. The flap opened and the two men emerged. Adam followed them down the hill towards the stream bed and the hole by the neem tree. Ravi was waiting there, though there was no sign of Sanjit. Adam hid behind a bush.

'I left my brother to guard the treasure here,' Shrisanth explained. 'Most valuable.'

He said it again, like a magic formula. He put his hand on the Brahmin's back as if to usher him towards the hole.

Adam stiffened. In his weeks of travelling with the Indians, he had learned more than a few words of their language. He had begun to understand their customs, most of all the intricate rules of their Byzantine caste system.

A man of lower caste, like Shrisanth, would never touch a high-caste Brahmin. It was as unthinkable as a manservant slapping his master.

The Brahmin felt the touch and began to turn. He opened his mouth, but before he could make a sound Shrisanth swept his legs from under him. The Brahmin fell forward on his face. Before he could move, Ravi sprang forward and grabbed his wrists. Shrisanth held his ankles while Sanjit – who had appeared from nowhere – kneeled over him. Sanjit put his knee against the small of the Brahmin's back, so that he was pinned like a butterfly. He undid the sash he used to belt his tunic, wrapped one end around each hand, and deftly put it about the Brahmin's neck. He crossed his wrists and pulled the sash tight.

Everything had happened so quickly, the Brahmin had no chance to resist. He could neither move nor make a sound as the life was squeezed out of him.

Adam saw it all from behind the bush. He was outnumbered three to one, and unarmed. The Brahmin meant nothing to him.

All those thoughts flashed through his mind in an instant. But he could not sit in the dark and watch an innocent man be murdered. He sprang towards Sanjit.

The murderer did not notice him coming. The other two were more alert. They had been keeping lookout for anyone who might witness their crime, and saw Adam the moment he broke cover. Shrisanth let go of the Brahmin's ankles and rose, drawing a long slim dagger from his robe.

Adam was unarmed. His only hope was to attract attention. The murderers had taken care to lure their victim to this secluded place; they would not want to fight off a large number of travellers.

There was only one problem. Adam did not know the word for help.

'*Baagh!*' he called.

It meant 'tiger'; it was the best he could come up with. He bellowed it out in his best quarterdeck voice, a voice that could reach the masthead in an Atlantic gale. He had to hope it would carry to the camp and wake some of the sleeping travellers.

Shrisanth paused, shocked to hear his silent companion in such fine voice. He stepped away from the Brahmin, raising the knife. If Adam lost the initiative now, he would be beaten. He did the only thing he could: he charged at Shrisanth, as if he meant to impale himself on the blade.

Adam came so fast, Shrisanth took a step back. At the last moment, Adam threw himself to the ground. Shrisanth tried to bring the knife down, but Adam was close enough that he slid underneath the blade and cannoned into Shrisanth's legs before he could strike. Shrisanth was knocked over.

Adam could have tried to wrestle the knife away. But that would have taken precious moments. Sanjit was pulling on the noose so hard it was a miracle the Brahmin was still alive. Adam lunged, trying to dislodge him from the Brahmin's back. Sanjit had no choice but to let go of the sash.

They rolled over, a tangle of limbs and bodies in the darkness. Adam punched and kicked and bit and clawed at his opponents. He could not afford to let them pin him down.

But there were three of them, and they knew their business. They didn't flail like drunkards in a tavern brawl. They put him in an expert lock, finding the pressure points when he resisted, and forcing him down.

Soft fabric slithered around Adam's neck. He jerked to try and get it free, but the murderers were too strong. The noose tightened around him, closing his throat. His vision swam; he went limp. A voice whispered in his ear, chanting something low and rhythmic like a prayer. It must be Shrisanth. Adam smelled the sweet cardamom on his breath again.

With his remaining strength, Adam thrashed backwards, smashing his head into Shrisanth's face. It broke Shrisanth's nose. He howled in pain and let go of the noose. Before he could recover, Adam lifted himself off the ground and threw Shrisanth off.

The cloth sash lay on the ground where Shrisanth had dropped it. Adam snatched it up. It was knotted at both ends for grip, with a coin or a pebble tied in one of the knots to give it weight.

Shrisanth stumbled to his feet. Blood gushed from his nose, but there was still strength in him. Adam flicked the end of the sash around his opponent's neck, as easily as casting a line. He grabbed the knotted ends and twisted them together, tightening until he felt something snap.

A blade lunged for him. Ravi had picked up the knife. Adam let go of the cord and twisted away so that the knife hissed past him. Adam grabbed the arm that held it with both hands and jerked it down against his knee. Ravi dropped the knife and wheeled away in agony as Adam snatched up the knife.

The odds had improved. Now it was Adam against Sanjit and Ravi. Ravi had a broken arm, and Adam had the knife. Adam checked the Brahmin, but he was lying on the ground, clutching his throat.

Adam, Sanjit and Ravi eyed one another, taking a moment to draw breath.

'Who are you?' Adam asked.

Ravi bared his teeth. 'We are the deceivers.'

'Go now, and I will not follow you.'

Sanjit shook his head. 'You have seen our true faces – you cannot live.'

He and Ravi edged apart, forcing Adam to turn to keep them both in sight. He raised the knife, brandishing it at them. Still they edged away. Did they both mean to rush him at once?

He heard a noise behind him. Only the rustle of a leaf, but his blood was up and his senses were fully alert. He glanced back.

There were more of them – half a dozen at least, dappled figures in the shadows under the neem tree. How long had they been there? Some carried knives; others had scarves ready in their hands.

'Now you die,' said Sanjit.

Adam couldn't fight so many. They closed on him like a pack of wolves. He circled, jabbing the knife at anyone who approached – but each time one stepped back, two more moved forward.

The futility of it overwhelmed him. He would die an unmarked death. The murderers would bury him in the hole they had dug; the other travellers would assume he had slipped away. No one would miss him because nobody knew he had been there. And all because he had intervened in a fight he could have avoided.

It was fate. He could never have let an innocent man be murdered – it was not in his nature. Whatever happened, it must be part of God's purpose for him, for better or worse.

The thought brought him calm. He feinted back, then suddenly drove forward so fast that the man opposite was taken off balance. The man took two steps back – and vanished with a scream and a thud. He had fallen into the hole that had been dug that afternoon. Adam leaped over it, through the gap that had opened in the ring of men. They followed quickly, but Adam was fast. He ran towards the camp, shouting defiance.

Voices answered him. Fire lit the night sky. At the top of the slope, men had appeared carrying torches. At last someone in the camp had heard Adam's shouts and acted on it. They were armed with the weapons of the poor – wooden axes, cudgels, even saucepans. In a pitched battle, Shrisanth's gang might have been able to fight them off.

But the deceivers did not like pitched battles. They preferred to lure their victims to deserted places, to fight in shadows. Light and crowds were poison to them. They fell back. They crossed the dry stream bed and disappeared into the night.

Emboldened, the men from the campsite gave chase. But the countryside was a barren place, and no one wanted to risk his life in the darkness. After a little distance, Adam saw the line of torches turn back

'Who are you?' hissed a voice in Adam's ear.

It was the Brahmin. He had a dark mark around his neck; his voice was hoarse.

'A man with secrets.' Adam jerked his head in the direction that Sanjit and his gang had gone. 'But not like them.'

The Brahmin gave him an astute look. Behind his eyes, Adam saw a sharp intelligence.

'I will keep your secrets for now,' the Brahmin decided. 'Say nothing.'

He turned around to meet their fellow travellers, trudging back from chasing away the murderers. They gathered, chattering excitedly. The Brahmin spoke, remarkably composed after what he had been through. He explained how Adam had stumbled upon the gang and effected a brave rescue. No one asked how a deaf man had overheard the attempted murder.

The Brahmin thanked his companions for their help driving off his attackers. One of his servants appeared and began distributing coins from a purse. One by one, the travellers took their reward and drifted towards the camp.

Adam went last.

'Come to my tent,' the Brahmin murmured.

Adam waited until the camp was quiet. It took a long time for his fellow travellers to settle; they were elated from their victory, and anxious in case the enemy returned. But at last Adam managed to creep up unnoticed to the Brahmin's tent.

The Brahmin sat on a cushion with two small cups of raki set before him. A chessboard was laid on the floor beside him. He had washed off the mud and blood and changed into a fresh silk robe. It was hard to believe that an hour earlier he had been fighting for his life – if not for the livid weal circling his throat.

Adam had not looked at him closely before. Studying him now, he saw a narrow face with high cheekbones, a trim beard, a straight back and stern eyes. He wore so many rings on his fingers that his hands clattered when they moved.

He offered one of the cups to Adam. The burning liquor nearly made Adam choke.

The Brahmin dismissed his servants with a wave of his hand.

'Since we know you are not deaf, and speak as clearly as I do, we can dispense with the dumbshow,' he said drily. 'Who are you?'

'*Nahgees*,' said Adam.

It meant 'nobody'. It was an obvious evasion, but the Brahmin let it pass.

'So. I am Chaudhury. A simple merchant travelling to my home in Holkar. You are Nahgees, a deaf peasant perhaps seeking work in the diamond mines. I was attacked by thieves – by chance you happened upon me and saved me. How many lies did I just tell?'

Adam stiffened. He glanced towards the tent door. An enormous pair of feet showed under the canvas flap where someone was standing behind it.

'I saved your life,' Adam said. 'Is that not enough?'

'Did you save my life?' Chaudhury sipped his drink and fixed Adam with those shrewd eyes. 'The men you saved me from were your travelling companions.'

'I did not know who they were. I still don't,' Adam added honestly. 'They deceived *me* as much as you.'

He thought back to what had happened.

'I think they adopted me into their company for just this moment. They meant to make it look as if I was the murderer. They hid a cup under my pillow, something precious. When it was found, and you were missing or dead, everyone would draw the same conclusion.'

Chaudhury's gaze bored into him – but Adam had nothing to hide. His voice grew hot with indignation.

'Did I fight like a man who was pretending? There are two bodies down by the neem tree that will tell you I fought in deadly earnest.'

'They could tell me indeed – if they were not dead. But they are insignificant. I have many enemies, and they would happily sacrifice two pawns in a greater game.'

'You are not a merchant.'

It was a statement as much as a question. The way Chaudhury spoke; the way he held himself; the command in his eyes: all said this was a man who held real power.

'It seems nobody is what he appears to be tonight,' Chaudhury said.

'Then how do I know I can trust you?'

'The very question I would ask you.'

'It is a stalemate.'

'Indeed.'

The two men regarded each other: Chaudhury in his pale silk robe, Adam in his tattered shift, crusted with dirt and other men's blood. Yet beneath the surface, an outsider looking in would have seen certain similarities between them: a strength of character; a nobility of bearing; a refusal to compromise.

Adam rose. He drew himself to his full height.

'My name is Adam Courtney,' he said in English, then switched to Hindustani. 'I am travelling to Holkar to find the man who murdered my family.'

He had hoped the confidence would earn him a measure of trust. Instead, Chaudhury sprang to his feet, his face wide with shock.

'Courtney?' he said. 'What witchcraft is this? Do you mock me? Or is this a conspiracy of all my enemies at once?'

Adam didn't know what to say.

'I have come alone.'

'You expect me to believe that? A Courtney in disguise, stalking me on my journey?'

Adam wondered if there was any corner of the earth where the name of Courtney was not known, and cursed.

'How do you know my family?'

'I am Panjit Rao, chief minister to the Maharajah of Holkar.'

Adam began to understand.

'That is where Hugo Courtney is stationed as the East India Company's ambassador.'

Panjit's face darkened at Hugo's name.

'So you confess you know him?'

Adam had to laugh at the fate that had brought him, through so many dangers and adventures, to this place. Perhaps he sounded slightly deranged. Panjit's hand went to the dagger in his belt; the feet behind the tent flap shuffled closer.

'You think this is funny?' Panjit demanded.

At last Adam managed to speak.

'I am laughing because we share a common purpose.'

'Do we?'

'Hugo Courtney is the man I have come to kill.'

A silence gripped the tent. The two men searched each other's faces for signs of deceit.

At last Panjit sat down. Adam did the same. Panjit snapped his fingers, and a servant came to refill the cups.

'I do not see how I can trust you,' said Panjit at last. 'But . . . your story is so incredible, it persuades me no man would ever expect it to be believed. Also, there is the small matter that you saved my life.'

'Who were those men who tried to kill you?'

'They were *t'uggee*,' said Panjit. 'A cult of thieves and murderers. They fall in with travellers on the road and lure them to their deaths. Thousands die every year. If they had succeeded, they would have buried me in the pit they dug and I would have vanished from this earth.'

'You knew about them?'

Adam was surprised a man as astute as Panjit would have let himself be led into that kind of trap.

'I know their kind,' the Brahmin explained. 'I was so vigilant, I thought you might be one of them. I could tell you were hiding a secret. But they came to me in the night, half asleep – and they knew my weakness.'

'What is that?'

'Greed.'

It was an unlikely answer. Everything in the tent was valuable and finely made, but none of it was ostentatious. Panjit had an austere air, almost like a monk. Adam's surprise must have shown.

'Not for myself,' said Panjit. 'For my mistress, the Maharani.'

'I heard she sits on the richest diamond mines in the world.'

'That is true. But it is not enough for the East India Company. They are an insatiable python, swallowing down every rupee they can acquire.'

Adam remembered what Cornish had told him.

'In Calcutta, I heard that Hugo Courtney has now been sent to win the company a monopoly over all the diamond trade of Holkar.'

Panjit steepled his fingers. His face registered surprise, but it was a weary sort of surprise: the acceptance of something long expected finally coming to pass.

'So.'

He looked up at Adam. For the first time that evening, his gaze was clear and without suspicion.

'You are a miraculous man, Adam Courtney. A deaf man who hears everything, a ryot who fights, an Englishman who would betray the East India Company.'

'Not betray,' Adam corrected him. 'I never owed them any loyalty.'

Panjit nodded, accepting the point. 'I do not know why the gods have sent you here, but I am glad of it. I will keep your secrets. More than that, I will give you the reward you deserve for saving my life.'

He drained his cup.

'I will take you to Holkar.'

ABYSSINIA, 1800

The hyena prowled the hills of the kingdom of Gondar. This was her hunting ground, and she knew the land by the kills she had made. She sniffed the night air and smelled blood on the wind. Blood might mean lions, and they were to be avoided – but it also meant food, and she had not eaten for three days.

She padded closer, slinking through the long grass. The scent brought her to a rise, looking down into a shallow depression. There were men. One lay on the ground – he was the source of the blood she had smelled – while four more stood over him, laughing and jeering as they kicked the body.

They did not see the hyena, but they must have sensed her presence. One looked up, but his eyes were feeble in the dark compared with hers, and the grass made her invisible. She kept still, and he did not see her.

He muttered something to his companions. With a final flurry of kicks at the man on the ground, they turned and walked away.

The hyena slunk out into the clearing, towards the man they had left behind.

Blood was pouring from his mouth, but the body was twitching. Contrary to what some of the local villagers believed, the hyena was not a scavenger. She would chase her prey until it collapsed from exhaustion, then dismember it and devour it alive. This time, someone had saved her the effort of the chase. The man's hands and feet were bound.

His eyes flickered open, white in the darkness. He tried to shout, but no sound came out – only more blood.

The rest of the hyena's pack were closing in, and she wanted the choicest meat for herself. Her claws rattled on the stones as she picked up her pace, trotting forward with open jaws.

The man's eyes widened as the hyena came closer. He writhed on the ground, struggling with the bonds that tied his wrists and ankles. He groaned and gasped, spraying blood which only sharpened the hyena's appetite. She could smell the fear coming off him, that unique musk that every animal secretes when it knows it is about to die.

The hyena snapped her jaws. The man rolled away, so that her long teeth grazed his skin. She pounced on him, digging her claws into his flesh while she sank her teeth deep into his shoulder. She bit again to tear a hunk off him.

A stone flew out of the darkness and struck her on the side of her head. Another hit her on the leg, so hard it almost broke the bone. The hyena howled with pain.

A girl walked out of the long grass into the clearing. She had two more rocks in her hands. Before she could hurl them, the hyena turned tail and bounded away, robbed of her prey. She would go hungry that night – but she would live to eat another day.

As many kills as you might make, there was always a more ferocious predator.

Sana watched the hyena run off. More animals were gathering on the edge of the clearing, drawn by the smell of blood. She could not hit them all. Instead, she walked towards them, banging the rocks together loudly and shouting at the top of her lungs, showing no fear. One by one, the animals slunk off.

Sana kneeled beside Paul and rolled him over. He had spat out so much blood it was smeared over his face, black in the moonlight. More blood was welling from the puncture wounds in his shoulder where the hyena had torn the flesh.

She found a sharp rock and sawed through his bonds. Paul moaned.

'Keep your mouth shut,' she hissed. She cut a strip off her tunic and balled it into his mouth. She tied another strip around his shoulder. 'You are bleeding too much. And there are more dangerous animals in the bush tonight.'

She took his arm to pull him to his feet. Paul rolled away, hugging himself like a baby.

'We must go,' Sana insisted.

She prised his hand free and hauled him up. She wrapped his arm around her shoulder to support him, then began to hobble away.

After a few paces, Paul stopped. Sana tried to drag him forward, but he stood his ground. He swung his arm in a broad circle, then made an empty gesture.

Where are we going?

Sana considered it. She knew they would not get far. They were in a hostile country and enemies of the king. There was nowhere they could find shelter, no one who would dare give them food. Paul's wounds would probably kill him, either quickly through blood loss or slowly through infection. The only advantage they had was that their enemies thought they were dead.

She could see in Paul's face he thought the same. She had to keep him moving, but he would not do that without hope.

'In the desert, you said there is water.' She spread her arms wide. 'Big water that takes you home.'

Paul nodded.

The ocean.

'Which way?'

The night was still dark, but the stars were fading. Far off in the east, a line of purple was starting to shade the horizon. Paul pointed to it.

'That is where we go.'

Paul never really knew how Sana kept him alive. Those first agonising days, he was so weak they barely travelled any distance. After three days, he could still hear the drums and horns of Goshu's army in the distance. They travelled by night and hid by day. Sana had an instinct for finding crevices and hollows they could crawl into. She raided farms and villages for food; every time she left him, Paul lived in terror she wouldn't return. But she always did, bringing eggs rustled from under hens, meat snatched from drying racks, and grain that had fallen out of the mill. She made Paul eat, though he choked and every mouthful was an ordeal. Chewing and swallowing had become alien movements, motions he had to learn again. He tasted nothing.

Days turned to weeks, then to months. They crawled up mountains, where the wind and the sun were sharp enough to blind them. They slunk across plains. They almost died a hundred times: of hunger, of thirst, landslides, bandits, wild animals and venomous scorpions. Once a cavalry patrol trotted ten paces away from the thorn bush where they were hiding. Other days, Paul thought he could not endure the misery of his existence any longer. In his mute way, gesticulating with his hands and contorting his face, he begged Sana to leave him to die. Every time, she forced him onwards.

Late in a cloudless afternoon, they crested a low line of desert hills and looked out. The land sloped away and there, in the distance, was the sea. It sparkled blue in the sunshine like a field of cornflowers and camomile.

Sana clapped her hands and laughed in delight. Paul smiled. He had rarely heard her laugh before.

'Is it real?' she asked.

He nodded.

'So much water . . . Where does it end?'

He shrugged. He only had the vaguest idea where they might be, an ocean he had never seen before.

From the hilltop, they could see along the coast to a small town. Whitewashed houses with flat roofs clustered around a bay, where dhows with triangular sails flitted about the harbour mole like gulls around a stranded fish.

'Who lives there?' said Sana.

Paul had no way of knowing. They had left Gondar far behind. There were neighbouring kingdoms he had sometimes heard mentioned at court, but those did not stretch as far as the sea. A pair of minarets climbed above the town's low skyline, from which he deduced it was an Arab town. Could they be back in Egypt? What if Bonaparte had conquered this place? They had walked so far, anything was possible. He wished he had a spyglass.

Avoiding the town, they made towards a promontory further down the coast. Palm trees fringed a white sand beach; gentle waves broke and raced up the shore. Sana dropped her walking stick, pulled off her tunic – by now not much more than rags – and ran naked into the waves. Paul did the same. They dunked their heads under water and shook their wet hair like dogs. They threw themselves into the breaking waves and let the ocean wash off the months of dust, sweat and fear.

Sana's wet body glistened in the sunlight. For all their meagre rations, she had grown in the months they had been travelling.

Her breasts had started to swell; hair was growing where it had not before. But at that moment, she was still a child.

'It is like you said!' she exclaimed. 'A desert of water.'

When they had exhausted themselves, they lay on the sand at the water's edge, letting the waves lap over their toes.

Paul knew they should move. Fishing nets had been strung between the trees at the top of the beach, and he could see smoke rising from a farmstead. If they stayed in the open, someone would find them.

But months of skulking and hiding had ground down Paul's fear. He closed his eyes, and let the sun bake him dry. Sana curled against him, her head on his chest and her arm thrown over his waist.

The sound of whistling woke him. Sana had risen, but it was not her whistling. Paul pushed himself up and looked around. A man in a white robe and sandals was walking down the beach towards them. Paul jumped to his feet – his body was stiff with caked salt – and pulled on his tunic.

The man was smiling, and apparently unarmed. His belly tended to fatness, and he walked with a bustling motion like a pigeon. But it was his eyes that made the biggest impression: bright, kindly and as blue as the sea.

Paul gaped. He had seen many faces since he arrived in Gondar: slaves from Juba with skin as black as night; lighter-coloured Amhara with their close-knotted hair; olive-skinned Arabs with hawk-like features – and every shade in between. But he had not seen a pair of blue eyes since he parted company with Sergeant Bastiat.

The man looked surprised to see Paul.

'*Salaam aleikum,*' he said in Arabic, with a small bow.

Paul returned the bow. He opened his hands, in a gesture that meant both 'greetings' and 'I have nothing'. Once, he could have replied in Arabic, but no longer; and though he had learned to speak it, he had never learned its script.

'*Português?*' the man tried. 'Swahili? Greek?'

Paul stared. The first two words meant nothing to him, but the third . . . At the very back of his mind, a compartment that had been closed for years suddenly opened: sitting in the schoolroom of his father's château, his hand throbbing from being rapped with a ruler as his tutor beat ancient Greek into him one word at a time.

He picked up the walking stick and drew figures in the sand, spelling out his name with Greek letters. The man squinted at it in surprise.

'Paul,' he read.

Paul pointed to himself. Understanding dawned on the man's face.

'Ilya Konstantinopoulos,' he introduced himself. And then, in Greek, 'You speak Greek?'

Paul opened his mouth, so that Ilya could see the void where his tongue should be. Ilya winced. He began speaking again in Greek, but too fast for Paul to understand.

A piercing cry echoed down the beach. Both men looked up. Sana had reappeared, running from the trees with an armful of dried fish. A woman in a white headscarf pursued her, brandishing a sharp filleting knife.

Sana ran to Paul and hid behind him. The woman raised her knife, jabbing angrily. She had bloody hands and stank of fish. Paul guessed that Sana had stolen the fish from a drying rack, and that this woman was the owner who had caught her.

Ilya stepped out and spoke rapidly in Arabic until the woman calmed. Ilya reached out a bag that hung around his neck and pulled out a copper coin. He gave it to the woman.

With a glare at Sana, the fishwife tucked the coin inside her bodice and stalked back to the trees.

'We cannot repay you,' Paul wanted to say. But he could not speak.

Sana might have said it in Arabic, but she stayed silent. She was not about to question a stranger's charity.

Paul bowed and pressed his hands together in thanks. Sana kept behind him, holding the fish close.

'She is with you?' Ilya asked.

Paul nodded.

Ilya sucked his teeth, studying the pair of them.

What must we look like? Paul thought. *A mute Frenchman and a thieving pubescent girl? And why did Ilya pay for the fish? What does he want?*

'You speak Arabic?' Ilya asked Sana.

Sana glared at him. But her eyes must have betrayed some kind of understanding, because Ilya continued, 'You have food? Clothes? A bed?'

Paul and Sana's silence answered his question.

'Then you will be guests in my house.'

Paul and Sana looked at each other. After months of travelling, they could read each other's thoughts wordlessly.

Why not? Paul's face said. *I'm tired and hungry.*

If he betrays us, we can kill him, Sana replied.

So they went.

Ilya led them to the port town they had seen. Its name, he told them, was Zeila. His house was one of the largest: white walls built of dry coral, with square turrets on the corners and tapered arches over the windows and doors. The ground floor served as a warehouse, now gated and locked, but the upper storeys held airy reception rooms. Black servants brought them sherbet to drink. Sana drank hers thirstily, while Paul sipped his cup. Losing his tongue had taken almost all his sense of taste, though the coolness was welcome.

'And now,' Ilya said, 'it is time for you to pay the price for my hospitality.'

Paul and Sana stiffened. Sana clenched her fists; Paul checked the door. Ilya looked horrified.

'Please. I did not want to alarm you. You are guests in my house. I want nothing in return except your story. How did you come to be here?'

Neither Paul nor Sana spoke.

Ilya studied his guests. Paul averted his gaze, but Sana stared boldly back.

'Why do you have blue eyes?' she demanded.

Ilya laughed. 'They run in my family. My great-grandfather was from Greece, from the fair-skinned peoples in Thessaly. He traded across the Levant. Gradually, he travelled further and further south – to Egypt, to Arabia, to Oman. Somewhere on his travels, he heard the legend of the Ark of the Covenant. Do you know it?'

Paul shook his head.

'The Abyssinians say that their first king, Menelik, was the son of King Solomon and the Queen of Sheba. They say that Menelik went to Jerusalem and brought the Ark of the Covenant back to this country.

'It is only a fairy tale, of course. But my great-grandfather heard this story and determined to find out the truth of it. Alas . . .' Ilya chuckled. 'He was not the explorer he dreamed himself to be. He did not make it across the desert. He returned here, poor and exhausted. He met a local woman, fell in love, married her, and turned his attention to trade again. We have been here four generations, but my ancestors' eyes always come through.'

He offered them a tray of sweetmeats. Sana took five and stuffed them all in her mouth at once. Paul took one and sucked on it.

'That is my story. I suspect yours is more remarkable.'

Silence hung over the room. Paul felt a familiar sense of dread – of being trapped in a cage. He could not possibly tell their story. He was a fugitive from the French revolution, a deserter from Bonaparte's army, and a condemned traitor from Gondar. Yet if they did not humour their host, what would happen to them?

'Begin with yourselves. Are you father and daughter?' Ilya tried.

Sana looked horrified.

'No,' she said.

'How did you come to travel together?'

Paul and Sana shared a look. They had entered the man's house and eaten his food. So far, he had shown them nothing but kindness. They should repay him, at least, with a little trust.

And if he betrays it, we can kill him.

The sweet had shrunk in Paul's mouth. He swallowed it down.

When did I become the kind of person who can think so carelessly of murdering his host?

Was this what the ibis-headed god wanted him to be?

Life had taught him he could trust no one, that he had to strike before he could be struck. The only surprise was that he still had any qualms.

He pondered that while Sana told their story, from the day Paul had found her in the ruined temple until the moment they had plunged into the sea. It was a fabulous tale: mighty armies and ancient kingdoms; scorching deserts and lofty mountains; murder, betrayal and bondage. For the most part, Sana told it badly, looking at the floor, chewing her hair, speaking in a monotone that at times became so indistinct Ilya had to ask her to repeat herself. Perhaps she was embarrassed. Perhaps their adventures were all she had known, and so she thought that all lives were like this. Paul could add nothing, except a few nods and grunts for emphasis.

But Sana's delivery could not rob the story of its drama. The facts were incredible. Ilya listened open-mouthed, interjecting occasionally but otherwise rapt.

'That is an extraordinary tale,' Ilya said when she had finished. 'All it lacks is a grand love affair.'

Sana blushed and gave him a cold look.

'But you are safe here. I can fill in other parts of your story that perhaps you do not know. King Goshu of Gondar did not live to enjoy his conquest. He had only been on the throne two months when his nobles tired of his rule and deposed him. The new king is a child, a puppet of the court. His nobles have become warlords, dividing the kingdom between them. Soon it will be anarchy.'

Paul supposed it hardly mattered. But he felt a measure of satisfaction, that vengeance had been done.

'France's invasion of Egypt is also ended. The army surrendered to the British nine months ago, though Bonaparte himself had returned to France many months before that.' He smiled at Paul. 'It is quite a catalogue of destruction you have left behind.'

And all of it pointless. Yostos and Goshu's scheming; Bonaparte's grand plans; Lefebvre's punishment: all dust and futility.

'Where will you go now?' Ilya asked.

Paul and Sana shared a glance. Neither of them had any idea. All that had kept them going those months was a vision of the coast. Now they were there, they did not know where to go.

'He wants to go on the sea,' said Sana suddenly.

'You are a sailor?'

Paul shook his head. Apart from the voyage on the *Orient* – something he would rather forget – the closest he had come to the sea was that afternoon, playing in the waves with Sana.

Ilya thought about it.

'I have ships,' he said. 'I could use a strong pair of hands – and I suppose you would not answer back to the captain.' He chuckled, not noticing the dark look Sana gave him. 'You are willing to work?'

Paul nodded.

'And for you . . .' Ilya turned to Sana. 'I can find you a place in my household as a kitchen girl or suchlike.'

'No.'

Ilya frowned. In the souks and the bazaars, he was used to stubborn negotiators. In his own home, he did not care to be contradicted, least of all by a teenage girl.

'I am offering you a good position. A home, food, security. In time, I may find you a suitable husband.'

He suggested the last possibility as if he were dangling a sweet before her. Sana's lip curled.

'I stay with Paul.'

Paul put out his hands, curled in fists with the index fingers pointing out. He rubbed the two fingers together. It was an Arabic gesture that he had learned from Abasi, to show that two people were inseparable.

Ilya saw the loyalty on both their faces.

'If that is what you wish. I suppose you have come through so much together that to separate you would be cruel. There may be space on one of my boats for a girl to cook and scrub.'

Paul bowed his head in thanks.

Later that evening, they lay in the blankets that Ilya had given them. Sana brought a lamp so she could see Paul.

Why are we going to sea? Paul asked.

Over the months they had been travelling, he had learned to communicate with Sana with facial expressions, rolls of the eye and hand gestures. It was trial and error to begin with, but now he could be surprisingly eloquent. Sana had learned to decipher his movements – and to make them herself. Their conversations were a strange mix of body language and speech, unintelligible to any outsider. For Paul, he barely noticed if she had said something aloud, or with her eyes or with a turn of her head: they were interchangeable.

'Do you want to stay here forever?' Sana asked.

They were in a foreign port, surrounded by desert for fifty miles in every direction. They knew no one; they were dependent on the kindness of strangers. Not a place to stay.

No.

'The sea is a way out.'

Where to?

'Where do you want to go?'

Paul shrugged. It was not a question he had ever in his life considered. He had gone where he was told: by his mother, by the army, by the Bishareen, and by the kings of Gondar. To have a choice was more than his mind could fathom.

'Back to your country?' Sana asked.

France?

He shook his head. His life there would be that of a fugitive, waiting every minute for the axe to fall. He had had enough of that for one lifetime.

He shrugged. *We will go where Ilya sends us.*

'Not forever.'

Paul turned Sana's question back to her.

Where do you want to go?

'Somewhere I do not belong to any man.'

Paul racked his brains for all the places he had heard of on earth. A kingdom that was not ruled by despots; a country where people were not merely grist to the mill of their tyrants' wars and vicious whims.

A memory came back to him. A salon at his mother's house in Paris; being allowed to stay up late to mingle with the important guests. A marquis from an ancient family had been there, handsome and alight with energy. The company had hung rapt as he recounted how he had become a hero in the war to liberate the American colonies from Britain.

'There are no kings there,' he had told Paul. 'The inhabitants choose their own rulers. They live in peace and liberty.'

Paul had not understood then, and now he had no idea how to communicate that to Sana. How to explain a country that she had never heard of, and he did not know how to find?

There is a place. He pointed west, then spread his arms wide. *Freedom.*

Sana wrinkled her nose. 'That is the way we came from, idiot.'

Beyond that.

'What is beyond?'

The sea.

Impatiently, she pointed in the opposite direction.

'The sea is that way.'

The sea is all around us. He waved his arms in a circle, trying to convey some sense of the globe. *A road that leads everywhere.*

'In boats?'

Paul nodded.

'Then we will go there. We will learn from the old man how to work the boat, how to find our way and how to travel on the sea. Everything we need.'

Paul thought of the small vessels they had seen in the bay. He thought of the mighty ocean-going ships of the French navy that had sailed from Toulon. Could a dhow survive a voyage across the ocean – if he could even find the Atlantic from this port?

Ilya will not let us sail his boat there.

Sana smiled. She did not smile often, and when she did, it always slightly unnerved Paul.

'We will take it.'

INDIA, 1807

The morning after the fight with Shrisanth and his brothers, Adam went to inspect the field by the stream bed. He thought he had come to the wrong place. All evidence of the assault had vanished. Shrisanth's body had disappeared, and the hole had been filled in. Adam wondered what had happened to the man he had pushed in. Was he under the earth? Had he been buried alive?

The only trace he found was a small brass amulet. It had been ripped off in the fighting and trampled into the earth. It showed a bare-breasted goddess with ten arms sticking out from her body like spider's legs. She held a trident on one side, and a severed head on the other. The goddess Kali.

Adam fixed the clasp and put it around his neck. It would help his disguise, but that wasn't why he did it. When he looked in the goddess's eyes, she seemed to speak to him of bloodshed and revenge. He wore it like a promise.

He and Panjit Rao left the group of travellers at the next town, waited two days, and joined another party on the road to Holkar. If their former companions had happened to spy Adam then, they would not have recognised him. His grubby dhoti had been burned; instead, he wore a long robe dyed in reds and yellows. He walked behind Panjit, carrying an umbrella to shade him from the sun. To all appearances, he was a favoured servant from a wealthy household.

'We are within the lands of Holkar now,' Adam said one night. They were sitting in Panjit's tent, playing a game of chess. 'Why not reveal yourself for who you are?'

Panjit picked up a knight – in this set, it was carved like an elephant – and rapped it down in its new position. He would study the board for ages in silence; but once he had decided his move he did not hesitate.

'I cannot be seen coming back, because I was not supposed to have left.'

Adam put that aside as he pondered his next move. He had often played against his father growing up, and excelled – he was used to winning. But in their many evenings together on the road, he had never managed to beat Panjit. Openings appeared in his ranks, but when Adam charged in, they turned out to be dead ends.

Adam advanced his bishop three spaces. *A good move*, he thought.

'What do you mean, you were not supposed to be away?'

'What do you know of Holkar?'

'Only what you have told me. That it is fabulously wealthy and coveted by the East India Company.'

'Their interest is not new. Hugo Courtney has been a visitor in our country for years. Already, the Company keeps two regiments of infantry stationed there.'

'I thought Holkar was independent.'

'Let me tell you how the Company conducts its business.' Panjit studied the board. 'First, they force us to sign a treaty in which the Maharani must reduce the size of her army – as a sign of good faith, of course. Then they say we are undefended, so they insist we accept a garrison of Company soldiers. Naturally, it is for our own protection, so we should pay the cost. One *crore* of rupees every year. Do you know how much is a *crore*?'

Adam shook his head.

'One hundred *lakhs*. Ten *million* rupees. That is why the fields are ravaged and the peasants flee the land. We have taxed them into ruin. Even with the mines, we cannot afford this much. But if we do not pay, they will say we are in breach of the treaty they made us sign.' He shrugged. 'Hugo Courtney has coveted those diamond mines since he set foot in India. He only wants an excuse to take them.'

'It sounds like piracy,' said Adam.

Panjit nudged a pawn forward. 'We tolerate it, because we do not wish to provoke war. But now Hugo Courtney is returning, I fear he will bring more demands – more soldiers, higher tributes, less freedom – until he forces us into war. We can only bend so far before we snap.'

'You went on a secret mission to look for allies,' Adam deduced. Panjit had exposed his pawn. Adam took it with his queen. 'In case it comes to war.'

Panjit did not deny it. 'Alas, the Company's power gathers over India. No one is willing to oppose them, and spies are everywhere. If the Company guessed where I had been, I think I would find what sort of protection their troops truly offered. That is why I travel in secret.'

He slid his rook forward, onto the square Adam's queen had just vacated.

'Checkmate.'

They sighted Holkar a full day before they reached it. They were travelling on a barren plain, broken only by clusters of tombs, when Adam spotted a bulge on the horizon. He assumed it was a pagoda; it was only after they had walked another mile, and it got no bigger, that he realised he had underestimated the scale. It was not a building, but a steep-sided hill. Smoke drifted above it. Was it a volcano?

Or perhaps it was a building after all. Closer still, he began to distinguish walls, turrets and battlements, as of a fortress. But if it was a building, it was on such a colossal scale it made Government House in Calcutta look like a dog kennel. A city?

Adam puzzled at it all afternoon, squinting through the haze. Only as dusk approached, when the red setting sun shone on its face, did he see it for what it was.

It was a hill, a city and a fortress all in one. The foundation was an eruption of treacle-brown basalt thrusting out of the plateau – a hill, Adam, supposed, though in contrast to the plain it felt more like a mountain. Where it had come from, only the gods knew. It stood in magnificent solitude, commanding the plain for miles. A broad river wound slowly near its base.

To the impregnable defences bestowed by nature, man had added improvements. Away from the base of the hill, strong walls made a perimeter many miles long. More walls rose behind them, wrapping the basalt in concentric layers of defences like a wedding cake. Inside them was a city, built in levels up the hillside to a citadel on its summit. Some of the buildings had been carved out of the rock; others were perched on precipices so sheer it looked as if a gust of wind might blow them off.

A few miles from the outer walls, Adam and Panjit stopped at a wayhouse. Horses were waiting for them: sleek, well-groomed steeds that must have come from Arabia. Panjit changed out of his merchant's clothes and put on robes more appropriate for his station: a long coat of green cloth embroidered with golden flowers; a red skullcap sewn with strings of pearls; golden armbands and diamond bracelets. He buckled on a sword with a gilded hilt shaped like a tiger. Adam stiffened. It was almost a perfect match for the dagger he had taken from Nativity Bay. He said nothing. There were many things he did not know yet, and it was wise to be careful.

Suitably attired and mounted, they entered the city through a monumental gate. Adam blinked. Outside the walls, the countryside was the same bleak land he had been travelling through for weeks: empty fields sprouting weeds; deserted houses blackened by war and fire. Inside the walls, it was like stepping into the Garden of Eden. Neat rows of crops flourished in rich soil. Fat mangoes and guavas bent the branches of fruit trees in their orchards. Water splashed through well-kept irrigation canals.

They crossed this paradise to the base of the hill. Here they were met by another ring of walls, another mighty gate, and the start of the city rising vertiginously. Every street and alley seemed to have been hacked out of the rock itself, with the buildings squeezed around them like birds on a cliff. When the residents could build no higher, they had added bamboo gantries onto their roofs or hanging off the sides like storks' nests, extending the dwellings into the air.

The city was a treasure chest, packed with every fancy and delight India could offer. The souks and bazaars ran for miles along the streets. Fragrant spices and richly dyed cloths; brass cooking ware and the golden bangles that Indian women loved; ivory and silk; tea from China, coffee from Arabia and opium from Bengal. And, of course, there were diamonds, glittering in the shadows of windowless shops. Adam paused to examine them. Some looked like no more than fragments of dirty glass, cloudy and opaque. Others had been cut, and sparkled like miniature stars. Long-bearded merchants guarded them jealously and whispered in their customers' ears.

As varied as the merchandise were the people. Adam could not believe how many were crammed inside the city walls. Pathans with long beards and scarred faces; weather-beaten Gurkhas with smiles as wide as their knife blades; Sikhs and Jats wearing rich gold earrings; Muslim women swathed in black from head to toe, and Hindu women in tight-fitting bodices and gauzy saris. There were dark-skinned Africans who made him think of Scipio, and even two white men in the uniform of French dragoons.

The one group he did not see were Englishmen.

'Where is the East India Company?' he asked Panjit.

His host pointed down the slope. From that height, the houses fell away so steeply that Adam could see over their roofs and down to the fields and the river. Outside the walls, upriver, stood two more buildings separated by a large dusty square. They were built of whitewashed brick and red-tiled roofs, straight lines and sharp angles without any decoration or ornament. They stood out like a formal brand on the landscape, an architectural rebuke to the cheek-by-jowl construction of the city.

'That is the British cantonment. Where the troops that *protect* us are quartered.'

A Union flag hung limp from a flagpole over the parade square, where a company of sepoys were practising musket drill. It was the flag Adam had fought under – and for – his whole life. Now, it was the banner of the enemy.

'Is that where Hugo lives?'

'Not in the cantonment.' Panjit pointed further out, where an elegant mansion stood among bungalows and gardens by the river. 'There.'

Gazing down on the house, Adam felt his pulse quicken. At last he was near the end of his quest. He felt the urge to charge back through the city that minute, break down the door and run Hugo through. But Panjit read his thoughts.

'Patience,' the Indian counselled him. 'We must speak with the Maharani first.'

It took almost an hour to reach the summit. The road wound up the hillside, sometimes so steep it turned into flights of stairs. It passed through massive walls, and over ditches that had been hacked out of the stone. At last they came through a domed gate decorated with painted tiles of tigers and leopards, and emerged into a wide courtyard. After the press of the city, it was like an oasis: a garden fringed with fruit trees and filled with flowers. Butterflies flitted among the blossom, and tropical birds swooped between the trees. There was nothing above them except the sky.

Panjit led them through anterooms into an audience chamber. Pillars rose around them, brightly painted in pinks and yellows, fanning out to make intricate vaults. Galleries about the walls were hung with coloured lamps, suffusing the room with variegated light. Guards in short trousers and tight-fitting tiger-striped jackets stood to attention around the throne, which was broad and flat, more like a bed than a chair, and covered in gold. It stood on gold legs with feet sculpted like a tiger's paws, and a golden tiger's head snarled out from its front. A wide crimson canopy fringed with gold had been erected over it. Behind it, a screened window gave breathtaking views over the whole kingdom.

But one thing was missing. The Maharani seemed to be absent. Instead, a little girl of about seven or eight had clambered onto the great tiger throne, lying on her stomach and cuddling a tiger-skin cushion. She wore a tight-fitting black dress embroidered with golden lotus flowers, lavishly trimmed with gold lace. Her dark hair was tied back in a long plait, and she wore a gold circlet around it with a glass bead dangling over her forehead.

Panjit kneeled and kissed the floor. Adam did likewise. The girl sat up and looked down at them, and as she did so, Adam realised he had been wrong on at least three counts.

First, the striped bundle she had been cuddling was not a cushion. It was a tiger cub, a puffball of fur and whiskers that was now energetically licking the girl's hand.

Second, the bead on her forehead was not glass. It caught the light as she turned, projecting points of white brightness across the room. It was an enormous diamond.

And third – from the way everyone was bowing to her – this was not some child playing where she should not.

'Maharani,' said Panjit in a deferential voice, 'allow me to present Mr Adam Courtney.'

The girl leaned forward to peer at them. She swung her legs over the edge of the throne, though her feet did not touch the floor. There was a tray of sweets beside her. She popped one in her mouth.

'I thought we hated Courtneys,' she said to Panjit. Either she didn't realise Adam could understand her language, or she didn't care. 'Why have you brought me another?'

'I believe this one is different.'

The Maharani sucked on her sweet. She fed one to the tiger cub, who licked it out of her palm.

'Why?'

'He saved my life. He is hunted by the East India Company. And he has a personal hatred for Hugo Courtney.'

'Why?'

She had spoken to Panjit again, but Adam was irritated at being discussed like a new horse. He stepped forward and said, 'He killed my family.'

The Maharani turned to look at him. Her eyes were heavily rimmed with kohl; her lips were painted in a rosebud. It created an unsettling effect, a woman's face overlaid on a child's.

'He is your family?'

'Yes.'

She nodded with understanding. Adam supposed feuds and dynastic struggles were not new to a queen, even one as young as this.

'But we do not want Hugo Courtney dead?' It was a question, aimed at Panjit.

'It would give the East India Company the excuse they seek to declare war on us.'

'Then let me kill him,' said Adam. 'You will be blameless.'

'You cannot,' said the Maharani. 'He is not here.'

That surprised Panjit as much as Adam.

'He has not returned from Calcutta?'

'No.'

'But he left Calcutta before I did,' said Adam. He remembered the East India Company litter-bearers he had seen racing along the road. 'He could have been here in half the time it took me.'

'Then he must have gone a different way.' Panjit frowned, trying to make sense of it.

But the Maharani had grown bored. She dangled a piece of brocade for the tiger, jerking it about to make the cub pounce and paw at it.

'I will send out my spies and see where he may be.' Panjit turned to Adam. 'For now, you will remain here as the Maharani's honoured guest.'

'A guest, or a prisoner?'

Panjit looked affronted. 'I am offended you even need to ask.'

Adam was not sure he believed Panjit. The next morning, he walked down to the citadel gate to find out. He was dressed Indian-fashion, in a brocaded coat and loose pantaloons that he had been given, but he did not put on a turban or attempt to disguise himself. That time had passed.

The guard saluted and opened a little postern to let him out on to the teeming streets below the citadel.

Not a prisoner, then, Adam decided.

He descended through the city, fending off the advances of beggars and stallholders, and the few prostitutes who were active even at this early hour.

He knew Hugo would not be at home. But he could not sit still in sight of his enemy's home. He crossed the fields around the foot of the hill, between the chattering irrigation channels and the fluttering birds, and reached the outer ring of walls. But that was as far as he was allowed. The guards on the outer gate smiled and made elaborate bows; they nodded earnestly when Adam spoke to them in his laboured Hindustani. But they would not open the gate.

Adam turned back towards the city. He trudged along until he was certain the guards were not watching, then ducked off the road into an orchard. He worked his way between the trees, hidden from sight, until he reached the red line of the outer rampart.

This was a remote section of the wall, away from any gate or tower. Some of the stones were loose; the fruit trees had been allowed to grow up against the wall.

Adam selected a tall and spreading mango tree and hoisted himself into its branches. The boughs sagged under his weight, but he climbed high enough that he was able to crawl out and drop down onto the top of the wall.

A gun boomed. Adam jumped; instinctively, he looked up, listening for the whizz of a cannonball and the thud of the impact. Was the fortress under attack?

Smoke drifted from the exercise yard of the cantonment, half a mile across the plain from where Adam stood. The sepoys were exercising their field guns. Adam watched them servicing the weapons, worming and sponging out, ramming in the new charge, pretending to load. They crouched beside it as the gunner jerked the lanyard.

A flock of birds flew up from the mango tree as the gun boomed across the plain again. It was a big piece, Adam noted, not field artillery but a heavy siege gun. And the sepoys were well drilled. They moved almost as fluently as Adam's own crew aboard the old *Diamond*.

Satisfied that no one had seen him, Adam crawled through an embrasure. The outer face of the wall was not in good repair. Loose stones and cracks in the mortar gave him plenty of hand-holds to climb down. In a few minutes, he was on the ground outside.

He gave the cantonment a wide berth and joined a road leading towards the river. These must be the officers' quarters – almost a little village of neat whitewashed bungalows set in their own gardens. Palm trees shaded the lanes that connected them.

At the far end, as large as all the other houses put together, was what must be Hugo's residence. A high wall surrounded it, and there was a gate across the drive, but no guards. The only people who watched it were a pair of beggars, a man and a young woman, sitting cross-legged in the shade across the way. Perhaps they were resting on their way somewhere else, for they could not get many passers-by there. Adam was surprised no one had moved them on.

The man rattled a bowl at Adam. Adam still had a few of the coins that Cornish had given him. He fished one out of his purse and dropped it in the man's bowl.

'Does Hugo Courtney live here?' Adam asked in Hindustani. 'Do you know when he will return?'

He did not expect much of a beggar, but it was worth trying to get something for his money.

The beggar shook his head, though whether in answer or because he did not know, or simply because the coin was not enough, Adam could not tell. The woman might know, but she was gazing at Adam with such a discomfortingly fierce stare that he had to look away. He supposed a young woman begging on the roads of India would have learned to fear what men might want of her. It must be a wretched existence.

He left the pair of them and crossed the road to the gate. Peering through it, he could see the house was a handsome mansion in the neoclassical style. It had a stuccoed frontage, and a semicircular portico held up by Grecian columns. With tailored lawns surrounding it, it would have been as much at home in rural England as in central India, apart from the tropical flowers in the flower beds, and the monkeys scampering through the trees.

Adam gripped the gate's iron bars. He stared at the house, as Hugo must have stared through the gate of Fort Auspice at the Courtney family home. Adam imagined how this fine Palladian house would look as a burned-out shell, its walls splashed with blood and vines curling through its shattered windows.

For now, there was nothing he could do. It would be madness to go any further. He could hear voices on the other side of the wall, out of sight behind a bush. He could not risk revealing himself too soon. He turned to go back.

There was a crack. Adam spun around just in time to see a hard round object flying towards him. It struck him square in the centre of his forehead and he collapsed.

INDIAN OCEAN, 1803

S ana tipped out a bucket and sluiced blood off the planks. Paul wiped his knife with a rag. At his feet in the bilge, the bodies he had gutted gasped their final breaths. Astern, the water churned as sharks fed on the gore Sana had dumped over the side.

'We will eat well tonight,' said Sana.

She took the knife from Paul, picked up one of the fish they had landed, and cut off its tail with a well-practised chop that the executioner in the Place de la Révolution would have admired. Paul could not watch without wincing.

At the stern, Mohammed, the master, smacked his lips. He had a wizened face, deeply etched from decades squinting in the sun and the wind, and three teeth, of which he was inordinately proud. He was not a gentle man – he would strike Paul with a rope end if he took in a reef wrong, and slap Sana if she got in his way – but he was not cruel. He looked after his ship, his cargo and his crew; he was kind when he could afford to be.

Paul did not want to have to kill him.

Sana passed the knife back to Paul. He took it, but for a moment she refused to let go. Blood from her hands dribbled over his fingers. Their eyes met.

When are we going to do it? she asked silently.

I don't know.

You have delayed this too long.

We have to be ready.

How much longer do you want?

She let go suddenly. Paul jerked back. He moved to the front of the boat and began parcelling a rope. Sana cleaned the fish. She put hooks through their jaws and hung them up on a line to dry in the sun.

How much longer?

Paul understood her impatience. Two years had passed – as best Paul could reckon in the unfamiliar tropical seasons – since they stumbled on to the beach and met Ilya. Two years plying the coast in the Greek's vessels, carrying ivory, cloves, hardwoods, cloth, tools and foodstuffs. They had travelled almost the whole length of Africa: the Red Sea ports of Massawa and Aden; the Swahili coast cities of Malindi, Mombasa and Quelimane; down to the Portuguese trading forts at Delagoa Bay.

Paul had become lean and strong, his body tanned nut-brown and rippling with muscles. Sana had grown, though no one had noticed. The child who had run heedlessly naked was gone. Living at close quarters with a boatful of sailors, Sana had become cautious with her body. She bound her hair in girlish plaits and wore a loose blue dress that smothered any evidence of the changes underneath. The crew were so used to her, they paid her no attention.

That would be useful when the time came to strike.

Paul had never meant this adventure to go on so long. He had thought they would be on the boat for a few weeks at most. They would learn how to handle her, much as he had once learned to ride a camel, and then they would set out for freedom.

But sailing was unfathomably complicated. It had taken him months to learn the names of all the ropes, how to read the wind and trim the sails and steer the right course. By the time he understood it all, he realised that the idea of him and Sana taking the ship by themselves was impossible. It was a heavy, two-masted *baghlah* dhow that needed a crew of thirty to handle.

He had also come to know how vast the continent of Africa was. On one night of shore leave, he had found a drunken Portuguese navigator in a tavern in Mombasa. Paul and Sana had plied the man with cheap arak and questions. What they learned was not encouraging. From the Horn of Africa, where they had met Ilya, to the southern tip of the continent, was some four thousand miles.

'And this . . .' The Portuguese had drawn a rough map with his finger in the alcohol that had slopped over the table. He jabbed his finger on the bottom of it. 'You know the real name for this? *Cabo das Tormentas* – the Cape of Storms.'

'Do people live there?' Sana had asked.

'There is a harbour, Cape Town. That is where the great trading ships call on their way to India and the East Indies.'

'Could two people get there in a dhow?'

Paul had shot Sana a warning look, but the Portuguese was too drunk to notice. He swigged his drink and shrugged.

'Nothing is impossible with God. But likely . . .?' Whatever else he had to say was drowned in a fit of drunken laughter.

In Quelimane, their fortunes had improved. Paul and Sana had been transferred to another boat from Ilya's fleet. Their new home was a smaller vessel with a single mast and a crew of ten. Paul had studied his shipmates, marking what each man did and how the work could be carried out if there were only two people aboard. In calm winds, he thought it might be possible.

They would still have to dispose of the crew. As well as Mohammed, there were seven others. After weeks at sea together, Paul and Sana knew them well enough to be sure that none of them would support an act of mutiny. Sana had no doubt what to do about them.

'Strangle them. You remember how?'

Paul shuddered. That was a chapter of his life he had tried to erase, though it lingered in his memory like a nightmare he could not shake. He refused to admit to himself that there had been a time when breaking a man's neck came as easily as shaking his hand. The thought filled him with horror.

But they could not delay much longer. They were in the right place. A storm had driven them past Delagoa Bay, further south than they would normally go. They had taken a few days to repair the boat and catch fish to replenish their supplies. Now they would turn north, for the long voyage coasting back towards Zeila.

By Paul's best guess, they were still almost a thousand miles from Cape Town. They would have to risk it.

It was mid-afternoon, and everyone was on deck. At the helm, Tenga the steersman kept a steady hand on the tiller. He was the latest addition to their crew, having joined them at Delagoa Bay. Beside him, Mohammed chewed on a wad of khat and surveyed proceedings like a lazy dog, occasionally stirring himself to bark an order. The others were busy mending ropes, tying nets and caulking planks.

'It is time,' Mohammed grunted. 'Come about.'

The men started to move. Sana picked up the gutting knife. Paul took a length of thin rope and looped one end around his fist, just as he had held the tarade in Gondar.

'I need a barrel of salt to pack these fish,' Sana called. 'Will someone fetch one from the hold?'

'Get it yourself,' called one of the crew.

'I am only a feeble girl,' she answered.

Grumbling good-naturedly, two others went below. That left six on deck. Still too many, but the best odds that Paul and Sana would have.

Sana moved towards the bow. Paul sidled towards Mohammed at the stern. He would strangle him first, then grab the tiller and force the boat around. The sudden change of direction would make the sail swing wildly. That should cause enough confusion that Paul could take on Tenga and the others.

The blood sang in his ears and bile rose in his throat. *You have done this before*, he told himself. But that had been under orders, for self-preservation. This was on his own account.

From nowhere, the ibis-headed god was suddenly in his mind. Paul had not heard the voice in years, but now it spoke like a long-lost friend.

To master life, you must hold it as light as a feather.

'What do you want, Samat?' asked Mohammed.

'Samat' was their name for Paul: it meant 'silent one'.

Paul had to distract the captain. He turned and looked out to sea as if he had seen something.

'What is it?'

Paul pointed – but, of course, he could not speak. With a grunt, Mohammed pulled himself up and came to the rail, shielding his eyes against the sun as he followed Paul's gaze.

This was Paul's chance. From the bow, he could feel Sana's eyes on him, waiting for the signal to wield her knife. He lifted his hand. At any moment, Mohammed would realise there was nothing to see and turn around again. Paul had to strike now.

He could not do it. The rope burned into Paul's palm like hot metal; he let it drop into the bilge. Over his shoulder, he saw Sana put down the gutting knife and shoot Paul a look of fathomless disappointment – the way his mother had sometimes looked at him.

'Who can she be?' Mohammed said.

Paul turned. Mohammed was not confused, or berating Paul for wasting his time. He was studying something.

Paul looked out to sea again, more closely this time.

There was a ship on the horizon, where he had pointed, as if he had conjured it from his imagination. It should not be there. From the navigator, Paul knew that the coast south of Delagoa Bay was a barren and inhospitable place. There were no people and no safe harbours – only hundreds of miles of rocky shore, lapped by vicious tides. The coastal traders avoided it because there was no one to trade with; foreign merchantmen steered clear so they would not be dashed to pieces.

'Look at this!' Mohammed called.

By now, everyone had come to the stern to study the distant ship. She was neither a dhow nor a cargo vessel, but a square-rigged warship. Paul could see the gunports chequerboarded down her side, and the figure of a ravenous shark baring its teeth from her bow.

On the voyage from Toulon, Paul had spent some time drawing the ships in the fleet, and learning their names. Now one of those unfamiliar nautical words swam back from the depths of his memory. She was a frigate.

And that was not the only memory she triggered. At her stern flapped a flag Paul had last seen tattered in the desert: the *tricolore* of France. He could read her name in French, too, painted on the bow. *Requin.*

He felt an old terror stirring. He looked west, where the coast of Africa made a low line in the far distance. He jabbed his finger towards it. His eyes pleaded with Mohammed to change course and run.

'We are nothing to them,' said Mohammed. He spat his wad of khat over the side. 'Except to trade.'

This was something they had done before. Ships' captains would pay better prices than you could get in the markets on shore and were less fussy about quality. Mohammed would offload the worst of his cargo, report to Ilya that it had been lost or spoiled, and pocket the takings, sharing his profit with the crew as the price of their silence.

Tenga set the ship on a heading to intercept the frigate. They closed quickly, for the frigate had also altered course to meet them.

The sail rattled down as Tenga brought them up against the frigate's hull. A rope was thrown up and made fast. The crew delved in the hold and brought up a selection of trade goods. A face appeared above, leaning from the frigate's side and beckoning them up.

'*Venez, venez.*'

On the frigate's deck, out of sight, the officers were conferring. They made no attempt to hide their voices, for they did not expect anyone in a boat full of African sailors to understand French. A gust of wind brought their words to Paul's ears down in the boat.

'She is too small to bother with.'

'But the crew. How much would they fetch in the slave markets?'

'Six hundred francs?'

'That would be something. Until the war starts again and we can get back to our proper business.'

Paul tried to attract Mohammed's attention, shaking his head in warning. But Mohammed was already clambering up the ladder. Paul grabbed Sana. He put his wrists together, hands splayed out, mimicking shackles.

Sana understood. She had not forgotten the months-long march with the Bishareen slavers. She grabbed Tenga, waiting his turn at the foot of the ladder, and whispered in his ear.

His eyes widened. He looked around uncertainly.

'Come on,' said Mohammed from the deck above. 'They have brandy for us.'

The rest of the crew had gathered around the ladder, jostling impatiently to go up. That persuaded Tenga. He climbed; the others followed. Paul hung back, leaning his weight on the gunwale. He had the fish knife in his hands, hidden from view, cutting into the rope that moored them to the French frigate. He sawed it back and forth, severing the fibres one by one.

Nobody noticed the rope end drop in the water as Paul cut through. Her crew were already on the *Requin*'s deck, enjoying the brandy that their hosts plied them with. The dhow began to drift away.

The gap between the two ships widened into open water. For a few precious moments, no one saw what was happening. Then there came a shout from above. Mohammed appeared at the frigate's side, scowling down on them with a brandy glass in his hand.

'What are you doing? Come back.'

Paul held up his hands, miming helplessness. On the frigate's deck, a sailor appeared with a rope and a boarding grapnel. He tossed it with a well-practised arm, and it sailed across the water straight for the dhow. Paul made as if to catch it, but his hands batted it away so that it splashed into the sea alongside.

'Clumsy halfwit!' raged Mohammed. 'I will beat you like a dog when I am back aboard my ship.'

Half an hour earlier, Paul had been within an inch of strangling Mohammed. Now, he felt a short-lived flicker of sympathy for the man he had served. Mohammed did not realise he was living out the last few moments of his freedom. The rest of his life would be spent in chains.

That was the way of the world. For now, Paul's only concern was to make sure he did not join the captain. The French sailor had hauled in the grapnel and thrown it again. The gap was now so wide that Paul didn't have to pretend to fumble it. It dropped short with a splash.

'Soon they will realise this is not an accident,' said Sana.

She had been untying the sail, ready to raise it at a moment's notice.

They won't pursue us, Paul thought.

The dhow was not worth the effort. With the crew captured, the French were already in profit. Their captain would not want to risk his magnificent ship getting any closer to the treacherous shore for such a feeble prize.

Paul nodded to Sana. Together, they hauled on the halyard to raise the sail. Normally it would have taken three men to do it, but Paul and Sana were fleeing for their lives. They hoisted the diagonal boom to the masthead and made it fast. The triangular sail filled with the wind, like a shark's fin cutting across the sea.

Paul grinned at Sana.

We have our boat.

And without a drop of blood being spilled. He took the tiller and settled on the stern bench. When he was comfortable with their heading, he turned to look at the frigate. By now it must be obvious that Paul and Sana were fleeing, but he could see no sign the *Requin* would give chase. There was some kind of commotion on deck, much movement and bustle, but no topmen putting on sail or bracing the yards around to change course.

A rumble sounded from across the water. The black gunports lifted, and twenty guns poked out their snouts. Sana blanched; Paul gave her a reassuring look. The French captain was trying to scare them with a warning shot.

But one gun would have sufficed for a warning shot.

The cannons fired. Not in unison but one after another, a wave of fire rippling down the frigate's side. With a chill of horror, Paul realised what they were doing. They weren't aiming to capture or dismast the dhow. They were using her as target practice.

Cannonballs flew all around them. Paul pushed Sana to the deck and threw himself on top of her, shielding her with his body. The scream of iron tore the air. Water splashed him from the spouts thrown up where the cannonballs landed in the sea around them. One ball struck the transom and unleashed a hail of splinters, some as much as a foot long. The dhow's planks were not nailed together – they were sewn. They shifted and warped under the impact, like a writhing snake. One ball passed so low overhead, Paul felt it tickle the back of his head. Another punched a perfect round hole through the sail.

And then it stopped. The gunners must be reloading. Paul braced himself for the next onslaught.

When it didn't come, he raised his head above the side and looked back. They had sailed further than he thought. The *Requin* had receded in the distance, so far she must be out of range. Her captain would not waste more powder and shot on them. Nor was he doing anything to put on more sail or change course to follow them.

Paul grinned with the elation of having cheated death once again. He tugged Sana up. She rose, rubbing her arms where she had been pinned down awkwardly. But she did not smile like Paul; she did not even look at the frigate. She was staring ahead.

Paul followed her gaze. The distance they had put between them and the frigate had brought them closer to the shore. The coast loomed high and dark and suddenly nearby. He could see the breakers foaming on the rocks.

He became aware of the wind. It was the reason they had escaped the French frigate so fast, a stiff easterly breeze speeding them towards the coast.

He gestured to Sana.

We need to come about.

This was a complex procedure on a dhow. The sail had to be loosened, and the whole yard needed to be pivoted around the mast. Even with a full crew it was an unwieldy manoeuvre. For a man and a girl alone, it was almost impossible.

Sana untied the sheet. The sail flapped and billowed, snapping out of her hands as she tried to bundle it up. Paul went to the front of the boat, balancing on the prow. The wood was slick with spray; the bow plunged down and reared up as the damaged boat rode the surging sea. Paul had no purchase to grip the heavy boom, let alone move it around.

The coast was getting nearer. The wind roared in his ears. If he did not bring the boom around quickly, the boat would be driven onto the rocks. He could not do it with his hands; instead, he wrapped his arms around the boom and kicked off with all his strength, using his weight to shift it.

With a creak of ropes, the boom swung around the masthead and on to the opposite tack. Sana scrambled to the stern and put the tiller over. Paul grabbed the untethered sail and pulled it around the mast. It bellied out as it started to catch the wind; if it filled, he would never have the strength to haul it in. He found the mainsheet tangled in the canvas and pulled it back. If he could just make it fast . . .

Halfway along the gunwale there was a wooden post for fastening the sheet. Moving backwards, Paul reached instinctively for it but felt nothing. Had he misjudged it? He looked back.

The post wasn't there. One of the cannonballs had bitten out a chunk of the hull, carrying away the planking and the post that had been attached to it. There was nowhere to tie the sheet down.

A gust of wind caught the sail. The rope snapped out of Paul's hand, so suddenly he was forced to let go or he would have been dragged overboard.

The dhow had already started to turn before she lost steerage way. Now she was caught halfway round, broadside-on to the rolling waves. The sea smacked into her side, battering and rolling her so hard Paul feared they would overturn. Only the cargo in her hold kept the boat buoyant.

Even without the sail to power them, the boat had not slowed. A current had them in its grasp and was dragging them on. Paul scanned the looming shore for any opening – a beach or a cove where they might bring the boat in safely. The black cliffs made an impenetrable rampart.

Now they were so close that he could see they were not sheer cliffs, but a series of rocky shelves rising out of the water. It made little difference. The boat would be smashed to pieces long before it reached dry land. Sana had grown up in a desert, and Paul in the middle of France. Neither of them had learned to swim.

They clung to each other, and to the boat. Paul kept one hand on the tiller, but it made little difference. The rocks were black, the water was black, the sky was black: everything was darkness.

The boat hit. Even though Paul knew it was coming, was braced for it, the impact was shocking. In the two years he had been sailing the African coast, he had run aground many times. Those had been gentle experiences – a jolt, and then the grate of mud or sand under the hull. This was nothing like that. The rock struck the boat with the force of a cannonball. The hull shattered; the mast toppled. Water gushed in. The battered timbers tore and twisted free from the cords that sewed them together. The planks floated off onto the sea, and were immediately hurled back with redoubled force by the waves. One hit Paul on the shoulder, so hard his arm went numb.

The boat was dying. If Paul and Sana didn't move, they would be pulverised with their ship. But the alternative was no better: to throw themselves into the foaming, chewing mouth of the waves around them. They were still too far from shore to touch bottom.

A massive object swung towards Paul's face. It was the broken mast, carried on the waves with the speed of a bolting horse. He threw himself back, just before it would have cracked his skull.

Sana was not so lucky. The mast hit her square across the shoulders and knocked her into the water. She cried out, but only for an instant. The sea swallowed her. Paul saw her body, a black shape in the water, being carried towards the shore like a piece of flotsam.

He opened his mouth to call for her, but the sound that came out was an indistinct, choking groan. He hurled himself off the shipwreck and into the water.

The mast bobbed a few feet away. Paul lunged to grab on to it – anything to help him float – but the current carried it out of reach. He was alone in the water.

He splashed and kicked and fought against the surging waves. It wasn't a fair fight. He had no strength left, while the sea's power rolled in from eternity. It toyed with him, tossing him up and throwing him down, like a kitten playing with a mouse. Even so, he lasted longer than he thought possible. He had to find Sana. Every time his head broke the surface, he shook the water from his stinging eyes and scanned the sea for her. In the dark chaos, surrounded by rocks and wave caps and broken pieces of the boat, it was impossible.

At last his strength failed, and he slipped beneath the waves.

HOLKAR, 1807

Adam was lying on the ground, eyes closed, breathing in the scent of jasmine. His head throbbed. He remembered a projectile flying towards him. He'd thought it must be a cannonball from the artillery in the cantonment.

If it had been a cannonball, his head would not be hurting. It would be pulverised.

He put his hand to his forehead and felt a hard lump rising. He winced and opened his eyes.

A child stood over him, maybe seven or eight years old. He wore a blue linen one-piece suit, with a frilled white collar framing a cherubic face, with golden curls and bright blue eyes. He was holding a cricket bat, scaled down to his size.

'I hit a six,' he said proudly.

An Indian woman in a voluminous sari bustled up behind him. 'Master Ralph,' she cried in English. 'Please what have you done?'

Ralph's young face creased with concern. He stared down at Adam.

'Or did you catch it?' He turned to someone Adam could not see. 'Is it out if he catches it, even if it went over the boundary?'

'I only caught it with my head,' Adam reassured him. 'You are not out.'

The boy stared at Adam as if he had grown a second head.

'He speaks English. I thought he was a blackie.'

'Ralph,' a voice reproved him. 'We do not use that language.'

The voice came from behind Adam – a woman's voice, gentle and cool. Adam craned to see who it was. The sun was behind her, so for a moment he was blinded.

'I must apologise for my son.' She saw the bruise purpling on Adam's forehead and gave a small cry. 'He has hurt you.'

She stooped into the shade. Her face swam into focus. Even in his dazed state, Adam could see she was exquisite. Her white skin bore no trace of the tropical sun, seeming lighter still against the raven-dark hair that framed it. But it was a brittle beauty, like porcelain: so flawless you feared it could not last. So fragile, you wanted to wrap your arms around her to cushion her from the world.

Adam made to get up. At the same moment, she leaned in to stroke a lock of hair that was matted to his bruise. Their heads collided, sending another jolt of pain through Adam. He flinched.

'I am so clumsy!' the woman cried. 'I am heaping injury upon injury.'

'Not at all, ma'am.' Adam got to his feet, brushing off the dust. 'We sailors have hard heads.'

Her eyes widened. He saw the question forming on her lips, but before he could think how he would answer it, her son spoke up with a dozen questions of his own.

'Are you really a sailor? Do you have a ship?' He looked down the lane towards the river, as if he expected to see a ship of the line anchored in its broad reach. 'How did you get so far from the sea? Why are you dressed like a native?'

'Ralph,' his mother reprimanded him again. 'You must not pester this gentleman. I must apologise, Mr . . .?'

Her eyes rested on Adam's. She was waiting for him to answer, and he did not know what to say. In all the months of plotting his revenge, all the hours of sleepless nights imagining what he would do, he had not anticipated this situation. His plans might succeed or fail on what he said next.

'Adam Courtney.' Looking into her eyes, he found he did not want to lie to her.

She put a gloved hand to her mouth. 'Oh! But I am Clare Courtney. Are we . . .' she peered at him, 'related?'

'I believe I am a distant cousin of your husband's,' said Adam.

'Hugo never spoke of you.'

'I would be surprised if he knows of my existence. Our branches of the family are . . . not close.'

'Yet here you are. As if by magic.' She stared at him, her eyes so deep Adam could not tell what might lie at the bottom. 'But I am forgetting my manners, keeping you on my doorstep when we have done you such injury. You must come and take tea.'

Adam knew it was dangerous. One careless slip might reveal his purpose, betray the fact that this was no chance encounter. He might learn more about Hugo – but the longer he spent enjoying the family's hospitality, playing with the boy, enjoying Clare's beauty, the harder it would be to do what he had come to do.

Ralph had been hopping from foot to foot while they talked, bouncing the cricket ball on the face of his bat. He grabbed Adam's hand and tugged him forward.

'Please come.'

'Please,' Clare echoed. There was an intensity in her voice that pulled Adam in directions he knew he should not go. 'For Ralph's sake.'

'I should be delighted.'

Unseen from the shadows across the road, the two beggars watched him go in.

They walked up the carriage drive, between the trim lawns and riotous flower beds, and sat on a veranda overlooking the river at the rear. A dozen servants brought tea, cakes, jellies and scones. If not for the water buffalo wallowing in the mud-brown water, the pagodas in the distance and a herd of elephants trumpeting on the far bank, they might have been in Surrey.

'What brings you to India?' Clare enquired.

The walk up the drive had given Adam time to concoct a story. 'Trade.'

She glanced at his clothes. If she was surprised to see a European in Indian garb, she did not show it – though there were many men, like Cornish, who took on the locals' customs.

'I guess by your attire you are not with the Company?'

'No, ma'am. I am here on my own account.'

A shadow crossed her face. 'Hugo will not stand for that.'

'Daddy says interlopers should be strung up,' Ralph volunteered through a mouthful of cream cake.

'You must forgive him,' said Clare. 'He is plain-spoken, like his father.'

Adam pushed back his chair. 'I should go. I do not want to put you in a delicate situation.'

'No.' Clare had grown agitated. The skin at her throat flushed scarlet; her cheeks glistened with sweat. The servant standing behind her began wafting her with a fan. The sight reminded

Adam of Lizzie in Cape Town, with her peacock fan and her sparkling eyes. He tried to put it out of his mind. 'Please stay. I get so little company here. The garrison officers . . .' She made a dreary gesture with her hand. 'And you must not be afraid of Hugo. He is away on Company business. Your secret is safe with me. But – let us talk of other things. Tell me of England.'

'I have barely been there six months in the last five years,' said Adam.

'That is more than me. I have lived in India through eight monsoons now. You know what they say in Calcutta – "two monsoons are the life of a man"? So I suppose I have lived four lifetimes here.'

'How did you come to be here?'

She waved the question away. 'Everybody knows my story. You do not wish to hear it.'

'I do,' he protested.

It was true. He wanted to know everything about her.

'I fell in love with Hugo. I married him and he brought me here. That is the sum of it.'

She said it offhand, but Adam could feel the pulse of emotion behind it. There was more she was not telling him. Before he could probe, she said, 'Tell me your story. Are you married?'

It was not the question Adam had expected.

'No, ma'am.'

'Do not call me that. You make me sound like an old maid. Surely a dashing young sea captain with such fine prospects must have a fancy or a sweetheart?'

'Alas, there are few opportunities for courting aboard ship.' Again, a vivid and wholly indecent image of Lizzie flashed in his mind.

Why can't I forget her?

'I am certain you must have left behind a string of broken hearts in every port,' she teased him. Then, veering suddenly. 'How do you find India?'

'Hot.'

'Indeed.' The servant began fanning Clare more vigorously. 'It is like this every year before the monsoon. Some days it is so strong I cannot even rise from my bed. Then the weather breaks, and the rains bring some relief. And the next year, it happens exactly the same.'

There was a pause in the conversation.

'Are you lodging in the cantonment?' she asked.

'In the city.'

'In Holkar? I did not know Englishmen were allowed there.' Again, the shadow of fear crossed her face. She kept looking over her shoulder, even when Adam was speaking, as if she was waiting for someone. 'But if you are family, you should stay with us. I could offer you a bed.'

She was looking away, so he could not see the intent in her eyes. On the face of it, her words were no more than courtesy. But again, he felt a current running under them that seemed to offer much more.

He was tempted to accept. He could not pretend to himself this time that it was to help his quest. Breathing in Clare's scent, watching as she licked away a crumb of icing from her cherry-red lips, he wanted more. He was stunned at the effect she had on him. He had endured so much hardship on his journey – murder, bloodshed, hostility, fear – that her soft entreaties were irresistible, like the pull of gravity.

For a third time, the memory of Lizzie intruded on his thoughts. He tried to shut the door on it.

She will be married by now, he reminded himself. *You made your choice. You will never see her again.*

'The Maharani's vizier, Panjit Rao, would not allow me to stay here,' he said. 'He insists that I stay in the city.'

'That is a pity. Ralph would have enjoyed having a playmate.' Clare's face was emotionless again, composed in bland politeness. 'Do you expect to stay long?'

'Until I have completed my business.'

'Your mysterious business. I think you are a man of secrets, cousin Courtney. Did you really come not knowing you might find Hugo?'

'I knew he was stationed here,' Adam allowed. 'His reputation—'

'Ah, his *reputation*.' Clare made a grand sweep with her arms. 'All the Courtneys have such *magnificent* reputations. You have seen the statue of my father-in-law, Gerard, in Calcutta?'

'I have.'

'Is it not marvellous?'

Adam could hear the sarcasm in her voice. He wasn't sure how to respond. Instead, he changed the subject.

'When is your husband expected to return?'

She tipped her head in ignorance. 'You know this country. Only the rains are predictable.'

'He did not share his intentions?'

'He tells me nothing.'

Adam thought for a moment.

'How long did you say you have been here?'

'Eight years in India. Four in Holkar.' She sighed and rearranged herself in her chair. 'Calcutta was tolerable, just. At least there was a little society. In Holkar there is nobody. When Hugo is away, I only have Ralph to play with.' She gave a sad smile. 'I have become a tolerable batsman and a very respectable medium-slow bowler.'

'Is Hugo away often?'

'The Company . . .' She waved her hand. 'He is devoted to his work.'

Adam knew he should ask more about what had taken Hugo away – and about what might have delayed his return. But that was not the question burning in his mind.

'Four years ago – did he go away for a long voyage. Six months or more?'

He knew he had overstepped the moment the words were out of his mouth. Clare went still, staring at him as if he had burst in on her in her boudoir. The silence stretched uncomfortably. Crickets chirped in the garden, and flies buzzed low over the crumbs on the plates.

'Where did you say you came from, Mr Courtney?'

'I travelled from Calcutta.'

'I mean, where is your home?'

'I was born at sea.'

'Of course.' She gave a dark little laugh. 'A piece of flotsam, washed up on the shore by the tides of fate. How poetic.'

'I think it is time for me to go.'

Adam rose, and this time Clare did not try to stop him. But though there were a hundred servants who could have shown him out, she escorted him to the gate. The day was getting on; the cricket stumps on the lawn cast long shadows towards the citadel.

Adam's head was filled with thoughts he dared not voice. Perhaps Clare was the same. Several times she turned towards him as if to speak, then looked away. But at the gate she clutched his arm, pressing herself close to him. Adam thought she must have tripped or lost her balance, but her feet were planted firmly on the ground and her dark eyes were fixed on his.

'Do not overstay your welcome,' she warned him. 'Holkar may seem a marvel of diamonds and spices and antique wonders, but it is a dangerous place. My husband will return before the monsoon breaks. When he comes, it will be more dangerous still.'

Without another word, she let him go and spun away. Adam watched her making her way up the path. In the dusky light, she seemed to glide across the gravel like a ghost, until she faded between the columns of the white house.

'You knew Hugo Courtney was not at home,' said Panjit. He sat on a cushion, puffing on a gold hookah pipe. Armed guards had brought Adam to his quarters the moment Adam returned to the citadel. 'And in any event, I expected you to stay within the city walls.'

'I did not know I was answerable to you for my movements.'

Panjit pointed through an open window. His apartments were in the north-east tower of the palace, with eagle-eye views looking down to the river, the cantonment and the British residency.

'You are my honoured guest. But I would be a poor host if I did not look out for my friend.'

'I can look after myself.'

Panjit blew a plume of apple-scented tobacco smoke into the air.

'Indeed yes. I would be dead if you could not.' He passed the pipe to Adam. 'Did you learn anything from your visit?' He nodded at the lump on Adam's head. 'I am sure you handled matters with your customary delicacy.'

'That was just . . .' Adam could not begin to think how he would explain cricket to the Indian. 'Bad luck.'

'I would say you are a man who attracts more than his share of bad luck.'

Adam couldn't deny it.

'How long until the monsoon rains break?'

'Three weeks, maybe four.'

'Clare – Mrs Courtney – said that Hugo will return before the monsoon.'

'So . . .' Panjit puffed out his cheeks, rolling the smoke around his mouth. 'That is something worth knowing.'

'I will have to remain until he comes. But I do not wish to outstay my welcome. I can find lodgings in the city.'

'Not at all. As I have said, you are the Maharani's guest.'

Adam knew exactly what sort of guest he was.

'Why are you keeping me here?'

Panjit exhaled. His face almost disappeared in a nimbus of smoke. 'I do not want Hugo Courtney to die until it suits my purpose.'

'But you said he was your enemy.'

'And he is. But he is not the only one. I must keep the Maharani's foes in balance.'

Panjit pointed to the chessboard. A game was in progress; the white queen had advanced deep into enemy territory. A black rook, bishop and three pawns surrounded her.

'My queen cannot move,' Panjit said. 'She could take any of those pieces, yes, but as soon as she does, she leaves herself vulnerable. She must stay still, and wait for her opponent to make a mistake.

'But I have other pieces to play.' He pointed to the white knight – the elephant – still in its starting position. 'The enemy does not know what I will do with him. Perhaps, if I play him at the right moment, I can spring my opponent's trap and mate his king. But I must wait until the time is right.'

He peered at Adam, in case he had not understood.

'You are the knight.'

'I feel more like a pawn. And I do not care about your power games. I am here for my family's honour.'

'That is why I must keep a close eye on you. To stop you acting before I am ready.' The veneer of courtesy disappeared, to be replaced by the naked exercise of power. 'You will stay as the Maharani's honoured guest, enjoying every courtesy and luxury we can offer.'

Smoke filled the room and stung Adam's eyes. Comfort and luxury meant nothing to him – all that mattered was killing

Hugo. But he could not do that until Hugo returned. There was no point forcing the issue until then.

'Will I ever be allowed to leave the city? As your *guest*?'

Panjit's eyes narrowed. 'Where would you go?'

'To Hugo's house.' Panjit began to speak, but Adam overrode him. 'His wife is lonely – she would welcome my company. She might let slip details of Hugo's plans. Or I could search the house when her back is turned.'

Panjit said nothing. He had his chess-playing face on, the frown of concentration he wore when he was calculating dozens of possible moves and their ramifications.

'Clare Courtney is attractive, is she not?' he said.

'I did not pay attention.'

The vizier broke into a smile. 'Now I know you are lying. Even a eunuch would have noticed her beauty. And I do not want you growing too close to these Courtneys.'

'If you could see in my heart, you would know that is no risk at all.'

'Indeed.' Panjit stroked his beard. 'The heart is an organ of air and fire. No man can tell all the things that are in it – even his own. I think it will be safer for you to stay in the citadel.'

'I met a man at sea who wanted to make me his prisoner,' Adam warned him. 'It did not end well for him.'

'You have misunderstood. You are not my prisoner.'

'What am I, then?'

'Waiting.'

Waiting. Out of the many challenges Adam had faced on his long journey, from the ruins of Fort Auspice to Hugo Courtney's doorstep, that was the worst: in Lesaut's prison; in the *Mornington's* hold; on the road from Calcutta; and now in the citadel of Holkar. Deprived of an outlet, his energy turned inwards, chiselling away at his soul. Though he tried to keep busy, every morning he found it harder to drag himself out of the sumptuous bed the Maharani had provided him.

Unexpectedly, it deepened his sympathy for Clare. Her prison was the invisible walls of her race, her sex and her status, but she was a captive as much as he was. He could not imagine how it must be, living such a life for years on end.

He told himself it was better if he did not call on her again. He had revealed too much of himself already. But he thought about her all day, obsessively, and at night he dreamed about her. He told himself it was because he was so bored, he had nothing else to think about.

He held out for three days. Then he went to find her.

It was the first time he had tested the bounds of his agreement with Panjit. No one stopped him leaving the palace, but again when he reached the gate of the outer walls the smiling guards would not let him through. He tried the mango orchard, but the trees near the walls had all been chopped down, and the gaps in the rampart repaired with fresh bricks and mortar.

Adam would not get out again that way. He suspected Panjit would have taken similar precautions elsewhere, but he walked the whole circuit of the walls anyway. It took him a full day. There were no trees overhanging the rampart, no ladders or ropes left lying about, no outbuildings he could clamber up. The guards who manned the watchtowers hailed him as he passed, friendly, but making sure he knew they saw him.

He returned to the city weary and defeated. Panjit smiled at him.

'Did you enjoy your walk?'

'Most invigorating.'

The impossibility of escape did not crush Adam's hopes. Instead, it goaded him on. He dreamed up more and more impractical schemes, each more life-threatening than the last. He could go out of the window and climb down where the wall gave way to the cliff face. He could strap himself to the belly of a cow and let it carry him out through the gate. He could make a giant kite from his bed sheets and fly down from the citadel to land on Clare's lawn.

At that point, he realised he had lost his senses.

You are not Icarus or Odysseus or some figure from myth, he told himself. *You are in a city of thousands. Men come and go all the time. There must be a way.*

One afternoon, Adam was sitting in the palace courtyard when two workmen came to repair the fountain. It was built in the shape of a life-size elephant: the spout was hidden in the trunk, so that when the fountain was turned on, water sprayed out of the trunk over the animal's back as if it was washing itself. But there was no water coming out that day.

'The wheel has jammed again,' said one of the workmen.

Adam watched, glad of any diversion and curious to see how the contraption worked. He expected the workmen to open some door in the elephant's belly. To his surprise, they went to a squat little building at the side of the courtyard, a square stone structure about the size of a single room. Adam had not paid it any attention, except to assume it must be some kind of storeroom. But now he looked closer, he did not see any door, only a small flight of stairs leading up to the roof.

The workmen climbed the stairs and kneeled. One of the men inserted a crowbar, and lifted one of the paving stones that covered the roof. Adam, down in the courtyard, could not see what was underneath it, but he guessed it must be some kind of opening or trapdoor.

The thinner of the two men tied a rope around his waist and slithered into the hole. The other man kneeled beside it, passing down various tools and pieces of rope.

They worked for about an hour. Suddenly, with a belch of air, a gush of water splashed out of the elephant's trunk and began to flow again. The man climbed out of the hole, soaking wet and filthy. They gathered their tools, replaced the stone and wandered away.

Adam waited for a few minutes after they had gone, then – as casually as he could – went up the stairs to the roof of the building. The crowbar had left scratch marks around the stone that had been lifted – and there was a sign, too: a small ideogram chiselled into the corner of the slab. Three curling lines, like waves.

'Has the city ever been taken by siege?' Adam asked Panjit later that evening.

They were playing their usual game of chess.

'Never,' said Panjit. 'Though many have tried.'

'I would have thought a determined army would have no difficulty starving the city out.'

'The orchards and gardens give us all the food we need.'

'And water? I have not seen many tanks.'

It was true. Everywhere he had travelled in India, in towns and roadsides and by temples or pagodas, one of the features was the large open tanks that collected water. In Calcutta, the Great Tank was the centre of town and a favourite spot for promenades. Yet in Holkar, despite its thousands of residents, there were only a few small pools.

Panjit studied his rook.

'There are springs under the mountain that feed all our needs.'

'Truly? Even for so many people?'

Adam had tried to make the question sound as casual as possible. But Panjit's antennae were sensitive to the faintest tremors of deception. He heard the motive in Adam's voice and raised his eyes from the board.

'Have you taken an interest in our plumbing?'

'If Hugo lays siege to the city, I want to be sure I am not going to die of thirst.'

Panjit's mouth tightened in a smile. 'Do not worry about that. Hugo Courtney's bones will have rotted to dust before Holkar runs out of water.' He moved his bishop and knocked over Adam's castle. 'Check.'

Adam puzzled over what Panjit had said. He felt certain there were things Panjit had not told him, and equally sure that the answer lay inside the building by the fountain. But the courtyard was near the Maharani's quarters. It was always busy during the day, and by night, guards patrolled it too often.

Then one day the Maharani went to attend a religious festival at a shrine in the countryside. Adam watched the procession depart: twenty elephants, with the Maharani in a golden howdah on a crimson saddlecloth. After she had gone, the palace was quiet.

That night, he crept out into the courtyard with a candlestick, a lamp and a small carpet. He waited behind a column. Fireflies blinked like an ever-changing constellation of stars; water gurgled off the stone elephant's back.

When he was certain no guards were coming, he crossed to the building and climbed the steps onto its roof. It was hard to find the slab he wanted in the dark, but he swept his hand around on the paving until his fingers felt the grooves of the carved waves.

There was a thin crack around the stone. Adam unrolled the carpet and put it on the ground beside him. He took the iron candlestick he had brought from his room, levered it into the gap and heaved.

The stone lifted clear. Adam slid it over the carpet to muffle the noise. From inside the hole, he heard the rattle of wheels and the splash of running water. Something was moving.

Adam lit the lamp and held it inside the hole. Everything inside was wet, so that the flame gleamed off every surface. The rattling grew louder.

The lamplight revealed, at last, the secret that lay beneath Holkar. It was a waterwheel, like the chain pumps Adam was familiar with from aboard ship, but on a larger scale. Scoops brimming with water were attached to a thick hawser that ran straight up a deep shaft and bent around a large wheel before descending again into the darkness. As each scoop reached the top, its water tipped out into a stone channel that led away into the darkness. It must serve the whole palace. The building Adam was on top of was what housed the machinery.

Adam held the lamp as far down as he could. He could not see anywhere near the bottom of the shaft.

'Only one way to find out,' he told himself.

He sat down on the edge of the hole and lowered himself in. The channel had a small lip, wide enough to stand on. Gripping the lamp in one hand, he sized up the waterwheel rattling past. The scoops were spaced about six feet apart. They didn't move quickly, but they were made of iron, and they came over the top of the wheel with a whipcrack motion that was enough to knock him unconscious if he mistimed his jump.

Years at sea had trained him well. He leaped, grabbed the rope like a backstay and hooked his feet around the hawser just as the next scoop came over.

It was like climbing the rigging in a storm in the middle of the night watch. The noise of the pulley thundered and echoed off the shaft walls, while at the bottom he could hear a churning noise like a high wind. Water rained down on him from the upturned scoops and ran in his eyes. He had to close the shutter on the lantern to protect the flame. His wet muscles stretched and groaned, but he could not loosen his grip or he would fall.

Gradually, the churning noise grew louder. It felt like he was slipping into the cold, hard entrails of a viciously lethal machine. Looking down, he saw the white froth of foam and the gleam of a wheel turning to drive the pulley. He waited until he was almost on top of it, then jumped, holding the lantern up above his head.

He landed in a pool of water, chest-deep. The surface was choppy with the turbulence of the scoops coming down into the pool, turning around the wheel and rising again full of water. A thick axle led away from the wheel and – by means of a series of gears – through a wall. Adam guessed that on the other side of the wall there must be men or animals driving the shaft, turning the wheels day and night to keep the palace supplied with water. In here, he was alone.

The lantern flame guttered. The jump had loosened the catch and the shutter had swung open. The flame heeled over. Even here in the bowels of the hill, a strong breeze was coming from somewhere.

Adam closed the shutter again, then breasted through the water with the breeze on his face. The pool was bigger than he'd expected – an underground reservoir so extensive the candle could only illuminate a small portion of it. The pulley he'd come down wasn't the only one. In the candlelight, he saw the shadow lines of other ropes rising into the darkness. Some were complex mechanisms like the one he'd descended by; others were simply buckets on ropes. This pool must supply the whole city.

The breeze grew stronger as he walked towards it. He had to cup his hand ever closer to the candle flame. He could feel a current in the water, pushing harder against him. Ahead, he saw a stone wall that marked the edge of the reservoir. There was an opening a few feet above his head, and a torrent of water pouring out of it over a weir and into the pool.

A wooden ladder was bolted to the wall beside it. Adam climbed up and peered into the hole.

He had been right. This was not a natural spring. He was looking down a brick-vaulted tunnel, bringing a stream to fill the reservoir. He couldn't see where it came from, but he could guess.
The walls were slick with moss and black with watermarks. It
must come from the river: after the monsoon rains, the stream
would rise to fill the tunnel. But this was the driest part of the
year, and the water was only knee-deep.

He splashed through, arms braced against the wall so he would
not lose his footing on the slick stones. The tunnel was longer
than he expected; the lantern started to burn low. He wished he
could blow it out to save oil – the tunnel was straight enough
that he didn't need it – but he had no way of relighting it. He
hurried on.

'At least it smells better than the drain in Port Louis,' he
muttered to himself. And then, 'Oh.'

The lantern went out. He was in darkness. Tendrils of claustrophobia started to creep around his insides, making him sweat.
But as his eyes adjusted, he could see a dim glow ahead. He went
on, more slowly. The stream was getting louder, but he could
hear a new sound – the chattering of frogs and crickets, and what
sounded like a nightjar trilling in the distance.

By the time he reached the end of the tunnel he could see
clearly. Moonlight poured through an iron grille where the water
entered. The grille was solid, but there was a ladder beside it,
leading to a trapdoor. The bolt was rusty, but Adam worked it
free. He lifted the hatch and came out into the clean night air.

He was in a small domed building – a tomb or a shrine – on
the banks of the river. It was built over the water, so that the tunnel entrance beneath was completely hidden. The trapdoor was
disguised to look like the paving.

But it was not empty. A fat-bellied man sat cross-legged on
the floor. He must have been deployed to guard the tunnel
entrance – he had an axe in his hands, and an elaborate helmet –
but he had not noticed Adam. He sat stiffly, his back to Adam,
staring across the river. Perhaps he was asleep, but he might
wake at any moment.

Adam stayed still. So did the guard. Unnaturally still – you
could not tell he was breathing.

On his travels, Adam had sometimes seen yogis in a similar state, a trance so deep they might as well be dead. It could last for hours, and Adam did not have that much time. He edged around for a better view. Could he creep past?

Then he laughed out loud. The man had been set to guard the tunnel, but not the way Adam thought. In fact, it was not a man at all. His face had a trunk, wide ears and two tusks jutting out – and it was made not of flesh, but of stone. It was Ganesha, the elephant god.

Adam touched the god's toe for luck, as he had seen pilgrims do at roadside shrines. In the distance, he could see the bulk of the citadel blocking out the stars, the glow of the few fires and lamps that were still burning at that hour.

He was out of the city. For a moment, he savoured his success.

Where next? He had done this to prove there was a way out, not because he wanted to leave Holkar. He had to go back. But his plan had some crucial flaws – he would never find his way through the reservoir and the pumping system without a candle or a lamp. And if he turned up at the front gate, Panjit would hear of it. He would work out how Adam had got out, and close up the route.

There was only one place to go.

In the moonlight, the bungalows of the British residence glowed as white as tombs. Adam flitted down the lanes between them like a ghost. It would have been easy – sensible, even – to enter through one of their open windows and find a lamp and a tinderbox. Adam passed them all.

His pulse quickened as he approached the great house. A servant dozed by the locked gate, but the wall was not high. Adam scaled it with the help of a palm tree and dropped into the garden. The mansion was dark – except in one corner room on the ground floor, where light glowed.

Adam crept up and peered in through the windows. It was the library: shelves lined with books, and an untended lamp sitting on a side table by a high-backed chair. The room was empty.

The lamp was what he needed; there was even a jar of oil sitting beside it. A servant must have been trimming the wick and forgotten to extinguish it.

The window was not locked. Adam hoisted the sash and climbed through. Clare must have been in the room that evening: her perfume lingered in the air, scenting it with camellias. She could not be far away. She would be lying in her bed, maybe right above him.

Against all reason, he found himself yearning to see her again. But that would be madness. He didn't know how long he had taken getting there, and he had a lengthy journey back. Dawn could not be far off. He could not risk being discovered.

He crossed to the lamp and picked it up. The bowl was half empty. He refilled it from the oil jar. That would be enough to see him home.

A sneeze echoed across the room.

Adam spun around. The jar, slick with oil, slipped through his fingers and smashed on the floor. Thankfully he had the wit to hold on to the lamp or he might have set the library ablaze.

Clare was sitting in the high-backed chair, her legs curled under her and a bottle of wine tucked beside her. The chair's wings had hidden her when Adam entered. Now she was staring at him, rubbing the sleep from her eyes.

Afterwards, Adam thought he should have run off into the darkness that instant. Let her imagine it had been a dream. But in the moment, his feet were rooted to the spot.

'What are you doing?' There was a tremor in her voice, but she appeared remarkably calm. 'Have you come to murder us in our beds?'

'I . . . ah . . .' The question had thrown him. He stumbled for an answer and realised he could think of no lie better than the truth. 'I needed to borrow a lamp.'

'That is the most preposterous excuse I have ever heard.'

'Indeed.'

She laughed. Adam relaxed a fraction.

Did anyone hear the jar smash?

'Is Hugo here?'

Her gaze flicked over him. The wine had left a red stain around her mouth, and her hair was tangled from sleep. Adam felt her eyes were asking him a question she could not voice.

'He has not returned yet.'

She uncorked the bottle and poured it into a glass that had been sitting by the chair leg.

'You cannot imagine the expense of getting tolerable claret to the middle of India, but it makes life here more bearable.' She waved the bottle at him. 'Would you care for a glass?'

Only a few dregs sloshed around the bottom of the bottle. Adam began to understand why she had fallen asleep in the library chair.

'Perhaps a different time. My hosts did not want me to leave the palace, and they will be displeased if they find I have gone.'

Clare nodded. The wine had started to make her eyes drift shut again.

'A gilded cage is still a cage,' she said softly.

The night was warm, but her dress was thin. Adam found a shawl on a sofa and laid it over her. He took the glass from her hand and put it on the table so it would not spill. Her breathing had slowed; her eyes were shut tight. She moved a little in the chair, sinking into a more comfortable position.

Without thinking, Adam leaned over and kissed her on the forehead.

Her eyes fluttered open; she smiled and murmured something.

Adam took the lamp and left her in darkness.

For the next three days, Adam became unusually clumsy. He walked into people. He banged his head on pillars, and tripped on doorsteps. He almost fell down a flight of stairs.

'I hope your stay with us has not turned you to drink,' Panjit joked.

The Maharani and her court had returned the day after Adam's escapade. So far as Adam knew, no one had discovered what he had done that night.

'I drink nothing but water,' Adam promised.

'You entertained yourself in our absence?'

'As much as I could, with what you allow me.' And then, seeing Panjit giving him a curious look, 'What?'

'When you start to accept what other men give you, I will worry you are not yourself.'

'You could always open the gates for me,' Adam answered.

The reason he had become so clumsy had nothing to do with drink. He was staring at the masonry, examining every tile and piece of stone. He lifted carpets when no one was watching; dropped fruits that rolled under furniture and had to be retrieved on his hands and knees; kept having to fasten his shoe.

And he found what he was looking for.

The slab on the building by the fountain was not the only one carved with the water mark. There were similar stones everywhere, often tucked in discreet corners or out-of-the-way alcoves. The aqueducts and water channels must run everywhere under the palace.

There wasn't one in Adam's room. But there was one in the corridor outside, and that was private enough. Servants rarely passed, and guards did not patrol it.

One morning, while the Maharani was holding her *durbar* and the court was occupied, Adam slipped out of his room, carrying a lamp and a sack. He lifted the slab as before and went down. The waterwheel, the reservoir and the tunnel were easier to navigate the second time. Soon he was crouching, soaking and naked, behind the Ganesha statue, changing into the dry clothes he had brought in the sack.

After the night in the library, he was not sure how Clare would react to seeing him again. But the gatekeeper opened the gate for him, and by the time he reached the top of the carriage drive, Clare had come out and was waiting for him in the shade of the portico.

'I hope you do not mind me calling.'

'I do not mind at all.'

The delight on her face was so real he could not doubt it. In fact, she was so gay and easy, he wondered if she remembered the incident in the library. But when they were seated, and the servants had brought trays of cakes and jellies, she said:

'I had the most curious dream last week. I was in the library, when I caught a strange man climbing through the window. He did not do me any injury – he only asked to borrow a lamp. Is that not the most unlikely dream?'

And then, in a voice so low only Adam could hear, she added, 'Say nothing. The servants are all Hugo's spies.'

'The most curious thing,' she prattled on, 'is that when I woke in the morning, my lamp was gone.'

They were sitting indoors. The heat was building before the monsoon, kettling it in so that the air seemed to steam. All the windows were draped with wet cloths to cool the air coming through. They put the room in a crepuscular half-light, so that Adam could hardly see Clare in the gloom.

They lapsed into silence. Adam sat on the chintz sofa, frustration mounting. His mind had suddenly become empty of things to say to her.

'Where is your son?'

'His ayah took him to the cantonment. Ralph loves to watch the soldiers drill. I think he must get it from his father.'

Another silence.

'How do you find Holkar now you have sampled its delights for a few days?' Clare tried.

'Even hotter than before. But it is a place of marvels. You must never tire of it.'

'I rarely enter the city. The Indians are jealous of their rights. They act as if an Englishwoman setting foot inside their walls might collapse the whole kingdom. I think they do not like Hugo.'

At the mention of Hugo's name, silence descended again. Hugo's presence hung over both of them, like the monsoon clouds massing overhead.

'How did you meet Hugo?' Adam asked.

Clare waved her arm. 'You asked me once before. Everybody knows the story.'

'I don't. But I would like to.'

He meant it. There was something bewitching about her – an unattainable beauty that made you long to touch her soul.

'My father arranged my marriage. But not to Hugo.' A smile played over her lips as she saw Adam's surprise. 'To a cavalry officer named Michael Leverett. He was young, ambitious and devilishly handsome. We cut quite a dash through London society. A charmed couple.

'Then I met Hugo at a ball. He was in London on Company business. He held my hand so tight when we danced, I thought he would snap my fingers. And the heat in his grip – like a man on fire. He danced every dance with me and would not let another man touch me. Even my own husband, when he came to claim me – Hugo gave him such a fearsome look he retreated in terror.

'We became lovers.' Her cotton dress clung to her in the heat, the thin fabric clutching every curve. 'Does that scandalise you?'

'No . . . Yes.' Adam blushed. He could feel her gaze on him, her eyes bright with delight at having trapped him. 'I do not think I can answer that question yea or nay without insulting your virtue.'

'My virtue?' She laughed. 'There was little concern for that, I was the talk of London. Of course, Michael heard of it. Do you know what he did?'

Adam shook his head.

'He went and bought two thousand pounds of East India Company stock. He thought this was his passport to riches. He thought if he connived with my infidelity – if he turned a blind eye – then Hugo would compensate him with some sinecure in Leadenhall Street. Nothing less than a directorship, you understand. He would not sell his wife too cheap.'

She shivered.

'But he underestimated Hugo. When Hugo sets his heart on something, he will accept nothing less than all of it. It was intolerable that any other should possess me. He would not settle for having me as his mistress: I must be his wife.'

'You divorced?'

'Do you know how hard it is to obtain a divorce? How expensive – and humiliating? I would have had to go before a court to prove my adultery. Not confess – *prove*. Of course, all London knew, but that would not be enough for a court of law. They would have demanded witnesses, bed sheets, the whole mess. My name would have been dragged through the gutter. And after all that, it would still require an act of Parliament to confirm the divorce.

'Hugo could have done it, of course. He would have bought every member of Parliament, if that was what was required. But he had a different plan. He went to Michael's club. In front of all Michael's friends, Hugo announced that he had been fornicating with me. I believe he was quite explicit in the details. My husband had no choice but to call him out to a duel. They met on Blackheath, and Hugo shot him dead through the heart.'

'I'm sorry.'

She waved Adam's sympathies away.

'Some people said Michael died for love. Others, less charitable, said it was his pride that killed him. The simple truth is that he died because he came between Hugo and what Hugo wanted.

'The funeral was in St James's on Piccadilly. A week later, Hugo and I were married in the same church. He even used the same flowers – you have never seen so many wilted lilies at a wedding.

'Our honeymoon was in Deptford. We sailed for India a week later. Some time afterwards, I realised that was the reason why Hugo was in a hurry to get rid of Michael – if it had taken any longer he would have missed his sailing. I was glad to go. London was poisoned against me. Even the common folk knew the scandal. I could not step down from my carriage without jeers and people spitting at me. I was invited everywhere, but only so I could be gawped at and gossiped about. I thought coming here would be an adventure, a chance to escape all that.'

She laughed softly. 'That was before I knew India. My card had been marked before I stepped off the ship. Calcutta was like London, but worse. A tiny society, and ten times the spite towards me. Holkar is lonely, but the garrison wives do not have claws like in London or Calcutta. And I have Ralph, who is everything.'

She shifted herself in her chair and rearranged her skirts.

'That is a very long answer to your question.'

'I should not have asked.'

'I am glad you did. Since I met Hugo, my story has not been my own – everybody thinks they know it before they meet me. You have given me the chance to tell it myself, and that is a precious gift.' She paused. 'You must think I am a terrible person.'

'No.' Adam was surprised at the vehemence in his voice. Her story had mesmerised him; he felt as if he was in a dream. 'You were caught in the storm of Hugo's ambition.'

Just like me.

It was on the tip of his tongue, desperate to get out. He wanted to tell her everything – to make her understand that he knew intimately what it cost to fall victim to Hugo. He could enlist her in his revenge.

One of the cloths that covered the window had come loose. Its corner flopped down, letting in a ray of light that pierced the gloom between them. Clare was radiant.

But she was still his enemy's wife.

A clock in the hall struck two.

'I should return to Holkar,' said Adam, 'before my hosts miss my company.'

'Will you come again?'

He knew he should not. He knew how dangerous this was, telling her half-truths that she only half-believed. Acting as if he was a gentleman paying a social call. He remembered Panjit's warning: *The heart is an organ of air and fire. No man can tell all the things that are in it – even his own.* Panjit was a shrewd man. Had he discerned some trace of the feelings that were now boiling inside Adam?

'I will come when I can.'

COAST OF AFRICA, 1803

Paul woke, and promptly vomited. Salt water and half-digested fish spewed out. More caught in his throat; he couldn't breathe. He forced himself on to his hands and knees, coughing and gagging until it came out in a stinking puddle on the rocks.

Only then did he remember he was supposed to be dead. The taste in his throat was so foul, he had to conclude he was alive after all. He looked around.

He was lying on black rocks, one of the flat shelves stepping out into the ocean from the cliffs. Seaweed and broken pieces of wood littered the tideline around him. A little way out, where the waves surged in, he could see the remains of the dhow wedged onto a rock in the sea. It was closer to land than he had thought. Further out, the ocean was empty. There was no sign of the French ship.

Something called behind him. Paul turned. A flock of birds was picking their way through the shallow rock pools left by the tide. They had white feathers fringed with black necks, and long, curving black beaks that they stabbed into the pools to catch fish.

They were ibis – twenty of them, at least. Paul stared. First the god had spoken to him on the boat, and now this. Why had he come back now? Was it to save him?

Bile rose again. There was an iron tang in his throat, a reminder that every time the god came to save Paul, blood was spilled. The god always demanded a sacrifice.

Sana.

Where was she? Unsteadily, Paul climbed to his feet. Black spots danced in front of his eyes; he felt light-headed. Every bone in his body ached as if it had been attacked with hammers. His feet slipped on the slick rocks and slimy seaweed as he stumbled along the shore, flopping like a scarecrow. The birds took fright and flew away.

The beach was empty. Sana was not there. Paul tipped back his head and gave a formless shriek from the depths of his soul. Had the god abandoned him again?

His gaze went up to the cliff top where the birds had flown. They had not settled, but were wheeling about with urgent croaks and barks. Suddenly the reason became clear. There was a figure, silhouetted against the sky. It was hard to make out, but even from that distance Paul could see the outline of a skirt and long hair blowing freely in the wind. She looked too tall for Sana.

Paul waved like a madman. The woman waved back. She called something that Paul didn't understand, pointing to her left. There was a cleft in the rocks, filled with loose stones that made a path. Paul scrambled up.

He reached the cliff top and thought perhaps he had died after all – if this was an angel sent to bring him to Heaven. How else to explain what he saw? She was the most beautiful woman he had ever seen. Abasi; the servant girls he had taken to his bed in Gondar: they had been young and nubile, but they were nothing compared to her. The only person whose beauty had come close was his mother. But he had only seen Constance in her later years. This woman was in the full flush of youth.

She was not African – or not like any African woman Paul had seen in his thousands of miles travelling the continent's coasts and deserts. She looked more like the girls he remembered from France, though infinitely more beautiful. Her blue eyes, the colour of the African sky, were clear and guileless. Her fair hair hung shimmering over her shoulders. Her lips were full, her skin burnished gold by the sun, and she wore a short dress that left her legs bare from the knee down.

Paul wanted to draw her, to capture and possess her grace. Who was she? He was desperate to know. If only he could speak – but maybe she would not have understood anyway, for when she spoke it was in an African-sounding language he didn't know.

He kneeled and wrote his name in the sandy soil with his finger. She backed away nervously, but her eyes widened as she saw the letters.

'Paul.' She read it effortlessly.

His name sounded different on her lips, lighter and sweeter. He longed to be able to talk to her, to hear her voice and to make her laugh. And she had understood what he wrote. Was it possible she could read and write French?

Tentatively, overcoming any fear of being in the presence of a stranger, she crouched and wrote her name next to his: 'Mary'.

He nodded, to show he understood.

'You speak English?'

He shook his head and wrote '*Français*' in the sand. Mary's face fell.

'I cannot read your language. But if you speak a little, perhaps I could make it out?' She pointed to her mouth, and then to his. 'Speak?'

Blushing, Paul opened his mouth so she could see inside. He hated to reveal his disfigurement. But he could not bear to let her think he was some kind of idiot.

She gasped and took a step backwards, as if ready to flee. The mutilation shocked her – the mark of extreme violence from a world she had never known. But she steadied herself and said, in a kindly voice, 'Poor thing. How did that happen?'

The moment she said it she realised it was a pointless question.

'Of course you cannot say. To have suffered this, and now to be shipwrecked . . .'

Impulsively, she stepped forward and threw her arms around Paul. He stiffened with the suddenness of it. He pulled back, but Mary would not let him go.

Something gave inside him. Whatever tension had held him together through the atrocities and abuse he had suffered, it was no defence against her simple kindness. He sagged in her arms. Tears flooded down his face, washing away the sea salt caked on his skin. He was like a child again, crying in his mother's arms – except that the one time he had done that with his mother, she had slapped him and sent him away for showing weakness. Mary hugged him closer, stroking his face. Her hair smelled of sunlight and fresh grass.

'Where did you come from?' she whispered. It was a rhetorical question: she knew he couldn't answer.

At last they separated.

'I must take you to my father. You need food and care and' – she looked at the rags he wore – 'clothes.'

A well-trodden path led along the cliff top among the trees. Mary started along it, but Paul grabbed her arm and pointed to the beach.

'What is it?'

Paul stooped again and wrote Sana's name on the ground. Mary squinted at it, opening her hands in incomprehension.

'I do not know what that means.'

Paul tried again. He drew stick figures beside each name: one for Mary, one for himself and one for Sana. Understanding dawned on Mary's face.

'Your friend? We found her an hour ago, further down the beach. My brother took her to our house. That's why I'm here, looking for you. She told us you were also lost.' She pointed to the stick figure, then down the path to make her meaning clear. 'Our home.'

Mary put out her hand.

'I will take you there.'

Mary was quiet as she led Paul along the path, uneasy with her emotional impulsiveness. She knew she was being reckless with her affections, but this man was in distress; she wanted to help him. They walked for about an hour, until they reached a rise that looked down into a small bay. Mangrove swamps stretched around it; a whale-backed hill guarded the entrance channel. The water in the main lagoon was so clear Paul could see the sandy bottom, rising to a white sand beach where a river discharged into the bay. Along the riverbanks, the jungle had been cleared into neatly fenced fields. Some had been ploughed for crops; in others, cattle grazed.

In the middle of the fields stood a large walled compound, half-way between a house and a fortress. It reminded Paul of the farms he had seen as a child in Normandy – solid buildings with stout walls that made the farmyard a courtyard. But this was different from those dank, grey buildings. The walls had been whitewashed with crushed shells, so that they sparkled like diamonds in the sunlight. Flowers ran rampant in the well-tended gardens that surrounded the main house inside the walls, and the orchards were in blossom. It was like a vision of paradise – though well defended. The gate was heavy enough to stop a cannonball, while the thick outer wall was pierced in many places with loopholes and embrasures.

Paul wondered how they would reach it. The mangroves seemed to make an impenetrable barrier, but when they got there he found that a path had been cut, and boards laid so they could walk through without getting their feet wet. Like the bay itself, it was well hidden. If you did not know where to look, you would never find it.

An ibis watched from the mangrove swamp, but Paul did not see it.

They carried on up a gravel path between the flower beds. Bees buzzed; the air was rich with the scent of fruit and blossom. Paul had been living off salt fish, rice and flatbread for two years. When he saw a fat plum bending the branch of its tree, so ripe the skin had almost split, he picked it without thinking and bit into it. Even without a tongue to taste it, he could feel the sweetness in the juices that filled his mouth and squirted down his chin.

Only when he had eaten it down to its stone did he remember his manners. His eyes made an apology, but Mary waved it away.

'There is plenty here. Take whatever you like.'

Two people had emerged on the porch of the main house – a man and a woman, both in their forties. Their faces were tanned and weather-beaten from decades under the African sun. The man was ruddy and blond; the woman paler, with chestnut hair. From the look they directed at Mary, Paul thought they had to be her parents.

'You have found another castaway.' The man gave Paul a searching look. 'Who is he?'

'He cannot speak,' Mary explained. 'He has lost his tongue. And I do not think he understands English.'

She turned to Paul and pointed to the man.

'Gert,' she said, speaking slowly and clearly. She pointed to the woman. 'Susan. My parents.'

Paul bowed. He did not understand what his hosts said, but he could see in their faces they did not trust him. The mother was giving Mary a curious look, while the father was examining Paul with undisguised suspicion.

'He can go to the guest room and clean himself up,' said Susan. 'I will prepare some food.'

Mary took Paul's hand to lead him away, but Gert stopped her.

'One of the servants can show him there,' he said. 'You help your mother in the kitchen.'

'But, Papa—'

'Do as you're told.'

While Mary followed her mother, with a lingering glance at Paul, he accompanied one of the African servants into the house. It was not lavish – certainly to Paul, who had grown up in the decadent luxury of *Ancien Régime* France – but it was warm and homely. Persian rugs and animal hides were spread on the mahogany floorboards, while the walls were decorated with many beautiful objects gathered from all over the world: tapestries, wood carvings, dried flowers and seashells. Paul took particular interest in the paintings. There were oil canvases that must have been imported from Europe; Ottoman miniatures executed with extraordinary finesse; pictures of ships at sea; and wild landscapes of India. The one he liked best was a watercolour, simply painted: a view of the beach and the bay they had passed, with a ship at anchor. It was sunrise, and the eastern horizon glowed with a beatific pink radiance. The picture was signed 'Mary Jansen'.

The servant brought Paul down a corridor to a small room at the end. There was a washstand and a wardrobe, and two sturdy wooden beds. Paul gave a cry of delight as he saw Sana lying on one of them, sleeping the way she always did, with her legs tucked up to her chest.

She opened her eyes.

'They found you,' she said. 'I could not make them understand. They do not speak Arabic.'

Paul seated himself on the opposite bed.

I do not speak their language either.

'What do you think they do here?'

I don't know.

'Could they be slavers?'

Slaving was rife on the coast, with Portuguese and local slavers exporting people to the slave markets of Arabia and India.

I don't think so.

They had seen plenty of slave barracoons on their travels down the African coast – squalid stockades jammed with humanity. If you did not see them, you could smell the stench coming off them, and hear the groans. There was nothing like that here. And of all the black people he had seen – the servants in the house and the workers in the gardens – none wore shackles or had brands on their skin.

'Maybe we have arrived in America,' said Sana hopefully.

Paul laughed.

This is not America.

'Or Cape Town?'

No.

'Then why are there white people here?'

Sana twisted one of her braids, chewing it like she had when she was a girl.

'Did you see the one with the golden hair? She is very beautiful.'

I didn't notice.

She reached across the gap between the beds and pinched him.

'Liar. You know she is beautiful.'

It was hard lying when you could not speak. Sana was so used to reading his face that it was impossible to hide his thoughts from her.

'Am I as beautiful?'

The question caught him off guard. He nodded vigorously – but not fast enough. Sana caught the hesitation. Her face collapsed into a scowl.

'Liar.'

She threw the pillow at him and stormed out of the door.

What does it matter? Paul asked, bewildered. But he said it silently, and nobody heard.

They ate with the family that evening. Though the Jansens might have misgivings about harbouring two unknown castaways in their home, hospitality prevailed. Sana and Paul were treated as guests.

When Paul came to the table, he found it was laid for eight. As well as Mary and her parents, there was a boy called Marcus, aged about twelve, who was such a perfect miniature of Gert that he had to be his son. He had a sister, Rachel, a little girl who had just learned to walk, with rosy cheeks and auburn hair. She spent the meal staring at Sana and saying nothing. The eighth chair, at the head of the table, was empty.

Gert said grace. Servants brought dishes of food: grilled fish, manioc cakes and fresh vegetables from the garden. They had started eating when the door banged open. An old man with white hair came in. He leaned on a walking cane, carved from ebony and with a warthog tusk for a handle. One of his legs was missing below the knee, replaced with a scarred wooden stump. The stump and the cane beat out a jerky rhythm as he limped across the room and threw himself into the chair at the head of the table. A servant hurried to fill his glass with wine.

'George,' Gert greeted him.

Paul noticed how his shoulders tensed the moment the old man entered.

George looked down the table. His eyes were hooded, his face etched with distrust. His gaze landed on Sana and Paul at the far end; he scowled.

'What are they doing here?'

Mary put her hand on his arm. 'I told you, Grandpa. These are the castaways I found on the cliffs.'

'And where do they come from?'

'Somewhere to the north. We cannot speak their language to ask them.'

'Their dhow was fitted out in the Arabian style,' added Gert. 'I would guess they come from the Horn of Africa.'

George jabbed at Paul with his fork.

'That one is not from Africa. He's a white man.'

'I'm a white man, and I'm from Africa,' Marcus pointed out.

'You're kin. That one . . .' Another dark look at Paul. 'Who knows what brought him here?'

'He nearly died,' said Mary indignantly. 'Nothing brought him here except chance. Bad luck that his ship foundered, and good luck that we found him.'

'Good luck?' sneered George. 'Did you stop to think what a white man was doing two hundred miles from anywhere, in a sinking boat with only a girl to crew it? How did he get here? Where was he going? What about the other ship?'

'He was attacked by pirates,' said Mary. 'Remember? We heard the cannon fire and went up on the cliffs to watch. You saw it.'

'She was a French frigate. And I saw the dhow sail up to rendezvous with her. How do you know our guest did not come from the ship?' He leaned down towards Paul. 'Are you a Frenchie? *Français?*'

It was the first thing anyone had said that Paul understood. He nodded, utterly surprised to hear a word of French.

'I knew it!' George's voice was loud with triumph, amplified by wine.

Sana could not follow what he said, but she heard the threat in his voice. She slipped her table knife into her lap, holding it ready to defend herself.

Paul put his hand on her arm to steady her. His hopes had soared. If George spoke French, they would be able to communicate. Paul could tell them his story.

But that one word seemed to be the limit of George's French. He turned to the others.

'What do you think he is? A deserter? A spy?'

'You think he deliberately risked shipwreck and cannon fire to come here to spy?' said Susan.

'Who would want to spy on us?' said Mary.

'More people than your little girl's mind can imagine.' George snapped a bone in two and sucked out the marrow. 'Do you know what happened to our family before I was born? They were driven out of England, accused of murder. Then they were driven out of Cape Town, accused of treason. Twice they made themselves prosperous, and twice they lost everything. They almost died in the wilderness.

'But, thank God, they reached Nativity Bay. I was born here, I have lived here my whole life, and – by God's grace – I will die here. But that has not happened by chance or good luck. The price of our liberty is eternal vigilance, keeping the prying eyes of the world well away.'

'Uncle Robert did not think so,' said Mary.

George's knuckles went white around the handle of his fork.

'He made his own choices. But it is one thing to go out into the world – it is another to invite it in to our home. Our sanctuary.'

He pointed to Paul and Sana again.

'Maybe they are what they seem, and maybe they are not. They will not tell us. But we did not invite them here. We owe them nothing.'

'They *have* nothing,' said Mary.

'That is not our concern,' said Gert.

'Papa,' Mary protested, 'you cannot speak about them as if they were not here.'

'They cannot understand,' answered Gert. He had a farmer's manner, direct and practical.

'Tell Grandpa we must help these people. We should let them stay with us as long as they want.'

Gert pursed his lips. 'Your grandfather is right. They do not belong here. When the next ship calls, we will put them aboard to take passage to Cape Town.' He peered down the table at Paul. 'Cape Town,' he repeated loudly, as if Paul was hard of hearing. 'You go to Cape Town.' He pointed to the painting of the ship on the wall. 'Ship. Cape Town.'

Paul nodded. He had not understood the conversation, but it was easy enough to read Gert's and George's attitudes in their faces and their voices.

He supposed he should be grateful. The shipwreck had shown what an impossible idea it had been, that he and Sana could sail the dhow to Cape Town by themselves. That they had survived was beyond lucky; that they found themselves sitting down to a fine supper, in a comfortable home, was a miracle. And now their hosts were offering to put them on a large, safe ship to take them to their destination. All that he had wished for over the years crewing the boat had finally been granted.

Yet now that he was here, he did not want to go.

An uneasy atmosphere hung over Fort Auspice in the following days. Paul could not leave unless a ship called, and no one knew when that would be. Until then, Paul and Sana were guests who did not know their hosts; strangers who could not speak; visitors who were not to be trusted. Through gestures, Paul offered to work in the fields, but Gert refused. Paul couldn't tell if it was from some vestigial sense of obligation to his guests, or fear that Paul would steal the cattle. Sana went to the kitchens and settled down to work. She asked no one's permission, and nobody stopped her.

Paul was left to entertain himself. He began to take walks around the property, down to the beach and around the mangrove swamps, up into the inland pastures. The fertility of the land astonished him. The cattle grazed fat, and crops grew in abundance.

On the third day, Paul was walking on the whale-backed hill that commanded the bay when he found Mary. She was sitting at an easel, with a palette of watercolours in one hand and a brush in the other. She was so engrossed in her painting, she did not notice Paul come up. He stood behind her, examining the picture over her shoulder. She had sketched the scene in pencil, and had begun painting it in. The colours she chose fascinated him: each one more vivid than the object it was portraying. The rocks were blacker, the sea a deeper blue, the mangroves more vibrant green. Overhead, the mid-afternoon sky was a hazy blue, but in the picture she had painted it in an explosion of reds, oranges, pinks and purples.

Paul coughed. Mary turned suddenly, smudging the mountain top she had been painting.

'Oh.' She smiled. 'You surprised me. Usually I am alone up here.'

Paul pointed to the painting, nodding and smiling.

'You like it?' She squinted at it appraisingly. 'I know it is silly – I have painted a sunset in the east, for one. Papa always tells me I should paint things as they are, even if that is drab and grey. But I want them to be bright.' She blushed. 'Listen to me prattling. I forget you cannot understand me.'

Her sketchbook and pencil lay on the ground. Paul picked them up, with a glance at Mary for permission.

'Of course. Do you draw?' she said in surprise.

Paul took the pencil. His fingers were calloused and hard, more used to knots and tar than paint and pencil now. But when he put it to the paper, it was as if the muscles in his arm were suddenly awoken from a deep sleep. Hardly aware of what he was doing, he drew a series of swift clear lines, then turned the pad around to show Mary.

She gasped. It was not one of his best pictures – done in haste, with hands that had almost forgotten how to draw – but it captured her flawlessly.

She put a hand to the lock of hair that was hanging down over her cheek, tracing one of the lines he had drawn.

'I am sure I do not look quite like that.'

Paul tore off the paper and gave it to her. His hand brushed hers as she took it; pencil lead from his fingers dirtied the sleeve of her dress. She tucked the picture in the pocket of her pinafore.

'I wish you could speak. I wish I could speak to you.'

Their eyes met. Hers were filled with frustration and longing; his with hope and uncertainty.

Or maybe words were not necessary. She was seventeen, and what she felt was new and overwhelming – a feeling that shivered through her body. The nearest sensation she could relate it to was when she sometimes walked to the top of the cliffs and peered over: the dizzying thrill of such great depths of danger, and the sea foaming below.

A noise sounded on the path up from the bay. A stone dislodged; a bird called in alarm. Running footsteps came around the corner. It was Marcus, flushed and bad-tempered. He glanced between Paul and Mary, and though he was only twelve he did not like the way his sister looked at the man. His scowl deepened. It made him look even more like Gert, Paul thought.

'Papa sent me,' Marcus said to Mary. He ignored Paul. 'You are supposed to be looking after Rachel while Mother has her nap.'

Mary didn't move. Her body tensed like a cat's.

'I will be down presently.'

'Papa said immediately.'

The two siblings glared at each other. Neither moved.

'I will go and tell him you disobeyed him,' Marcus warned. 'You know what he will do to you.'

'I am grown-up now. He cannot belt me like he used to.'

'There are other things he can do.' Marcus's voice turned spiteful. 'Maybe if I tell him you were up here alone with the castaway, he will not wait for a ship to take him away. Papa will cast him out for the lions to eat.'

He had found her weakness, as only a brother could. Mary snatched up her painting equipment and folded away the easel with a bang. The wet paint on the canvas was smeared beyond repair. She stalked away down the path. Marcus lingered a moment longer.

'Stay away from her,' he warned Paul. 'She does not want your attentions. You understand?'

Paul hadn't comprehended a word that had been spoken. But he understood perfectly.

Everything was upside down. The almanac on Gert's desk said it was October, but the plants outside shouted spring. Flowers carpeted the ground with rampant colours. The trees were in bud, the sky a cobalt blue. Every day the sun rose higher; every day the weather grew warmer. Corn sprouted in the fields, while the pastures sounded to the bleating of young kids and the lowing of calves. It was a bountiful time.

Yet a cloud hung over Paul. An invisible wall seemed to have sprung up between him and Mary. He hardly saw her: she was forever being sent on errands to examine distant cattle herds, or assess some new patch of land, miles away, for clearing. When he did see her at meals, she was seated at the far end of the table. She kept her head down, staring at her plate, and said little.

Gert treated Paul with undisguised hostility. Marcus followed his father's lead. Apart from Mary, the only member of the family who showed Paul any kindness was Susan, Mary's mother. When she heard that Paul could draw, she gave him paper and pencils to occupy him. In return, Paul gave her a sketch he made of the house, surrounded by flowers. She liked it so much, he began drawing more: the farmhands, the bay, the twisted mangroves, and the wild animals that roamed nearby. He bound them into a portfolio with some thread he had found, and presented it to her.

'Thank you.'

She smiled as she turned through it, delighting in the familiar scenes captured so well. Each picture burst with tiny details Paul had included: a monkey throwing fruit from a tree at a passing cow; a bird preening itself on an elephant's back, while the elephant raised its trunk to douse itself from the river; a baby mouse using a banana leaf as her cradle.

Susan stopped at the second-last picture. It was of the yard in front of the house, bustling with farm workers getting ready to tend the fields. Mary was there, too, mounted on horseback. Paul hadn't meant to draw her, but somehow, even in the background, she had become the focal point of the picture.

The smile on Susan's face faded to something wistful and sad.

'So that is how you see her.' She closed the book. 'You probably think I do not understand. But I have not forgotten.' Paul wasn't sure if she was speaking to him, or to herself – and he did not know what she was saying. 'When Gert came here, a hunter who had lost his way, he was the first man I had ever met who was not either old enough to be my father, or familiar enough to be my brother. I was seventeen, about as old as Mary is now. I was helplessly in love.' She sighed. 'Mary is a sweet girl, but she knows nothing of life beyond the safety of Nativity Bay. Her father will protect her at all costs. And that is probably for the best.'

She handed the album back to Paul.

'You keep it. It will remind you of your time here with us, when you are gone.'

All Paul understood was that his gift had been rejected because he had drawn Mary.

Sana found him later that afternoon. He had made a small fire in the forest, and was feeding the pages from the album into it, one by one. Sana gave a queer smile when she saw what he was doing.

'They hate us,' she said.

Paul didn't agree. It was not hatred he had seen on Susan's face. Gert's rudeness, too, and the grandfather's, did not stem from hate. They were afraid, though Paul did not know why. He couldn't imagine how anyone living in this isolated Eden could fear anything.

They feared things that were outside the walls. They feared Paul even more, because he was inside them. But even with Sana, who could understand him better than anyone, he did not have the means to explain it.

'It would be different if you were a girl. They pay me no notice.' Sana sounded pleased about that. 'Do you know what I have found?'

Paul shook his head.

'There is another way out – a little gate hidden in the back wall. The kitchen maids use it to fetch herbs that grow by the river. They do not know that I have seen them, but I know where the gate is. They keep the key in an alcove in the kitchen fireplace.'

What good is that?

She gave him a dark look. 'It is always good to have a way out. You of all people should know that.'

Paul lay in his bed that night and could not sleep. The moon shone through the window and danced on his eyelids. His mind churned. He could not stop thinking about Mary: her smile, her grace, the way her golden hair blew around her face in the wind. He thought of her breasts, cinched up by the waist of her dress, and imagined running his hands over them.

The thoughts made him swell up. He felt ashamed, but more than that, he was gripped with desire that he did not want to let go of.

'Paul?'

Mary's voice. He opened his eyes, and saw her face in front of him. He must be dreaming.

'Come.'

She took his hand. It was the first time he had touched her since she found him on the cliffs: her skin was soft and cool. She pulled him up – then stepped back with a gasp as she realised he was not wearing anything. Thankfully, the sheet covered his erection.

'I will wait outside,' she said. 'There is something I want to show you.'

Paul glanced at Sana in the neighbouring bed. She snored softly, coiled into her usual ball. He did not wake her, but rose and dressed and padded silently after Mary, down the deserted corridors and out into the night. The stars quilted the sky with light, bright and clear, while in the trees the forest murmured with the sounds of its nocturnal inhabitants.

Mary took him to a small gate in the back wall, mostly hidden by an acacia tree. She slipped out a key that was hanging on a string inside her bodice and undid the lock.

'I stole it from the kitchens,' she said. 'Papa does not know I know where to find it.'

Paul smiled, uncomprehending but blissfully happy. They pushed through the narrow gate and walked side by side down to the river. An eagle owl hooted in the trees; in the distance, Paul heard the roar of a hunting lion. Should he have brought a gun?

They paused on the riverbank, their bare toes squelching in the mud.

'There.'

On the far side of the river, a herd of elephants ambled slowly along. The moon and the stars lit up the plain with silver light, a mirror-world where nothing was quite real. The elephants swished their trunks through the long grass; their young played and skittered around their parents. They were untouchable, majestic beasts, like something out of legend.

'Do you ever feel that you are stuck on the wrong side of the river? That there is something grand and magnificent happening on the other bank, but you cannot cross?' Mary's voice shivered with emotion. 'Just once, I would like to go over and run with the animals.'

If Paul had known what she was saying, and been able to reply, he might have told her that walking in the world among beasts was not like gliding through a dream. People got hurt and broken. But he could not speak, and so he stood beside her, admiring the great animals and their serene progress across the plain.

Mary was not still. She swayed on her feet; she twitched her head with birdlike movements. She stood so close to Paul she jostled his shoulder.

Paul looked down and realised she was staring at him. Her eyes were wide with purpose, her lips parted.

He leaned down and kissed her. If he was not sure at first that it was what she wanted, her reaction left no doubt. Her body tensed; she turned into him, pushing herself against him. He felt the swell of her breasts press against his chest.

They held the kiss for what seemed an eternity. Then they broke apart, staring at each other with wild and ravenous eyes.

'It is how I always thought it would be,' said Mary, softly.

They kissed again, longer this time, until they could not breathe. They ran their hands over each other's bodies – chastely at first, then more daring, exploring the contours like unmapped landscapes.

A branch snapped in the trees behind them. Probably only an animal foraging, but it broke the spell. They were beyond the walls, and lions were not the only dangers in the night.

'We should go back,' Mary said.

Adam's days slipped into a pattern. Every other day, he would slide open the slab in the hall and make his way through the watercourses to the shrine by the river. Nobody in the palace noticed his absence, and he always made sure to be back by evening.

'You seem spirited,' Panjit complimented him. 'Life in Holkar agrees with you.'

'I can do nothing until Hugo returns. I thought I might enjoy myself.'

'That is well. Revenge is good, but if it is all a man eats, then his soul withers.'

Every night, Adam lay in bed and repeated his pledge to his father.

'I will find the men who did this and I will kill them.'

Every night, it was a bigger struggle to push away the image of Clare's face when he said it.

Another time, Panjit might have been more curious about the changes in Adam. But the Brahmin had the concerns of running a kingdom, and there was much business to conclude before the monsoon arrived. Even their chess games were less frequent than before. Adam was left to visit Clare as often as he liked.

By silent agreement, they did not talk of Hugo again. Guilt nagged Adam: he should be using the opportunity to find out more about his enemy. He felt Hugo's presence pressing around them like the heat. But he knew if he mentioned Hugo, Clare would ask him to leave. And he did not want that.

Instead, they walked by the river and took tea on the veranda. Adam played cricket with Ralph, who delighted in bowling him out.

'There is no room for cricket aboard ship,' Adam complained. 'You have me completely at a disadvantage.'

'You have a boyish spirit and Ralph enjoys your playfulness,' Clare told him. They were drinking sherbet on the veranda.

Ralph was at the far end of the garden, climbing a tree. 'He has no friends, only his ayah and me. A boy that age needs more than old women to play with.'

'You could send him to England.'

Though Adam's schoolroom had been the quarterdeck, he knew most of his fellow officers sent their sons to boarding school to be educated.

Clare shuddered. 'That is what my husband wants. I know it would probably do Ralph good – but it would tear my heart in two. Ralph is all I have.'

Adam didn't hear her. He had leaped to his feet and was shouting at Ralph.

'Get away from that tree!'

Ralph looked back. He had crawled along a branch and now seemed to be stuck. The reason was just beyond him: a large brown bole sticking out from the branch, surrounded by a moving cloud. A hornet's nest – and its occupants. They were unlike any insect he had encountered before, as big as a man's thumb.

'Jump down!' Adam called.

Ralph did not move. The branch was too high, and he was paralysed with fear. He tried to scrabble back towards the trunk, but his movement shook the tree branch, bringing out an even greater cloud of angry hornets.

'If he stays there, they will sting him blind.'

Adam was running across the lawn. He ducked under the tree, ignoring the hornets flitting about, and held up his arms.

'Jump!' he called.

Ralph clung to his branch. 'I cannot.'

'Jump,' Adam said. A hornet buzzed his cheek. 'I will catch you.'

He kept his voice calm but firm. It was the voice he had used aboard ship many times, coaxing green recruits or frightened boys up and down the rigging. Many captains would leave it to their boatswains to drive the men aloft with the short end of a rope, but Adam had found that helping sailors master their fears was a surer way to earning loyalty.

It worked again now. Ralph slowly loosened his grip. He slid off the branch until he was dangling by his fingertips, then dropped into Adam's arms. Adam moved swiftly away from the tree and put Ralph down on the safety of the lawn as Clare came running up. She embraced Ralph and wrapped him in her skirts, stroking his hair – though her gaze was fixed on Adam.

'That was brave and kind.' Her eyes brimmed with gratitude. 'I wish I could thank you as you deserve.'

Adam shook off the compliment.

'You should have someone remove that nest.'

He knew their friendship could not last. The rains were coming: every day he felt the charge building in the air. Even if Hugo didn't return in time – and as the days passed, that seemed increasingly possible – the monsoon would fill the river and flood the tunnel. Adam's escape route would be cut off; he would have no way out of the city for months.

One humid afternoon, he arrived at Claire's house and found it deserted. The gatekeeper was not at his post. The cricket bat leaned against the stumps on the lawn, but there was no sign of Ralph or his nurse.

Adam pushed open the front door. A heavy stillness hung over the house. The wet cloths that covered the windows let in chinks of light that captured the dust in the air. His footsteps echoed loudly on the floorboards. From the cantonment, he heard the great guns exercising like distant thunder.

But there was another noise. A low moan, like a breeze through a crack in a window – except that all the windows were wide open, and there was no wind.

Adam followed the sound down the corridor to the library. The door was ajar; the noise was a woman crying. He knocked gently. When there was no answer, he entered.

Clare lay on the chair, wearing only a petticoat. Her eyes were red, her face was wet with tears, and there was a weal down her cheek where she had scratched herself.

'What has happened?' Adam cried. And then, with a dreadful premonition, 'Where is Ralph?'

Clare was sobbing too much to reply, but she managed a gesture at her writing desk. A letter lay on it, recently opened. Crumbs of wax from the broken seal littered the floor. The ink was smudged with fresh tears.

Adam picked it up. Clare did not stop him. His eyes went instinctively to the signature at the bottom, and he felt his stomach clench.

'It is from Hugo.'

The letter was dated two days earlier. If it had arrived already, Hugo must be close. The long summer that Clare and Adam had enjoyed together was about to end. But that was not what had made her so distraught.

Adam read the letter.

I wish to inform you of new arrangements I have made for our son's schooling. Until now I have acquiesced to your wishes to keep him with you, but it is past time to prepare him for his station in the world. He will attend Eton College. I have secured a berth for him on the Earl of Abergavenny, *Indiaman. He will go to Calcutta, and sail for England as soon as the monsoon allows.*

'He is taking Ralph from me.' The words were torn from her breast.

'You could go to England with him.'

'Hugo would not allow it. He wants me close, locked up in a strongroom with his other treasures.'

She looked desolate – a beautiful statue that had been smashed to pieces. Adam wanted to comfort her. Without thinking, he put his arms around her and cradled her to his chest. She hugged herself against him. He bent over her, smelling the warmth of her hair and the spice of her perfume. He stooped to kiss the top of her head.

As he did, she tipped her head back to look at him. Clumsily, their heads knocked together, just as they had on the day they met, when Adam had been felled by the cricket ball. Except this time, it was their mouths that met.

Adam's lips touched hers, like a gull brushing the water. He tasted salt from her tears, and sugar from the sweet she had been eating. He smelled the scent she had dabbed on her neck.

He opened his mouth. Maybe he meant to apologise, but before the words came, her mouth had opened and was pressing against his.

She is Hugo's wife, a voice insisted in his head.

He didn't care. He kissed her back, long and deep. Her body tightened in his embrace. He felt the heat throbbing off her through her thin shift.

At last she pulled back.

'Not here,' she breathed. She kissed him again. 'Upstairs.'

She had already grabbed his wrist and was pulling him down the corridor to the staircase. Adam didn't know where the servants had gone. They had all disappeared.

'Where is Ralph?'

'I sent him to the cantonment to watch the soldiers with his ayah. I could not bring myself to tell him the news.'

They were on the staircase. Clare was almost dragging him up. As she turned on the landing, their bodies collided again. She pulled Adam against her, making him press her against the wall.

Something nagged at the back of his mind, but his mind did not heed it. He was drunk on her. They were like two animals freed from their cage, giddy with the release of their pent-up desire. He tugged on the laces of her dress, so hard he ripped the fabric. She was more frenzied still. She tore his shirt open from his neck to his navel. He shrugged it off, as she dragged him up the second flight of stairs to the top floor of the house.

They went through a bedroom door and onto a broad bed. Gauze curtains draped it to protect against mosquitoes. Inside was a cocoon of soft, hazy light.

Clare wrapped his hair in her fingers and clutched his head to her breasts. He bit down on her nipples and she gasped. She arched her back, pushing herself against his belly.

Their bodies glided against each other. Clare curled her legs around the backs of his thighs. She wrapped her arms over his back and sank her nails into his skin. She bit his lip and pulled his hair and kicked her heels against his buttocks.

She climaxed before he did. She was still crying out when Adam came, pouring himself into her with deep thrusts.

They lay there afterwards, their bodies drenched with sweat; Adam could feel an exquisite pain on his back where Clare's nails had drawn blood.

She ran a finger down his chest.

'Did I frighten you?'

He could barely speak. His body felt battered, as if he'd been battling a storm. His senses were glutted with sex.

Clare rolled over and closed her eyes.

'Hold me,' she commanded, and Adam obeyed. He wrapped her in an embrace, his hands cupped over her breasts and their legs spooning together.

He did not know how long they lay there. Inside the tent that the mosquito netting made, they were in a perpetual twilight haze. After the echoes of their love-making had died away, the house had fallen into silence.

Where are the servants? Adam wondered.

He remembered what Clare had said to him: *The servants are all Hugo's spies.*

At last Adam felt Clare's body go limp. Her breathing eased. Under his hands, he felt her rising and falling in a deep rhythm. She was asleep.

He untangled himself and rolled away. His clothes lay across the floor, but he did not dress. Instead, he left the room and padded naked down the corridor.

In his visits to the house over the past weeks he had seen every room downstairs, and a few of the reception rooms on the first floor. Until today, he had never had an excuse to go to the top storey. He searched quickly, opening every door he passed to see what was behind it. Mostly bedrooms, furniture covered with sheets and sheets covered in dust. There was a nursery, with regiments of lead soldiers lined up on parade in front of a wooden castle, that gave Adam a moment of guilt thinking of Ralph. Had the boy heard Adam and Clare? Adam peeked out of the window, but there was no sign of Ralph in the garden. The cricket bat still lay abandoned by the stumps.

The last door, at the end of the corridor, was what Adam was looking for – a study, with a wide desk facing the window. Adam pulled out the drawers, rifling through them. He was not sure what he was looking for.

The first item he found was a pistol, a beautiful weapon with gold chasing and a hammer shaped like a tiger's paw. When Adam picked it up, a ball rolled out; he sniffed the pan and smelled powder. Clearly Hugo was a cautious man.

He worked through each of the drawers in turn. They were stuffed with papers too tedious and complicated to study: manifests, bills, dispatches. Adam thumbed through them with growing impatience. If Clare woke, or the servants returned . . . In the distance, he could hear the sepoys exercising the guns again, shot after shot, like a drum marking time. An elephant trumpeted. He could not stay much longer.

One more drawer. He nearly left it. It was not worth the risk just for more account books. But this was Hugo's inner sanctum. After so long on his quest, Adam was desperate to know everything he could about his enemy. He opened the last drawer and pulled out a fistful of papers.

A door banged downstairs in the house. The noise startled Adam; the sheaf of papers slipped from his hands and spilled over the floor.

He swore. The house was coming alive again. He heard servants calling to one another, opening shutters and pulling cloths off the windows. The guns had fallen silent, but there was a commotion in the garden. People were shouting, boots stamping and elephants trumpeting. Had they broken into the garden?

Adam had no time to see what it was. He took the gold-chased pistol and fled down the corridor back to Clare's room.

Clare was awake. She had put her petticoat on and was being laced into her dress by an Indian maidservant who had appeared as if from nowhere. The maidservant gasped at Adam's nakedness.

'Get away from here,' Clare hissed. Her face was screwed tight with fury. 'And for God's sake get dressed.'

Adam's breeches and shirt were hung over a chair. A servant must have retrieved them. Adam struggled into the breeches, his panicked fingers fumbling with the buttons.

'Not in here!' Clare cried. She was not angry, Adam realised – she was terrified. 'Another room. If he finds you like this, he will kill us both.'

Adam had managed to get into one leg of his breeches. Pulling on the other, he grabbed his shirt and hopped towards the door. He grabbed the handle to open it and . . .

The door swung out a split second before Adam touched it. Adam stumbled forward, into the man on the landing. The man was taken completely off balance. He stepped backwards. His foot caught the top step of the staircase and slipped. Windmilling his arms, he began to fall, eyes wide with shock.

The stairs were solid marble, curving down two storeys. Falling to the bottom would crack a man's skull open. Without thinking, Adam reached out and clasped the man's hand. His grip was solid. Adam took the strain and heaved the man upright until he found his footing.

The man shook his hand free. Adam moved away. Belatedly, he realised he was still wearing nothing but his breeches, with another man's wife in the bedroom behind him.

'Who the devil are you?'

The man Adam had saved advanced from the staircase. He was huge. Adam stood six feet in his stockings, but this man had another six inches on him, and breadth to match. He had jet-black hair, green eyes, and a deep scar across his cheek that gave him a permanent sneer. His scarlet uniform was heavy with gold braid, with the star of the Order of the Garter pinned to his breast.

The guns Adam had heard were not exercising: they had been a salute. The elephants in the garden were part of the official travelling procession.

Hugo Courtney had returned. And Adam had saved his life.

Skirts rustled from the room behind Adam. Clare had managed to dress in a green gown, though it did not hide what she had been doing. Her hair was unkempt and she had powder and lipstick smeared over her face. In the close corridor, you could smell the sex radiating from every pore of her skin.

'Welcome home,' she said. Her voice was cool and poised.

Hugo stared at her as if he wanted to wring her neck.

'Who is this?'

He didn't look at Adam.

'Captain Adam Courtney. I think you are related.'

Adam's and Hugo's eyes locked. The world seemed to stop as the two men stared at each other across the landing, each man's eyes mirroring the other's hatred. Adam had waited months for this moment. Now here he was, face to face with his enemy.

And he was unarmed.

'Well, husband . . .' Clare seemed to be enjoying the moment, and it occurred to Adam that perhaps her dalliance with him had only ever been a way of hurting Hugo, the only way she could. 'Will you not defend my honour?'

With a roar of fury, Hugo sprang at Adam. Adam retreated, but Hugo moved with surprising speed for a man his size. He grappled Adam and drove him back into Clare's bedroom. Adam could not hold Hugo's weight. He went down with Hugo on top of him.

Adam was pinned to the floor. He was not a weak man, but Hugo's weight crushed down on him. He did not try to dislodge it. Instead, he grasped Hugo tight and hugged him closer. If Hugo had space to swing a clean punch, he could knock Adam senseless with a single blow. Adam's only chance was to keep him at close quarters.

Hugo realised it, too. He pulled away, bucking like a stallion to shake Adam's grip. Adam dug his fingers into the fabric of Hugo's coat. For a moment, it held him. Then, with a shrug of Hugo's broad shoulders and a tearing of fabric, it split in two. Hugo reared up, fist drawing back to strike.

But though he was strong, it was a long time since he had fought someone who could hit back. Adam had been doing it all his life. With reflexes honed in the melee of quarterdeck brawls, he reached up with both hands. One hand closed around Hugo's wrist; the other smothered the knuckles of Hugo's balled fist and gripped it tight. Hugo's arm was immobilised.

Before Hugo could wrestle free, Adam twisted his hands. Hugo screamed with pain, but Adam continued twisting. If Hugo resisted, his wrist would snap. He had no choice but to roll with the motion, off Adam and onto the floor.

Adam sprang to his feet. The pistol he had taken from Hugo's desk lay on the dresser. He snatched it up and pointed it at Hugo before his enemy could rise.

'I have two fresh battalions of sepoys outside.' Hugo's lip was bleeding; his right hand hung limp. 'If you kill me, you will never escape.'

'And if I let you live, you will let me walk out of here?'

'We can discuss that.'

'And did you *discuss that* with my family when you murdered them?' Rage swelled in Adam's heart. 'There is nothing to discuss. Everything was decided years ago.'

Without another word, he pulled the trigger.

Hugo started to move – but he was too close. Adam could not miss. The tiger's-paw hammer snapped forward. A spark flashed in the pan. A puff of smoke turned the air white and bitter.

But there was no bang – only a muted pop and a wet fizzle.

Sitting in the desk drawer for months in Hugo's absence, soaking up the humid air, the powder had gone damp and rotten. And even if Adam had had fresh powder, there was no time to reload.

Hugo rose, his face black with pain and anger. He swung at Adam; Adam blocked the fist with the pistol barrel, but the blow was so strong it knocked the gun from his grip. The pistol flew away and landed under the bed.

'Now we are more fairly matched.'

Adam would happily have killed Hugo with his bare hands. But – he knew from experience – it is surprisingly hard to kill a man without a weapon. Particularly if that man is six inches taller and forty pounds heavier than you. He circled away, scanning the room for anything he could use. There was a vase on the dresser with some wilted flowers. He hurled it at Hugo; Hugo dodged and it broke against the wall. Hugo retaliated with a brass ewer on a dressing table. It hit a mirror and smashed it. Dozens of wicked shards cascaded over the floor.

Adam was barefoot; Hugo still wore his riding boots. He crunched over the broken glass as he strode to the bed, put his foot against the bedpost, and heaved on it with both hands. His strength was immense. The post was two inches thick, but he snapped the wood like a stick of sugar. The canopy sagged and collapsed. Now Hugo had a club in his hand.

He hefted its weight, surveying Adam in triumph.

'Adam Courtney. The hero of the Royal Navy. You are a long way from the sea now.'

'You know why I am here. I came to avenge my family.'

Hugo grinned. 'I do not intend to give you that satisfaction. Instead, you have allowed me to complete what I began in Fort Auspice.'

'You do not deny it?'

'Deny it?' Hugo leaned closer. 'I enjoyed it, and I will enjoy killing you even more.'

Adam had seen the way Hugo broke the bedpost. One swipe of the cudgel would be enough to dash his brains out. Clare must be nearby, but she had fled. Whatever she and Adam had shared, it was over now that Hugo had returned. She would not save him.

'Wait.' Adam dropped to his knees. 'Have mercy. Have you not killed enough Courtneys?'

'No.'

Hugo's face split in a leering grin at the sight of his adversary losing his courage. It might have been entertaining to make Adam grovel a while longer, to prolong the pleasure of his victory. But he had just returned from a long journey, and his patience had run out. He swung the club at Adam's head.

Adam was not defenceless. As he kneeled on the floor, pretending to beg for his life, he had picked up a broken fragment of the mirror – a piece of the wooden frame, with a sliver of glass emerging from it like the blade of a knife. He brought it up now, driving straight for Hugo's belly.

Hugo saw the glitter of the blade halfway through his stroke. He jerked back in time to avoid the jagged point that would have ripped him open. The club swung over Adam's head and struck the wall.

Adam jabbed at Hugo again. Hugo sprang back, brandishing the club in defence. Adam might have got inside his guard if he had followed up the attack, but Hugo was in the middle of the field of broken glass. In his bare feet, Adam couldn't get close enough.

Hugo's attack had left the door unguarded, with only the bed in the way. In one bound, Adam leaped on the bed. With another, he sprang off the mattress and out of the door. He ran down the stairs to the first-floor landing. There were pikes on the wall in the front hall. If he could grab one of them, he would have a fighting chance against Hugo.

Shouts sounded from the ground floor. Boots thumped on the lower steps. Looking down, Adam saw red-jacketed sepoys advancing up the stairs. They had heard the smashing of furniture as Adam and Hugo fought, and come to investigate.

Adam might have talked his way past them. It was a brave sepoy who would defy orders from a white man. But Hugo appeared, leaning over the banisters from the top floor.

'Stop him!' he bellowed.

The sepoys lowered their muskets. Adam turned. If he ran down the corridor, they would have a clear shot at him. He opened the nearest door, dived in and slammed it shut.

He was in a large first-floor dining room, with tall windows overlooking the front of the house, the roof of the portico and the grounds beyond. It looked as if the house was under siege. The garden was filled with soldiers, field guns and elephants. Hugo had brought an army with him.

And some of them were at the door. Musket butts thudded against the wooden panels. Adam put his shoulder against it, but he was outnumbered. His bare feet slithered on the mahogany floorboards, varnished as slick as ice. He would not be able to hold them.

He stepped aside and let go. The sepoys stumbled through the door. Adam stuck out his leg and sent one sprawling to the floor. His musket flew out of his hands and skidded away. Adam grabbed it. Before the second sepoy could gain his balance, Adam punched him in the stomach with the butt of the musket, then again against the side of his head. The man went down.

More men were coming. Adam was trapped. He ran to the window, but it was latched fast. The sepoy he had tripped was getting up.

'Courtney!'

Hugo strode in, kicking the prone sepoy aside. He seemed to have grown still taller in his rage, a towering presence. Only the dining table stood between him and Adam.

Except that Adam had the musket. In his haste, Hugo had entered unarmed. Adam pulled back the hammer and checked the pan was well loaded with dry powder. Hugo stopped abruptly.

More soldiers flooded into the room behind him. The sight of Adam with his musket trained on Hugo threw them into confusion. Even if they had been prepared to shoot, Hugo was in their way.

'You will not live to enjoy your victory if you shoot me now,' he warned Adam.

'At least I will die knowing I fulfilled my father's wishes.'

The gun in Adam's hands stayed rock-steady. He only hoped that word of what he had done would somehow reach Rob.

'So will I.' Hugo gave a small shake of his head, a man discovering unexpected wisdom. 'I wonder, do we avenge our father's sins – or suffer for them?'

Adam had no answer. He knew there was a truth in Hugo's words, but his mind was such a whirl he could not contemplate it. *You know what is true*, he told himself. *You must kill Hugo.*

He curled his finger around the trigger. Hugo's eyes narrowed, the look of a cornered animal with no hope of escape. Adam put his cheek against the musket to sight it, though at that range he could not possibly miss.

A scream sounded from the door. Not a woman's scream, but the cry of a child in anguish. Ralph stood there. He was wearing a soldier's uniform, a replica of Hugo's, with a wooden sword and a wooden pistol. He must have dressed up to welcome his father home, every inch the brave soldier. Now his face was a mask of tears, his lip quivering and his eyes red.

'What are you doing to my daddy?'

It was too late. Adam had already pulled the trigger. But in that instant as the spring uncoiled, Hugo's words played again through Adam's mind.

Do we avenge our father's sins – or suffer for them?

Was that what he wanted to inflict on this child? The boy he had played cricket with, who had looked at him like a surrogate father.

Jump. I will catch you.

All of that crossed his mind in the split second before the hammer struck the spark. It was enough. Adam moved the barrel of the musket – only an inch or two, but enough to make the difference. The ball flew over Hugo's shoulder and hit the door frame next to Ralph. Jagged splinters flew off and struck the boy's face. He clutched his eye and sank to the floor, howling in pain.

Hugo did not glance at his son. Triumph blazed in his eyes.

'You missed your chance,' he told Adam. 'Just like the rest of your family.' He stepped aside and turned to the sepoys. 'Kill him.'

Adam's ears were still ringing from the shot he had fired. The reply – half a dozen muskets crashing out at once – deafened him. But his reflexes were faster than the sepoys'. He threw himself to the floor, behind the dining table, so that the bullets went harmlessly over his head and smashed through the window behind.

Before anyone could move, Adam hurled himself after them. The broken glass gave easily under his weight, though shards left deep cuts over his naked arms and torso. He ignored the pain.

He had landed on the roof of the rounded portico that projected over the front steps. He vaulted over the edge and slid down one of the ornamental pillars, gripping it with his knees like a mast. Trails of blood from the cuts on his chest smeared the white stucco red. A servant stood on the steps, gazing at him in disbelief. Adam almost knocked him over as he landed on the balls of his feet and turned to sprint away.

He would not get far. The drive was blocked by a dozen elephants draped in rich red saddlecloths and gilded howdahs, standing in a row like carriages lined up after a ball. Beyond them, the garden had turned into a parade ground. Indian sepoys in bright red coats and white shorts stood in long ranks, muskets ready. They looked uncertainly at Adam.

'Stop him!' Hugo's voice bellowed across the lawn from the upstairs window.

That decided the sepoys. The front rank spread out, moving towards Adam to circle round him.

Adam ran straight into them. In their midst, they couldn't fire for fear of hitting their own men. He ducked and weaved between them. Hands grabbed for him, but his skin was slick with blood and sweat and they could not get hold of him. He saw an upturned musket raised to strike, and ducked away just in time.

From the corner of his eye, he saw the tree that Ralph had been playing in a few days earlier. The hornets' nest was hanging off the high branch. The servants had not yet managed to remove it.

Adam ran towards it. The pursuers dropped back, scared off by the huge yellow-jacketed hornets buzzing around the tree. Adam climbed into the tree and along the branch where Ralph had got stuck. He reached up and grabbed the nest with both hands. Hornets started to emerge. Bolts of pain lanced through Adam's skin where they stung him, but he kept hold until he had twisted the nest free. It vibrated in his grip with the furious buzz of a thousand angry insects.

With all his strength, Adam hurled the nest at the nearest elephant.

The nest broke against the animal's hide. A cloud of insects swarmed out of it like smoke from an explosion: shocked, frightened, driven to rage. They swarmed up the animal's trunk and into the folds of its eyelids, stinging blindly in their anger.

The elephant reared up on its hind legs, trumpeting in panic. The gilded howdah with its velvet curtains was shaken free. It crashed down and smashed on the ground. That only spooked the elephant more. It thundered away, with the broken howdah dragging behind.

Panic was infectious. The other elephants in the train broke away from their handlers and began blundering about. Their mahouts hurled themselves from the animals' backs. The garden became a melee of thundering beasts, human screams and animal shrieks. Some of the sepoys were trampled underfoot; the rest separated and fled. The elephants charged blindly. Statues were destroyed, flower beds crushed, trees uprooted. Adam saw Ralph's cricket stumps disappear into the earth under a great grey foot.

As everyone fled, Adam ran against the crowd towards the nearest elephant. The rope that had fastened the howdah to its back trailed down its side. Adam ran alongside it, feeling the earth shaking under his feet. He snatched the trailing line, took a good grip and swung himself up. Dust swirled around him, punctuated by hornets caught up in the maelstrom. The rope bucked and cracked; if Adam had let go, he would have fallen under the pounding feet.

But it was not so different from climbing rigging, and Adam had done that often enough. He hauled himself up the rope onto the animal's back, spread-eagling himself across it to stay on.

He had meant to charge the gate. But the animal had shaken off its reins and was in no mood to take orders. It had sniffed the river and decided that was the safest place. It charged around the side of the house and across the lawn to the water. All Adam could do was cling on.

The elephant trampled down the muddy bank into the river. The water calmed it. Adam felt its huge legs begin to slow, moving easily. He scrambled to his feet, balancing on the beast's back, then dived into the water. He swam upstream, battling the current. It would not be long before Hugo came looking for him.

Soon he saw the dome of the little shrine rising on the right bank. He swam to it and hid himself in the dark water under the arches that supported it out of the water, just as the first sepoys reached the river.

He didn't know how long he spent treading water there. The river poured through the hidden entrance into the channel behind him, but the grille was fixed tight and he could not get through. At nightfall, the sepoys gave up the search. Adam scrambled out into the shrine and let himself into the tunnel through the trapdoor. Without a light, he had to feel his way in darkness, listening all the while for any sign of pursuit. When he reached the waterwheel he barely had the strength to hold on as it lifted him back to the palace.

He had escaped. But that was no consolation. He had had his chance to kill Hugo and he had thrown it away. Now Hugo was warned, Adam would not get another opportunity. How would he explain it to Rob? He had failed.

The palace was dark; everyone was asleep. Adam replaced the flagstone and returned to his room. A light came from the crack under his door: one of the servants must have lit a lamp for when he returned. He went in, desperate to lose himself in the oblivion of sleep.

But the day had one more surprise in store for him. The room was not empty. Panjit sat on the bed. He had the chessboard laid out and was studying it hard, halfway through a game he must have been playing against himself. He took in Adam's appearance: half-naked, filthy with blood and mud from the river, every muscle sagging with exhaustion.

'Each time I think I know what to expect from you, you manage to surprise me.'

'Hugo has returned,' said Adam.

'I know. I heard your encounter from here.' Panjit took a piece off the board and turned it between his knuckles. 'Everything you have done has been against my purpose. I was not ready for you to kill Hugo Courtney. But having had the chance, I wish you had done it.'

Again, Adam felt the bitter shame of failure. 'What will you do?'

'Hugo will come for an audience with the Maharani tomorrow. We will find out then what he wants.' Panjit gazed at Adam with a weary look in his eyes. 'I was keeping you back for my endgame. Now you have ruined my strategy.'

'I am sorry for that.'

'If I cannot use a piece to attack or defend, you know the only other use for it?'

With a sudden jerk of his hand, Panjit swept the white knight off the board. The piece shattered on the stone floor.

'Sacrifice it.'

Adam could not sleep. He tossed and turned on his bed, but every way he lay made his wounds throb. Worse was the pain of what he had done – and not done. He thought he might spend the rest of his life trapped in that moment, the gun pointed at Hugo and his finger on the trigger. If only Ralph had not appeared. Adam would have avenged his family, saved Clare, and delivered Holkar from Hugo's threat.

But if his aim had been true . . . He imagined Ralph's face covered in his father's blood, watching Hugo shot down in front of him. The games of cricket and hide-and-seek would have been forgotten. Ralph would have dedicated himself to revenge, just as Adam had, just as Hugo had. The wheel of violence that had crushed so many Courtneys would have turned again, into another generation. A kind and gentle child would have been turned into a monster.

Would he change what had happened, if he could? He didn't know.

Guards were posted on Adam's door. In the morning they brought him food, and fresh clothes, but they would not let him out. Even to relieve himself, he had to use a chamber pot in the corner. Through the high window, he watched the shadows inch around the courtyard. It was the hottest day he had known. Down in the cantonment, the sepoys were exercising their guns again. The noise rumbled across the mountain like thunder, promising relief that never came.

Around five o'clock – as best he could tell – trumpets sounded. Down on the plain, he saw a knot of red-jacketed men ride through the outer gate into the city. Soon afterwards, a knock sounded on his door.

'You are summoned.'

The court was packed into the durbar chamber. The Maharani sat on the huge tiger throne in a shimmering dress of azure silk. An enormous diamond pendant hung between her eyes, with more diamonds dangling from her ears, draped around her neck and studded in the rings and bangles she wore. It was almost as if she wanted to flaunt the wealth of her kingdom to the man who wanted to take it. The tiger cub lay curled on a cushion at her feet.

'Stand here.'

The guards manoeuvred Adam through the crowd, to a place between two pillars. Dressed in his Indian clothes, complete with turban, he would hardly be visible in the crowd.

Trumpets and drums announced Hugo into the room. He had scratches across his face, and a black eye that spread almost to the scar on his cheek. He stalked across the audience chamber, shoulders hunched, brushing off the courtiers who tried to halt him in the middle of the room. He carried on until he was towering over the throne. The little Maharani had to crane her head back to look at him.

He did not bow or offer any courtesy.

'I have come from Calcutta with a message from the East India Company. We demand certain changes to the treaty between Holkar and the Company.'

'What terms do you offer?' said Panjit.

'First, that you increase the subsidy you pay the Company by ten lakhs of rupees.'

There was an intake of breath from the assembled courtiers. It was an astronomical sum. To pay it would mean vast taxes on them.

'Second,' Hugo continued, 'that the new regiment I have brought from Calcutta be garrisoned here in the citadel. For the Maharani's protection,' he added.

Adam knew what that meant. Accepting a garrison within the palace would be tantamount to surrendering the city. The Maharani would be Hugo's prisoner.

Panjit showed no emotion.

'Is there anything else?'

'One other demand. That you surrender any subjects of His Majesty King George who have sought refuge in Holkar.'

Panjit's face was a model of innocence.

'The Maharani does not permit the hat-wearers to enter her city.'

'Are you so certain?'

Hugo's gaze swept across the room. Adam knew he should duck behind the pillar, but he stood his ground. He would not retreat from Hugo ever again.

He did not have to. Adam stood taller than almost any man in the room, but Hugo saw only a turban and tanned skin, half-hidden by a helmeted guard in front. His eyes missed Adam and moved on. He grunted.

'Those are my terms. Any failure to comply with them will be counted as an act of war. What is your answer?'

The room went quiet. There were hundreds of people, but the only sound was the low murmur of Hugo's translator speaking to the Maharani. She sat stiff-backed and proud under her canopy – a girl who held the lives of thousands in her hands.

She spoke.

'Her Highness the Maharani has considered the proposal of the East India Company,' Panjit translated. 'For the well-being of her subjects, and for the sake of amity with the Honourable Company, she accepts your terms.'

Adam saw disappointment flicker across Hugo's face: a hunter robbed of his sport. He had *wanted* the Indians to defy him, so he could make an example of them.

'*All* the terms?'

'All the terms,' Panjit confirmed. 'The subsidy will be increased. Your soldiers will be welcomed into the citadel tomorrow morning.'

'And the fugitives?'

'We will search the city tonight. If we find anyone, they will be waiting for you when you arrive tomorrow. Then you may do with them as you wish.'

Silence fell. Hugo's face writhed with emotions: suspicion, triumph, greed. He twitched and snorted.

He had won. But even in victory, he could not resist one last act of cruelty. As he turned to go, he saw the tiger cub snoozing at the foot of the throne. A smile twisted his lips. With the hard toe of his boot, he kicked it in the ribs.

The cub yowled and leaped to its feet, fur bristling. It saw its attacker and did the only thing it knew. It sprang at Hugo's leg.

The Maharani might have tamed it, but she had not defanged it. Its claws were pointed, its teeth sharp, and its young jaws were strong enough to break bone.

It never touched Hugo. Adam did not see Hugo draw his sword, but in a blur of movement, the blade cut through the air and struck the leaping cub on the side of its neck. The cub was knocked to one side. It flew across the floor and landed in a heap of fur, blood gushing from the deep gash in its throat. The blade was so sharp, it had cut clean through the artery.

The Maharani screamed. She jumped down from her throne and ran to the cub, cradling it in her arms as its lifeblood pumped out and ruined her silk dress.

The crowd shuddered and drew back. The guards tightened their grips on their weapons and looked uncertainly at Panjit. Hugo was unconcerned. He wiped his bloody blade on the throne's cushions, then turned to look around the room. He brandished the sword, challenging anyone to defy him.

Panjit stayed still. The crowd was silent. The only noise was the soft sound of the Maharani, weeping.

Hugo tossed his head disdainfully.

'The little tiger may pounce,' he said, 'but if she bares her claws she will feel the taste of my steel.'

With a glance at Panjit, he strode to the door.

'I will return tomorrow.'

NATIVITY BAY, 1803

'Where were you last night?' Sana demanded.

Paul rolled over. His head was clouded; his eyes refused to open. All he wanted was to lie in bed and nurse his memories of the night before.

'I woke and you were gone.' Sana jabbed him in the ribs. 'You did not come back for hours.'

I went for a walk.

'Alone?'

Paul didn't answer. Sana drew back, her mouth tight with anger.

'Be careful. These are not good people. If they think you have betrayed them, they will hurt you.'

At breakfast, Paul did not dare look at Mary for fear of giving himself away. He felt sure Gert and Susan must see the guilt written across his face. Sana banged about like a cannon that had broken loose from its moorings. She bashed her cutlery, spilled the milk and broke her plate.

'Something in the air,' said Susan. She was staring at Mary, who would not return her gaze. 'Your Papa thinks you should ride out to the village at Ekuseni today. The chieftain has two fine bulls he is willing to sell. It would do you good to be away from here for a little while.'

'I do not care about cattle,' said Mary.

'Then you should learn,' snapped George. 'It is your inheritance.'

'More like my cross to bear.'

'Mary,' her mother reproved her.

'You cannot treat me like a child. I am a grown woman now. Do I not get any say in my life?'

Mother and daughter glared at each other. But before they could say any worse, the door slammed open and Marcus burst in.

'There is a ship!' he cried. 'Tacking towards the headland, making straight for us.'

Gert rose. 'Is it the Frenchman we saw?'

'An East Indiaman.'

As ever, Paul did not understand the words. But he could see Marcus was pointing out to sea, and that Gert snatched up a spyglass from a stand on the wall. He guessed what it meant: a ship to take him away. He looked down the table and met Mary's eyes. The emotion that passed between them would have been obvious to anyone, but the others were seized with the news of the ship and did not notice.

Or maybe Susan did. She cleared her throat to get Paul's attention.

'I'm sure you will look forward to being on your journey again.'

They went out to the headland to watch the ship approaching. She was a stoutly built ship, broad-beamed for carrying cargo but well armed, if the row of gunports down her side was any guide. A figurehead of a buxom woman leaned out under her bow, exposing the tops of her breasts to the waves, and the red-striped ensign of the East India Company streamed from her stern.

Paul could not watch her without dread in his heart. But it seemed from their reactions that the others recognised her.

'The *Seven Sisters*,' Gert said. 'Captain Talbot. He was here two years ago.'

'He will want some ivory, and fresh beef, I warrant,' said Gert. 'Best get the slaughtermen to kill some cattle. And the tusks from that great bull elephant we brought down in July – that will fetch a good price in Cape Town. I will be able to buy that new plough we need.'

'And the captain will want feeding,' said Susan.

The family scattered to prepare for their guests. By the time Paul got back to the house, Sana had already packed a bag with her belongings – a few hand-me-down dresses of Mary's she had been given – and was sitting on the bed ready to go.

Paul rolled his eyes.

The ship is not even here yet.

The Indiaman anchored in the bay and dropped a boat. The family gathered on the foreshore to welcome them. Talbot was first out of the boat even before it had touched the beach, splashing through the surf. He was a large man, with a full face made red by sun and many bottles of wine over the years. He wore his sandy hair long, tied back in a queue. Everything about him was large: the fists which shook hands with his hosts; his smiling mouth and sagging jowls; the belly which bulged over his belt. The only exception was his eyes, which were small and pig-like.

He had arrived from India and had brought gifts for all the family. There were bolts of silk cloth for Susan and Mary, an elephant carved of ivory for Marcus, and a doll for Rachel. Gert received a new saddle. George was given the princeliest gift of all: a gold-hilted knife, its handle carved in the shape of a tiger with ruby-red eyes. Talbot tousled Marcus's hair – 'You have become such a big lad since I saw you last' – and bowed to Mary. 'You are quite grown-up. It is as well your father keeps the location of your home a secret, or you would have suitors dashing themselves on the rocks to get here.'

Mary blushed and made a sort of curtsey.

Talbot turned to Paul and Sana.

'And who are these two?'

'Wayfarers,' said Gert. 'They were shipwrecked up the coast. We took them in, of course.'

'We hoped to prevail on you to take them on to Cape Town,' said Susan.

'Of course.' Talbot took a pinch of snuff from his snuffbox and gave an almighty sneeze. 'My ship is full, but we can make space.'

He gave them a smile through watery eyes. Paul and Sana did not return it.

'Now, let us see if there is anything we can trade to our mutual profit.'

He turned. Another man had got out of the boat and was striding up the beach. He was the biggest man Paul had ever seen – well over six feet tall and broad in proportion. He wore a striped coat of some brightly dyed Indian fabric,

'Hugo . . . ah . . . Constable. The supercargo.' Talbot introduced him. 'You know John Company do not like to see any of their precious trade lost through wastage or neglect.'

Hugo shook hands. Even Gert, with his strong farmer's grip, winced. Hugo stared into each of the family's eyes, like an astronomer searching for a distant star.

'So these are the famous Courtneys,' he said. 'I have heard of you.'

Gert frowned. 'Not much, I hope. We keep ourselves to ourselves, here.'

'Of course.' Hugo sniffed the air, breathing in the warmth of Nativity Bay as if it was a long-lost home. 'If I had such a paradise to call my home, I would not want to share it.'

'You will not find our hospitality lacking,' said George sharply.

'No indeed,' said Talbot. He was sweating; all his bluff good cheer had evaporated in the presence of the supercargo. 'The table at Fort Auspice is the finest you will find between Cape Town and Muscat. I can vouch for that.'

'Then I will relish it,' said Hugo, licking his lips.

Two more places were laid at dinner that night for Talbot and his supercargo. It should have been a gay evening, with fresh company and news of the outside world to celebrate. Instead, it reminded Paul of the banquets at the king's palace in Gondar. The food was lavish, the wine flowed freely, and everyone was as comfortable as if they were sitting on knives.

The reason was Hugo. He was never less than polite, but he exuded malevolent energy like a prowling wolf. When he cut apart his food, there was something terrifying in the action. The candles in front of him seemed to burn brighter than the others. Somehow, all conversation started and ended with him.

He showed particular interest in his hosts.

'Your son is Sir Robert Courtney, the famous fighting admiral?' he asked George.

George scowled. 'A better admiral than a son.'

'Yet I owe him a great debt.' Hugo shovelled another forkful of meat into his mouth. 'He roams the seas like a tomcat in the farmyard, keeping them free of vermin and making it safe to trade.'

'His place was here,' said George. It sounded feeble, an old man's lament.

'He has a son, too, I believe.' Hugo continued as if George hadn't spoken. 'Lieutenant Adam Courtney?'

'Cousin Adam,' said Mary. 'He came here years ago. He must be grown-up now.'

'You have not seen him recently?'

Hugo's gaze fixed on Mary like a beam of sunlight escaping storm clouds. She was seated opposite him. Normally she dressed demurely, but tonight she seemed to have loosened the neck of her dress, and at the same time cinched in the waist more tightly. It showed off her figure and emphasised her breasts, in a way that had Susan pursing her lips in disapproval.

'The last time I saw him I was ten years old.'

'And now you are . . . twenty?' Hugo guessed.

'Seventeen.'

'I would not have thought it. You are a fully formed woman.'

Was it a gallant remark? At the head of the table, Gert's face was tight with fury. Susan frowned; Marcus looked ready to spring out of his chair. Mary herself was less offended. She gave a smile, taking it as a compliment.

Hugo ignored the discomfort around him.

'Now you are grown-up, you must think what to do with your life.'

'She stays here,' said Gert.

'That would be a waste. A woman of your beauty could go anywhere she chooses. There would be no palace in Europe that would be closed to you. Kings and dukes would vie for your hand. I am certain if you asked, the gallant Captain Talbot would be willing to give you passage on his ship, at least as far as Cape Town. What do you say, Talbot?'

Before Talbot could reply, Gert pushed back his chair and stood. He had been drinking more than usual that night, and it made him unsteady.

'My daughter is going nowhere!' he shouted. 'Either hold your tongue or get out of my house.'

Hugo didn't move. 'I was merely paying a compliment to your daughter. I am afraid in Calcutta I am quite starved of the company of accomplished young women.'

Gert stared at him. Hugo held his gaze, unyielding. Talbot fiddled with his napkin, while Mary looked bewildered between the men.

'Sit down,' George told Gert. 'You are making a damn fool of yourself.'

Paul endured the meal in complete misery. Not understanding what was said, he had to watch the way Hugo stared at Mary, and the way she seemed to delight in his frank attentions. The sight of her in her low-cut dress – a way she had never showed herself before – drove Paul mad with thwarted longing. He mashed his food between his teeth and nursed the injustice. Hugo was rich and important. No doubt he came from a fine family. He could speak to Mary in her own language and make her laugh. Why would she not prefer Hugo to Paul – a penniless castaway, a man who did not even have his own tongue.

Paul thought how he must appear through Mary's eyes. A loathsome cripple, a gibbering pauper. He burned with shame for his disfigurement. For the first time, he wished Sana had left him to die in Gondar. Even being torn apart by the hyenas would have been a better fate than suffering a life without love or dignity.

In his misery, he paid little attention to the conversation. If he had, he might have noticed how often in the stream of unfamiliar words the name 'Courtney' was mentioned. He might have been struck how similar it was to the name he had assumed in the French army – 'Courtenay'; he might have thought back to the battered edition of *Moll Flanders* he had found inscribed with his mother's maiden name, Constance Courtney. He might have begun to ponder how common that surname really was.

Sana heard the name, but it meant nothing to her. She was watching Paul. After their time together, she could read his thoughts in every twitch of his face. She could see how he was suffering, now that the bitch with the golden hair had found someone she liked better. At last Paul could see what Sana had known all along: that this girl was vain and inconstant.

It was good that the ship would take them away. She would have Paul to herself again.

She reached out and squeezed his hand under the table. He looked at her in surprise. She smiled, to remind him he was not alone, and he returned it with a look that spoke of the pain in his soul.

The dinner ended early: no one wanted to linger over their food. Talbot and Hugo returned to the ship. Gert and George summoned the farm manager, a Nguni tribesman named Jama whose grandfather, Inkunzi, had come with the Courtneys when they first settled at Fort Auspice. Inkunzi had been the chief herdsman for a mighty queen whom the Courtneys had defeated in battle. As the queen's wealth was in cattle, and as the Nguni loved their cattle as tenderly as their own children, it had been a position of great honour and power. His family had been managing the Courtney family lands ever since.

'Lock the gates tonight,' said Gert, 'and summon our workers to the fort.'

Jama frowned. 'Do you expect trouble?'

'*Isala 'kutshelwa sabona ngomopo,*' said George, using Jama's own language. *A man who does not listen for danger will find out his mistake when the blood flows.* 'Those men who came for dinner were our guests, but I do not trust them.'

Jama nodded. The Courtneys had not survived so long at Nativity Bay without a healthy dose of caution. He sent runners to fetch the strongest of their workers from their kraals and unlocked the armoury to break out the stands of muskets that the Courtneys kept ready.

'We will keep watch all the night,' Jama promised. 'If even an ant stirs, we will see it coming.'

From the bedroom window, Paul watched the men take up their positions on the walls of the fort. Again, his mind went back to Gondar, to Yostos's warriors seizing the gatehouse as soon as the king was dead.

Did I bring this here? It was a paradise before I came. Now there are guns, and war is on men's lips.

He went to bed, but could not sleep. Knowing this was his last night at Fort Auspice drove him to despair. When he thought of how Mary had flirted with Hugo at dinner, he beat the pillow with rage. But the thought of being parted from her was even worse.

Sana couldn't sleep either. She rolled out of her bed and climbed into Paul's, as she had done so many times. When she was smaller, she could almost curl into the curve of his back. Now she had grown so much she stretched the full length of him, cupping herself into the undulations of his body.

She had been given an old nightdress of Mary's, but she wasn't wearing it that night. Paul could feel her naked skin warm against his own. Her breasts pressed against his back, while her pubic hair grazed against his buttocks. She threw her arm over him, so that her hand rested on his stomach.

He felt himself begin to harden. It horrified him: in their years together he had come to think of Sana like a daughter. He tried to concentrate on other things, to control himself, but the more he tried, the more he could feel himself swelling up. He told himself she was a child; she did not know what she was doing.

But it was not a child's body pressing against him any more.

'Are you sad?' she whispered.

He nodded.

She kissed him on the nape of his neck.

'It will be good to be gone from this place. We will be alone together again.'

'Mmmm.'

The hand on his belly moved slightly lower. She kissed him again, this time on his shoulder blade. Paul knew she was only trying to comfort him. She could not realise the effect she was having.

Sana tugged on his shoulder, rolling Paul towards her. In the narrow bed, her face was inches from his. The moonlight shone on her dark skin, on her bright eyes and her glistening lips. There was an expression on her face, fierce and vulnerable, that was entirely new to Paul.

She leaned forward and kissed him on the lips.

Paul responded automatically. His body convulsed; his mouth opened. Sana took it as encouragement. She pressed herself against him, writhing like an eel. She was awkward and inexperienced, but fired with determination. Her teeth knocked his as she forced her tongue between his lips; their noses jostled clumsily.

The soft skin of her breasts rubbed against his chest. Her hand reached down and took his penis, pushing it against her pubis.

Paul pulled back. Sana clung on tighter. Her mouth was so tightly locked on his, her teeth caught his lip and made it bleed when he finally got free. He stared at her, both of them wild-eyed and panting hard.

What are you doing?

'I wanted to make you feel better.'

She reached for his cock again, teasing it up. He snatched her hand away, shaking his head. Sana's eyes narrowed.

'I thought you loved me.'

I do love you. But . . . He made the gesture he had made once before to Ilya – two fingers rubbing together side by side. *You are my friend.*

Tears glistened in her eyes. He had never seen her cry before.

'I saved your life.'

The confusion on his face spoke more clearly than any words.

What does that have to do with it?

'I love you.'

Then, horrified by what she had said, she sprang off him and ran out of the door.

Paul did not try to follow her. He lay on his bed, dazed. For so long, he had seen Sana as she had been that day he rescued her from the necropolis: a scrawny child in need of protection. Without him noticing, she had grown into a young woman, full of a young woman's needs and desires.

His body seethed with frustration, which only deepened his guilt. What sort of a man was he, to respond to her that way? His mind rebelled. But at the same time, he could not forget the tears in her eyes. He had done that to her, and he hated himself for it.

He was still lying there, knotted in misery and self-loathing, when a soft knock came at the door. He made no sound; he was not sure he could face Sana again yet.

The door edged open, admitting a crack of lamplight.

'Are you asleep?'

It was Mary. Paul pulled the sheet over himself just as her head peered around the door.

'I came to say goodbye.'

He beckoned her in. She closed the door and set her lamp down on the dresser, filling the room with a warm glow that dispelled the steely moonlight. She sat on the bed beside him, her legs tucked up under her nightdress.

'Where is Sana?' she asked, noting the empty second bed.

Paul pointed out of the window.

'You look sad,' she said. 'Is it because you are going away?'

Paul gazed at her, helpless. All his anger from dinner was forgotten now she was here. There was so much he wanted to tell her: how beautiful she looked; how much he would miss her. But language was a wall between them that neither could cross.

The frustration showed on his face as anger. Mary drew away.

'Perhaps I should not have come. I only wanted to say goodbye.'

No.

It emerged as a strangled grunt from his throat. Gesturing to her to wait, he wrapped the sheet around his waist and went to the bureau. He took up the sketchbook and pencil he had borrowed from her.

She understood what he wanted. She settled back on the bed and held herself still. The lamplight softened the lines of her body and surrounded her with a radiant nimbus. Paul felt the same trance-like magic creeping over him that he had felt in the temple in Egypt. An invisible tendril seemed to stretch from his eye to the tip of the pencil, bypassing all thought and will. He forgot where he was, who he was – even that he was there. All that existed was Mary, taking shape in curves and shades on the paper.

There was no clock in the room, so he didn't know how long it took. At last he finished, trembling with the effort. He put her name and the date on the back.

'Let me see,' said Mary, holding out her hand.

Shyly, he gave her the paper.

'You have made me beautiful,' she gasped. The delight on her face transcended words and sang in his heart. 'Is that how you see me?'

She looked up from the picture and her gaze met his. In that moment, the walls that had stood between them seemed to dissolve. Her face shone gold in the lamplight, open and willing. Her eyes said everything that needed to be said.

Paul leaned in and kissed her. Tenderly, softly, full on the lips. She moved towards him, putting her arms around his shoulders and drawing him close.

They parted for a moment to draw breath. Mary tugged the sheet away, exposing the full length of Paul's body. She gazed at him wide-eyed, as if she had been admitted to a secret. She traced her fingers down his chest, over his hips and along the shaft of his erection.

'You are beautiful,' she told him. 'Beautiful.'

It was one of the few English words he knew, and he thrilled to the sound of it. In all his life, no one had ever said that before. Silently, he mouthed it back to her. He unlaced the bodice of her nightdress and tugged it off her shoulders, revealing her full breasts. He ran his hands over them, squeezing and cupping them in a way that made her groan with desire.

She wriggled out of the nightdress and stretched out on the bed. They came together again, more urgently this time. Instinct took over. Sana's attentions had primed Paul's body; Mary was almost as eager as he was. She pulled him on top of her. For a moment they fumbled awkwardly as her unpractised hands tried to guide him to the right place.

She cried out when he entered her. He paused, but at once she grabbed him and drew him in deeper, biting her lip against the pain. He felt her body resisting him, but she would not let him stop. Gradually, she opened to him. They relaxed into a rhythm, slow and tentative at first, but then faster, rising like a wave climbing to a peak. The rhythm rose. The wave climbed to unfathomable heights, curling over but still carried on by the irresistible force of its own power. At last it broke. Paul flooded into her, again and again and again. He wrapped his arms around her and hugged her to him. Their bodies shuddered in unison, glistening with sweat, as the pleasure washed through them.

'I have never done that before,' Mary whispered in his ear. They lay tangled together on the damp sheets. 'And now that I have, I never want to stop.'

Paul stroked her hair. For maybe the first time in his life, he was perfectly happy.

'Let us run away together,' she said. 'Somewhere my papa cannot disapprove or send you away. Somewhere we can be free, like my great-grandfather Jim did when he came here with Louisa.'

Paul wished he understood what she was saying. He could see it was important – something she wanted him to know, rather than simply endearments. He smiled, shaking his head slightly to show incomprehension.

Mary put her hand on his chest. She made a walking motion with her fingers, across his skin and then into the air, extending her arm towards the window until it was pointing at the night sky sparkling with stars.

'Together,' she said.

Paul understood. He kissed her. He closed his eyes, savouring the sweetness of her lips, the brush of her tongue inside his mouth.

But already his mind was starting to turn with practical details. They would need food, supplies, a gun for hunting and ammunition. Then there was the question of how they could get out of the fort, with Gert's men standing guard on the walls. They could not have chosen a worse night.

And at the back of his mind, always, the fear that he had misunderstood Mary; or that she would think better of running away from her family; or that some other stroke of fate would intervene to stop him.

He opened his eyes.

He had not heard the door, but now it stood ajar. Sana stood in the gap, almost invisible against the dark corridor behind. How long had she been there? What had she witnessed?

Even if she had just arrived, she had seen enough: Paul and Mary, naked, locked in an embrace and smeared with each other's fluids. Paul met her gaze, and what he saw would stay with him forever. Her face had twisted in a terrifying snarl, worse even than the hyenas in Gondar. Eyes flared, teeth bared, every muscle quivering with hatred. A guttural growl trembled in the back of her throat, sharpening to a hiss as it escaped her lips. She spat at him. Then she turned and fled.

'What will she do?' Mary cried. Her golden skin had gone grey with shock. She snatched up her nightdress and pulled it on. 'Will she tell Papa?'

Paul was already halfway into his trousers and shirt. Gert was a strict father, and George even more uncompromising. If they knew what Paul had done with Mary, they would thrash the hide off his back – or worse. Then there was Sana. She had had the look of a wild animal; there was no telling what she might do.

Later, Paul might feel guilty that he had forgotten about her in his plan to run away with Mary. For now, all that mattered was speed and escape. He went with Mary quietly down the corridor to the pantry. They filled two sacks with provisions – flour, rice, salt beef and other food that would keep – and grabbed a jug of Gert's cider. Every second was urgent, but when Mary caught his eye they started giggling like children. They both knew this was madness. What if they were discovered? If they were not discovered, how could they ever survive the African wilderness? But it was a wonderful kind of madness that they refused to let go. If they stopped to think, they would not dare to do it.

For all his fears, Paul's heart was filled with joy. Everything he had suffered in his life was worth it if it had led to this moment. At last he was in command of his own destiny, with this beautiful woman who – miraculously, inexplicably – loved him.

'It would be better to take horses,' Mary mused. 'But I do not know how we can get them out of the gate with all Papa's men guarding it.'

Paul shrugged, not understanding. He was more concerned with finding a weapon. They would need it for hunting, and for defending themselves if necessary. Euphoria had not made him completely insensible. In the back of his mind, he knew Gert would not let his daughter run off unstopped. He would come after them to get her back.

He mimed a shooting motion. Mary nodded.

'All the muskets have been distributed to the men. It will have to be Papa's hunting rifle.'

The rifle was kept in a rack in the dining room. Paul and Mary went there quickly. The room was dark, and Mary had not brought the lamp. Paul felt around on the wall for the gun. His hands ran over the brackets that should have held it, but they were empty.

'It is gone,' said Mary.

Only one man was allowed to carry that rifle. Gert guarded it jealously; Paul had seen Marcus get a clip around the ear even for touching it. But Gert was supposed to be in bed.

'What the hell do you think you're doing?' said Gert's voice behind them.

The words needed no translation. Paul turned slowly, arms out in surrender. The joy in his heart turned to ash. Gert stood in the doorway. Moonlight streamed through the window and shone on the blued barrel of the hunting rifle in his hands.

'What are you doing with my daughter?'

He stepped forward. Paul had the wall at his back and could not move. Gert saw the sacks by Paul's feet, spilling over with food. His mood darkened.

'I save your life, feed you, clothe you, take you in as one of my own family – and this is my reward? That you will steal my own daughter from me?' He raised the rifle. 'You are no better than a wild animal.'

'No, Papa,' Mary pleaded. She stepped forward, putting herself between Paul and her father. 'He loves me.'

Gert's hands tightened around the rifle so hard Paul feared it might go off by accident.

'Have I raised a harlot in my own home? I expected better of you, but I should have known. George warned me you were too much like your uncle.' He sniffed. 'Whatever you think you feel for him, it is only some girlish fancy.'

'I am not a girl any more.'

As she spoke, Mary moved forward into the patch of moonbeam. The light shone through the thin cloth of her nightdress, silhouetting her naked body beneath. It hid nothing: the unlaced bodice, the tear at the neck where Paul had pulled it off her, and the dark bloodstains that spotted the fabric between her thighs.

Gert's eyes widened with shock that hardened to fury.

'What have you done?'

The moment seemed to last forever. Gert, Mary, Paul – and the gun between them. Paul could see Gert's knuckles tensed on the trigger. In his rage, even his own daughter standing before him might not stop him firing. Paul started to go forward, trying to put himself in front of Mary to shield her. Gert's hunter's eyes caught the movement almost before Paul had begun. He swung the rifle towards him.

Paul had faced death so many times it was a familiar experience – but this time something was different. He did not hear his mother's voice, or even the bird-headed god's: they were silent. The only thought in his mind as he stared down the barrel of the gun was *Mary*. To die now, having tasted such bliss, was almost too cruel. And yet, strangely, it did not frighten him.

But Gert was an outraged father, not a murderer.

'Get out of my house,' he growled. 'Get out and never let me see you again. And you . . .' He turned to Mary. 'We will speak of this with your mother in the morning.'

Paul did not understand what Gert had said – only that he would not be killed. He glanced at Mary, and saw the pain of parting written on her face.

'You must go. *Go*,' she repeated, pointing to the door.

Paul wanted to cling to the moment. To savour her face, to gaze into her eyes until she understood his love for her. Gert would have none of it. He grabbed Paul by his collar and dragged him to the front door. Paul glimpsed Mary's stricken face framed by golden, dishevelled hair, mouth open as if to call something after him. Then the door slammed and she was gone.

Gert marched Paul across the yard to the front gate. Jama waited there, talking softly with his fellow guards. Gert sniffed the night air.

'Any sign of trouble?'

'The night is quiet.'

'Open the gate.'

They removed the heavy bar that locked the gate and heaved it open a crack. As soon as it was wide enough for a man to pass through, Gert gave Paul a hard shove between his shoulder blades. Paul stumbled out.

'If I ever see you again . . .'

Remembering that Paul could not understand, Gert stopped speaking and shook the rifle at him in a gesture that needed no translation, keeping his eye on Paul until the gate crunched shut.

Paul was left alone outside the fort. He stood there for a moment, stupefied by all that had happened. All he wanted was to be back with Mary. To be taken from her, he felt some part of his soul had been ripped away.

He wanted to curl into a ball and sob until he shrivelled away – but he could not stay where he was. What if Gert decided to use that rifle after all? Paul stumbled away across the field, legs moving independent of any thought. Where did Gert expect him to go? Was he supposed to go aboard the ship, for Cape Town? But that thought was unbearable.

Gert had acted in anger. Perhaps by morning his temper would have ebbed. Susan would calm him, Mary would plead for him, and Gert would relent. Or else Mary would find a way to creep out and join Paul.

Everything would be better in the morning.

He crossed the open field and entered the line of trees at its edge. He could wait there, undisturbed, until dawn.

Belatedly, with a stab of guilt, he remembered Sana.

Where is she?

He wished they had not argued, and he wished he could talk to her to explain. It still stunned him that she thought Paul might be attracted to her romantically.

What could she have been thinking?

If he had considered more carefully, he would have realised that there was only a year or two's difference in age between Sana and Mary. But he did not see them that way. To him, Mary was in the full bloom of womanhood, while Sana would always be a little girl to him. He hated to think of her on her own. What if she never came back? What if the last words she had spoken to him were words of anger?

He crouched there, sobbing silently. Thorns and branches scratched his arms, but he did not mind. There was something pure and clarifying in the pain. He snapped off one of the branches – one with a particularly large thorn near its tip – and scraped it against his arm over and over again, until the blood ran freely and he could not feel it.

Lost in his grief, he did not hear the rustling leaves. Even the soft snap of a twig did not intrude, nor the warmth of another creature's energy radiating just behind him.

Something tapped his shoulder. In an instant, Paul's senses were alive again. What if the smell of the blood running down his arm had drawn predators? A moment earlier, he had thought he wanted to die. Suddenly, he wanted to live so much it hurt.

He spun around with a low cry. Sana's eyes gleamed out of the darkness, caught in a shaft of moonlight that pierced the tree canopy.

She said nothing, but simply stared at him ferociously. Clearly she had not forgotten, nor forgiven him.

How did you get out? he mouthed.

'The side gate. There are no guards there.' She spoke in a whisper, her voice no louder than the chatter of insects.

How did you find me?

'I saw you come out.' She looked him up and down, no hint of pity. 'They threw you out, then.'

He nodded, though it had not been a question.

'I thought they would.'

He had no response.

'It is good.'

No.

'Yes.' She gripped his shoulder, her small hands digging so deep between the bones he gasped in agony. 'We must go before the bad men come.'

He gaped at her.

What do you mean?

'Men from the boat. With guns.' She gestured to the fields beyond the trees, the open ground leading up to the fort. 'They are coming.'

He barely understood her. Bewildered, he put his face through the foliage to see what was out there. His eyes had adjusted to the darkness in the woods, and out in the fields the moon was shining strong and bright. He saw clearly: the pale walls of Fort Auspice, sparkling with the crushed shells ground into the mortar; the glow of the sentries' lamps; the long grass in the pasture, stretching down to the lagoon. And – only a few paces in front of him, keeping close to the shadows thrown by the trees – a dozen men crawling on hands and knees.

Their skins shone pale in the moonlight: white men. He did not recognise them, though they must have come from the ship, but he knew in a heartbeat why they had come. They carried themselves with the same purpose as the Tigréan warriors he had seen coming for the king of Gondar on the hunt, all those years ago. All were armed with many weapons.

Gert was right to distrust Hugo.

They crept past towards the walls of Fort Auspice. Every sinew in Paul's body stretched taut to snapping.

What should I do?

He ought to warn the others, but if he revealed himself, then he would have no protection. Hugo's men would shoot him dead.

The walls are strong and well defended. Gert's men are ready.

He wanted to believe that was enough – but the thought of Mary sleeping unawares behind those walls preyed on his heart.

'We must go,' hissed Sana.

A shot ripped open the night. The flash of the musket blinded Paul; he closed his eyes, even as the image lingered on his eyeballs. It had come from the walls. Gert's precautions had worked. His sentries must have seen Hugo's men approaching. The attackers, expecting no resistance, had been taken by surprise.

They responded quickly. The night became a storm: guns crashed, and muzzles flashed from inside the cloud of powder smoke that swirled around the gate. Gert's men kept up a brisk fire, while the attackers had to fire and run before the defenders could pinpoint their positions. But they could not hide. The defenders lit flares that threw back the curtain of night with a burning white light that was as bright as day.

There was no need to warn the family now, and nothing Paul could do to help. Paul watched from the trees, like Gondar again, seeing Yostos's and Goshu's armies battle for the throne. This time, the outcome did not seem to be in doubt. The walls were strong, and the gate well defended. In the light of the flares, the attackers could not get close. Whatever Hugo's purpose – Paul still had no idea why he should have launched this attack – it would fail.

But Hugo was not ready to give up yet. While his men peppered the front wall with musketry, Paul saw a smaller group slipping away into the darkness around the side of the fort. Looking for another way in, no doubt, but they would be disappointed. The walls were well maintained all around the compound, and the only other door . . .

Paul froze. He turned back to Sana and gestured towards the back of the fort.

When you came out of the side gate, did you lock it?

She shrugged, and did not meet his eye. He remembered how distraught she had been when she left, how furious with him. If she had blundered through the gate, would she have thought to lock it behind her?

Sana had said it was unguarded. If the attackers found the unlocked gate, they could get in. Mary and her family would be massacred.

Paul pointed through the trees in the direction of the fort. He made to go, but Sana grabbed his hand.

'This is not our fight,' she hissed.

The family saved our lives.

'They threw you out. They hate us.' She tugged his hand. 'If you go back, they will kill you.'

He was not sure who 'they' were – Gert, or Hugo's men, or simply the Fates that had been trying to kill him ever since the revolutionaries came for his mother. But he could not sit there and watch Mary and her family be massacred.

Could he?

Endure anything, say anything, become anything. But promise you will survive.

Constance's words were suddenly so real, it was as if she was standing there in the forest with him, as if the hand clutching his wrist was his own mother's.

You have endured worse than this, Paul told himself. *You survived.*

The shooting by the gate continued. The staccato rhythm res-onated inside him like the drums that had marched his mother to the guillotine. He had stood there that day, a few paces away, and done nothing.

If you go back, they will kill you.

The gunshots grew louder. A thought began to smoulder at the back of Paul's mind – an image of the bird-headed god in the Egyptian temple.

To master life, you must hold it as light as a feather.

Was that the message the god had given him? To let go of everyone else in order to protect himself? In the desert, in Gondar, and aboard Ilya's boat, he had killed men, or planned their deaths, or watched them die so that he would survive. Whatever attachments he felt, he had severed those bonds to save himself.

But he could not do it to Mary. His feelings were too strong. The weight of his mother's charge seemed to lift away; his life counted for nothing next to Mary's. He felt as light as a feather.

And suddenly, he understood what the god had been trying to tell him that day in the temple.

He pulled free of Sana's grip and began running towards the house.

HOLKAR, 1807

Adam lay stretched out on his bed, fully dressed. The stifling heat spurred a memory he had almost forgotten in the past weeks: the night he had found Lizzie in her cabin. What had happened to her? She must be married by now. He hoped she was happy.

He remembered their parting – her hope that he would give up his quest to live with her, and his harsh dismissal. Had he made the right choice? All he had achieved was death and ruin – yet the man he had come to kill was alive and triumphant.

A bar of light glowed under the door. Someone was coming. Adam sat up, just as the door swung open. Panjit came in, carrying a lamp. His face was lined with cares, made deeper still by the shadows of the flame.

'Have you come to arrest me?'

Adam had been waiting for it. He knew what Panjit had to do. Panjit shook his head. 'Not yet.'

'You should,' Adam urged him. 'I am what Hugo wants.' Enough people had suffered for the cause of his revenge. He would not drag down this proud city as well. 'Bargain with Hugo. Offer him my head. I think he is so furious with me, he would drop his other demands just to get hold of me.'

'Do not underestimate his appetite for our diamonds,' said Panjit with a weary smile. 'Or overestimate your own worth. Hugo does not know you are here.'

Adam was confused. 'He must suspect it. Otherwise, why insist that you hand over any fugitives?'

'Hugo suspects many things. But according to my spies, he believes you escaped down the river and away from here. He has had his cavalry scouring the countryside for you all day.'

'Then why—?'

'His wife has run away, and she has taken their son. Hugo is mad with jealousy and fury. He thinks she has sought refuge here.'

'Why would he think that?'

Before Panjit could reply, the door opened again with a squeak of hinges. Adam looked up to see a slim figure standing there. She was wrapped in a shawl and veil, but even so, he recognised her. He had been entwined with that body only the day before.

Clare pulled off the veil. Raven-dark hair tumbled over her shoulders. She did not approach Adam, but stood stiffly in the doorway, like a winged bird hiding in the undergrowth. Her face was bruised. She had not escaped Hugo unscathed.

'Where is Ralph?' said Adam.

'The Maharani's doctor is seeing to him.' Her voice was so low it almost disappeared. 'A splinter pierced his cheek.'

Adam bowed his head, torn by guilt. For the thousandth time, he wished his bullet had hit Hugo in the chest and ended everything.

'Why are you here?'

'I cannot stay with Hugo.' She touched the bruises on her face. 'Life with him would be a living death.'

'But you are not safe from him here. Tomorrow he is bringing his army to occupy the citadel.'

Adam glanced at Panjit. Why had he brought Clare here? If Hugo found Clare in Holkar, it would not just be her life in danger. Hugo would use it as a pretext to punish the whole city.

The old Indian had closed his eyes, and seemed to be snoozing.

'Panjit Rao has offered to smuggle me out of the city,' said Clare. 'By the time Hugo learns I am not here, I will be far away.'

'You cannot outrun him,' Adam warned. 'There is nowhere in India his power does not reach.'

'You think I do not know that?' She shook her head. 'No one better. That is why I have come to you.'

'I had my shot at Hugo.' Adam's voice was flat with despair. 'I missed. He will not let me get near him again.'

'Perhaps there is a way.'

Panjit had listened to their conversation in silence, his eyes shut. Now he sat up, alert and with such an intent smile that Adam knew he had been waiting for this moment. He had a plan, and he had manoeuvred Adam and Clare like pieces on his chessboard to achieve it.

But what was the endgame?

'I think the knight has one more move to make.'

Clare and Ralph left before dawn. They slipped out of a back gate, hidden in a curtained palanquin, with four servants and a small detachment of soldiers to protect them.

Adam watched them go. A knot twisted his stomach – so many emotions he could not reconcile. Memories played through his mind: cricket on the lawn and tea on the veranda; Clare naked in bed; Ralph screaming as he clutched his bleeding face.

The palanquin paused while the guards opened the little gate. The curtains swung back; Adam glimpsed Clare. Ralph lay beside her, his head on her breast. His right cheek was wrapped in bandages; he was asleep. Adam guessed the Maharani's doctors must have given him opium for his pain.

Clare had seen Adam. She reached out a hand through the curtains.

'I hoped you would be here.'

'I came to say goodbye.'

She leaned forward, trying not to disturb Ralph.

'It does not have to be goodbye. If you succeed in our plan today, you could follow after us. We could be together.'

Her lips were open, her eyes wide. The yearning on her bruised face was almost as painful to see as Ralph's injury.

'I would give everything I had if I could make you happy, make Ralph whole again.'

Hope flared in her eyes. 'You will come with me?'

He gazed on her fragile beauty, so vulnerable and inviting. It was tempting to succumb. But in his heart, he knew that it was impossible. Whether he killed Hugo or died in the attempt, he could not give her the love she needed. They had nothing in common except Hugo. Alive, Hugo's dark gravity was what bound them together. Dead, he would linger like a ghost between them, driving them apart until they hated each other.

'I cannot.'

A desperate note came into her voice. 'I need you.'

'You need love, and safety, and I can give you neither.'

The desperation hardened to anger.

'You are just like all the other men,' she said bitterly. 'Happy to come into my bed, and gone when you are needed.'

She had spoken too loudly. Ralph stirred in his sleep. He mumbled something, then rolled over, burying his face between his mother's breasts like a newborn baby.

'You deserve better than you have had,' Adam told her. 'I hope, for your sake and for Ralph's, that you will find it.'

The gate had opened. The palanquin bearers moved forward. Clare withdrew her arm and let the curtains drop closed. Adam's last sight of her was a bruised face streaked with tears.

The knowledge that he had done the right thing was little comfort. He had hurt her and her child; that would be a guilt he would always bear.

There was only one consolation to be had now.

In the citadel, a servant brought Adam a fine suit of clothes. Adam dressed slowly, feeling the rich fabrics against his skin. All his senses were heightened, as if a blindfold had been taken off. He fully expected to die that day.

He put on the shirt, the loose trousers of dazzling white silk and the sash around his waist. Last of all, he put on the coat that Panjit had given him. The richly embroidered cloth was stiff, but immaculately cut and sewn. The only flaw was a small knot under his left armpit that dug into his ribs. He ignored it.

From his window, he saw the troops mustering in the cantonment: four thousand red-jacketed sepoys in straight lines. They had elephants in their vanguard, and more elephants harnessed to the great siege guns in the rear. When they started marching, the dust rose like storm clouds.

Hugo is taking no chances, Adam thought.

He looked for his cousin, but could not pick him out. He was probably on one of the elephants.

The Maharani's guards arrived in their tiger-skin jackets to take Adam down to the gates. They put a chain around his wrists, but otherwise they treated him with respect. They must have known he was going to his death.

The city was deserted. The bazaars were closed; even the beggars had disappeared. The people waited indoors, furtive shadows behind shuttered windows as the procession passed.

The Maharani and her court had already assembled in the courtyard by the inner gate at the foot of the hill. They had formed up on three sides, in front of the red stone arcades that lined the square. The Maharani was mounted on a baby elephant with a tiger-skin saddlecloth. Panjit sat astride a white horse beside her, flanked by guards. Neither of them gave Adam a glance.

Trumpets blew outside the walls. Drumbeats answered them from within. The gate was hauled open. The elephants leading the Company army were so huge they could not get through the gateway with the howdahs on their backs. They waited outside, while the troops marched in.

The square was broad, but the sepoys filled it and still left men outside beyond the gate. Adam watched as they filed in, rank after rank. The heavy coat grew heavier still as his sweat soaked through it; the knot under the arm dug into him. Adam had to endure it. With his hands chained, he could not shift it.

Thousands of soldiers filled the parade ground. Not one of them made a sound. They stood in perfect lines, leaving an aisle down their middle that led like a blade straight from the gate to where the Maharani waited.

Outside the gate, the lead elephant kneeled. Hugo dismounted from the howdah and strode forward. He wore a coat of black cloth embroidered with dazzling golden thread in the shapes of tigers and elephants. A troop of guards fell in behind him as he walked between the files of men and approached the Maharani.

'Your Majesty.' Hugo's harsh voice whipped around the square. 'I have come to complete the terms of our agreement.'

The Maharani nodded. A courtier came forward, carrying an iron key on a silk cushion.

'The key to the citadel,' said Panjit. 'Quarters are prepared for all your men. You will find chests containing ten lakhs of rupees waiting for you.'

'And the fugitive?'

'We did not find your wife.'

Hugo swelled with anger. Adam thought he might order his troops to open fire that moment, but Panjit carried on calmly,

'We did, however, discover a rat lurking in our sewers. Perhaps you will accept him as fulfilment of our bargain?'

Panjit signalled to the guards. They nudged Adam forward with the tips of their bayonets, out from where he had been hidden behind the Maharani's elephant.

Hugo stared. Surprise lit up his face, turning to savage joy as he took in the chains on Adam's wrists, and the full scope of his victory.

The Maharani's guards stepped back. Adam was left in space in front of Hugo.

Will Hugo kill me at once? Adam had gambled everything that he would not.

The coat seemed to have shrunk so tight around him he could not move. The knot in the fabric pressed into his flesh. Adam held Hugo's gaze and ignored the pain.

'We will accompany the Maharani to the citadel and take possession of it,' Hugo said to the colonel beside him. 'We will put the prisoner in her dungeons.'

He leaned closer to Adam. Almost close enough.

'I have a servant who will see to you. A jailer who used to work for the Tipu Sultan and bears a grudge against Englishmen. He has a particular talent for inflicting pain. He will ensure that the last of your line of the Courtneys does not die with a whimper, but screaming in agony.'

Adam edged closer. Almost in range . . .

'If I die with your blood on my hands, I will die a happy man,' he told Hugo.

Hugo started to laugh. But it died on his lips as Adam started to move. The chains fell from his wrists as if by magic. His free hand moved to the bulge inside his coat. It was not a button or a knot of cloth. It was the pommel of a knife, smooth and round and sewn into the lining so expertly that from the outside you could not see it at all. A short blade, but at that distance Adam could plunge it straight into Hugo's heart.

There was an enormous bang from behind him. Something whizzed past, inches from Adam's shoulder, trailing red sparks and smoke. Instinctively, Adam turned back and saw more smoke billowing from what looked like a trunk of bamboo. Then, following the missile's trajectory back around, he saw the colonel next to Hugo clutching his chest. An iron rod three feet long was sticking into his heart. Blood pumped out around it, staining his scarlet uniform coat a darker shade of red.

More of the explosions sounded all around the square – like cannon fire, but pitched differently. They were not shooting balls, but bamboo sticks attached to iron points that streaked through the air and skewered the formations of infantry. One had so much power it went through a man's belly and out of his back, through the next man, and into a third man behind him.

Adam had never seen such a weapon before. It was like a gunpowder-fired javelin. He had no time to wonder at it, for he only had one thought: Hugo. He lunged with the knife.

But the Holkaris had fired too quickly. The rocket had given Hugo just enough warning. He was already fleeing towards the gate, and as the corridor of men contracted around him, Adam could not get through. He grabbed a musket from a sepoy who had been impaled on a rocket, sighted it on Hugo's fleeing form, and fired. The weapon was inaccurate. Blood showered Hugo's coat as the head of the man beside him exploded, but Hugo was untouched. Before Adam could find powder and shot to reload, Hugo vanished into the crowd.

Hands grabbed Adam and pulled him back. He turned to fight – but it was Panjit's guards, dragging him into the shelter of the arcade. One handed him a rifle and ammunition pouch; the other a sword belt and a curved scimitar.

Adam buckled on the belt and slung the pouch over his shoulder. The rifle was already loaded. He squinted down the barrel, searching out Hugo in the melee, but could not find him.

Panjit had appeared, still on his white horse.

'You should have killed him when you had the chance!' he shouted.

'You should have given me ten more seconds.'

Panjit grimaced. 'One of our rocket-men lit his fuse too soon.'

He looked up at the battlefield. The square was running red with blood, like the scuppers of a man-of-war. The rocket barrage had stopped, but only so the Holkari troops could move in with their spears and bayonets. The sepoys were surrounded, too hemmed in to organise any kind of defence and unable to get out through the gate, which was blocked with the trampled bodies of men who had tried to flee.

'It will be harder to win the battle with Hugo still alive,' said Adam.

Their plan had depended on killing Hugo with the first blow and relying on confusion to rout the leaderless troops.

Panjit drew a pistol and aimed it into the melee. A sepoy havildar who had been making good use of a long pike went down.

'If we must die, better a bullet in our heart and the battle cry on our lips, than to be slowly strangled by the East India Company.'

He kicked his horse and charged forward, slashing and cutting with his sword. A sepoy stumbled towards him, waving his musket like a club. Panjit avoided the blow and chopped deep into the man's neck with his scimitar. Blood from a severed artery spewed over the white horse's flanks.

Adam followed. After so many months in hiding and captivity, his heart sang to have a sword in his hand and enemies in front of him. He fought with savage joy, every hit and thrust precisely aimed. The sepoys could not stand against him. They broke and fled, clambering over the mountain of bodies that jammed the gateway. Many were trampled underfoot and added to the pile.

'Clear the gate!' bellowed Panjit. 'Clear the gate!'

The order made no sense to Adam. As long as the sepoys were penned in the square, they were easy pickings for the Holkari troops. Letting them out would give them the chance to get away.

Then a trumpet sounded behind him, and all became clear. The ground trembled as a company of Holkari cavalry galloped out from the streets behind the square. They lowered their lances and charged, running through the fleeing sepoys and crushing them under their horses' hooves. They closed around the survivors like a noose, clearing the courtyard and herding them towards the gate. The dam broke: the press of humanity pushed aside the bodies jamming the gate and rushed out, with the cavalry in close pursuit.

Some of the sepoys kept up the fight. These were a knot of battle-hardened warriors who understood that panicked flight would seal their own death warrants. They kept up a regular fire, covering their retreat. They could not hope to win, but they could do enough damage to hold off the cavalry. Ahead of Adam, a bullet plucked one of the lancers off his horse and knocked him to the ground. The horse, freed of its rider, turned to bolt. Adam ran to it. He grabbed the bridle with one hand, wrapped the other in the horse's mane, and hauled himself onto its back. Seizing the reins, he guided it towards the gate.

The gardens beyond the city had become a battlefield. Routed sepoys crouched behind walls and trees in the orchards, trying to find shelter from the Holkari counter-attack. The cavalry rode them down ruthlessly. Irrigation canals were clogged with bodies and ran red with blood. One man was pinned to a mango tree by a spear that went through his body. Adam saw another man's head lopped off like a melon.

Adam steered his mount away from the fighting as much as possible. Hugo had managed to get out of the square and onto a horse. Adam glimpsed him in the distance, riding hard towards the cantonment with only a few men around him. Adam kicked his horse forward, driving it to a gallop. He was not a practised rider, but the horse was flawless. It vaulted ditches and fences and cut swathes across the fields, freshly ploughed for the monsoon rains to come.

Some of the other Holkari lancers saw what he was doing. They spurred up, riding in a loose formation around him. Adam was glad of their company, for he could see more red coats in the distance. Not all of Hugo's troops had been defeated yet.

One of the lancers, a commander in a splendid golden helmet and a crimson sash, came alongside Adam. He grinned at Adam, and even in so much danger, Adam had to smile back. The wind streamed in his hair and whipped his coat behind him. He felt exhilarated, like being on his quarterdeck under full sail and clear skies, with a stiff breeze scudding him along.

And then the lancer disappeared. The horse galloped on, but there was no one guiding the reins. Adam glanced back to see the man lying in the dust behind him. His mangled body had been torn almost in two.

A bang echoed across the plain. Startled by the sound, the horse stopped so suddenly that Adam was almost thrown from the saddle. He grabbed on and reined the horse in, clinging for his life until it calmed. He looked forward.

He had come out from an orchard on to the open ground that surrounded the city. The last remnants of the defeated Company army were picking their way across the plain, battered and limping. It looked like a victory.

But a new army had appeared. A line of sepoys, three deep and almost a mile long, formed up with artillery and war elephants. It was as if the massacre in the courtyard and the rout through the fields had never happened. These were fresh troops, their white cross-belts gleaming in the sun and their red coats unstained.

They must have come in secret. That was why Hugo had taken so long to arrive from Calcutta. He had been travelling across India gathering an army. He had anticipated Panjit's trap and sprung one of his own. Adam could see Hugo on his black horse, behind the lines now and consulting with his staff officers. It looked like two regiments at least – several thousand men, a massive counterpunch to throw against the city.

Adam had to warn Panjit. He turned the horse and galloped back, chased on by another thunderous roar of cannon fire. The Company army had started to advance. Some of the Holkari cavalry, too eager in their pursuit, suddenly found themselves in range. They were shot down before they knew what was happening.

The face of the battle was turned upside down. Many of the defenders, assuming victory, had flooded out of the city to kill the stragglers and loot the dead. Their officers shouted at them to re-form, but the Holkari troops did not have the discipline of the sepoys and were slow to react. Many ran with whatever they could carry; they were cut down by the skirmishers advancing in front of the main army. Others formed straggling lines; they, too, were cut down by ruthless volleys of well-drilled musketry.

At the gate, Panjit was standing up in his stirrups and screaming orders. The mound of bodies had jammed the gate open. Panjit shouted at his men to drag the blockage away, but too many of them were fleeing from the onslaught and did not heed him. Others tried and died for their obedience. A cannonball came so close to Panjit that it hit the foreleg of his horse. The leg was snapped off; Panjit managed to jump clear as the horse collapsed. It thrashed and screamed, flailing with hooves that were as dangerous as bullets. Somehow, the maimed animal was even more frightening than the wounded men. Panjit dispatched the beast with a shot from his pistol.

Artillery fire smashed into the gatehouse. Shattered bricks rained down; the great gate was knocked askew on its hinges. Other cannonballs hit the piled-up bodies in the gateway, throwing up fountains of severed limbs and gore. The men who had been going to move the bodies stumbled back, blinded by blood.

Through the swirling red dust, Adam saw a monstrous shape moving forward. It was a war elephant, and in its pomp it looked like an incarnation of Ganesha, the elephant god who strikes down all obstacles. Lightning flashed from its back where sharpshooters rained fire down at the men on the walls. The gateway, previously inaccessible to the great beast, had been brought down by cannon fire. It marched through the ruins, head down, trampling the dead and the rubble under its mighty feet.

'Fall back!' shouted Panjit.

He hobbled across the square, while his men streamed back into the city. Panjit followed, but the fall from his horse had injured his leg. He limped after them, falling behind – an easy target for the marksmen on the elephant's back.

Adam was still mounted. He swerved, crouching low over the horse's neck as he urged the beast forward. The horse could smell the elephant coming. His nostrils flared; his ears sat flat. Bullets rained around them and clattered off the paving stones as the horse streaked across the courtyard.

Panjit heard the thunder of hooves behind him. He turned, expecting to make a final stand, and might have shot Adam if his pistol had been loaded. A moment before Adam reached him, he recognised Adam's face. Adam leaned down from the saddle, reached out an arm and scooped up Panjit, landing him unceremoniously over the horse's back.

The extra weight slowed the horse. Behind them, the Company infantry were flooding into the courtyard. Adam jerked the reins left and right, sending the horse on a crazy meandering path so that their enemies could not get a clean shot. The rumble of cannons sounded louder.

'We must reach the inner defences,' gasped Panjit.

Adam nodded. The ground rose as they entered the city, cantering up the road that climbed the hill. The streets were empty; everyone had fled. Ahead, the stout bastion of the second ring of walls loomed over the houses. The gate was closed, but someone saw them approach and cracked open a small door within the main gate. The horse would not get through. They had to abandon it and hope it would find its way to safety.

Adam stumbled in, his arm around Panjit's shoulders. As soon as they were through, the door was shut and bolted behind them. The guards looked shocked, but there was a determination in their faces that gave Adam hope. They would fight.

'You must get your leg seen to,' Adam told Panjit. It was badly broken. Blood poured from a hole where a fractured stump of bone had punctured the skin.

The Indian must have been in extreme pain, but he showed no sign of it. He shook Adam off angrily.

'There is no time. The Company will be here any moment.'

The walls shuddered under the impact of a cannonball. Hugo was bringing forward his artillery. The Holkari guards took up position on the walls, ready to fire.

Adam kneeled. He cut a strip of cloth off his coat and wound it around Panjit's leg, tying it fast with two more strips torn from his shirtsleeves. The stiff fabric just about passed muster as a splint.

'This fortress has stood impregnable for a thousand years,' said Panjit. 'We will not lose it now.'

Another gun fired, reverberating through the mountain under their feet.

NATIVITY BAY, 1803

Gert was back in the house, and had just poured himself a glass of brandy to settle his temper, when the first shot sounded. He leaped out of his chair even as more shots sounded, a rattling volley of gunfire. Shouts of alarm came from the men on the walls.

'What is happening?'

Susan had appeared, in her nightdress and shawl, with Rachel cradled in her arms and Marcus at her side.

'This is some evil cooked up by Captain Talbot and his supercargo.' Gert was already moving towards the door. 'We were fools ever to let them land. Take the children to the larder and bolt the door.'

Susan and her children went to the kitchens. Gert ran out into the courtyard. The defenders had lit Bengal fires on the walls – tubes packed with red sulphur and antimony that burned with a blinding blue-white light. They lit up the compound and the surrounding fields brighter than moonlight. The attackers could not approach without being seen. Instead, they were pinned back at the edges of the field, hiding in the shadows. They could not fire without giving away their position, and the Qwabe marksmen on the walls took full advantage.

Gert found Jama.

'How many of them?'

'Maybe thirty. They have come in strength.'

Gert swore. 'Artillery?'

'No.'

'That is good.'

From the bay, the *Seven Sisters*' guns could easily reach the walls of Fort Auspice. Gert guessed Hugo and Talbot had planned to take the fort by surprise, not expecting such well-organised resistance. Now that the men were committed, the ship could not open fire without risking hitting her own men.

The battle had settled into a slow rhythm, cautious and tactical. That suited Gert. He guessed it was not the battle the attackers had planned to fight. They would have expected surprise and a quick, overwhelming victory. Now that he had denied them both those advantages, Hugo's men were reduced to feints and potshots.

The fort was well supplied and could stand a siege for weeks. And if Hugo tried to bring the ship's cannon into play . . . Well, the bottom of Nativity Bay was littered with the bones of ships that had tried that ploy. Gert would mount one of Tom Courtney's old nine-pounders – nearly a hundred years old, but still clean and sound – and see what a few balls of heated shot might do to the *Seven Sisters*.

'What in hell's name is happening?'

George had come out of the house. Instead of a cane he carried his rifle, using its butt as a crutch to help him walk.

'They will try to get around behind us,' he warned. 'Do you have men on the rear walls.'

'As many as I can spare,' said Gert tersely.

The reality was, he did not have enough men to guard the whole perimeter of Fort Auspice. He had concentrated his forces where he expected the attack, at the front gate. So far, his decision had been vindicated.

'I will go and check the rear.'

'You should be with Susan and the children.'

'Do not presume to order me,' George snapped. 'This is my home. The first time I had to fight for it I was two years old. I will not cower like a woman now.'

'The situation is well in hand.' Gert could not hide his impatience with his father-in-law. 'Muskets and cutlasses will make little dent in our walls. Probably, the ship's crew fancied themselves pirates and thought they could catch us off guard. We have taught them different.'

'Pirates?' said George with a hollow laugh. 'This is not some whim or sport. They came here with a purpose, and they will not give up until we or they are defeated.'

'That will be soon enough.'

While they spoke, the battlefield had fallen silent. Now, the fighting erupted again in a furious volley near the front gate. Gert left George and rushed to the ramparts. Others came running, too, concentrating their strength to fight off the attack.

'This must be their last throw,' Gert said to Jama.

He closed one eye, watching the darkness beyond the orb of the Bengal fires. As soon as he saw the spark of a flame, he opened the other eye and loosed his shot. A satisfying cry told him he had hit the mark.

'When they retreat, send two of your best trackers to follow them. I want to be sure they return to their ship. We . . .'

Down on the open ground in front of the gate, a man ran forward. It was a suicidal move: if he came into the light, a dozen rifles would be ready to take aim at him. He stopped a distance away, cocked his arm and hurled an object into the air.

It was still in flight when a volley of bullets struck him. He stumbled back, jerking like a puppet. Gert felt a grim satisfaction – one less of the invaders.

But the man had served his purpose. The canister he had thrown arced over the wall and landed inside. For a moment, it lay on the ground, the only hint of danger a red glow where a fuse smouldered.

Then it exploded.

The fireball flashed bright in the courtyard. Fragments of metal flew out. They did little damage: most of the defenders were too far away to be badly hurt. But they were farmers and hunters. Though spears and guns did not frighten them, they had never faced a weapon like this. Some fled; others threw themselves to the ground. Musket balls peppered the walls as the attackers renewed their assault. A grapnel flew over and hooked on. Gert ran to it and cut the rope. He heard a thud on the far side of the wall as the climber was dropped on his backside.

'To your posts!'

In the courtyard, Jama was trying to rally the dazed and frightened defenders. He bellowed like a bull, pulling men to their feet and pointing them towards the walls. The battle hung in the balance.

Suddenly Jama fell silent. He clutched his heart, doubled over, and fell face first on the ground.

Gert stared. He had known Jama all the years he had lived at Nativity Bay. Both men were keen hunters, with an eye for a game trail and a gift for stalking prey. Jama had stood as godfather to Marcus, and Gert had presented Jama's son with his first spear. To lose him was second only to losing one of Gert's own family.

Yet in his grief, one more dreadful fact stood out. The wound was in Jama's back. He had been shot from behind. Somehow, Hugo's men had managed to get into the courtyard.

Gert knew how to handle a gun. He could track game, read the wind, aim and reload with speed and precision. If he had been a soldier, he would have realised that his best hope was to hold his men together and use their combined strength to fight off the invaders; if they broke ranks, it would be every man for himself.

But he was not a soldier. He had thought they were safe inside the walls of Fort Auspice. Now that certainty was lost, he did not know how to react. His men were by the walls, his family were in the house, and the enemy had come between them.

'Back!' he shouted. 'Back to the house!'

HOLKAR

The Holkaris battled ferociously. Adam had fought with crews who would rather see their ship burned to the waterline than surrender it, but the Holkaris were even more determined. They made the Company troops buy their lives dearly. They fought them from house to house, through the bazaars and workshops and public squares, all the way up the hill. For every Holkari who fell, at least five sepoys died first. Blood flowed down the steep streets in streams.

But the defenders were pushed back. As with a rising tide, they could resist the advance but not stop it. If they held a position too long, they would be surrounded. Again and again, Adam was forced to retreat before he was cut off. He ran along the rooftops, leaping between the close-packed houses; slithering down onto the wooden balconies; ducking in and out of buildings. Once he ran through a room where a family of eight cowered behind a curtain. The youngest, a newborn baby, was clamped to its mother's breast so it would not cry out. Adam left them there and hoped the sepoys would be merciful. Further down the hill, where the Company troops had consolidated their gains, women were already coming out of their houses, offering the soldiers gold and brass to spare their homes. The soldiers took the treasures they were offered, and then they took the women.

Still the Holkaris retreated, further and further up the mountain towards the citadel. The ancient walls had not been built to resist modern siege guns, and Panjit did not have enough men left to fight off all the sepoys. Hugo's brutal plan had worked. He had sacrificed almost a full battalion, but in return he had destroyed the cream of the Holkari army.

Adam had no doubt that Hugo had accounted for it in advance. He would know to the last rupee how much each sepoy cost – his equipment, his training, his use to the Company – and how many lives it was worth spending. For the diamond wealth of Holkar, Adam knew, he would sacrifice every one of them.

From the rooftops, Adam searched through the smoke for any glimpse of Hugo among the advancing troops. Adam had a good rifle – all he needed was one shot but Hugo kept well back.

He found Panjit again on the walls above the gate to the citadel, at the summit of the hill. Both men were bloody, bruised and powder-stained.

'How much longer can we hold out?'

The noise of battle was so loud, Adam had to shout in Panjit's ear. He shrugged. 'The citadel is strong. But . . .'

They looked in each other's eyes, one warrior to another. Both knew they were losing.

'Is it fair to ask the men to keep fighting?' Adam asked.

He would never yield, but he could not demand the same of the Holkaris.

'Better to die like tigers than lambs.'

'There are ways to escape.' Adam thought of the underground water tunnels he had used to visit Clare. 'There must be other forces in the countryside you could rally.'

Panjit tapped his leg. It had bled much more since Adam bound it; the fabric of the splint was soaked through.

'I cannot run.'

Adam reached out to embrace him. Panjit flinched away. Even in the heat of battle, the dictates of the caste system could not be compromised.

'I will die beside you,' Adam promised, 'and hope Hugo dies first.'

The citadel gate shuddered. The summit of the hill was high enough that the Company gunners could not elevate their cannons enough to bear. Instead, they had brought up an elephant, a great old bull with tusks so heavy they dragged along the ground. They goaded it on, pricking its hindquarters with spears to enrage it. It charged forward to get away, slamming its head into the gate as if it was felling a tree.

Adam loaded his rifle with extra powder and took aim at the elephant's head. The beast was bucking and rearing so violently, it was hard to get a true aim – but Adam was used to fighting with the swell of a ship beneath him. He tracked it carefully, then fired.

The shot crashed out. The ball flew straight where he had aimed it, clean on the animal's forehead – above its trunk, between its eyes, and below the armoured cap that covered the top of its head. Adam watched the bullet strike.

But there was no fountain of blood or wounded cry. Instead, the bullet bounced off the grey hide, like a cricket ball hit against a wall.

'The head is like iron!' Panjit shouted at him. 'Aim for the lungs!'

Adam stared in confusion. He had precious little notion where an elephant's lungs might be, and even less idea how he might hit them when the animal was hurling itself about in a raging frenzy. He reloaded, using so much powder he feared he would split the rifle barrel.

The old bull hit the gate again, an impact that shook the whole wall. The gate splintered. The elephant drew back, crouching on its haunches for another charge. The men around it put up their spears, letting it gather its strength for a moment. They knew the gate could not withstand another blow. Behind the elephant, sepoys were fixing bayonets for close quarters fighting.

Adam scanned the enemy lines for Hugo. At the bottom of the slope, he saw a black figure mounted on a horse. He raised the rifle, but before he could take the shot the figure retreated behind a building.

There was no time to wait for him to emerge. The elephant was coming again. The men with spears pressed forward, jabbing at it and driving it to new rage. It tossed its head in fury. One man, too daring, came in range of the swinging trunk and was knocked off his feet. His head slammed into a wall and he fell, unmoving.

The elephant raised itself. As it did, Adam saw the knuckles of its spine running down its back towards its tail. The skin was stretched taut over the bones, rippling as the beast moved.

Adam was no hunter. But men were animals, too, and he had seen enough die in combat to know where they were weakest. Men might survive all manner of gory blows to their fronts, but they would be paralysed at a stroke when a blade cut their backbones. He sighted the rifle again, aimed and fired.

The effect was instantaneous. The elephant dropped to its haunches in a sitting position, crushing one of the drivers behind it. It put up its head and bellowed in agony. It pawed the ground with its front feet, shaking the earth, but it could not move. Adam's shot had hit true and shattered the beast's spine.

He felt a wave of pity for the animal. He wished he could put it out of its pain, but he could not get a shot. He looked for Hugo instead, again in time to see him retreating to shelter.

As long as the elephant lay dying, nobody could get close to the citadel. Sepoys surrounded the animal and began pouring fire into it. Blood flowed from the many holes they made, pouring into the street. It took an age to die. The sepoys were exposed to fire from the defenders on the walls, so that their blood mingled with the dying beast's.

'They will not get the gate open now,' Adam exulted.

The gate opened outwards, and the dead elephant lay in front of it. If Hugo's men tried to move it, they would pay a heavy price. Already, more of the Maharani's troops had appeared on the walls. They laid down a devastating fire, clearing the streets below the citadel. The sepoys, who moments earlier had been readying for the final assault, were forced back. Many did not make it, but lay in a sea of bodies.

When there were none left in range to kill, the battlefield quieted. For about half an hour there was silence, except for the screams of the fallen. To ears deafened by gunfire, they were hardly noticeable.

'Will they retreat?' said Adam.

He didn't dare believe it. But even Hugo did not have an infinite supply of men, and he had paid a heavy price to advance this far. Perhaps the walls of Holkar would remain inviolable after all.

'Would you give up?' said Panjit. 'So close to your goal?'

Adam knew the answer.

'Offer to treat with him. Say you will give me up, in exchange for the city.'

If it was the only way to get in arm's reach of Hugo, he would happily do it.

'You know what kind of man he is,' said Panjit. 'He would take you, and then he would renew his assault.'

A memory came to Adam's mind, studying Shakespeare by lamplight in his father's cabin as a boy. He murmured the words under his breath. "'I am in blood stepp'd in so far that, should I wade no more, returning were as tedious as go o'er.'"

'Hugo has staked the whole might and prestige of the East India Company on this attack,' said Panjit. 'He would rather die than fail here.'

Adam cracked a weary smile. 'In that, I can oblige him.'

A commotion from down the hill signalled that the assault would be renewed. The earth shook again to the tramp of elephants.

'They are desperate.' Adam pointed to the bull elephant's carcass, which had finally stopped twitching. 'They will not be able to ram the gate with that blocking the way.'

A pair of elephants emerged from the buildings at the foot of the slope. They were not armoured with skullcaps; instead, they had howdahs on their backs, mounted with swivel guns. Only small-calibre cannons – anything heavier would have broken the elephants' backs with its recoil – but the added height meant they could reach the top of the walls.

Adam did not bother to aim for the animals. At that distance, the bullet would have bounced off. Instead, he aimed for the men servicing the guns.

What are they planning?

The guns were so small they would not dent the walls.

By now it was the middle of the afternoon. The clouds pressed low, insulating the battlefield with its own heat. Smoke, grit and moisture filled the air. It seemed the clouds must burst open any moment with the long-awaited monsoon, but still they held on. Adam wished the rain would come. When it did, the storm would wash the streets clean and turn every grain of gunpowder to porridge. Hugo would have to retreat.

In the gloom, Adam saw the glow of a match on the back of one of the elephants as the gunners touched the fuse.

'Get down!' he ordered, ducking behind one of the battlements.

Most of the men followed suit, but not all. They felt safe on top of their walls. There was little chance the cannonball would hit them.

But the cannon was not loaded with round shot. It belched flame, shooting out a tin case about the size of a wine bottle. The fire from the gun ignited the powder charge in the case, ripping it apart and spreading the contents across a wide arc.

A cloud of metal flew over the ramparts, buzzing like a swarm of wasps. The contents of the canister – rusty nails, pieces of wire, spare musket balls and other scraps of metal, mingled with the jagged remains of the case itself – made a deadly hailstorm of iron. It hit any man who had not been quick enough to hide. The fortunate died quickly as the metal fragments buried in their brains, sliced their arteries or diced their faces. The less fortunate were maimed for life: eyeballs gouged out, tendons severed, bones smashed. They collapsed, screaming. Some stumbled off the ramparts, fell into the courtyard below, and were mercifully silenced.

Adam, crouching behind the battlement, was spared. The scrapshot flew by on either side, but did not touch him. As soon as it had passed, he leaped up, rifle ready to attack the gunners while they reloaded.

But the gunners on the second elephant had been waiting for the Holkaris to show themselves again. As they did, the second gun fired. Again, a blizzard of metal fanned over the ramparts, a mincing machine for any man caught in it. Adam threw himself to the floor just in time. A scrap of iron buzzed past his ear and left a long shallow gash in the side of his head. Many were not so lucky.

Those who survived were in no hurry to get up. The first gun might already have reloaded, and they had lost too many men. But in the instant that he had had his head above the parapet, Adam had seen that the sepoys were advancing again. They flooded forward, dodging around the elephants and running up the slope towards the gate under cover of the cannon fire. They carried ropes and scaling ladders.

Adam risked another glance. The Company troops were at the foot of the walls. Some had clambered on the back of the dead bull elephant and were using it as a platform. Others took cover behind it, where fire from the walls could not reach them.

'They are coming,' Adam warned.

It hardly needed to be said. Bamboo rattled against the outer walls as the first ladders were hoisted into place. The rungs quivered as the sepoys began to climb.

'Up!' Adam shouted. 'Do not let them reach the walls!'

Reluctantly, the Holkari rose from their hiding places. Some fired down on the massed troops, while others reached through the embrasures and pushed the ladders away. One or two of the ladders toppled back into the crowd, scattering the troops behind. But others were already so heavy with the weight of men on them that they could not be budged.

Adam cracked off a couple of shots, aiming for the officers where he could find them. The men on the ground were so numerous, it made little difference. Everything had become automatic: cleaning out the rifle; ramming home the new bullet and wadding; priming the pan; darting out from cover to take the shot, and then ducking back again before anyone could take aim at him. Smoke filled the air and brought on an early twilight.

In the darkness and the press of men, Adam almost missed the light glimmering in the distance where the elephants still stood. Hugo had climbed on the elephant's back and was shouting orders at the gunners. He wanted them to fire again. It was madness: at that range, their scattershot blast would kill as many of their own men as the Holkaris. But Hugo had more lives to play with, and he was willing to spend them profligately.

The gunners were less willing. Adam could see them remonstrating with Hugo – a brave effort, but also wasted. Hugo snatched the match from the gunner's hand and touched it to the cannon himself. Another killing spray of iron and lead raked the ramparts. Many of the sepoys – the boldest, the ones who had been first up the ladders – were cut to pieces. But there were more below to take their places, and precious few defenders left. The final blast had taken everyone by surprise. The battlements were swept almost clear.

The sepoys reached the top of the ladders and poured over the wall. No one remained to oppose them – except for one man, who would not yield. Panjit faced the invaders with his leg splinted, one hand gripping a crutch and the other holding a sword. One of the sepoys came at him, musket raised like a spear to skewer him on the bayonet. Panjit swayed out of the way of the lunge and ran the man through with his sword, grimacing with the agony of the effort. The blade stuck in the corpse; hobbling on one leg,

Panjit could not get it free. Another sepoy charged at him, and Panjit had no defence.

Adam saw a weary look cross Panjit's face, the resignation of a man who has given everything, and failed at the last. A man ready for death.

Adam still had the loaded rifle in his hand. He fired it at the sepoy, knocking him into the soldiers behind. Before they could regroup, Adam hooked an arm around Panjit's shoulders and dragged him back.

'Let me go!' Panjit shouted. 'Let me die with honour!'

'I would rather you lived.'

The sepoys were coming again. Adam reached down, picked up a dead man's musket, and hurled it at the men coming after them. They tripped over it, which bought him a few more precious seconds – enough time to reach the safety of the guard tower. He slammed the door shut and bolted it, just as a bayonet struck, quivering, into the wood.

'You should have let me die.' Panjit did not sound angry, only sad. 'We have lost.'

'What about the Maharani?' Adam demanded. 'Where is she?'

'In the palace.'

'Will she surrender?'

Panjit shook his head. 'She knew the risks when she chose to fight, rather than sign Hugo's treaty. She will see this through.'

'Then Hugo will go to find her.'

Panjit gave Adam a look that was half admiration, half despair. 'You still think you can kill Hugo?'

'Perhaps not.' Adam plucked one of the pistols from Panjit's belt and reloaded it. 'But I will die before I stop trying.'

He glanced at the door. The invaders had given up trying to break it down. There were easier pickings to be had in the fortress, and they could always come back later. But if he opened it, there would certainly be someone ready to stick him with a bayonet.

Panjit read his thoughts.

'There is another door at the foot of the tower. From there, a passage leads to the kitchens, and then to the throne room.'

'Let's go.'

'You go. I will only delay you.'

'I need you to show me the way.'

Panjit could not navigate the twisting stairs with his broken leg. Adam heaved him over his shoulders and carried him down. Outside the tower and across the courtyard, they could hear the Company soldiers flooding the citadel – but they had not found their way into the palace yet. The passage was deserted; so, too, were the kitchens. The fires were cold, with only the scent of fat and spices lingering in the air. With Adam half-carrying, half-dragging Panjit, the two men hurried through them, down a connecting corridor and into the main banqueting hall of the palace.

The moment they entered the hall, the sounds of battle grew louder. All was lost, but a few pockets of resistance held out. Most of it seemed to be coming from the throne room next door. Adam and Panjit went through.

The great mahogany doors had been thrown open. A makeshift barricade blocked the outer doorway: rubble that had been blasted from the walls; wooden screens; chests and tables. The golden throne had been chopped into pieces and added to the pile. The tiger-jacketed bodyguards kneeled behind it, firing into the courtyard beyond. Several already lay dead. The Maharani paced behind them, a tiny figure shouting encouragement. She was still dressed in her finery, with the diamond diadem on her forehead and her hair braided back.

She gave a little cry when she saw Panjit.

'I thought you were dead.'

'The day is not yet finished, Highness.'

A deep roar rumbled through the palace, shivering the furniture and shaking dust from the tapestries on the walls. At first Adam thought the siege guns had opened up again; then, as it rolled on, he thought someone must have fired the fortress's powder magazine.

Panjit recognised it first.

'Thunder,' he said. 'The monsoon is breaking.' A tear of frustration slipped from his eye. 'If it had only come an hour sooner.'

Through the doors, Adam saw the first drops of rain begin to fall on the courtyard. Dark wet spots appeared on the paving stones, singly at first, but quickly blotting into each other.

All the force of the clouds was unleashed at once, nine months' worth of pent-up moisture dropping like a landslide. It battered the ground and pummelled the hard earth. It hammered against men's skins and stung their eyes blind.

The Maharani's guards, in the shelter of the throne room, were spared. They could reload and fire at will, while their enemies – caught in the open – had no protection. The sepoys retreated to the edges of the courtyard, taking shelter under the arcades and in palace buildings.

The rain was falling so hard the drops ricocheted off the ground, making a fine mist. No one could fire a musket, except the men inside. They could pick their enemies off at will.

'We are not safe,' Adam warned Panjit. 'They will find another way in soon enough. We do not have enough men to guard all the doors.'

Panjit nodded. 'The west tower. We can defend ourselves—'

He broke off. The pace of firing had risen. Beyond the broken door the day was almost dark as night, but in the gloom they could see sepoys regrouping again. Their officers shouted and kicked and beat them with the flats of their swords, driving them out of their hiding places into the centre of the courtyard. In their rear, Adam saw Hugo striding about, bellowing orders and beating any man who shirked or straggled. Adam snatched a musket, but in the milling crowd he could not get a clean shot.

The sepoys formed up in a line. They made an unmissable target, and the defenders shot many down. But even with ten times as many men, the Holkaris would not have been able to kill them all. And they were running low on ammunition.

The Company troops were drenched and battle-weary. They wanted to be dry and warm, and to be allowed to plunder the palace. Without waiting for a command, they lowered their muskets and charged for the throne room doors.

A final volley of Holkari gunfire cut down the front rank of the sepoys. The men behind them surged on, stepping on the bodies of the fallen to climb the barricade. The Holkaris jabbed their bayonets and swung their weapons like clubs, but they were too few to stem the tide. The sepoys swarmed over the wall. One by one, the defenders were butchered.

Only Panjit, Adam and the Maharani were spared. The sepoys spread out around the room, making a semicircle around them. Violence smouldered in their eyes, a hair's breadth from massacring the survivors. But they had their orders, and even in the lust of battle they knew the price of disobedience.

A dark figure loomed through the curtain of rain. Hugo Courtney strode in, through the broken doors and the splintered remains of the barricade. He was soaked, his black hair plastered to his forehead and his shirt stuck to his skin. A cut bled from his cheek. None of that mattered now. He had won.

The Maharani stepped forward. She did not reach Hugo's chest, but she faced him unbowed. Her strength would have been astonishing in a woman twenty years older; in this child, dressed up in her full finery like a doll, it was breathtaking.

'I will surrender my palace and my treasure. All I ask in return is that you treat my people with mercy.'

There was no one to translate. But Hugo had studied her language in secret, hiding his talent to deceive his adversaries and listen in when they thought they could not be understood. Now, he did not have to pretend.

'You had your chance to treat with me,' he said in flawless Hindustani. 'Now, I will take everything.' He ran his eye over her little girl's body, and the face with the rosebud lips painted like a woman's. 'I will treat you exactly as I am going to treat your kingdom. Indeed, you will feel it most *intimately*. And you . . .' His gaze swung to Panjit. 'I will make you watch everything I do to her. You will learn the price of betraying me.'

Adam hoped the Maharani could not understand the true meaning of what Hugo threatened. But even at her young age, she recognised the intent: the age-old evil of a predator.

'No.'

She took a jewelled dagger from her belt. Raising it high, she charged at Hugo, a battle cry on her lips.

It was an extraordinary sight – the princess, little more than a girl, charging towards the giant like David against Goliath. Her skirts flew around her legs; the diamond diadem flashed like lightning. The watching sepoys were so stunned, none of them moved to stop her.

Hugo was not so slow. He drew his sword and extended the long blade. The Maharani was almost on him. Even if she had seen it, she did not have time to change course. Perhaps she did not want to.

The point of the sword pierced her dress and sank deep into her heart. Her body seemed to fold in two. With a small gasp, the Maharani collapsed in a heap of silk and blood. Her dagger fell to the floor. Hugo reached down, yanked the diadem off her head and slipped it in his pocket.

'A pity,' he remarked to Panjit. 'I would have enjoyed breaking her in, teaching her a little obedience.'

'The same way you teach your wife obedience?' said Adam.

'Do not mention her. I am a jealous husband, and *you* . . .' Hugo jabbed the sword at Adam. 'You cannot afford to provoke my temper.'

'You may have defeated me,' said Adam, 'but your victory is empty. Clare has left you.'

'She will not escape. There is nowhere in India she could go that I could not find her.'

'You are a powerful man,' Adam agreed. 'You will probably find her, eventually. But you will never see your son.'

Hugo went very still.

'My son?'

'She brought him here,' Adam said. 'She thought the Holkaris would protect him.'

Hugo stared at Adam, eyes burning with suspicion and doubt.

'What did you do?'

'What did you do when you found your enemy's children?' Adam held Hugo's gaze, letting his fear stoke itself to a white heat. 'Did you have mercy?'

'What did you do?' Hugo's voice had risen to a roar. 'Where is my son?'

'A place where you will not find him.'

Hugo could not contain himself. With a roar, he charged at Adam, sword outstretched to run him through. Adam backed away, but he could not go far. He was almost against the rear wall. The only way out was the high window from where the Maharani had once surveyed her kingdom. The wooden screen had been torn away to make the barricade; on the other side, there was nothing but thin air and the sheer face of the mountain.

If Hugo had been in control of himself, he could have pushed Adam back at the point of the sword until Adam's only choices were the blade or the drop. He could have had his men do it, closing the noose around Adam until it throttled him.

But Adam had goaded Hugo to a fury. This was the kill he had waited half his life for. Like a lover craving the touch of his beloved's body, he had dreamed of the sensation of his sword sliding through Adam's flesh, accomplishing his father's quest. Now, that was the only thought in his head as he lunged at Adam.

Adam had one thought, too. He reached inside his coat and felt for the knife that Panjit had hidden there, still snug in its lining. He pulled it out, brandishing it at Hugo.

A triumphant smile curled Hugo's lips. Against his own weapon, the dagger was nothing more than a needle. Hugo's sword would be buried in Adam's heart up to the hilt before Adam could even scratch Hugo with it.

Hugo drove the point forward. Adam stood at the window's edge, framed by clouds and falling rain. He did not try to move forward or take his guard. He was resigned to his fate.

At the last minute, he jerked his wrist. The knife rang against Hugo's sword. It could not withstand the force of his blow; it snapped off at the hilt. Hugo roared with triumph.

But the little blade had served its purpose. It had diverted the stroke, pushing the sword away so that it whistled past Adam's side. Adam was inside Hugo's guard – unarmed, but that did not matter. He did not have to live to defeat Hugo. He only had to kill him.

Hugo's body collided with Adam. Hugo drew back to strike again, but Adam was faster. He wrapped his arms around Hugo, hugging him so close he could smell the sweat on the nape of his neck.

Then he stepped back off the window ledge.

NATIVITY BAY

T he battle had become a nightmare. By the time Paul reached the gate, the Bengal fires had burned out, leaving the compound in darkness that was broken only by the flash of musket fire. Everything was chaos. No one wore uniforms, so a figure glimpsed could not be identified as friend or foe. People ran helter-skelter like a herd of gazelles panicked by a lion.

The main gate stood open. Not smashed off its hinges by cannon fire or battered down with hatchets – the party who had entered by the side gate must have opened it from the inside.

One by one, the remnants of Fort Auspice's defenders returned to the house. There were not many of them. Hugo's men followed, pressing home their advantage. It reminded Paul of that terrible night in the mountains of Gondar: left for dead, the hyenas circling around him for the kill.

Mary must be in the house.

He ran across the compound to the kitchen, praying no one would pick him out as a target. The kitchen door hung open, spewing smoke, though the fire in the hearth had been put out hours ago. Two men lay across the threshold: one white, one black, both dead. Paul stepped over them. Ten paces later, it occurred to him that he should have searched them for weapons. He ought to turn back, but his legs kept carrying him inexorably forward. He had to find Mary.

Where can she be?

He ran down the corridor, throwing open doors to the various storerooms. No one was there. Ahead of him, he heard the savage sounds of close combat: the ring of steel; the roar of guns discharged at point-blank range; the grunts of men locked in tests of strength. Through broken windows, he could see into the other wings of the house, like pictures hanging in a gallery. Furniture was overturned and smashed. Smoke billowed. Spent wadding fell to the ground and set the carpets alight. Soon the fire spread to the curtains and upholstery, licking up into the wooden roof beams and the thatch. Half the house was ablaze, though that did not stop the battle. The fire became another source of weapon. Men snatched burning pieces of wood and used them as clubs, or pushed their enemies into the flames to set their clothes alight.

Through the uproar and destruction, he heard a child's scream cut through the din. He followed the sound down the corridor towards the drawing room. The smoke was thicker here. He dropped to his knees to crawl on the floor, where the air was clearer – and came face to face with a sprawled-out corpse. A boarding axe was buried in his skull; his features were so masked with blood that Paul almost didn't recognised them.

It was Gert. The sight froze Paul; he nearly gave up. Then the screaming came again. He could not fail Mary.

He climbed over Gert's body and carried on. More bodies littered the corridor, dead and dying together. Their blood and guts and brains smeared the walls, while an infernal red light from the burning building throbbed through the smoke.

The roof might give way at any moment. If Paul was caught under it, he would be buried alive. He got to his feet and ran. Slipping on blood, tripping on corpses, choking on smoke and gunpowder residue, he charged into the main living room. Through the shattered windows, he saw men retreating across the compound towards the gate. Their work was done.

But one remained. Hugo stood by the door, his sword raised. Paul stopped short, thinking the blade was aimed at him. Then he saw Mary.

She lay on the ground, pinned under one of the fallen roof timbers. Rachel lay in her arms, inches below the beam. Mary must have seen the beam falling and thrown herself over her sister to protect her.

Hugo stood over them. Mary said something that Paul could not hear. Whatever Hugo replied, his words hit Mary like a bullet. She flinched, then gathered her strength and tried to heave the beam off herself.

Hugo seized Rachel's hair and dragged her away. Rachel screamed louder, weeping and beating her tiny fists. Hugo laughed. With a casual swipe of his sword, he cut the toddler's throat. Her screams choked off. She tottered for a moment, then fell into her sister's arms. Mary clasped the dying child to her breast, while Hugo stood over her. He spat on the dead child and said something Paul could not understand.

A cutlass lay at Paul's feet where someone had dropped it. He snatched it up. With the fire raging, there was no time to take guard or put up a defence. He charged at Hugo.

HOLKAR

Hugo and Adam fell with the rain. Even in mid-air, they did not stop struggling. They wrestled and fought, as if one could still claim victory by killing the other before the impact finished them both. The cliff face rushed past. The ground rose sickeningly fast to meet them.

At least I have avenged my family, Adam thought.

He wondered if Phoebe and Rob would ever hear of it, far off in England.

The two falling bodies hit the ground. The impact shocked Adam: he had expected death to soften the blow. Instead, he felt it through every bone in his body.

And yet not so hard as rock. The ground was yielding, cradling them as it slowed their fall without breaking their necks. There was a rustling, a snapping, and then a hard bump as they finally came to rest.

Adam looked up, amazed to still be alive. He saw sticks, straw, and rain pouring over him through a broken roof. He smelled animals and dung.

They had fallen into a thatched shed at the bottom of the cliff. The straw had cushioned their fall, while the bamboo rafters had acted like springs to absorb their momentum. When the bamboo finally snapped and dropped the two men into the building, the fall merely knocked the wind out of them.

Both men sprang apart, circling each other. The moment Adam got to his feet, he felt a stab of pain shoot through his knee. The fall had hurt him, after all. Hugo appeared unscathed. He had been holding his sword when they went through the window: he had let it go as they fell, but it had dropped with them and landed beside him. He plucked it out of a pile of straw, taking a few experimental swipes to see that the blade was still true. A smile spread across his face.

'I've never met a man so difficult to kill,' he said.

Adam didn't reply. Hugo was already moving towards him. Adam had to keep his distance, while desperately scanning the room for a weapon.

A *katiyal* hung from a hook on the wall. It was a kind of Indian billhook, a long-handled knife whose tip curved ninety degrees into a wicked hook. The knife was sharp on both the inside and the outside of the curve, while the end was honed to a point like a needle. Adam had seen toddy-tappers use them to harvest coconuts. They would reach the fruit off the tree with the hook, then use the blade to split it open and husk it.

Adam snatched it. He had to turn to grab it, exposing his side to Hugo. Hugo saw the opening and lunged. Adam managed to bring the *katiyal* around to parry the blow in time. Metal rang on metal. The *katiyal* was forged from a single bar of iron, so that the vibrations shivered all the way through the handle. Adam almost dropped it, but Hugo was coming at him once more. Adam flung up the billhook and deflected the blade again.

The movement put all his weight through his damaged knee. Adam gave a shout of pain. He tried to hide it from Hugo, but that was impossible. He backed towards the door, lurching with each step.

Hugo came in low, cutting at Adam's weak leg. The *katiyal* blocked the sword, but the force of the blow knocked the flat of the knife against Adam's knee. Adam cried out. Hugo followed up quickly with another feint that Adam, in a haze of pain, could only swipe at. He swung at thin air, while the blade cut inside his guard and sliced for his stomach. It would have disembowelled him, but at that moment Adam's leg gave out. He collapsed, so that the blade only nicked him. Blood welled into his shirt.

Hugo stepped back and beckoned Adam to get up. He was baiting Adam like a matador with a wounded bull, though there was no one to see and no crowd to applaud. Perhaps he was performing for the ghosts of his ancestors, Gerard and Christopher and Guy Courtney.

Adam did not want to be his sport. But he would not die sitting on his backside in an Indian hovel either. He pushed himself up, gritting his teeth. The *katiyal* weighed on his arm like a rock.

He backed away, out through the door into the rain. Each step was agony. Hugo followed, but not quickly. He was enjoying watching Adam's suffering.

They had come out into a lower part of the city, built on a natural terrace on the hillside below the palace. Adam recognised it: he had been there before. It was on the main road up to the citadel. In happier times, there would be bazaars and crowds thronging this place. Now, there were only the bodies of those who had resisted Hugo's army as they passed through, like the leavings of the tide. Sheets of rain drummed on the road and sluiced the blood away.

The townspeople had fled; the soldiers were all up at the palace. The only living things Adam saw were two beggars crawling up the street, hunched over in their rags against the rain. No doubt they had come to loot the dead before the army returned.

Hugo rolled the sword in his hands.

'Even if you kill me,' Adam called, 'there is one thing you will not have.'

'What is that?'

'The Neptune sword. The birthright of the Courtneys – the true Courtneys, not their bastard cousins – given to us by Sir Francis Drake himself. The weapon that killed your grandfather.'

Hugo paused. He wiped the rain from his eyes.

'Your father has it. When I am done with you, I will sail to England and take it from him. Now that the French are defeated at sea and he is a cripple, I no longer need his services to protect my shipping.'

An image assailed Adam's thoughts: Hugo standing over Rob's bed and Rob helpless to defend himself. Adam forced it out of his mind.

'My father gave the sword to me. I brought it to India, to kill you with.'

Hugo laughed. He pointed at the ungainly *katiyal*.

'You appear to have mislaid it.'

'I have hidden it. If you kill me, you will never find it.'

'A weapon so valuable will turn up eventually. When it does, I shall hear of it.'

'I have buried it deep and safe.'

'So be it.' Hugo pushed a lock of hair from his forehead. Beneath it, hidden until now, Adam saw the crater of a terrible burn scar on his temple. 'The days of Francis Drake and the chivalrous Courtneys are ancient history. This is a new era, for new men. I control the richest diamond mines in the world. I can forge another weapon, that will make your Neptune sword look like a tinker's trinket.'

He took his guard. In a fair fight, with equal blades and in good health, they would have been well matched. But Adam was bleeding and hobbling, holding a cumbersome tool instead of a weapon. It would be a short fight.

Adam's eyes cast around for anything he could use to stave off the inevitable: a piece of rubble; a fallen weapon. There was nothing close enough. The cobbles had been swept clean, apart from a few small mounds of horse droppings. Behind Hugo, the two beggars continued their inexorable progress, but they would not join the fight. They would wait until it was over, then dart in to take what they could.

Adam stooped, scooped up a handful of the droppings, and hurled them at Hugo. He aimed for Hugo's eyes, thinking he might blind him – but Hugo reacted instinctively and averted his face at the last moment.

The manure struck him on his temple, a bullseye on the burn mark that Adam had seen. The dung had been softened by the rain and was not hard, yet the effect on Hugo was extraordinary. He froze, the sword drooping, frantically pawing his head as if his hair was on fire.

Adam did not understand what had happened. But he knew he had a chance.

NATIVITY BAY

Paul rushed at Hugo. He had not fought with a sword since he was a boy: there was no subtlety or finesse in his attack. He just swung at Hugo with every drop of rage in his heart.

Hugo was not prepared for it. He raised his sword and parried the blow, but he did not have the strength to repel it. The sword was beaten aside. Before Hugo could recover, Paul raised the cutlass again and swiped at his head.

Hugo saw the stroke and swayed out of the way. Not quick enough: the blade sliced deep into his cheek. Blood welled and poured down his face.

Paul brought the cutlass back for a final blow. But Hugo was strong as the Devil. Even with his cheek flapping open and blood running out of him, he was dangerous. He let go of his sword and grabbed Paul's arm, so quickly Paul did not have time to pull away. Strong hands wrestled the cutlass from his fist. Paul's fingers, slick with sweat and blood, could not keep their grip. The weapon fell to the floor.

Hugo held on to Paul's arm, digging his nails into the skin until it bled. With the other hand, he smashed a fist into Paul's face. Paul's head snapped back.

'Are you another one of the Courtneys?' Hugo hissed. The hole in his cheek made his voice wet and rasping. 'Or simply their dog?'

He punched Paul again, but this time, as the blow landed he let go of Paul's arm. Paul was knocked over. He stumbled away and sprawled on his back amid a pile of ash and debris.

Hugo picked up his sword and strode across the room. He towered over Paul, framed by flame from the burning house. White bone gleamed through the blood flooding from his cheek. He raised the sword.

Lying there, helpless, a memory flashed into Paul's head: The road to Gondar; the Kitzera placing the noose around his neck. Certain he would die.

He put out his arm. His fingers closed around something round and hard that fitted perfectly in his palm. Just where he'd known it would be – the bird-headed god had not deserted him. It was a lump of wood that had broken off one of the roof timbers, still burning. The heat seared Paul's hand and sent a jolt of sheer pain up his arm, but he only had to hold it for a moment.

He did not realise he was screaming. He cocked his shoulder and hurled the ember with all his strength. It struck Hugo's temple and exploded like a firework. Sparks flew everywhere. Some went in Hugo's eyes, blinding him; others scattered onto his clothes and into his hair, setting it on fire.

Hugo turned and ran. Paul never forgot his last sight of him: a ghastly vision of blood and flame and charred flesh, a face torn by agony so it was no longer human.

Something gleamed on the ground beside Paul. It was the golden tiger-handled knife that Talbot had brought. Paul picked it up with his left hand and hurled it into the darkness after Hugo. It struck him between his shoulders, but only with the haft. The knife bounced off and fell on the ground.

It was a feeble parting shot, but it might be enough to quell any thoughts Hugo had of returning. He stumbled under the impact, regained his balance and kept on running.

Paul let him go. He had to save Mary.

HOLKAR

Adam charged at Hugo. They were only five paces apart; he should have covered the ground in no time. But he had not made allowance for his damaged leg. The wound slowed him, and gave Hugo time to react. Hugo raised his sword, ready to deliver the *coup de grâce*.

Then Adam seemed to trip. Just as Hugo swung at him, he stumbled forward. The blade passed over Adam's head. Adam flung out his arms as if trying to gain his balance.

He had not lost his balance. His outstretched arm did not touch the ground. Instead, it lunged forward and thrust the *katiyal* past Hugo's left foot. Hugo began to move, but Adam was already drawing the weapon back. The curved end hooked Hugo's ankle and pulled it forward. On the wet ground, he could not keep his footing. He was pitched backwards, screaming. He tried to get up, but the *katiyal*'s sharp inside blade had sliced clean through his Achilles tendon and he could not move his foot.

Adam stood over him. This, finally, was what he had sacrificed everything for. He wished he had the Neptune sword. That would be the right weapon for this triumphant moment, not some rusting farm tool, but the *katiyal* would have to do. He raised the blade.

Hugo said nothing. He would not beg for mercy. Adam searched his eyes for any sign of pity or remorse. There was only the same fury that had always been there.

'I did not kill your son,' he said.

It mattered to him that Hugo should know. Not for Hugo's comfort, but so that Hugo would go to his grave knowing Adam's true character.

Hugo's shoulders slumped.

'You should have,' he whispered. 'This does not end here. This feud . . . it will take your children, and your children's children. Sons will avenge their fathers, and those sons will have sons of their own.'

Adam paused. He tried to think of his cousin Mary, of his Aunt Susan and Uncle Gert, and all the others that Hugo had murdered. But in his mind's eye, all he saw was Ralph. Did he want to see his own children grow up, fearing every day that the boy he'd once played at cricket would come to hurt them? That was no way to live a life.

Adam could not forgive Hugo for what he had done. But when he looked at his opponent sprawled on the ground, his blood mingling with the rain, he saw a man defeated. He had lost his wife and son. He would never walk again without the aid of a stick. All the riches of Holkar would not compensate for that.

His father's voice came back to him. In the cabin at Nativity Bay, gripping Adam's hand. *Find the men who murdered our family and kill them.* Adam had followed his father's instructions faithfully. He had tracked Hugo across an ocean and a continent. He thought of the men he had killed to get here: the *Diamond*'s crew who had died at Port Louis; Lesaut, blown from the barrel of his own cannon; Talbot, eviscerated in a Calcutta whorehouse. He thought of Clare, alone with her son – and Lizzie, whom he had rejected because he could not let go of his quest.

If you choose hate over love, what do you have left?

Was this justice? Or was it merely vengeance?

With the clarity of battle, he saw clearly at last. He had come all this way thinking that revenge was a destination, a definitive full stop. But now he stood on the threshold, he understood that revenge was not an ending at all, but merely prolonging the fight. A comma, a moment of fleeting satisfaction before the suffering continued. He had to let it go.

Forgive me, Father.

Without a word to Hugo, Adam tossed the *katiyal* aside. It clattered on the wet stones and skidded down the slope as Adam turned away. It was time to go home – to begin the long journey back to England. He would tell Rob what he had done, and hope for his father's absolution.

Steel scraped on the ground behind him. Adam looked over his shoulder. Hugo had risen, sword in hand, balancing on his one good leg as he drew the weapon to stab Adam in the back.

Perhaps Adam might have outrun him, even on his hobbled leg. But his strength had drained from him; his legs turned to wax and he could not move.

I've made my choice. Now I must live with it.

He turned, so at least he would take the blow in his front. As he did, a movement caught his eye – a dark figure rising behind Hugo, as if his shadow had come to life. It was the beggar Adam had seen earlier – though suddenly transformed from a wretched corpse-picker to something terrifying and powerful. He had cast off his cloak, revealing a shaven head, and a naked torso that rippled with muscles unlike any beggar Adam had seen. He had picked up the *katiyal*, wielding it with the easy grace of a man who is accustomed to killing tools.

Hugo sensed the danger. He turned, and as he did, Adam saw an extraordinary change come over his face. The shock of recognition, and – for the first time since Adam had seen him – fear.

'How did you find me?'

Hugo brought up his sword. Before he could strike, the beggar swung the *katiyal*.

It was a blade made for hacking through the sinewy fibres of coconut palms. Mere human flesh and bone presented little resistance. Hugo's neck barely shook as the blade severed it. His head toppled from his shoulders, landed with a splash in a puddle, and rolled away down the hill.

Adam gaped. The beggar stood over Hugo's headless corpse, and though it seemed impossible he should know who he had killed, there was an unmistakeable charge of triumph in his eyes, as of a long-held debt finally repaid.

'Who are you?' Adam shouted.

The two men stared at each other. Adam did not think he had ever seen the man in his life before, and yet there was something about him that resonated deep within him. Like looking in a shattered mirror, seeing your own reflection at once familiar and strange. His eyes, Adam noticed, were blue as the sea.

'Who are you?' Adam said again, into the rain.

The second beggar came up beside her companion. She was a young woman, maybe not yet eighteen, but the look she gave Adam was so pitiless it chilled him to the core of his soul.

She pointed at Adam and said something. Adam did not recognise the language, but he guessed the meaning.

Should we kill him, too?

Adam felt weightless, as if his life sat in the pan of a scale that had not yet come into balance. As if everything he had done, or not done, was being judged.

The beggar gave Adam a curious look, as if he, too, half-recognised something he could not name. He frowned, then shook his head. With a sigh, he took the girl's hand and walked back down the hill. They both vanished into the rain.

Adam wanted to follow. There was so much he needed to know: who they were and how they had come to be in that place; why Hugo had recognised them, and why they had killed him. But all his strength had been spent. Pain throbbed in his wounds as he sank to his knees. The rain soaked him to the skin until he shivered with cold. The cut in his side had started to clot, but he had lost a lot of blood. Perhaps he would die there with Hugo, their bodies lying together until the vultures picked the carcasses clean, and no one could tell one man's bones from the other's.

'Adam?'

The first time he heard the voice, he thought he had slipped into dreams. Or perhaps he had died, and this was the voice of his ancestors welcoming him.

'Adam?'

He opened his eyes. Now he was certain he had died, for he was looking into Panjit's face, staring down at him with concern. He was still in the road, with Hugo's body lying motionless a few feet away. How could Panjit have got there?

Panjit pulled Adam to his feet. Over his shoulder, Adam saw that there was a small square building behind him with its door standing open. The water ideogram that he had searched out so often in the palace paving slabs was carved into the lintel above it.

'You got away through the irrigation tunnels,' Adam said in wonder.

'After you and Hugo went through the window, I took advantage of the confusion to escape. I knew it was impossible to survive that fall – but I also knew that if any man could do it, it would be you.'

'Did anyone follow you?'

'There are many passages through the mountain.' Panjit was still limping; Adam could not imagine how he had worked his way through the slippery, tortuous passages by himself. 'It will take the Company soldiers weeks to find them all, especially without their leader.' He nodded to Hugo's body. 'I see you had your revenge.'

'Perhaps.'

Adam thought about telling Panjit how it had happened, but it was so extraordinary he could not be sure he had dreamed it. There would be time to ponder it later.

Panjit looked at the corpse and wrinkled his nose.

'There will be others. The East India Company is like an enchanted serpent. Cut off one head and two more appear. We cannot save Holkar now.'

He gave Adam his arm. Leaning on each other, the two wounded men hobbled their way down the road that led out of the city.

'Our battle is over.'

NATIVITY BAY

Mary lay on the floor, still pinned by the roof beam. Her arms cradled her dead sister. Her eyes were closed.

The beam was charred and scorching hot, but Paul's hands did not feel it as he gripped it and heaved. Arms strengthened by years at sea lifted it off her and threw it aside. A huge section of roof that had been propped up by the beam collapsed in a blizzard of sparks and dust. Hot embers blew over him. His skin blistered; his clothes started to burn. Mary did not move. Paul grabbed her arms and pulled her free of the debris, out of the door into the courtyard. Only when she was safe did he drop and roll over, smacking himself frantically to put the fire out.

The compound was deserted. Anyone who was not dead had fled the burning house, whose flames were licking high into the night. Paul lifted Mary and carried her in his arms, like a bridegroom with his bride, to the marula tree that grew in a corner of the yard. He laid her among its spreading roots, propped against the trunk as if she was dozing on a summer's day. Her eyes were closed, her nightdress ghostly white. For a moment, it was possible to believe she was only asleep.

Paul cupped his hand under her chin and lifted her head. Frustration at his muteness swelled inside him.

I am sorry, he wanted to say. *I tried to save you. I love you.*

Her eyes blinked open, though a grey film seemed to cover them like a layer of soot. Her strength was fading. Her golden hair had been burned off half her scalp; her flawless skin was blistered and mangled; blood and filth covered her body. Yet when Paul looked at her, the person he saw was the angel who had found him on the beach.

'I love you,' she whispered.

Her eyes closed again. She put her hand on his heart, and Paul did the same. Through the thin fabric of her dress he felt the faint beat, slower and slower.

At last her breathing stopped; her body slumped. Paul threw his arms around her. Her blood soaked his shirt; when he squeezed her tight, the burned skin on his hand screamed with pain. She was dead.

A tug on his shoulder spun him away from his grief. If he had had a weapon, he would have buried it in her before he saw who it was.

It was Sana. Her eyes burned in the firelight, and there was blood on her hands and arms that said she had not escaped the battle.

'We must go.'

Paul ignored her. He pointed to Mary, and the tears streaming down his cheeks spoke more than any words

'She is dead,' Sana agreed. There was no sympathy in her voice. 'They are all dead. But we are alive.'

Paul wished he had not let Hugo go. He wanted to run down to the beach and slaughter every man he found. He would set their ship on fire and burn them all alive, then scour the globe to find every one of their families and kill them, too. But what could one man do? Hugo would be back aboard his ship by now. Paul could not even swim to get there.

Sana's hand closed around his. Her firm, cool touch seemed to draw the heat out of him. He began to tremble violently, his body convulsing with silent sobs.

Sana's grip stayed tight. Like a mother with a rebellious child, she pulled him away and led him out of the gate towards the river, while the last remnants of Fort Auspice collapsed and burned behind them.

CALCUTTA, 1807

I t was strange hearing English spoken again. Walking through Calcutta, listening to the men and women flirting and conversing, Adam realised how much of a stranger he had become to his own people during his time away. The buildings that had seemed so grand when he arrived now felt prim and starched. The people who drove past in their carriages, braying and preening, were a different species.

Months had passed since the battle of Holkar. His wounds had healed and he walked easily. He was dressed as a sailor, in canvas trousers and a checked shirt which Cornish had provided, with a sailcloth bag hoisted over his shoulder. Adam kept a firm hand on the bag. Tucked inside were the two fragments of the Neptune sword, now safely retrieved.

He was alone. After travelling hundreds of miles together, he and Panjit had parted ways at Benares, where the great trunk road met the Ganges.

'Where will you go?' Adam had asked.

'There are parts of India that are still free of the Company's rule. I will find a kingdom that has not yet been conquered and carry on the fight.'

Adam had almost shaken Panjit's hand, then remembered the caste rules and halted himself. But Panjit did not pull away. He had wrapped his arms around Adam and hugged him tight.

'Whatever other people may think, the gods will not say I defile myself if I touch you. You bring nothing but honour.'

Adam had embraced his friend, aware of the compliment he had been paid. When at last they separated, Panjit had taken a small leather bag from inside his coat and pressed it into Adam's hand.

'A souvenir of Holkar. Something to remember us by.'

The bag was heavy, bulging with hard edges. When Adam peered inside, he saw the glitter of diamonds. He had pushed it back towards Panjit.

'You have greater need than me.'

'Consider it your reward for your services to Holkar. It is a long journey back to England, and you will have to pay your way. Besides . . .' Panjit had unbuttoned his coat and opened the folds, revealing four more similar bags tied to his belt. 'I have enough of my own.'

'Then be careful who you share your fire with on the road. I will not be around to rescue you from the T'uggee next time.'

'Careful?' Panjit had laughed. 'You bring danger like dung brings flies. I will be safer by far when you are gone from this country.'

The words still brought a smile to Adam's face, many weeks later. But there was also a harder truth in them. He was a fugitive and an outlaw. There were only two powers in Calcutta that could get him back to England – the Royal Navy and the East India Company – and he had made enemies of both. Nor could he assume a false name. Calcutta was an incestuous society; every white face was known the moment it arrived. To appear in Calcutta would bring down all manner of scrutiny. Even a common seaman would be noticed.

He looked across the brown Hooghly river, at the fleet of Indiamen anchored in the stream, and wondered how he would ever get back home.

NATIVITY BAY, 1803

Paul gazed across the sparkling blue lagoon, at the Indiaman hoisting her anchor. The sky was clear; the sun shone. The day paid no respect to the horrors of the night before. The only clue was the thin column of smoke rising into the sky from the ashes of Fort Auspice.

The *Seven Sisters'* anchor broke the surface with a splash of white spray. Her crew raised it clear and made it fast to the cathead. Sails were set, and the ship nosed her way through the narrow channel that led out of the bay. Paul climbed the whale-backed hill and watched her go, until she was a speck on the horizon.

When he was certain she would not return – when he could delay the moment no longer – he went to the beach and up the path that led to Fort Auspice. The dagger he had thrown at Hugo lay on the ground, trampled into the soft earth. He let it lie there.

From the outside, all was well. The gate stood open as if in welcome. A few pockmarks gouged out of the white walls were the only clues to what had happened.

As he stepped through the gate, the picture changed. Bodies littered the ground. It had only been twelve hours, but many had been stripped half-bare by the scavengers. A jackal looked up from one of them, its muzzle covered in blood. It gave Paul a piercing stare, then went back to its meal.

He forced himself on, up the stairs and into the remains of the house. The embers were still warm; smouldering timbers burned the soles of his bare feet.

He went to Mary's room. He rifled through her clothes – dresses and petticoats she would never wear again. He buried his face in them, trying to breathe in her scent, but they only smelled of smoke.

He found her paintbox under her bed and took it to what had been the living room. He meant to keep it as a memento, perhaps to paint a portrait to take with him. But when he tried to remember how she had been, the image he saw was a charred corpse.

A wave of fury overtook him. He threw the box to the ground and smashed it. He picked up one of the paints, daubed it on his hands, and in frenzied letters wrote, '*J'aura mon revanche.*' But when he read it back, the words only seemed to mock him, hollow and empty.

He had to bury the Jansen family. He found Rachel in the living room where Hugo had killed her, and Susan in the doorway. She must have been shepherding Rachel and Mary out of the house; a bullet had killed her instantly. Gert was in the corridor. Flames had burned away the axe haft and much of his skin, but the axe-head remained buried in his skull. George, too, had been badly burned. Paul identified him by the missing tibia where his wooden leg had been, and the walking cane that lay under him. It had been cut in two; he must have died using it to defend himself.

It took longer to find Marcus. Paul eventually dug him out from under a collapsed wall. The boy's mouth was full of dust, and his fingertips were worn bloody and ragged from trying to claw his way from under the masonry before it crushed him. He had been buried alive.

Last of all was Mary. Paul tied a strip of cloth over her face so he did not have to look at her.

He found a spade in one of the farm buildings and began to dig near the back of the compound. The ground was hard; it took heavy effort to break the soil. Sana sat on a tree stump, her legs curled under her, munching a kei apple. Paul gestured to her to help, but she did not come. She had put on one of Mary's dresses, a blue one that had been Mary's favourite. It was too big for her. The neckband hung too far down her chest, and the hem dragged in the dirt when she walked. Paul wished she wasn't wearing it.

The Jansen family needed a big grave. By the time it was a foot deep, Paul was drenched with sweat and every muscle ached. He welcomed the pain.

'It makes no difference,' Sana called from her stump. 'They are dead.'

He knew she was right. What did he owe them? Even Susan, the kindest, had been wary of him; Gert and George had been openly hostile. But in these few weeks they had been the nearest people to family he had known since his mother died. More importantly, they were Mary's family. He was doing this for her.

At last he had made the hole deep enough. He laid out the bodies, then gathered rocks and rubble to cover them against scavengers. He mounded the earth over it. Lastly, he found flat stones to act as grave markers and scored the family's initials into them, scratching the stone again and again until his hand was blistered from holding the knife. He set the stones at the heads of the graves, and laid wild flowers beside them.

It wasn't enough. He wanted to pray, like he had prayed when he was a child and still believed in a benevolent god – but his mind was blank. He could not remember the words.

All the books in the living room had been destroyed by fire. But George's office was in an older part of the house that had a brick-vaulted roof and a stout door. Hugo's men had broken in – the lock on the strongbox had been smashed, and papers scattered around the room – but the fire had not taken hold. Much of the office was as George had left it: a pen stood upright in the ink-stand; a ledger lay open on the desk. And on the shelves, among the account books and almanacs, there was an old Bible.

It was a very old book. It was printed in Latin, but Paul thought he might remember enough of his schoolboy lessons to read it. He took it to the grave, rested it on a rock, and turned the pages until he found a psalm. The words fell into his memory like drops of water in a deep well.

Yea, though I walk through the valley of the shadow of death, I will fear no evil . . .

He wished he could say the words aloud. He wished he could believe them. He said them in his head and hoped that they would serve.

Wind rustled the pages and blew them back, exposing the inside front cover. The flyleaf was covered in writing – different inks and different hands and many different times, judging by how faded some of the letters were. Spidery lines connected the words.

It was a family tree. Paul studied it. Near the bottom were the names he recognised: Mary, Marcus and Rachel; Gert and Susan above them; George above that. George's parents had been called James and Louisa; James's parents – very faded – Tom and Sarah.

Tom had had three brothers: Dorian, Guy and William. All had married and had children, and those children had had children of their own, until the family tree had so many branches that someone had pasted in a second flap of paper to continue it. Paul read the names, wondering what stories lay behind them: Francis, Christopher, Gerard, Robert, Adam, Theo, Constance.

He blinked. At the same time, his eye caught the heading written at the top of the page. The words were so old they had faded almost to the same brown as the paper, but under the bright African sun they became legible: *The Courtney Family*.

Constance . . . Courtney. The same name he had seen written in the front of his mother's childhood book. But surely that was impossible. It must be a coincidence – one more grim joke played by a fate that had tormented Paul all his life. The alternative . . .

'What is it?'

Sana had come up behind him, silent as usual. Paul pointed to the words on the page, but of course she could not read them. How could he tell her? Though she could read his face, the thoughts in his heart were so complex he could not explain them.

She pushed the book closed. It had taken so long to dig the grave, the sun had dropped behind the trees. Shadows lengthened from the forest. Soon it would be dark, and the bodies in the house would draw out the carrion eaters again.

'We do not want to be here when night falls.'

Where else can we go?

Standing over the graves, a new depth of despair opened inside him. The painful labour of digging had barricaded him off from it, but now grief and guilt overwhelmed his defences and crashed through.

If Sana had not found him with Mary – if she had not fled out of the side gate and left it unlocked – the walls would not have been breached. The family would have held off the assault. Mary would be alive.

It was all my fault.

The thought was like a lion's paw clawing at his soul, ripping it to ribbons. In a frenzy, he snatched up his knife. Its point was blunted from gouging the initials into the gravestones, but it only had one more stroke to make. He would plunge it into his heart.

Forgive me, Mother.

He raised the knife.

A hand, small but strong, gripped his wrist. He wrestled against it, but he was exhausted, and Sana had a tenacious strength. She prised his fingers off the hilt, pulled the knife from his hand, and tossed it aside. Paul made to go after it, but she planted her feet and held him back, arms locked like wrestlers or dancers.

Their eyes met.

Let me die. The words were written in every tear on his face.

'No.'

It was my fault.

How can I make her understand?

He looked at the graves, then slowly tracked his gaze across the compound to the kitchen gate hanging open on its hinges.

'It was not your fault. I opened the gate.'

But it was a mistake. You did not know what you had done.

A terrible thought.

Did you?

A sly look came into Sana's eyes. She held his gaze with pitiless clarity; there was nowhere to hide from the monstrous thoughts that crashed through his mind like hammer blows, each driving the spike in further.

You left the gate unlocked deliberately.

She did not deny it.

You let the attackers in.

Her impassive face showed no emotion.

You let the family die.

Did she understand what he was trying to say? All strength had left him, and Sana no longer had to hold him back. He dropped to his knees in front of her.

Why? All I have ever done is protect you.

Her eyes narrowed with scorn. 'You would have died in the desert if not for me. All the times you thought you saved me – I saved *you*. Who killed the Frenchman? Who found water in the desert? Who rescued you from the palace guards and the hyenas, and who guided you to the sea?' She stood over him, glaring down mercilessly. 'Look at me.'

Paul stayed where he lay.

'I will not let you die now,' Sana whispered, and in his grief he could no longer tell her voice from the bird-headed god's. 'You still have something to live for.'

He looked up at her, like a child staring at its mother.

What?

'Revenge.'

In the dark depths of his torment, the word was like a glowing ember. A tiny spark, but enough to kindle hope in the ashes of his soul.

How?

Sana wrinkled her nose as if it were the most ridiculous question. 'Find the man who did this. Kill him.'

Paul lifted a limp hand towards the lagoon and sketched a vague, all-encompassing gesture.

He has just sailed out of the bay. He could go anywhere in the world.

'We have time. We can find him.'

Paul shook his head. His thoughts were a mosaic of pain, and Sana's words simply added to the confusion. Constance; Abasi; now Mary: everyone he loved had died, while the cruel and violent – Bonaparte and Lefebvre, Goshu and Hugo – had gained power.

His mind went back to the temple in Egypt, that scorching hot day. He thought of the picture he had seen on the wall: the god with a pair of weighing scales, a human heart in one pan and a feather in the other.

The god was justice. The god was judgement. The god was Nemesis.

J'aura mon revanche.

He had daubed it on the wall in a fit of madness, not knowing where the words had come from. Now he realised it was not madness, but the god speaking through him. Not a helpless plea, but a promise.

Did Sana leave the gate open deliberately?

He would never ask her, and she would never say. But she had not wielded a sword or a gun. She had not murdered the family. She was not to blame, any more than Paul was. Only one man carried that guilt.

I will have my revenge.

The promise gave him strength. The cords that had been severed in his soul knotted themselves back together like scar tissue, thicker and stronger than before.

He had one name, no way of speaking it, and all the oceans of the earth to scour. Was it possible? He thought back over the past day, like a scavenger digging from scraps. Hugo had come from India. He had said his name was Constable, but Paul had a suspicion that the name Courtney would also help to find him. He had mentioned Calcutta.

Is that enough?

Paul could be patient. Another ship would call at Nativity Bay, maybe in a month or a year. He would be waiting when it came.

Endure anything, survive anything, become anything. He had the god's promise. *Justice comes to every man.*

He rose to his feet. Sana stretched out her hand, and Paul took it. They went out through the gate together, into the immense unknown darkness beyond.

CALCUTTA, 1807

Adam stared at the river. The sun was setting, painting the sky a delicate confection of pinks and golds. Behind him, the streets were coming alive after their mid-afternoon slumbers. Lamps were lit, drinks poured, and the cream of society emerged to take their pleasures.

He had not paid attention to the passing time: someone was bound to notice him soon. He had meant to hail a boatman to take him to one of the ships so he could sign on for the passage, but his legs refused to move. His body was tensed, as if waiting for something.

A figure was walking along the embankment towards him. He did not see it clearly, but the gait or the shape of the face struck a familiar chord in him. He turned away in case he was recognised.

It was too late. The figure stopped and stared.

'Adam Courtney? Can it be?'

He had spent three days in Calcutta fearing he would be recognised. Yet now that it had happened, the sound of the voice brought only unabashed joy. He turned, a smile spreading over his face. Lizzie March stood there, a parasol cocked over her shoulder, looking at him with an expression that shifted from delight to bewilderment to anger.

'The wandering adventurer. The hero who chose revenge over love. Have you won your battles, slayed your dragons?'

'Miss March.'

He started to raise his hat to her, but she was more forward.

'You held my heart in your hands and then you left me. I have every right to hate you.'

She smiled, displaying a self-possession that unnerved Adam.

Is she angry with me or not?

She moved towards him, came up close and studied his face, as if the journeys he had made were etched on his skin, the stories he could tell reflected in the glistening of his eyes.

'I thought I would never see you again,' she said.

He longed to touch her. Of course it was improper, he reminded himself.

'Nor I you, Mrs . . .?'

She laughed. 'You do not need to be so correct. I am still plain old Lizzie March.'

'Your husband . . .? The dashing major?'

'The marriage did not happen.'

Adam felt a tremor in the pit of his stomach. 'What happened? Surely no man in his right mind would have jilted you?'

'You are very gallant.' Lizzie stuck out her tongue at him. 'Has it crossed your mind that perhaps I jilted him?'

'But . . .' Adam tried to process this turn of events. 'What about your mother?'

Lizzie looked as if she despaired of him.

'I decided I would not live my life according to what she had arranged for me. If I must be poor and disreputable, that is my choice.'

'How have you lived?'

'I have taken work as a governess.'

She flicked her hand as if to say *it does not matter*, and Adam felt he had suddenly become the most boring, flat-footed conversationalist imaginable. What had happened to the easy laughter they had enjoyed on the *Mornington*?

'Have you had no other suitors since?'

Single English women in Calcutta were like flowers in a desert. There was no shortage of thrusting young men looking to pluck them.

'Not a day has gone by that I have not had a proposal of marriage. Sometimes three before breakfast.' Lizzie's eyes danced with mischief. 'You may be sure I have left quite a trail of broken hearts across all Bengal.'

'But why—'

'Because despite your impulsiveness, your single-mindedness, there is only one man I love, and every minute since you left I have prayed that you would come back here. Silly, I grant you, but I know my own mind.' She twirled the parasol. 'I tried to find you, but you had disappeared. Months later, I heard that a man named Hugo

Courtney had been killed in a distant province. I feared it might be you, under a different name – though, of course, Hugo Courtney was so well known here I knew it could not be you. Still, I wondered . . .'

'Hugo Courtney was my cousin. I was with him when he died.'

'So you got what you wanted.' She stiffened, pulling back. 'The revenge you sought.'

'No.'

Even remembering it made him feel dazed. He continually puzzled over that extraordinary day in Holkar. Had he done right? Honoured his father? Found justice for his family? He had questioned his choices a thousand times, never finding an answer. Always, his thoughts came back to the beggar who had killed Hugo, his blue eyes staring at Adam like some ancient god of judgement.

'I had my chance for revenge. I could not take it. I do not know if that makes me a hero or a villain.'

Lizzie went quiet. She stared at him, scanning his face to try and understand his riddles.

'I think you did the right thing.'

'It is a long story.'

'That is what you said the night we met,' she reminded him.

'You said I was fortunate you had plenty of time to listen.'

'I still have time.'

They gazed at each other, and suddenly Adam realised he must say what was in his heart or lose the chance entirely.

'I never want to be parted from you in all my life,' he blurted. For the first time since he had landed at Nativity Bay, his heart felt whole again. 'If you will have me.'

Waiting for her to reply felt like the longest moment of his life – though it lasted mere seconds.

'If fate has brought us back together, it must be for a reason.'

She leaned up and kissed him, her lips gentle and forgiving.

Afterwards, they walked together down the ghats along the Hooghly. The ships in the channel tugged their anchor cables as the current pulled them downstream, longing for the river mouth and the open ocean where they belonged. Adam smiled.

'We have a long voyage ahead of us.'

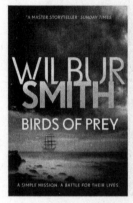 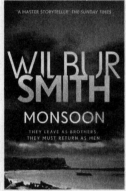 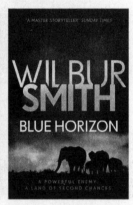

BETRAYED BY BLOOD. FREED BY FATE.

GHOST FIRE

Inseparable since birth, Theo and Connie Courtney are torn apart by the tragic death of their parents.

Theo, wracked with guilt, seeks salvation in combat, joining the British in the war against the French and Indian army. On a personal mission he meets the beautiful, innocent Abigail, with whom he falls madly in love. But when their tryst is discovered, Theo is left outcast in the wilderness, desperately fighting for his life. Determined to reclaim his honour and save Abigail, Theo does whatever it takes to survive.

Connie, believing herself abandoned by her brother, and abused and brutalised by a series of corrupt guardians, makes her way to France, where she is welcomed into high society. Here, she once again finds herself at the mercy of vicious men, whose appetite for war and glory lead her to the frontlines of the French battlefield in North America.

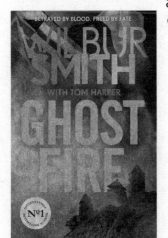

As the siblings find their destinies converging once more, they realise that the vengeance and redemption they both desperately seek could cost them their lives . . .

AVAILABLE NOW

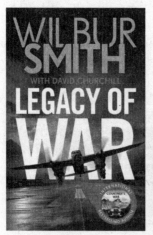
 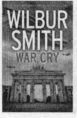 

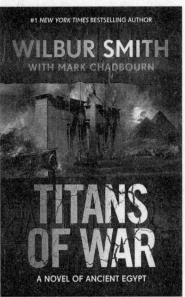